RIVERS OF GOLD

FOR INFORMATION, INCLUDING PERMISSION TO REPRODUCE THIS BOOK OR ANY PORTIONS CONTAINED THEREIN, PLEASE VISIT WWW.DUNNBOOKS.COM.

PUBLISHED BY DUNN BOOKS. FIRST PAPERBACK EDITION NOVEMBER 2015.

THIS TITLE IS ALSO AVAILABLE AS A DUNN BOOKS EBOOK, AND AS AN AUDIBLE DIGITAL AUDIOBOOK.

AN EARLIER EDITION OF *Rivers of Gold* WAS PUBLISHED BY BLOOMSBURY USA IN 2010. THIS VERSION CONTAINS NEW MATERIAL NOT PREVIOUSLY PUBLISHED.

LIBRARY OF CONGRESS CATALOGING-IN-PUBLICATION DATA IS ON FILE WITH THE U.S. COPYRIGHT OFFICE.

ISBN: 978-0-9962082-0-8

DESIGNED BY ARCHIE FERGUSON.

DISTRIBUTED BY BOOK MASTERS, INC.

MANUFACTURED IN THE UNITED STATES OF AMERICA.

RIVERS OF GOLD

BOOK
1

A NOVEL

ADAM DUNN

DUNN BOOKS

GLOSSARY'S IN BACK

TO THE CABBIES,

AND

MY FAMILY,

AND

ERIC AMBLER, KINGSLEY AMIS, MARTIN AMIS, ANIRUDDHA BAHAL,
J. G. BALLARD, IAIN BANKS, PETER BENCHLEY, JOHN BURDETT,
ANTHONY BURGESS, RAYMOND CHANDLER, LOUIS DE BERNIÈRES,
SEAN DOOLITTLE, JOHN EARLY, DAN FESPERMAN, CHARLES G. FINNEY,
ALAN FISHER, ALAN FURST, WILLIAM GIBSON, PETE HAMILL, DASHIELL
HAMMET, THOMAS HARRIS, COLIN HARRISON, JOSEPH HELLER, CARL
HIAASEN, MO HAYDER, J. ROBERT JANES, JOSEPH KANON, THOMAS
KELLY, PHILIP KERR, DINAH LEE KÜNG, JOHN LAWTON, DENNIS
LEHANE, ELMORE LEONARD, MICHAEL MALONE, DOMINIC MARTELL,
COLUM MCCANN, DEON MEYER, JIM NISBET, CHUCK PALAHNIUK,
ORHAN PAMUK, CLAY REYNOLDS, JOHN SANDFORD, STEVEN SHERRILL,
DANIEL SILVA, SHANE STEVENS, P. J. TRACY, JOHN TREVANIAN,
ANDREW VACHSS, JOSEPH WAMBAUGH, EDWARD WHITTEMORE, AND
ROBERT WILSON

FOR TELLING ME

EACH IN HIS OR HER OWN WAY

TO SHUT UP AND WRITE

The fish might have been asleep, save for the movement
dictated by countless millions of years of instinctive continuity:
lacking the flotation bladder common to other fish and
the fluttering flaps to push oxygen-bearing water through
its gills, it survived only by moving. Once stopped, it would
sink to the bottom and die of anoxia.

—**PETER BENCHLEY**, *Jaws*

Old men didn't talk about this, not even to each other. Just bore the truth
of it, the change of life. You learned something about the world when you
lost your sexual desire, you saw things differently, how tormented young
men were, how stupid and out of control.

—**COLIN HARRISON**, *The Finder*

Poets that lasting marble seek
Must carve in Latin or in Greek;
We write in sand, our language grows,
And, like the tide, our work o'erflows.

—**EDMUND WALLER**, "Of English Verse"

You're a saint in a world where the only cardinal sin is to be bored,
And you'll do what you love, you'll love what you do,
you won't ask what it's for.

—**THE VERLAINES**, "Angela"

They've got cars big as bars, they've got rivers of gold,
But the wind goes right through you, it's no place for the old . . .

—**THE POGUES**, "Fairytale of New York"

PART I

TEABAGGING CHARYBDIS

STEPPING OUT

WE'RE THREE LIGHTS FROM THE FRONTIER.

The frontier, of course, being defined as the last green light beyond which stretches a solid column of reds, like Chinese lanterns. The frontier is my aim point, the hinge of possibility, the variable that will determine (a) the amount of time you will spend in the cab and (b) the amount of your fare. It helps me to calculate whether or not I'll be late, and if so, how late, and whether I call, text, or browse. If I'm working, it also determines whether I can shoot out the window for background material I can Photoshop in later, since the speed of the cab is usually somewhat proportional to its distance from the frontier. For my purposes, a good rolling glide of about thirty miles an hour at least one hour after sundown produces just the right effect of blurred dynamism. New York is truly the city that never stops moving, and the trick of my trade is to capture this motion at its most evocative—and lucrative—moments.

If I'm making sport with a playmate in the backseat, the frontier tells me how much time I have before the cab slows down and the driver looks in his mirror at what we're up to, which affects the complex algorithm of Taxi Sex—oral is best on smooth straightaways of guaranteed duration, furtive gropings and dishabilles better at low speeds when flanked by other, higher vehicles or along narrow streets affording increased pedestrian views, full-groin revelation out of the question in stop-and-go traffic, unless that's what you're into. Personally, I find it preferable only while traversing bridges at night.

Then again, sometimes just being alone in the back of a taxicab, watching the infinite streams and whorls of the city streak by like passing galaxies, is preferable to Taxi Sex. After all, the city may try to kill you, but at least it doesn't give you an earful of whiny complaint. None that stays within earshot for long, anyway.

This cabbie has his timing down pat, he's got a good foot, he's maintaining a two-to-three-light gap, keeping his speed in a range using controlled deceleration rather than braking, which means that barring construction, accidents, police convoys, cable trucks, or anybody from fucking Verizon, we should sail down to the meet at moderate speed, minimum cost, and merciful lack of aggravation. Good incentive for a good tip.

And it's comfortable. My chariot this evening is the venerable Ford Heifer. You know this vehicle as the Crown Victoria. Designed with rear legroom in mind, it's roomy enough for a man to properly and thoroughly adjust his equipment. I can hardly remember what it was like before the city adopted the stretch cabs, and I can't imagine how people tolerated the smaller ones—no, how people actually *fit* in them. When I was still an assistant, carrying rental lights along with cameras, lenses, bipod, tripod, batteries, cords, and extra memory, there was just no way anyone could be back there with me, even though sharing the fare meant saving a few bucks. Now that I have the discretionary capital, I hardly consider sharing a cab. Unless the model is exceptional and she's prepared to come across. I'm in this game for one thing, and I don't gladly suffer those who waste my time. I've lost enough of that already.

At least this cab's clean. I speak from painfully accrued experience when I say that drivers maintaining clean cabs should be awarded—how, exactly, I'm not sure, probably free gas, at nine bucks a gallon they certainly wouldn't say no, and it'd be good incentive for all the others to clean up the crumpled receipts, discarded water bottles, hair, cigarette foil, gum, roaches, used condoms, vomit, lighters, vials, and other assorted detritus of transit that shake loose from us like dandruff wherever we go. If you are going to engage in the extreme sport of going down on a woman in the back of a taxicab (not, I repeat, *not* for amateurs), take my advice—do not kneel on the floor.

We're on Columbus Avenue, just passing the old Natural History Museum, which finally joined the others and closed down *temporarily* last year. This makes for an elongated stretch of darkness, which isn't brightened much by what little trade is visible as we drift south. There was a time when this part of town was alive with restaurants, bars, clubs, stores, and markets. It's a much more depressing scene than the one Bruce Weber might have shot back in the day. There's plywood over two thirds of any commercial property on every block along the avenue, covered with illegible graffiti and strewn along its base with trash. The few lights visible at street level come from the handful of remaining restaurants open for business, and even this is refracted through layers of security barriers and industrial-sized doormen. Above these, lights still glow in people's apartments, though the lower floors sport the same wrought-iron window guards once reserved for the parlor floors of townhouses. Even twenty feet off the ground, New Yorkers take no chances.

—Scyooz me, mohn. Ees okay I take Broadway all de way dohn and go across Feefty-sebahn Street? Feefth eez teddible raht no.

—Yes indeed. No trouble at all.

It's *street*, with that machine-gun-rolled *R* from behind the front teeth, rather than *stweet*, left behind from a pulling back of the lips. That plus the short vowel-heavy last-name-first on the license suspended in the scratched plastic partition between the seats (Omo), plus the deep velvety brown skin which looks so good under halide lights, plus the lack of pungent body odor, rules out Haitian in favor of African. He's asking if he can leave me across the street from the meet instead of driving up in front from Fifth, which ordinarily would piss me off, but since we're making such good time, I'll get a chance to stretch my legs before the gathering, have a smoke, maybe check out the night's diversions at Nobu 57—smoothly fleshed but pampered, spoiled, and temperamental, with daddy complexes and engineered overbites. I don't need to hang around the bar getting soaked beforehand. I'm properly primed, no more, no less.

Indulge me. Renny's Rule Number Five: Proper Preparation. It's a big night for me, one that promises to turn drab dingy December 2012 into a *very* merry Christmas, should all go as planned. Which means I've taken the time to accessorize. A polish of the crystal face on my Jaquet Droz. A hefty shot of Ronsonol for my sterling Zippo (Elsa Peretti), three sharp spanks on the rump of a fresh pack of Davidoffs. Each measure punctuated in turn with sips of the perfect Manhattan: Basil Hayden's, a dash of sweet Tribuno, and most important, three teardrops of Angostura orange bitters, shaken to a froth over as much ice as will fit, served only in stemmed Waterford. *One's not enough, two is too many, three is just the beginning.*

All of this is really to prep the persona, get just loose enough, just numb enough, to get through an otherwise intolerable time. It's a hell of a thing to have to act grateful to someone you despise, to try to coax him out of enough money to justify a job you hate.

But that's what it takes, at least if you want to keep moving forward. I do what I do because I need to, and because it enables me to enjoy the lifestyle hitherto taken for granted. Think there's a reward for loyalty, merit in hard work, honor among leaders? Not in this town, not anymore. There is prosperity, and then there's survival.

There is no comparison between the linoleum cell on Thirty-seventh Avenue in Queens, where my mother sits at the window slowly going mad, and my parlor floor-through one-bedroom on Manhattan Avenue, in Manhattan, where I sip my Manhattan. Maybe you think I'm vain or shallow. I'd say I'm a realist living in unreal times and making the best of it. Carpe diem, dipshit.

A pothole in the spine jolts me back to reality. We've reached Columbus Circle. Between Trump Palace and the Mandarin Oriental, this area once had everything going for it. These days the going's gotten tougher. The Time Warner Center was finished years ago, but the abandoned renovation of the Columbus Circle subway station left the surrounding streets jagged and torn. The fountain was refinished in time to revert to its former role as one of the city's largest latrines. All along the roundabout's southern rim, shantytowns line the boarded-up frontages of stores. In the semi-enclosed subway entrance at the corner of Fifty-eighth and Ninth, there's a black market where you can buy anything from gasoline to guns most nights. Tonight the streets are empty. The people are all indoors. Or in taxicabs.

You can tell real New Yorkers from gawking tourists by the way they sit in a cab, lips parted, mouth slightly open, so they don't bite off their tongue when the driver makes a point of hitting every hole in the pavement. The tourists milling about the safe havens in front of the big, well-defended hotels are the ones telling each other the San Remo's the Dakota and the Dakota's the Beresford. There's a cluster of ambulances at the entrance to the Mandarin Oriental; some VIP must have choked on his osetra. They've just arrived—the EMTs clamber down out of their trucks, wave to one another in world-weary recognition, and light up in unison. They're in no hurry, and there's no IV on the stretcher, so they'll be bringing down a bag, maybe more than one. This is the sort of New York moment best captured with my trusty 35-millimeter Marathon Cyber SEX. Four frames: Bring Out Yer Dead.

Traffic's crawling and I'm itching for a Davidoff, but there're cops all over the place, and my driver would probably have a heart attack if they saw me light up. It's no longer possible to enjoy an indoor smoke legally, which is why the speaks have portable air filters as standard equipment (they don't have much else). More on those later—to serious business first, before the serious business of pleasure.

True to his word, after skillfully circumnavigating the Circus Columbus, the driver drops me precisely at the Fifty-seventh Street light halfway between Fifth and Sixth, an incongruous location for a useless traffic signal (if it was put there to ease crosstown congestion, it's a dismal failure). This driver has been excellent—street-savvy and swift—which means there's no point in trying to recruit him. Either he hasn't been here long enough or he's on someone else's payroll, and I'd just be chiseling in, which could have serious repercussions, depending on who else is using this cab to what ends. I swipe my Urbank Electrum through the slot, leaving a generous tip. Share that which you have (or at least that which you have been preapproved for) with those who have not.

Tonight's first meet is for a fat new *Roundup* magazine contract. The second meet concerns the Specials. One should never, ever rely on one sole means of income.

This stretch of Fifty-seventh, I like to think of as the Street of Dreams. At its eastern boundary, the Survivors—Tiffany, Bulgari, the Louis Vuitton flagship store with its exquisite staircase (I've repeatedly told L that I want to have her on that staircase, and she's repeatedly promised me that, should circumstances permit, I will). Thrusting westward: the new Throb store in the old Ascot Chang location—I covered the opening for *Raid*, two and a half grand direct-deposited into my Urbank account *the next day;* the perpendicular ski jump of the 9 West Building (you can skip the restaurant beneath it); the aforementioned Nobu 57 (no comparison with its downtown progenitor in food, decor, or clientele); and my beloved Rizzoli store, my refuge from chaos. I pray this bookstore won't close down like all the others. When things get too much and I need some quiet time, I hide out in a corner in the upstairs photography section for hours. Every man needs a sanctum sanctorum from the Charybdis of need, including his own.

The first meet is at Shelley's, an Italianate sit-down spot with a laughable interior but dependable seafood. What they also have, however, and where Marcus Chalk (editor in chief of *Roundup*, media mug par excellence, and my current meal ticket) goes when he means business, is a private dining room downstairs in the wine cellar. It'll probably be Marcus; his mousy but effective assistant, Diane; Johnette the Lesbian AD (my biggest obstacle in any *Roundup* job); and Fabryce from marketing (whose inevitable advances I hope to avoid, though I suspect he'd make a good client for Specials).

Shelley's private dining room: a wood-trimmed, marble-floored terrarium with walls made of wine. Marcus Chalk sits at twelve o'clock at the round table, Fabryce to his right, Johnette to his left, Diane at six o'clock, closest to the glass door (presumably in case her boss needs her to run out to throw herself in front of a FedEx truck), and at about four-thirty, closest to a corner with a stool suggestively set, an empty chair for me. (The prick.) Smiles and soft handshakes all around, except from Johnette, who owns a grip like a forceps made for bovine breach births. I sit down and dial up my best Obsequious Compliant.

Let the games begin.

Obligatory pleasantries, anecdotes, and tales of petty outrage are put through the conversation hopper in due course. Food is perfunctorily ordered, lightly and nearly all vegetable or marine, except Johnette's, a *tagliata* extra rare. (My stomach contracts. Johnette has jet-black razor-styled hair, dead-level bangs in front, and a severe fantail, cut off mercilessly mid-neck, that looks uncomfortably like an SS helmet. Sitting under Johnette's withering glare can be unappetizing enough, but doing so while watching her saw through hunks of bloody meat is downright disturbing.)

—Renny, we've booked Johnny Retch and Miyuki for the cover story. All next year's Dolce, Canali, and Giovanni Kwan, Chalk intones in his trademark Boardroom Baritone, the overheads casting a fine patina over his smooth coriander dome.

Fashion photography was something I did to pay the bills. That was the plan, anyway, before the bottom fell out of the art market four years ago—a harbinger of worse things to come. I had talent, I had contacts, I had a portfolio made up of girls I knew and others I'd picked up. But what caught the eye of guys like Marcus Chalk were my cityscapes, long washes of light and shadow play in motion, an animation of staid facades and gridlocked intersections—think Berenice Abbott on meth, shooting digital. It's a technique I worked up with X, though I don't want to think about X now. If I do, I'll want a drink. Then another. There'll be time enough later to torture myself with memory. Right now I've got things to do. *Roundup*'s monthly circulation runs to a million downloads. No matter how much I dislike these people, it's all about the ducats.

—Just what is it you're looking for?

—We want more of what you did for *Diazanon*, the Hollywood issue, Fabryce lisps, his eyes sliding over to his BlackBerry.

Diazanon is *Malathion*'s sister magazine for the West Coast. They flew me out there last spring for a weeklong shoot. I was lucky enough to get paid just before the EIC was found in somebody else's Brentwood house with two naked teenage boys, one of whom was already catatonic from an overdose. Things haven't been quite the same between the two rags since, though there's been no buzz yet about a formal breakup.

—Just with a little less *motion*, Johnette says in her icy snarl, biting off the last word.

—Yes, Renny, we're looking for the same urban backwash effect you've been doing, but not so much that it detracts from Johnny and Miyuki. A bit less movement in the background, a bit more contrast to bring focus to the actors and the clothes. You understand, Chalk says regally, pouring on the professional indoor sincerity-speak.

You prick, I want to snarl at him. Can you even spell *photography*, or do you have people who do that for you?

But I say:

—Of course. You want something a little more toned down, lowlight, maybe fewer lightscapes?

—We don't want any *lightscapes*, Johnette says in her warmthless, gen-der-neutral voice.

It's nice to see Johnette hasn't gone all warm and fuzzy on me. You need to be able to count on some things in life.

Johnette continues mercilessly:

—How do you do those anyway, do you just shoot out the window of a moving taxica—

The food arrives, allowing me to regroup. I can hardly look at my sea-food bruschetta, but I take a few obligatory nips to look busy. Mousy Diane, who looks like she hasn't eaten or slept in a week, is about to tear into her calamari when Chalk abruptly sends her out on some meaningless errand. Fabryce can't stop toying with his BlackBerry, probably lining up a date at Splash. Johnette glares from beneath her steel bangs, the serrated edge of her steak knife turned toward me, dripping blood. I'd rather be anywhere than here.

This is how it happens.

There are moments of such unforeseeable synchronicity that they actually make you Believe. This is a good one. My phone gives a double-thump heartbeat in my jacket pocket, which tells me Prince William is ready to meet, which means he's got next week's speak number. This is a legitimate excuse to cut the *Roundup* meeting short if it gets too unbearable. Business is business.

Then Marcus Chalk says:

—Okay, Renny, September cover's yours. Twenty thousand. Sign here.

And then my phone gives out the soft sample of a tritone from a Balinese gamelan. That would be L. Her timing has always been uncanny (I think she really is a witch).

Now I just need to get out of here. I make a show of reading the contract, but only the payment catches my eye. I scrawl my signature across the bottom of each page with my titanium Thoth and hand them all back to Marcus Chalk, who wordlessly cosigns and hands me back one full copy. (You'd think by now digital signatures would be legally binding—fucking lawyers.)

Any further conversation is perfunctory; the main business has been transacted, my presence is no longer required or even desired. The feeling is mutual. The end of dinner is a blur. Without quite knowing it, I'm out on the sidewalk, trying to hail a cab, check my messages, and suck down as much of a Davidoff as possible. Luck is with me—I hail a Ford Friesian. Best kind of cab, really, since I'm alone. While hybrids are righteous and good and blah blah blah, those separate seats make serious backseat cavorting well nigh impossible. If you stick with the third-row bench seat, you risk the ire of a pissed-off cabdriver, who knows what you're up to and (a) is worried you'll get him a ticket from cops with nothing better to do than hassle him, (b) worried you're going to make a mess back there that he'll have to clean up later, or (c) wants to watch. Since more and more cabs have cameras in them, it's not a good idea to risk an altercation over anything other than the fare (unless you're already in business with him).

First things first. A short exchange with Prince William, and we're set to meet at the Broome Street Bar & Grille at ten. A good spot for me, since it's practically a straight shot across town from where he knows I'm heading now, and since it's high-profile without being exclusive and down-market without lacking class. He'll give me the new speak number, I'll get the word out to my Special clients and add a Fast Forty to the twenty I just signed up from Marcus Chalk. I love it when my legal and illegal paydays overlap.

Having attended to logistics, I turn to the not-to-be-forgotten matter of pleasure. L desires some time off later this evening from the man who thinks he is her fiancé, and could we perhaps meet at our usual spot around ten-thirty, ten-forty-five?

This is how it happens.

The Friesian groans up Fifty-seventh, leans hard left on Seventh (throwing my erection and me into an uncomfortable configuration against the armrest), and we're on the downtown glide path through the neon hell of Times Square.

●

Capitale is a modern temple to indulgent exclusivity; how it survives is beyond me. From the moment you pull up in front of those fluted columns, those stately carved capitals spelling BOWERY SAVINGS BANK (a charming holdover from Gotham's storied past—nobody actually *saves* anymore, not with a zero percent interest rate), past the stone lions and stone-faced security thugs into the glorious main chamber, all Corinthian columns and friezes and mosaics and gel-tinted spots.

Here, the children of privilege giggle and pose and sniffle and flirt, lit up by a hundred flashbulbs, for the pleasure of the leering older crowd who can actually afford such a place. In here, every banker is a pasha, every fund manager a khan. This is the domain of the hyphenated name, indoor shades, and hectares of pampered, succulent, magazine-quality flesh. It will either turn your stomach or make you hard. Or both.

This is where I live, by choice as well as necessity. I may not always be thrilled with it, but I've learned to go with the flow.

This is the great fluid confluence of endless possibility.

Let the games begin.

I'm needing some high-octane fuel after that meet at Shelley's, so I join the horde by the long draped bar, behind a gazelle in sandals with straps reaching all the way up beneath her short pleated skirt. By the time we get our drinks, I've already forgotten her name. She waves a kiwirita around while I carefully balance a massive double Mumbai martini for the obligatory exchange of digital cards. Here, it's permissible, even encouraged, to gawk (whereas Outside, we all studiously avoid making eye contact—these days it can get you killed). So my less than surreptitious appraisal of her décolletage and gluteal musculature does not earn me a kiwirita shower.

It's not long before I see the first familiar face, and the gazelle apparently doesn't like my company, because she's gone with an audible *Nice meeting you* and a muted *Call me* before I sit down at one of the tables along the perimeter of the dance floor (DJs only tonight, but it's too early for this crowd to achieve the requisite chemical boost for a floor show). It's the usual Rogues' Gallery: Here are Luigi, and Chas, and Euan and Timo, and Joss and Tory and Dylan and Siobhan. These are my clients, for better or worse.

—I didn't think you'd all be out on a Tuesday, I offer from behind my Mumbai.

—Tuesday's the new Thursday, quips Tory.

—Monday's the new Friday, adds Chas.

—Wednesday's the new Saturday, Dylan puts in, eager to catch up.

—And *every* hour is happy hour! they chorus, laughing and clinking glasses and inadvertently mixing ingredients. The joyful squeals of adult children at play.

—Here's lookin' at you, kids, I intone, finally starting to relax.

—So, Dr. Feelgood, pipes Timo, got the new number yet?

Timo's a spoiled fucking brat who knows nothing about discretion. But he's also a client, and business is business.

—You'll be the first to know, I assure him with my best wry-insider grin. I should be getting it later tonight.

—You *always* get it later at night, Luigi guffaws through his Negroni. (He's a client, too, but for carnal rather than chemical services, and I'm not in on that end of the business, strange as it may seem.)

—Pig, Joss sighs in disgust. (I wonder if Luigi has had her, too. Joss would seriously freak if she knew where he's been ensconcing his conch. I would have tried for her by now, but Renny's Rule Number Two is No Client Coitus.)

—But you *will* let *us* know first, yes? Your benefactors? Timo drawls, tipping his martini toward me for emphasis.

The prick is playing the boss for his friends, trying to suggest that my access to this party and others like it is due to his patronage. He sees me as some shiny piece of rough trade in from the boroughs to hobnob with Manhattan's hoi polloi, a chance find adding a dash of edgy color to his safe, easy life. Whatever. The getting here was good. I spent thirty-four minutes on my knees, ministering carefully to the clitoris of the senior publicist from the PR firm that set up this party, taking her just to the edge of bliss and bringing her back, over and over, until I finally induced a climax so concussive that she actually passed out. (I really should call her.) I tell myself to relax. I don't need the shit I will surely get if I lose steady customers, but I also don't need to *take* any shit from a brat like this, client or not. Without me, they won't find the speaks, and if they don't find the speaks, they can't buy my Specials. I lean forward and say in a low voice:

—I *said* you'd be the first to know.

It's momentary, a fleeting thing, but the shift is palpable. Timo blinks, the bated breath of the congregation eases out, and Joss gives me an appraising look that says, *Not tonight, but soon.*

But not tonight. I make my goodbyes with just enough haste. There's more business waiting for me at Broome Street.

●

I call Prince William that because (a) he's British, and (b) he can make money out of thin air. How he came to work for our boss, Reza, I have no idea, but it's a natural fit.

I might not be in my position had we not met at the launch party for Moan cologne at the Flatiron Lounge, sponsored by *Pyrethrum* magazine. I was shooting for the mag, he was there because he's got The Knack. (Any party, anywhere, any time, he'll know about it before it happens.) Over round after round of ginger-pear-basil-aspic martinis (those with The Knack never see a bar tab), I told him how I was funding my digital media classes at Pratt with magazine work. He told me I should be at Parsons or the Art Institute (like I could have afforded that at the time). His accent was mesmerizing, his speech hypnotic. He told me that he'd parlayed two double-default mortgages into one of the new three-thousand-square-foot loft conversions in the Mink Building in Harlem for no money down. That's how fucking slick he is. Plenty of players can trade up these days with the glut of housing on the market, but Prince William cleaned up, no mistake.

I know a sales pitch when I hear it, but the Prince was a cut above the rest. He recruited me for Reza with the skill of a master angler, all in a night's work. And when the money started flowing, I was hooked. That was then and this is now, and the wheels on the bus go round and round. Life in the Big Apple in 2012 isn't about pride or principles, it's about survival. And you have to survive to thrive.

Tonight the Prince is at the far end of the bar under the chalkboards, chatting up a pair of buzz-cut birds in tank tops, perhaps planning a three-some. Even if they're lesbians, that wouldn't matter to him, he'd simply see them as yet another challenge. Prince William could talk the devil himself out of a pitchfork; he can certainly talk a couple of dykes too young to be set in their ways into a surf-and-turf. The Brits have this sense of restraint about them, which explains how they get away with such excess. Not just in speech but in print—English-style text layouts are so much more pleasing to the eye, all em dashes and no quotation marks cluttering up dialogue.

My arrival alters the balance of the equation, however, and the two girl-girls take their tattoos out the door (though the shorter one compliments me on my hair, was that an ever so slightly hetero twinkle in her eye?), kindly leaving us their seats. Prince William sits facing me on the stool closest to the wall. I sit next to somebody who might very well be a bum (or an NYU student), where I can face Prince William and also see partway into the back room, from which an interesting kind of noise emanates.

—Driving off potential playmates was not the intention.

—No worries, good sir. They know how to find me. One if not the other, mayhap both.

We always talk like this, he and I. It's not an affectation. Prince William talks the way I'd like to in another life. People always think I'm gay because I speak in complete sentences and use BIG WORDS. Or else just because of my hair. In an age of enhanced communications, the first casualty is speech.

Bon vivant though he is, the Prince looks moody and apprehensive tonight. He's drinking his usual gin gimlet, which I complement with a heavily iced G&T. Out of the corner of my eye over the rim of my first slug, I see him slide the matchbox down the beveled lip of the bar, our bodies blocking all view of the transfer. I put my glass down next to it, which will facilitate a surreptitious pocketing on my next pull. Prince William is going on about something Reza's been saying, something about increasing volume, but I'm not catching all of it because there's an altercation brewing outside the window just across from us, probably over a fucking parking spot, and because standing in the doorway of the back room is a strawberry blonde in a ribbed halter top with a silver navel ring in the middle of the most defined abdominals I've ever seen on a white woman. She's partially shadowed by the spiky, leather-covered carapace of an enormous male of indeterminate species (biker? ball player?), but she's checking her cell phone. Men, for the record: A woman with a man and her cell phone in hand should be classified as Keeping Her Options Open and therefore a viable target. I ease out my iPhone.

—Renny, you listening, mate? This is serious, the Prince says seriously.

—So is this, I reply, thumbing up iHook. This handy little app (created anonymously online, a gratis download) is tailor-made for those looking to connect on the sly while still in sight of a significant other, or in this case, standing right next to him. The woman with the cobblestone stomach is obviously bored with her present company, and a gentleman should never let a lady rest unamused. It's not long before our eyes connect. One thing that hasn't gone out of style is the age-old technique of using bar mirrors to make eye contact, thus avoiding the possibility of being caught staring at someone else's girlfriend, thereby inviting assault or murder. Twice in two minutes is the rule, and I can see the look of wry surprise, the connection, and that exquisite moment, the only two people in a crowded room sharing a secret. I thumb over my introductory message (iHook can beam up to twenty feet between phones without making a call and blowing your cover, a handy resuscitation of old technology): BORED? (A text is usually accompanied by a sig file consisting of a photo of oneself and contact information.) She juts out her chin a bit to hide the smile, turns her face toward her company, and crosses her arms at the border of her halter top, her phone in her lower hand, pointed my way. I'm only halfway through my drink before I get the reply: WITH SOMEONE. MAYBE LATER. She looks over at me to make sure I've gotten the message (I experience again that luscious sensation of speaking a language only we two understand) before turning back to her eurypterid boyfriend.

Prince William, who has been following the whole vignette in the bar mirror, drops his head and sighs through his nose, his mouth in a tight-lipped smile, and raises his glass.

—My dear Renny, you are truly fucking incorrigible. I admire that in a man.

—It's the scandalous company I'm forced to keep, I reply, clinking glasses.

—Look, *do* try to make Reza happy, Prince William says, and I'm surprised, because it sounds like there's genuine concern in his voice. He's got quite a nasty temper, you know. We have to move more product, period. Full stop.

—No worries, mate, I say through clenched teeth around an unlit Davidoff, leaving a twenty on the bar. *À bientôt.*

I have to cross the street to light up, because it's always better to hail a hack on the far corner so you don't lose money sitting at a red light. Also, the altercation outside the bar has turned nasty, two neck-tattooed behemoths in jumped-up pimpwear (one black, one Latino) screaming an endless stream of *muthafucka*s at each other. This is street stupidity; there are probably sixteen cameras on them now, between the security cams on the traffic lights and the phones of the crowd come-a-gawking. Traffic's against me, I can't cross, there's an empty Ford Heifer parked right in front of me, but the driver's on *his* fucking phone and waves me off. Asshole. Luckily, an empty Ford Friesian rolls up neatly behind the Heifer, and I've got the door open, and I hear the scuffle on the street coming closer, and then there's a scream (man? woman?) and I hear someone shout something like *stigmata*, and car doors are opening and now several women are screaming (Get in the cab) and men are shouting and cursing (Get in the cab, Renny) and the driver of the Heifer in front of us is out on the sidewalk wrestling the black guy to the ground, and now I can hear sirens (RENNY, GET IN THE FUCKING CAB) and I'm in the cab and the driver locks the doors and stomps on the gas and the motor gargles to life and I see the belligerent Latino frozen with his hands at his sides staring down the laser beam coming from beneath the muzzle of a weird-looking pistol held rock-steady in the hands of the bum/NYU student I was sitting beside in the bar and the Friesian lumbers across West Broadway toward the river and the highway and I'm gone.

•

—What kind of gun was it? L asks me over her *caipirinha*.

—I don't know. It looked weird. Kind of like Will Smith's gun in *I, Robot*.

We're snug at the front-window table at Ouest. No matter how crowded the bar gets, L always seems to be able to get this table. She likes it because she can hide behind the framed clips in the window, but she can still see out on the street. With her particular beauty, she's always a little uncomfortable in public, but it's really just because she has to keep a watchful eye out for the man who thinks he's her fiancé. She doesn't explain, and I don't ask. She says he travels a lot. I figure she uses him for a sugar daddy, or maybe window dressing to ward off any annoying family pressure. I don't know and I don't care, because as long as I can keep fucking her with no strings attached, it doesn't matter whom she's with or what story she tells. You'd feel the same way, believe me.

I'm still a little shaky from earlier. It isn't clear to me what happened; maybe it was just one of those random rootless acts of violence that happen so often these days, a mistimed glance or an overheard utterance leading to carnage. The cops put it down mighty quick, but what were they doing there? Broome Street's a legit bar, been there since before I was born, it's not a speak.

Being here now with L, getting lost in her eyes, watching her exquisite mouth, and knowing what pleasure it can bring, is taking the edge off. The man who thinks he is her fiancé must realize that although he can put a ring on her finger (which I've never seen her wear), he cannot possibly hope to keep her to himself. There is too much passion in her, too much sexual fire banked behind a facade of stylish gentility (she's an investment banker, or so she says). After our much too brief first date, she took me shopping at James Perse in the West Village, walked in on me in the back dressing room as I was changing, and proceeded to give me the blow job by which I have since measured all others. In the backseat of the Heifer on the way back to my place that night, we achieved everything but St. George–style penetration (and not for lack of trying). When I'm with her, I feel like ancient European royalty instead of a freelancer from Queens. Prince William and Reza and my Specials clientele and the whole miserable *Roundup* crew and the NYPD and every thug in the city can all go fuck themselves raw. I've got L, she's *mine*.

For the next few hours, anyway.

We read each other's signals effortlessly, and not soon enough we're in the back of a Toyota Jersey en route to my place, oblivious to the outside world as we drink deeply from each other's mouths, our fingers whispering beneath fabric and the rising heat from her body diffusing through mine. I am delighted to discover she is wearing the tuxedo-style panties I bought her at Kiki de Montparnasse in SoHo. (Clearly, the man who thinks he is her fiancé has not familiarized himself with her lingerie collection and thereby deserves his fate.) We maintain discretion from the backseat of the cab through the front vestibule and down the hall to my apartment, where she silently eases up behind me as I'm fumbling with my goddamn keys, smoothly pulls down my zipper, and deftly wraps her hand around my painfully stiff cock (I never wear underwear when I'm stepping out for the evening), letting out an appreciative grunt at the absence of pubic hair and the presence of the condom I put on in the men's room at Ouest (maintaining an erection indefinitely is not a challenge when I'm in L's presence).

I've barely managed to get the damn door open when she shoves me against the inner alcove wall, slamming the door shut with her magnificent ass, her tongue lighting a trail from my mouth to my balls to my brain stem. Now I've got her pushed against the front door, her skirt up around her waist, one of her powerful legs wrapped tightly around my ass, her tuxedo undone, and liquid fire between us. I recognize the suburbs of her first climax when she starts moaning softly in Czech.

—*Prosím nezastavit.*

The challenge at this point is to stave off my own orgasm as long as possible (L is multi-orgasmic; my record is four of hers to one of my own, and every time we're together, I try to beat that). Every man has his own method, of course, from the commonsensical (reciting the alphabet backward) to the tedious (counting backward from a hundred by sevens). My own prolonging agent is the Mana Mana song from the Muppets, a time-honored method that never lets me down. Try it sometime and see.

Mana ma*na* (do do do-do-do . . .)

—*Slyšte!*

*Mana ma*na (*do do do-do . . .)*

—*Těžší! DÁT TO MĚ!*

*Mana ma*na (*do do do-do-do, do-do-do, do-do-do, do-do-do-do-do-do-do-do-do!)*

—Ó BŮH!! ZAMÝŠLÍM PŘIJET JEDNA TISÍCINA ČASY!!!

And once again we leave this vale of tears all too briefly for one of shimmering golden stars.

ON THE SET

SANTIAGO LIKED THE view from Vernon Boulevard and Fiftieth. Sitting in the little park by the 7 stop, the last one completed before the Greenstreets program was shut down to save money, he could look across the river from Queens toward the skyline of Manhattan and wonder if the city would try to kill him again today.

Probably not. It was his day off, which meant he'd have time to make the run up north with his father and be back in time for his second job. Traffic and other conditions permitting, it would be a round trip of some four, perhaps five, hours. Since it was currently four A.M., he would, as usual, go straight to work when the store opened at ten and let his father take the van home to unload. As for many cops, Santiago's second job was doing retail security work, which was plentiful around town, as the surviving stores and restaurants needed all the help they could get. Santiago was a rent-a-cop for Barneys, twelve-hour shifts of standing around looking menacing for the rich, or at least those who still had good credit.

It would be a fairly quiet drive; he'd loaded up his iPhone with Manzanita and Tomatito for the ride. His one contribution to his father's van was an adapter for the dash radio, on which his father had relented after Santiago played him a Juan Luis Guerra track from his phone over the Bose speaker system at the audio place. Santiago always planned ahead.

A chilly breeze came up off the river, bringing with it a nice whiff of a passing garbage barge. Santiago shifted his weight from one cheek to the other, adjusting himself so his gun wouldn't dig into his back.

Not that he'd have much need for it, even sitting by himself on a park bench in Queens at four in the morning, as the bars shut down and the drunks windmilled their way home (or wherever they went). Detective (third grade) Sixto Fortunato Santiago stood six-five and weighed between 220 and 230, depending on how recently he'd been to his parents' house for dinner. His most prominent features other than his large eyes were his outsize hands, which had the look of leather well broken in. His hands were the product of years in his father's machine shop, on the steel press, the English wheel, the lathe. Every family member took a turn in the shop, but Santiago had racked up the most hours by far. Smoothly worn calluses extended from the base of his palms to his fingertips. A woman once told him that his hands felt like polished wood as he moved them over her body. The woman was long gone, but her observation had stayed with him, a parting gift.

As the youngest of four children, Santiago had taken plenty of shit as it rolled downhill from his sister and two brothers. His asshole brother Rafa had been especially cruel, viewing his younger sibling as a servant/ scapegoat/punching bag put on earth for his own personal use. Santiago always gave as good as he got, but the difference in age and mass favored the elder. That had changed during Santiago's fourteenth summer, when his father got him a job on a Poland Spring water truck through a friend. The awkward Santiago, in the middle of a growth spurt and unused to his shifting size and weight, spent twelve-hour days humping five-gallon jugs and thirty-six-bottle cases of water into offices and delis all over town. That was when he first started learning about the city, its staggered lights, the traffic patterns, the best shortcuts between boroughs to use at rush hour. The city had opened up and out, expanding his sights far beyond his Fort Tryon neighborhood.

At the end of that summer, at the start of a blistering, humid Labor Day weekend, Santiago's asshole brother Rafa had started in on him over some meaningless shit that neither remembered, right when Santiago had gotten home from a particularly grueling shift. Without thinking, Santiago had synchronized the relevant muscle groups from shoulder to wrist, mas- sively built up by the power of DNA, time, and water, and sent one huge fist along a dead-level trajectory into his brother's solar plexus, aiming for the wall three feet behind Rafa's back. Rafa had sat down on the floor and puked all over himself, their mother had come running and screaming, and Santiago had been banished to the shower by his beaming father, Victor, who surreptitiously gave him a hearty pat on his broadening back.

Later that weekend, Santiago had experienced for the first time the sublime joy of a girl putting her mouth around his penis.

There had been nothing said, but a subtle shift in family dynamics had occurred. There'd been no more bullying, no more leaning on *hermano pequeño*. Santiago knew he had crossed the invisible barrier between childhood and something more: He could feel it in his carriage and gait, and the rest of the family knew it as well. His brothers had stopped bothering him, even warmed toward him a bit. His sister, Esperanza, with whom he'd always had the best relationship, became a trusted confidante who backed him whenever he cooked up a story to feed their mother, on whom Santiago's burgeoning popularity with the neighborhood girls was not lost. His father, Santiago knew, did not buy his bullshit for one second but subtly toed the line. Santiago knew that he could not lie to his father and that Victor knew it as well. Their relationship deepened accordingly, something Santiago was privately fiercely proud of, living as he was in a time and place where over 20 percent of fathers abandoned families before the firstborn reached first grade. Victor Santiago was differently made, and his youngest son realized it at a crucial time.

Twice-tapped brights from down Vernon Boulevard brought Santiago off the bench. Victor's van glided smoothly to a stop by the Café Brasilia, and Santiago climbed in, wordlessly plugging his iPhone into the dash and thumbing up his playlist, trying not to think about the large, heavy-looking shape behind them in the cargo area, hidden under an old mover's blanket. Jesús Alemañy's golden trumpet fanned out from eight speakers.

The van was typical Victor. It was a fourth-generation Honda Odyssey originally seized in a drug raid. Santiago had steered his father to a police auction after a rare argument. Victor originally wanted to buy one off a guy he knew in the Bronx, an entrepreneur in the booming black market for hybrids, but his son the cop put his foot down. For two thousand cash, Victor had driven it off the auction lot, straight to his machine shop, where he spent the next six weeks breaking it down and rebuilding it. He junked the old cylinder head and bored out the cylinders another hundredth of an inch, machining a new head and valve covers himself. A metalworker he knew in Brooklyn forged him a new crankshaft and pistons. He ran stainless-steel lines to new stainless-steel brakes and bolted up a whole new stainless-steel exhaust system. New stainless tank and fuel pump, new alloy radiator, a larger oil cooler, ECU remap, lightweight alloy rims (not too fancy, Santiago didn't want the neighborhood *vatos* all over the van) on premium all-weather tires. Santiago helped out stripping the cabin, which was braced, plumbed for the Bose system, then outfitted and upholstered over several weekends by some guy named José from Jersey whom Victor knew. For an unspecified amount of cash, José replaced the factory front seats with eight-way power adjustables from a top-of-the-line Lexus. (Santiago didn't want to know.) Wherever possible, Victor obtained the maximum warranty available on the new parts. The paint job was good but unremarkable (though Victor had the body and frame taken down to bare metal and sprayed with a chemical rust inhibitor before painting, courtesy of a fellow *plátano* he knew from home who now ran a body shop in the South Bronx). At a glance, the van looked like every third people-mover on the street. Closer inspection hinted at the humdrum Honda's hidden potential; one time behind the wheel turned the most diehard skeptic into a true believer. Santiago christened it the Ninja Van.

Victor wheeled them around for the riverside loop north, up 278 and over the Kosciuszko Bridge to pick up the Cross Bronx Expressway (skirting the toll off the Triboro Bridge), slotting them smoothly up I-95 away from the city, the opposite lanes forming a single sclerotic artery of immobile semis, reefers, and tankers, inbound at a geologic pace to help the city survive one more day. Not for the first time, Santiago thought that blocking this crucial stretch of roadway, along with maybe one tunnel or bridge, be it barricade or bomb, would cause the city to crumple to its knees like a man kicked brutally in the balls.

They spoke little as they left the city behind, watching the sprawling slums give way to derelict suburbs full of empty housing developments, artifacts of a boom gone bad. Santiago cherished the fact that he could simply sit with his father on a long drive without having to say anything. There were times when he thought the city would triumph, not by physically killing him but by filling his head with so much noise that he would want to check out voluntarily. When he was growing up, there was always a spare set of bunk beds in the tiny bedroom where Santiago and his brothers were crammed, for relatives and close friends emigrating from the DR to the city and points north. Santiago had gone to the overcrowded George Washington High School on Audubon Avenue, which he'd always thought of as a zoo with a loading zone. And joining the department had plunged him headlong into the freak parade that was life in New York City at the turn of a century and millennium.

It had been Victor who'd given him the unimaginable gift of privacy.

It was partly the result of diligent hard work, part windfall, and part historical accident. Victor's machine shop had prospered enough to support his growing family, though not enough to get them out of the cramped rental walk-up in Inwood, a north Manhattan neighborhood just starting to turn in the 1990s. September 11 had thrown everything up in the air. That night Victor had come home with extra-fine-particle filter masks and goggles and told them in no uncertain terms, glaring at his youngest son, that anyone going south of Twenty-third Street should wear them at all times or he would beat the living shit out of them. Santiago was put to work sifting rubble for bodies and directing traffic in and around Ground Zero for two weeks, and he wore the gear every day, showering twice daily. Fourteen bronchial cases in his unit later, Santiago thanked the Virgin and her blessed son for his father's foresight, although he tended to see his father as more of a shaman from an older time, when having such mystical vision was considered a blessing and not some voodoo bullshit to be buried under canon law.

Victor had paid close attention to the government's response to the attacks in the subsequent months, as the family tensed for financial disaster. When the Fed cut interest rates to 1 percent, Victor had borrowed as much as he thought he could recoup within one year, invested in new plant and equipment, and, over time, paid off the loan early. When Santiago had asked his father why he agreed to be penalized for early repayment, Victor had cuffed him a good one across the side of the head, snarling, "*Carajo*, you wanna save a few bucks, or you wanna be debt-free ASAP?"

The gambit paid off. As the city recovered, the shop got more work, and with its new equipment and some new hired hands (though Santiago and his siblings still put in at least ten hours a week on top of their day jobs), the receivables column in Victor's ledger got longer. Santiago began noticing *The Wall Street Journal* lying around the shop alongside the *Post*, the *Daily News*, and *El Diario*. The night of the first airstrike on Baghdad in '03, Santiago (who by that point was living in Long Island City and liking it) had been summoned back up to Inwood for dinner. Over his mother's heavenly *chivo picante*, *lambí guisado*, and *mofongo*, washed down with glacial bottles of Presidente, Santiago and his siblings were informed that Victor was making a bid to buy the building where his shop was located. Gasps of *ay* and *coño* went up from everyone except Santiago and his mother, who nailed her asshole son Ricardo a good one on the back of the head for his profanity. After dinner, while the others whooped it up with cigars and rum, Santiago confronted his father and asked him just what the fuck he thought he was doing.

"You want another one?" Victor replied, raising a cocked backhand. Though not, Santiago recalled fondly, without a smile—just as well, since by this time Santiago had nearly a foot and a hundred pounds on his father.

Once again, Victor's foresight brought his family unprecedented prosperity. Soon he owned not just the building housing his company but the apartment where he and Santiago's mother lived. Victor had kept a wary eye on the city's exploding real estate market, and Santiago often overheard his father muttering and grumbling to himself in the shop as he read the papers—things like "*Perra*, you take your fucking ARMs and shove 'em up your ass."

Since just before 9/11, Santiago had lived in a third-floor walk-up in a well-kept prewar apartment building on Vernon Boulevard. It was a two-bedroom with plenty of space and light, there being few skyscrapers in the neighborhood at the time. Santiago had little furniture with which to clutter it up. He'd worked on the kitchen slightly to indulge his keen interest in cooking, and turned the living room into a makeshift home gym with state-of-the-art Precor equipment bought on the cheap (more choice pickings at a police auction, there being no end of raids and seizures of homes occupied by pharmaceutical entrepreneurs). The owner of the building, a tough old Jew named Hiram, had cashed out when property values peaked in '06, and the new owner (some hedge-fund kid from Manhattan who never even visited the building) jumped in with both feet, leveraged to the hairline, thinking the market would never drop. Drop it did, and violently, over the course of the next two years, in every borough but Manhattan, and while trying to track down the new owner to find out why the building had no heat one January, Santiago discovered that said owner had thrown the keys at Urbank and disappeared (ahead of a host of creditors and an SEC investigation of his fund). Once Urbank repossessed the building, Santiago and his fellow renters were offered buyouts.

Once again, Victor Santiago had displayed shamanic foresight and timing. When asked, he had advised his son to buy the apartment outright, counseled him on the finer points of first-time mortgage application

("*Cabrón*, you tell them you want a thirty-year fixed at this rate, that's all, they try to sell you some horseshit deal, you tell 'em to go fuck themselves in the ass"), and co-signed the loan with some tender words of advice for his youngest ("You miss one fucking payment, just one, you're out in the street, I don't give a shit, you come crying to me, I'll piss in your face, *claro*?"). So Santiago had the monthly sword of Damocles hanging over his head, but the apartment was *his*.

Suddenly, his mind was brimming with possibilities. He did two things immediately: He applied for a second job, at Barneys, on the referral of a brother from his unit who also worked there; and he celebrated his first night as a homeowner with a girl he knew from Inwood named Anilda, who fucked him so hard he had bruises and friction burns on his groin and thighs for three days.

Victor's move on his youngest son's behalf was unprecedented, and there were some angry words around the dinner table when the news was broken, but the old man stood firm, and by this time neither of Santiago's asshole brothers would even think of getting in his face over this. His sister, for her part, bought Santiago a George Foreman grill (the big one with the griddle on the side) as a housewarming present, and he began to consider that life might just actually be sweet.

Santiago's mother had thoughtfully prepared some highway snacks for them, since he and Victor agreed that all the road food along I-95 would gag a subway rat. For fifty miles, they munched intermittently and blissfully on grilled poblano peppers stuffed with fresh crabmeat (which she had thoughtfully picked over for shells), and Santiago reminded himself for the umpteenth time what a lucky SOB he was, even as a part-time security guard and a full-time street cop with the Citywide Anticrime Bureau, easily one of the most dangerous jobs in town.

Victor brought him back to earth abruptly when, on the outskirts of New Haven, he asked, "How's it going with your new partner?"

Santiago sighed. "Could be better," he said wearily.

●

Thirty-six hours earlier, Santiago had nearly checked out forever when two morons bent on killing each other over a fucking parking spot had trashed a weeklong investigation of the drug trade flowing through the city's bars.

It was nothing new. The market lay just beneath the surface, the demand was always there, it was a matter of asking around until you connected. No surprise, really; since Bratton and Kelly had kicked the dealers off the streets so they wouldn't scare off well-moneyed tourists, the trade had simply moved indoors. Tourists liked having good illegal drugs to accompany the legal ones just as much as native New Yorkers did, and with cops working multiple jobs to raise enough weakened dollars to keep their heads above water, well, the usual graft was getting unusually thick.

It was compounded by the fact that the city's drug merchants had set up a triple-tiered trade for cocaine. First came top-of-the-line powder ($250 a gram), then heavily cut rock ($10 a vial), then the dreaded *paco*. This new South American import was a waste product of the refining process that had become a profitable way to dispose of even the last dregs of a shipment. It was blamed for a quarter of all the overdoses in the city, as well as a third of violent drug-related crimes. Combine that with 10 percent inflation and 12 percent unemployment, a hiring freeze in a police force already cut back 20 percent from its 2008 size, soaring food prices, and annual tax hikes, and you had a recipe for apocalypse.

The one thing that could be counted upon to prop up the city was tourism. Not that New York was Disney World, far from it. But with the government's unprecedented spending binge, the dollar had dropped through the floor, and just about anyone from anywhere else could afford to live it up in New York—hey, it's a *safe* big city, the FBI says crime is at its lowest point in half a century! So, word had come down from City Hall via NYPD high command: Keep the knuckleheads down. Young Arab swingers flush with petrodollars, jetting in on private planes to the Big Apple to do all the drinking and fucking they couldn't do at home, well, they tended to get turned off when a *paco*-crazed junkie drove a stolen SUV into the lounge bar where they were making time with those loose American girls. Well-scrubbed German families converting stronger euros to weaker dollars tended to "turn around and advance" back to the nice safe EU with a quickness when an overheard comment—or, God forbid, eye contact—between locals led to whole magazines being unloaded in classrooms, movie theaters, and subway stations.

And then there were the speaks, which the NYPD couldn't begin to get a handle on. As per their namesake, the speaks were illegal bars; unlike the ones of old, however, these floated with no fixed address through scores of buildings left vacant by the real estate crash. A bar would vanish from one address only to pop up at another. The mechanism was a phantom network that broadcast the next location of each speak with little advance notice. No one knew how the information was transmitted, which made it all but impossible for the cops to crack. Not that any of this would have come up on the cops' radar if not for the fact that the speaks provided excellent cover for all sorts of criminal activity, from drugs to prostitution, and even that would've gone unnoticed in the carnage that was New York City in 2012 if not for the body count such nightlife racked up. Vice, Narcotics, and Homicide were undermanned, overwhelmed, and outmaneuvered. The cheerleaders of chaos and entropy were thriving and diversifying, while the home team of law and order was in the ICU.

Then some genius had dreamed up the Citywide Anticrime Bureau (CAB). Basically a revamping and expansion of the anticrime units in place at most precincts, CAB was a task force aimed at holding back the rising tide that utilized street-level undercover work. Officers from any division in the NYPD could volunteer. Units were organized under local area commanders, all veterans, with each unit spearheaded by field teams in undercover taxicabs backed up by what remained of the uniformed department, organized into flying squads. CAB units, as per their namesake, had citywide jurisdiction, authorized to use deadly force when necessary. Then came the incentive: CAB cops racked up points based on collars made and cases cleared, a merit system designed to retain seasoned veterans (who were otherwise leaving the force in droves) as well as attract fresh young talent. To sweeten the pot, the panjandrums of One Police Plaza dangled the golden bough: Detectives who reached a predetermined point level earned a transfer to OCID, the Organized Crime Intelligence Division, long held by most cops to be the Valhalla of the NYPD.

The scheme worked at first. Young cops of Santiago's age, with new families and mortgages to feed, eagerly signed up for CAB detail. New transfers from all departments began swelling the CAB ranks, pooling their experience and competing in a cavalier fashion that irked some of the more established police classes, such as the Homicide dicks. With their shiny shoes and metallic suits, the murder cops considered themselves the landed gentry of the department and did not care for the young guns driving all over their turf in their dirty fucking taxicabs. But they had no choice, being up to their trouser pleats in bodies. Crime was spiking, the force was shrinking, and the city needed to be thrown a lifeline. CAB was a child of the age, dubbed by one *Times* reporter as "the biggest little shakeup in the history of the NYPD."

Then Aubrey Bright happened, and the new CAB unit nearly died at birth.

It was only natural that, as the CAB field teams jostled to turn crime into job credits, different minorities would take the lead in different locales. Which member would go undercover depended on the "set," or situation. Latino cops worked Latino sets, black cops worked black sets, and so forth. Aubrey Bright, an up-and-coming twenty-two-year-old fresh out of uniform, had taken point to work a black club in the Flatiron District, home to a number of boisterous nightspots that often hosted assaults, stabbings, and shootings, as well as a river of drug traffic. Aubrey Bright had gotten decked out in his best Sean John, sidled on the set with his best hustle-and-flow, and been made in about five seconds by a notorious gangsta rap star known as MC Cancer, and an equally notorious drug dealer, both stoned to the eyeballs, in the club's best booth near the back, each enjoying his own personal bottle of Cristal and a below-table blow job from a female staff member employed by the club for that very purpose.

Aubrey Bright had been dragged out the back door to an adjacent parking lot by the rapper and the dealer, who beat him to a cracked wet pulp before the dealer emptied a full Glock magazine into his body. The murder was recorded by a security camera atop one of the parking lot fence posts; after shooting Aubrey Bright, the dealer pulled down his pants and waggled his genitals at the camera lens. The pair then jumped into a Lincoln Navigator SE and roared out of the lot, with the left-side wheels rolling over Aubrey Bright's corpse, collapsing his rib cage and skull, and splashing viscera across the tarmac. By the time the CAB backup team caught up, the rapper had wrapped the SUV around a Dumpster half a block down the street. In the ensuing firefight, 112 rounds were fired, a large number of which ended up inside MC Cancer. The drug dealer survived by running out of ammo, then repeating his earlier genital gesture, at which time one of the field team officers subdued him with a Taser shot to a sensitive area. All of which was recorded on the phones of more than a dozen gawking bystanders.

It was a cascading nightmare that never seemed to let up. First the CAB unit was taken balls-first over a cheese grater by the media, with much hand-wringing and shit-eating being done for the cameras by the mayor, the police commissioner, and the head of CAB, who was summarily dismissed and promptly made for points unknown. Then the arraignment, in which the playback from the club's security camera was shown as evidence by the (black) prosecutor, causing the (black) stenographer to vomit. The (white) defense attorney tried for a clemency plea before being loudly and profanely fired by his client, who had to be hauled kicking and spitting from the courtroom by burly (black) bailiffs, to be sentenced in absentia. The (black) judge gave the defendant life without parole in record time; the (black) officers involved in the shooting were exonerated and publicly lauded by the commissioner.

That the officers were black evoked little sympathy in the black community; in the public's eyes, said blacks were blue. WHERE DO WE GO FROM HERE? was the title of a mournful editorial over the byline of one of the *Times*'s most prominent black columnists, while the cover of a high-profile black scholarly journal featured a cartoon of a whirlpool with one dark arm visible, on which was written BLACK YOUTH in dropped-out type. Black community leaders scheduled a coordinated series of civil disobedience gatherings citywide, for which absolutely no one showed up. Aubrey Bright died on a Monday night; an ominous silence had descended over the city by Wednesday afternoon.

Everyone knew what was coming, which was why CAB wasn't disbanded despite nonstop howling from the City Council and numerous community groups. Captain McKeutchen had called his boys together; he was grandfatherly in his own way, Santiago thought, if your grandfather kept blown-up color stills from his latest colonoscopy on his office wall. After giving them a short speech about duty, honor, and riding out the storm—"Like an impacted turd, this too shall pass"—he'd sat down heavily in his reinforced chair and, for the first time in unit memory, started cleaning his service weapon, a two-inch S&W Airlite 340PD .357 with a five-shot cylinder, grunting, "The odd one's for me."

Thirty seconds later, Santiago was the first CAB cop to the armory, plowing right over a pair of tense uniformed rookies demanding M-16s; he managed to talk down a panicky duty sergeant who was fortifying himself with a bottle of Ten High he didn't bother to hide. After a brief shopping trip through the ordnance locker, Santiago took his pickings out to one of the unmarked cabs. He'd floored it up the Henry Hudson Parkway,

Victor in his hands-free headset helping him coordinate, racing the sun as it careened toward the Palisades, as though eager to hide from the coming storm. Once back in his parents' neighborhood, he'd stopped at a gas station on Dyckman Street, topped off the tank, checked the oil and tires, and strong-armed the nervous attendant into giving him two extra five-gallon jerricans of gas and a case of Poland Spring half-liter water bottles.

For the next three days, as rioting spread throughout the city, Santiago had lived in his taxicab, Victor in his headset, a dashboard solar charger for his iPhone and the police radio chattering nonstop, a twelve-gauge Benelli M4 Tactical semiauto cradled in his huge hands. Santiago didn't know why his CO was allowing him to do what he was doing, which was against the entire NYPD rule book, but he was supremely grateful. He checked in with McKeutchen regularly on his command line, wanting to make sure that if he were hung out to dry, he'd do what he could to see that his boss would be spared.

Those had been a bad three days. The department essentially set up security islands north of the fortified Ninety-sixth Street barricade, dubbed "The White Zone" by the media in Manhattan, one around 181st Street to guard the George Washington Bridge, one at 168th Street to guard Columbia Presbyterian Hospital, which was starting to overflow with Harlem's wounded, and 116th Street to guard Columbia University, where the more radical protesters were teargassed and clubbed and dragged around the corner to St. Luke's Roosevelt Hospital on Amsterdam Avenue, while their vocal support—those with lots of pins on their backpacks—disappeared in a hurry.

Up in Inwood, Santiago was more or less on his own, but the neighborhood was having none of it. Surly Latinos (many with chests bared) wielding an impressive array of weaponry both legal and illegal stood watch in front of their homes and businesses. Santiago made food runs between his parents' house and his father's shop, delivering large amounts of fried plantains and *pollo guisado* from his mother's kitchen to Victor and some of his staff, who had effectively barricaded themselves in the shop; Victor sat on the roof of the building with binoculars, his iPhone, and Santiago's service Glock. Santiago didn't blame his asshole brothers for not helping with the vigil, as they had families of their own to watch over, while he himself was single. His sister was doing triage work at Mount Sinai, coping with the overflow of wounded, though well protected by a squad detailed from the nearby Twenty-fourth Precinct—another favor from McKeutchen, who claimed it dovetailed with department policy to protect all hospitals during the riots.

Excepting the occasional roving posse car, nobody came near the old taxicab with the big scowling Latino at the wheel and an enormous shotgun poking out the driver's-side window. He'd stuck his badge high up on the left side of his jacket, so that any trigger-happy uniforms or ESU teams wouldn't blow him away by mistake, and listened to the reports of fires and looting coming in from East New York, Brownsville, Bushwick, Bed-Stuy, East Flatbush, Crown Heights, Greenpoint, Borough Park, Hunts Point, Mott Haven, Soundview, Morrisania, Parkchester, Tremont, Fordham, Hollis, Jamaica Estates, and Hillcrest. When the storm subsided as abruptly as it had begun, the death toll would be twice that of the 1993 Los Angeles riots, with untold numbers of wounded; property damage was estimated at half a trillion dollars. The media later reported that the most sought-after items from looted stores were iPhones, liquor, and PlayStation 5s.

Santiago had traced a meandering route along Fort Washington Avenue, around Fort Tryon Park and the Cloisters, across Nagle Avenue to Dyckman Street, up and around Fort George Hill, down the western border of High Bridge Park, and back along St. Nicholas Avenue. He kept a wary eye on all the stairwells descending from the elevated 1 subway line, as well as the exits from the A train terminus at 207th Street. There wasn't much he could do about the Broadway and Henry Hudson bridges, but he knew from his radio that squads from the Thirty-third and Thirty-fourth precincts, as well as DOT teams, had set up twin checkpoints (later reinforced with the few local National Guard units just back from Iraq). Officially, Santiago was detailed to the bridge details; off the record, he was off the reservation.

Santiago hadn't done much reflecting about the riots or their place in the city's history. Other than immediate thoughts of his family, he found himself remembering his days coming up in Traffic, long before his transfer to CAB, and his old partner Bea Goldberg, a wizened old Jewish lady from Sunnyside, looking to see how big a pension she could rack up before the department cut her loose. Santiago had been a happy young buck in those days of boom time, before the credit and real estate busts. The city had revealed another side of itself to him, one of infinite possibility and prizes for the taking. He couldn't wait to get to work in those days, nailing one stolen car after another, collaring joyriders, car thieves, and chop-shop couriers. He'd learned how to do research, rapidly run down histories (criminal, credit, employment, or medical), find patterns in seemingly meaningless reams of data, spot a mope on the move from a great distance. It was so easy. He'd just drive to the nearest school, wait for the most expensive car to roll up, and pounce. He remembered being chided by his partner for profiling, a concept he readily employed. "Bea, honey," he drawled, feeling oddly paternalistic toward the ancient dwarf sharing his radio car, "you call it like you see it. If you see some knucklehead barely old enough to shave behind the wheel of a brand-new SL95 AMG, you stop him on principle. Ninety-nine percent of the time, you either got credit card fraud or grand theft auto. If you don't, you just say, 'Have a nice day.' All it takes is a few minutes of time on your computer, and these badges we wear say we can stop whoever we want, whenever we want. At the end of the day, we get more collars, the city gets fewer people defaulting on their credit cards or using stolen or fake ones, and the department maybe even gets a few bucks selling the cars we seize at auction. Everybody wins except the knucklehead who deserves to lose anyway. See?"

"*Nu*, right you could *effsher* be, but as it is, *boychik*," conceded Bea Goldberg. "Even verse, ven young you are, but since ven the vorld vuz easy? Esk any Jew."

Bea Goldberg was always one for folk homilies. She never badmouthed anyone, never raised her voice, never cursed, and Santiago loved her for it. She was an oasis of warm harmlessness in a population bursting with anything but. He liked to give her "Goldbug hugs," sincere embraces carefully designed for her tiny, delicate frame (he would have crushed her otherwise). But for all her kindness, Bea Goldberg was beset over the years by a spectacular series of physical ailments—viral pneumonia, rheumatoid arthritis, acid reflux, tendinitis, constipation, heart murmur, and bunions. Still, she never complained.

Santiago knew there was something unusually wrong at the beginning of their last shift together, about six months before his transfer to CAB and the riots, during one of those daylong drenching New York rains that sent the cockroaches scurrying up the pipes into peoples' apartments to escape the deluge. Bea Goldberg came on shift looking like a wet rag, and once inside the radio car, slumped against the passenger window.

"You okay, Goldbug?" Santiago asked nervously. Chronic fatigue was a daily condition with Bea Goldberg, given her medical history, but Santiago sensed something further amiss.

"Tired is vat I yam," Bea Goldberg said in a ragged voice just above a whisper. "Okay you drive?"

Drive Santiago did, like a bat out of hell, straight to the emergency entrance of St. Vincent's Hospital on Seventh Avenue (now subsisting on federal aid), where he threatened to arrest two paramedics lighting up if they didn't move their fucking bus clear of the admitting bay. The shouting went unnoticed by Bea Goldberg, who had lost consciousness almost immediately after Santiago pulled away from the station house. Santiago jammed the navy blue Traffic Malibu nose-first into the admitting bay, left the motor running, and carefully carried the comatose Bea Goldberg inside (Jesus, she weighed *nothing*, nothing at all, even in full uniform), where he got into a shouting match with a bitchy West Indian nurse who was nearly his own size. The last he saw of her, Bea Goldberg was flat out on a gurney, being slammed through a set of double doors bearing the words AUTHORIZED PERSONNEL ONLY BEYOND THIS POINT in angry red letters. Santiago then turned slowly to look at the half-dozen or so faces in the admitting area, waiting, offering only the same look of fear and helplessness. He steeled himself as best he could for the wait.

Although he'd been watching the clock, Santiago lost track of how long he'd stood there waiting for news. It seemed that a smiling, jovial young doctor bearing the name tag ZUCKERMAN simply materialized in front of him and told him with jarring bonhomie that Bea Goldberg's leukocyte count was down through the floor, acute neutropenia, the cancer already at end-stage, would he be able to contact her family? The happy young medicine man then swerved off toward an anxious-looking couple behind Santiago whom he cheerfully informed that the malignancy in their five-year-old's liver had already metastasized, there was nothing they could do, they'd try to keep him comfortable, and would they please come this way? And off they went, Dr. Zuckerman waving to the nurses at the admitting desk.

Santiago had stood in the middle of the waiting area, Bea Goldberg's uniform jacket, hat, and belt gathered in his huge hands, utterly at a loss for which violent emotion surging through him to indulge first. He watched the second hand of the hospital clock make a full revolution (though he could not, and later would not, remember what time it was). At some point a cool breeze blew in through his mind, as though from far offshore, and he had his iPhone in hand before he knew it. Within a minute he had an ID on a Dr. Marc Zuckerman, St. Vincent's Hospital (Cancer Center), and in a second minute, the jaunty doctor's ride, a silver BMW Z7 M coupe, brand-new. The third, fourth, and fifth minutes involved processing, and the sixth minute got the wrecker dispatched. Within forty minutes, Dr. Zuckerman's Z was on its way to the police impound on Eleventh Avenue (a half-cleared yard left fallow since the city's Atlantic Yards renovation project collapsed in '08), where it would stay lost for a month.

Bea Goldberg didn't last a month. Santiago went through the motions with the one relative he could locate, a cold, whiny spinster from Milwaukee who complained nonstop about costs and why the hell the NYPD wouldn't pick up the goddamn tab, best to leave her there, it was the only place she was ever halfway comfortable. Santiago voiced the appropriate responses, which seemed to come from someone else's mouth; he would not remember these later.

Once a year, on the anniversary of their first patrol together, Santiago drove out to the sprawling necropolis that was the New Calvary/Mount Zion Cemetery in Sunnyside, Queens, and placed flowers on Bea Goldberg's gravestone (at least the one that said her name in English—he couldn't read the Hebrew).

Santiago had skidded a bit after that. Did some unprotected drinking, some binge screwing. Got into a couple of fights (including one where Bea Goldberg's replacement, a crew-cut young gringo with biker tattoos and a penchant for conversational use of the word *kike*, had ended up face-down and unconscious in a fifty-five-gallon trash barrel). The second time he showed up at his parents' house for dinner with combat-torn hands, his mother reached up, cradled his face, and said, "*Querido*, I don't know what's wrong with you, but whatever it is, fix it or let us help you fix it." Victor, standing behind her, conveyed with his scowl all Santiago needed to know. He'd already heard talk of the new CAB unit. It was just a matter of getting the paperwork pushed through.

Within weeks of Bea Goldberg's death, Santiago was spit-shined in full dress uniform, talking to the ugliest, sloppiest, most repulsive police-man he'd ever met, an obese captain named McKeutchen who somehow knew about Bea Goldberg and Santiago's fondness for her. McKeutchen dropped Santiago's file on a desk strewn with all matter of rank-looking food residue, peered out at Santiago with watery blue eyes all but lost in rolls and loaves and sheaves of fat, and said, "I need you to do something for me. I'll tell you what it is when the time comes."

And not long after the riots, he assigned Santiago to an undercover taxicab with a new volunteer from ESU named Everett More.

•

"He doesn't talk," Santiago explained. "At least not unless you ask him something. He's always reading, right up until go time. When we're on the set, he blends right in, talks if he has to, picks up on things people around him are saying, and sort of copies them. That's probably why my boss chose him, he's so"—Santiago searched for the right word in Spanish—"*anodino*. Nondescript. I mean, you don't see him, you kind of see him in a roomful of other people, he's like furniture, he just disappears. He's the kind of guy you might sit next to at a bus stop or on the train, and five minutes later you wouldn't be able to remember what he looks like."

Victor appeared to be mulling this over as he veered off I-95 for the Long Wharf exit. Santiago could see the enormous Q Bridge span arcing over the Port of New Haven's anchorage channel against a backdrop of massive oil tanks. This was usually the point where he began to feel slightly nervous, for reasons he could not entirely articulate. It wasn't just that the bridge was crumbling for lack of repair funds in the state budget. Sure, what they were doing was blatantly illegal, and McKeutchen would probably have his ass and his badge if he got caught, but there was something more deeply unsettling about the exchange. As if they were watching one of the support pillars of the bridge, now covered with vehicles, begin to sway, then crack, right before their eyes.

Victor rolled them down a cracked and potholed Long Wharf to the second row of harbor cranes, then hung a sharp right by a checker's booth toward a towering nest of oil stacks, behind which the railroad tracks were mixed up in a seemingly meaningless pattern (though Santiago remembered the first time he and his father made this run, nearly a year ago, when Victor explained that this was one of the largest rail hubs in New England, moving freight the length and breadth of the northeast corridor). Santiago could see the warehouse, an amorphous concrete box laden with soot and graffiti, a tattered Dominican Republic flag draped in a barred window—*all clear.*

There were no cell phone calls, no horn honks, the corrugated aluminum door slid up, and the Ninja Van slid in. A short, stocky Dominican in stained coveralls appeared in the doorway of a makeshift office (where he'd watched their arrival on a CCTV monitor linked to a network of cameras hidden in and around the warehouse) and pointed them toward a kind of monkey-bar lattice of I-beam girders forming a giant set of shelves on which sat hundreds of shrink-wrapped pallets of cargo. About midway down the length of the mass sat an old orange three-wheeled propane crane, and in front of that sat a reinforced pallet made of pressure-treated wood. An electric pallet jack stood nearby, a wallflower at the dance.

Victor wheeled them around, backed the van up to the midpoint of the mass, and popped the slow-motion tailgate release. Santiago climbed out, stretched, and wished for the hundredth time that this would go quietly, which he knew would never happen. Victor and his friend (a fellow *plátano* named Luis whom Victor knew from God knew where) were Dominicans of a common age and generation, wherein polite conversation meant shouting into each other's faces at the top of their lungs. Santiago cursed under his breath and walked around to the back, pulling the old moving blanket off the cargo they'd hauled up from the shop in Inwood. It was a Perkins Sabre M215C, an inline six marine turbodiesel that Victor had spent a full month rehabbing. Luis, who ran a fishing trawler when he wasn't working the loading docks, would have more than two hundred horses on tap in any weather, enough for him to reach the striper and porgy grounds well south of Morris Cove. Luis's family would eat well in the weeks to come.

As would Santiago's. This pleased him no end, for reasons more avaricious than familial. Santiago was under no illusions as to the congenital vulnerabilities of his tribe. Diabetes. Tachycardia. Atherosclerosis. Not so for him. Santiago lived largely on fish and vegetable dishes he prepared himself, and performed a demanding series of abdominal exercises each morning without fail. Not into yoga was he.

Luis worked the crane, Santiago helped maneuver the motor out of the van, and they all swung it over onto the reinforced pallet. Victor pulled a handwritten list out of his pocket, and father and son walked to the wall of pallets. For the next thirty minutes, with Santiago sweating and constantly checking his watch, they cherry-picked their way through a cubic acre of dry bulk food. Bagged bunches of garlic. Flats of canned beans. Plastic sleeves of tortillas in three flavors. Huge cans of condiments and plastic jugs full of spices. Screw-topped boxes of premixed soup stock. Pints of pickled peppers, mixed dried mushrooms. High-fiber cereals, low-fat granola bars. Chips and crackers and cookies galore. And (Santiago sweating, grunting, cursing in three languages) one fifty-pound sack of rice for each household in the family, arranged on the floor of the Odyssey's cargo bed like flagstones.

Grasped right hands and *abrazos* between Victor and Luis signified the end of the exchange. Having covered their haul with the moving blanket, Santiago slid wearily into the passenger seat, grateful for the adjustable lumbar support. He had an eight-hour shift waiting for him back in Manhattan. Victor waited until Luis had checked outside and waved them on before wheeling back to Long Wharf, then heading for the interstate.

Half an hour later, coasting through Milford, Victor asked his son whether he trusted this new guy More. *"¿Usted confía en este tipo?"*

Santiago pursed his lips in thought. *"No sé. Demasiado pronto para decir."*

Too soon to tell.

•

Still, he had to admit that More had been pretty fucking fast out the door when Santiago called the code word *stigmata* (More's idea, the weird fuck), and that big *atacante* with the blade—who could have easily filleted Santiago while he was rolling around with the *mayate* on the pavement—had stopped dead in his tracks when More stuck the nasty little laser gun in his face. It reminded Santiago of the weird-looking piece Harrison Ford carried in *Blade Runner*. No tremor in his hands at all.

No hesitation.

Quick.

Focused.

Santiago figured that had to count for something.

IN THE SHADOW OF THE TITTY BAR

IT'S BEEN A BUSY MORNING ONLINE. Got the particulars for the *Roundup* shoot from my indispensable assistant, Marty. Marty is a photographer's dream: does everything for you but take the pictures. Handles the shoot setups, books the location, rents the equipment, handles all transport and logistics, and makes himself invisible yet always within reach while on the shoot. All I have to do is show up. It's a good way to make trade connections and surreptitiously build my other client list, for Specials. Not to mention the endless supply of models for hire, all of them willing to do anything (or anyone) for their chance to one day fill the lens. Thy name is humanity, Vanity.

The shoot is a week from tomorrow, at the Eyrie from eleven to four. Additional models: two. Lighting: floor, floods, and an oscillating icosahedron (fuck! I *hate* the soccer-ball light, it's a twenty-thousand-dollar accident waiting to happen, and I'm the one on the hook for the rentals). The best/worst news is that Tony Quinones will be back from Cannes in time to be our stylist. Tony Q did the costumes for *The Snake*, a drama about a love triangle of gay sewage workers in Manila that's this year's odds-on favorite for the Palme d'Or. Tony is the kind of gay caricature who gives other gays a bad name (though he's always good for a few Specials for himself and his so-called *Queue'terie*.) As long as Johnette stays out of my face, this should be my easiest (and biggest) paycheck yet, courtesy of the rising young Retch and the delectable Miyuki (not to mention Marcus Chalk, cool and distant in his glass Olympus on Eighth Avenue).

Work. I sigh.

This is the sort of day I used to spend with X, going out with nothing but a camera and a MetroCard and drinking in the city through my lens. We were a natural fit—X was a model who didn't like modeling, I was a photographer doing rag work to get by. She shared my fixation with *city glances askance*, the concept of capturing motion in an otherwise stillborn frame. She wasn't just about Newton and McMullan, like the rest of her tribe; she knew Pellegrini's and Gottfried's work and had a grasp of photography beyond the jargon. We would go into all sorts of places to get shots—crawling around under the anchorages of the Brooklyn, Manhattan, or Verrazano bridges, the gatehouse of the reservoir, City Tunnel 3, even the abandoned shafts for the Second Avenue subway. We'd put them all through my editing software and post them on my site in miniature book formats. The city was different then, a place of possibility and opportunity without menace, all warmed by the presence of X. That was when I shot my Mall Series, which I consider my best work. I have these four frames, enlarged, hanging on the wall opposite my bed. It's less painful to think of X when I'm looking at the one good tangible relic of that time. After the crash, after she was gone, the only other thing left of those times were the taxiscapes.

I'm remembering this, and fighting the pain and the need for drink it brings, when I get the message from Prince William. The message is a photo of an old city subway token, the kind you see in the Transit Museum or on T-shirts and coffee mugs in any cheesy tourist curio shop in Times Square. (My mother, deep in her personal twilight zone, still hoards them.) This is code to check in with him from a street phone for the location of the drop, and then I have to run the Subway Labyrinth.

Reza insists on it, and what Reza wants, Reza gets. I understand the logic. The best way to shake a tail is in the subway, and Reza doesn't even want me using a pay phone in the same borough as the speak I'm about to supply. This may seem strange and inefficient, but it's the best way we've worked out to supply the speaks, and no one's been busted yet, ever. The cops can't tap a pay phone unless they've staked it out first. Maybe that's why they were watching Broome Street last night? I should pass by the bar again soon and check the location of the nearest phones . . . Nah. Just nerves.

Knowing I'll be riding the rails to some less than stellar spot in the outer boroughs (Reza again; he says the farther out from Manhattan you go, the fewer security cameras there are around—the last time I had to go from

Queens Plaza out to Roosevelt Avenue, then double back to Queensboro Plaza, then up to fucking Ditmars Boulevard—Reza is more paranoid than I am), I dress down in jeans and army surplus for the occasion. The speaks should be humming tonight. There's one in Williamsburg, where the partially employed crowd will be slumming it, then another on the LES, then the mother lode: Le Yef, which tonight is in the old Toy Building on Madison Square, vacant lo these many moons since the big toy manufacturers all went broke last year. I might be able to move the whole shipment in one night. Even Reza won't be able to bitch about that.

I wish I were in better shape. I definitely did *not* need that shaker full of nightcaps after L left. Maybe if she stayed the whole night just once, it might keep my mind off X. There's a certain moodiness that sets in after episodic sex. It's not exactly a vacuum, but you do tend to notice the sudden emptiness that much more.

Crossing Amsterdam at 103rd, I see the Irish Bull on his cell in front of his truck, parked outside his pub, which I call the Drunk Factory. The Irish Bull is a contractor (did all the renovations himself) who opened here last year in the space occupied by an old Italian restaurant that closed abruptly at the end of December (as did a whole slew of restaurants around here when their leases came due and no one could make the rent hikes—same old song). Cheap, noxious pubs are always in demand, though—if anything, people drink more when the economy's in the shitter—and this one pulls in the jocks with their beer guts and soccer jerseys, as well as the sort of females who go in for them, the Spandex Brigade, all tube tops and lip gloss and Ultras and whinnying laughter. You can always hear when it's closing time from the shouts and fights, and in the morning you can gauge the previous night's volume by the number of vomit sites.

Even from half a block's worth of boarded-up storefronts away from the subway stairs, I cannot escape the inevitable reek of shit wafting from the underground. When the budget cuts began, the MTA was already in the hole. The unions were arguing for pay hikes despite a big budget deficit, and the mayor wasn't having any of it. It made headlines for a while, but money—or lack of it—always wins in the end. The MTA didn't budge, the state wouldn't kick in any cash, and the transit budget was slashed right along with Sanitation and the cops. The subways and stations were pretty clean before the crash; I wonder if now they're more like what Walker Evans or John Conn captured in their lenses.

—SUSAN!

I haven't even cleared the turnstile and some crazy homeless guy is screaming right in my ear. Perfect.

—SUSAN LOWINGER!

The derelict has not been homeless long enough for his hairstyle to grow fully formless. He must have had a reasonably well-paying job until recently, his hands and face not yet weathered by a full cycle of seasons without shelter. His wheeling eyes and slack jaw, however, betray the extent of his mental deterioration, the vast gulf separating his former self from where it is now. He's also picked up the Scent, the indelible pong of the unsheltered, a combination of urine and ashes that every New Yorker equates with The Bottom. There is nothing distinctive about him, nor is he the only one of his species wandering aimlessly about the station, engaged in spirited dialogues with invisible interlocutors. Once again I am caught without my trusty Marathon Cyber SEX. Two frames: On the Way Down. Whoever Susan Lowinger is, she's somewhere high above this fetid wet tunnel, well protected from its lost, damaged denizens.

One good thing—the train's just arriving at the platform as I swipe my MetroCard and get pole position behind one of the support girders (the rule is, stay out of the slipstream and out of the line of sight; minimize your friction and you minimize your chances of confrontation). People stopped believing the reports about lower crime rates years ago, the city churns out such propaganda to keep the tourists from being scared away. I keep to myself behind my titanium polarized wraparound bedroom eyes. I'm itching to check my messages, but you don't pull out your iPhone below ground if you want to keep it (and the blood inside your body). It's only one stop south to Ninety-sixth, not quite long enough for anything to happen; we're all cloistered at one end of the car, since there's a snoring vagrant at the opposite end whose stink makes my eyes water, even from here. I've taken subways all my life, I don't intend to stop because the city's in a tough spot, though if I can, I'll take a cab. However, duty—Reza—commands.

Changing at Ninety-sixth for the northbound 2 train, I feel the tingling onset of the anxiety of Borough Crossing. Manhattan is the innermost of the five, it's the most modern, the most built up, the richest, the most stylish. Anyone moving to NYC does so with the idea of at least spending time in Manhattan; most could not afford to *live* there. It's the city's gravitational center, recent difficulties notwithstanding. It's also the best-protected borough. During the riots, the police simply cordoned off Harlem. Nothing happened to Manhattan—not the important parts, anyway. Nothing. Brooklyn and the Bronx and fucking Queens, you could see them smoldering from miles away. I was on a photo shoot in Ireland at the time, but I remember seeing the residual smoke as we came in to land three days later, and how many police cars there were on the tarmac. My building on 104th was inside the police cordon, close to Columbia and Morningside Heights. Don't get me wrong, I would never live on Park Avenue or the Upper East Side or some other sterilized honeycomb; if you're going to live in New York City, you've got to be where you can *feel* it. The trick is not to be where the human waves can wash you and your home away. I heard horror stories from friends in Brooklyn Heights, Park Slope, Prospect Heights, Windsor Terrace, Fort Greene, Astoria, Long Island City, Forest Hills, Hamilton Heights, and Kingsbridge, places where the mix is too pureed, where the different ingredients are too blended together. This is the sort of conversational road it's never safe to go down in a bar, but I digress.

So to the Bronx. One good thing about the subway system is that as long as you're on it, you don't usually notice the areas you're passing through. I mean, who really wants to go hoofing around East 149th Street in the Grand Concourse? Here, riders are subdued, they know where they are, they're keeping as low a profile as possible. Once I switch to the southbound 5, I have to steel myself for what comes next.

East 138th Street, Point of No Return. Abandoned gas stations—unless it's a big oil company, there are no independent stations anymore, and even the franchises are fewer and farther between. I can't remember the last time I saw a Shell or Hess logo. What happened to them? I hate walking around out here, I feel so fucking exposed (you would, too, if you had my hair). Bodegas. Hybrid maintenance shops. Claptrap storefronts selling repackaged nickel hydride and lithium ion batteries and cheap Chinese-made solar laptops. It's really not that much different from Canal Street back in Chinatown, only here it's so much more spread out, wider roads, less hope, more decay. What I really hate about this is that it's so fucking *familiar*. I might as well be back in Jackson Heights, but without even the South Asian flavor, I *hate* the Bronx. Why would anyone live here?

Here I am, at the corner of East 138th and Alexander Avenue in the South Bronx, waiting for Reza's man, standing in the shadow of some disgusting strip joint near the Third Avenue Bridge called Felicity. I feel like

I'm in a Lou Reed song. No, actually, I feel like I'm standing in somebody's crosshairs. I fire up a Davidoff and pull on it furiously.

Which reminds me to check my messages. I turned off my iPhone for the underground journey, but if anyone's going to try for it out here, at least I can see them coming from far enough away to call the cops. I've got an emergency phone app called Red Flag with which I can instantly notify Reza to abort the drop—probably invented by the same enterprising soul who wrote iHook. When I've got service, I'm stunned to find a string of calls with no messages from Prince William. Before I can call him back, a battered Nissan Hereford pulls up, and I see Arun gesturing frantically from the driver's seat.

About Arun. Basically the black sheep of a respectable Indian merchant family, Arun felt he wasn't cut out for the family business. He'll spin you some yarn about driving a cab while attending a Jain religious school to take his vows, renounce the world, and become a mendicant monk in search of enlightenment. This is pure bullshit. Whether he dropped out or was kicked out of school, Arun is obviously a fuckup whose family cut him off. It's not really surprising that he came to drive a cab (although he's usually flying on premium smoke—how does Arun beat the TLC drug checks?). No such cannabinoid calmness for the Jain wonder boy today, though. He's all amped up about something. I climb in the back and he pulls away, careful to signal and not squeal his tires. (This is a bad sign. He's not usually this cautious.)

—Renny, mahn, Eyad's dead.

—What the fuck are you talking about?

—I just goht the text message from central, mahn, eet says police found a body the other night and just got DNA identeefeecation. They gave Eyad's name and license numbah. They say eet looks like there was torture involved, Arun says, rolling his *R*'s Hindi-style.

Oh, shit.

—Renny, *yaar*, what you theenkeeng? Arun asks, his wide eyes on me in the rearview. He's nervous, his hands are strangling the wheel, he'll need to self-medicate soon or he'll start jumping curbs.

Think, Renny, think. You've planned for contingencies. Get what you came for, then get out of sight.

—Drive me to Queens, I say in my steadiest voice (Christ, I could almost believe myself).

—Where you want to go, mahn?

—Jackson Heights. Thirty-seventh Avenue, by the G stop.

He nods, still scared but relieved to be moving toward familiar turf. I don't know if he lives there, but if you're Indian and you drive a cab, Jackson Heights is one neighborhood you know.

—Where's the package?

—The usual place, *yaar*.

I hunch down in the backseat, cursing under my breath, trying to get my fingers beneath the GPS panel without having to put my knees on the floor of the cab. In '08, when GPS systems in taxicabs became mandatory, a lot of drivers started bitching about the heat coming through the driver's seat from the monitor built into the partition showing ads and offering touch-screen maps and news feeds for tourists. Since by law the fleet is supposed to be all-hybrid by next year, lots of owners have been buying hybrids with off-set monitors retrofitted in existing partitions to save money. A few observant souls like Arun noticed that this adjustment permitted a small, unnoticeable, and fucking-hard-to-reach space inside the partition manifold. A space just about big enough for a standard-size Blu-ray case. Or a similar-sized case holding two concentric rings of pharmaceutical-grade Ecstasy tablets in perfect birth-control-pill formation. Two hundred doses at two hundred dollars each is a Fast Forty, which is what should be brought back to Reza. You do that, you get paid. You don't, you might end up like Eyad, beaten and burned and God knows what else.

This system is what brought Arun to work for Reza and me to work with Arun. Reza likes things to work well, and people in his organization generally do. Eyad is an aberration. I don't know who's behind it. If it was a random thing, maybe some Arab blood feud, Reza would let it slide. If there's a crew jacking cabs in the network, they'd better get the hell out of town, fast. Reza doesn't like interference, and he's got people who can straighten things like this out, fast.

Come to think of it . . .

Nah. Just nerves.

•

For the long ride home, I pull out my iPhone and wireless stereo headset and thumb up a playlist titled UNDER THE COVERS. In tribute to Eyad's memory, I select all my covers for the Cure's "Killing an Arab," the first one by Rickets, their version of Dinosaur Jr.'s cover of the Cure's "Just Like Heaven," off the Tad Kubler Memorial Burn Unit fund-raiser ('09):

I can turn
And walk away
Or I can fire the gun
Staring at the sky
Staring at the sun
Whichever I choose
It amounts to the same
Absolutely nothing

Too bland, everyone said so. I thumb up last year's Smallpox cover of the Rickets version, muscled up with more feedback and distortion:

I feel the steel butt jump
Smooth in my hand
Staring at the sea
Staring at the sand
Staring at myself
Reflected in the eyes
Of the dead man on the beach
The dead man on the beach

Not enough. I thumb up the best from the Craig Finn Memorial Liver Transplant Foundation compilation ('10). Blood Clot's interpretation of the Smallpox version of the Rickets cover destroys them all. For sheer sonic monstrosity, nothing beats Blood Clot (electric kettle drums, three bass guitars, and oboe):

I'm alive
I'm dead
I'm the stranger
Killing an Arab.

Staring out at the South Bronx while heading for Queens is like looking at old photos of the city back in the day. Nothing ever changes here. Gentrification is supposed to be the great engine of change in NYC, but there are whole swaths of the city untouched by progress (I should know, I'm from one). Every time the economy goes up, people in the outer boroughs count on their neighborhood being the next Tribeca (rolled eyes, complaints of rising rents and Starbucks infestation). When the economy tanks, people wonder why they're still living in squalor. It all comes down to money, and the money's in Manhattan. Period. Full stop. You don't think it's out here, amid the abandoned factories, crumbling tenements, and festering projects, do you? No no no. Out here, it's FLATS FIXED signs and roadside fruit vendors and carjackers. Out here, it's going nowhere slow.

I'm making myself jumpy as hell, and I'd kill for a Davidoff. I've heard all the stories. Reza, the Russian mob's Manhattan Man. Reza, the one-man criminal empire. Money-laundering Reza. Mack Daddy Reza. Reza, King of the Speaks.

But this is the first time I've heard of a death—a violent death—connected with Reza's network. Even if it was only Eyad (there probably won't be a police investigation, nobody cares about cabdrivers), it's nerve-wracking when terminal violence comes to someone you *know*. And why Eyad? It couldn't have been Reza, that doesn't make any sense. Even if Eyad skimmed a whole Fast Forty, Reza could probably make that back in under a week. Why go to the trouble? It must've been something else, but who or what, I have no idea.

Jackson Heights in June smells like cardamom and diesel exhaust. Arun drops me exactly where I told him, doesn't come to a full stop, just keeps rolling, on familiar ground, off for some relaxing smoke and sex (both probably courtesy of Reza).

I'm home.

Trudging wearily past all the DO NOT BRING ROTI IN STORE! signs, I head down the old familiar stand of brown brick apartment houses stacked like so much cardboard. No architectural flair, no spark of vitality, just lumps of brick and mortar, anthills for the masses.

Trudging up the stairs of my mother's building to apartment 3A, I remember the need to signal confirmation. I send Prince William a photo of a baseball squarely in the pocket of a catcher's mitt. Subtext: package received. Then I unlock my mother's door.

Can one describe a smell as empty? There's been no life here for years, only a sense of slow entropy that makes the flue on my arms crawl and inexpressible sensations fight in my stomach. My mother's house is always tidy, nothing out of place. Look closer and you'll see dust built up behind easily accessible areas, discoloration of the wallpaper up near the air vents, cobwebs round the radiator pipes. My mother sits, as she always does, in the kitchen chair she dragged to the window overlooking the street on the day my father died. She's added to it through the years, made a little station for herself, a small table, a pad with a pencil, her needles and yarn. But her main activity is staring at the street, the Sentinel of Thirty-seventh Avenue, as though expecting my father's truck to come rumbling up under the window, him jumping off the back rail by the levers, just in time for dinner. I don't think my mother has cooked a meal since I left for college.

—I'm home, Ma, I say to the ghost in the chair.

She turns her head slowly, not so much moving her head as altering her horizon. The movement is mechanical, devoid of organic fluidity. She stares without seeing, slowly raising one hand toward me in a way that makes my throat constrict. I know I'm supposed to give her a hug and a kiss, and I will, like the dutiful son that I am, but honestly, it's just too sad. My mother is hunched, wizened, existing somehow in a mental fog. As I approach her to do my filial duty, I am hit by the awful medicinal stench of decay, not like the scent of the homeless but the vinegary stink of medically slowed putrefaction. *Age.*

—How are you, Ma? I say, taking her hand and kissing her on the forehead.

My mother hasn't received the sort of news that took my father from us, the succession of reports beginning with the three most terrible words in the English language (*We found something*) that confirmed the spots on his lungs and the disagreeable numbers of his blood chemistry. My mother keeps alive by the usual alchemy of takeout food, the occasional supplement from caring neighbors around holidays, and the ever increasing pool of medicines foisted upon the elderly. None of these really matter. The portion of my mother that gave her vitality, direction, spark, fire, and glowing ember, that all died with my father. The remainder of my mother, who sees only the ghost of my father when she isn't looking at the glowing box that tells her what the world is, is suffering from *time*. And there's only one cure. I hate myself for saying that, for even thinking it, but it's true. Dad, you fuck, why'd you have to die? Forget about me, don't you see what you did to *her*?

—My sweet boy, she says, holding one of my hands in both of hers, white shadows in veined vellum. Over her right shoulder I see The Photo, the one of my dad, healthy and smiling in his DSNY greens and fat orange garbage gloves, beaming out at a world preparing to consume, reclaim, and recycle him in the great landfill of Mother Earth. I want to get out of here.

—Are you eating well, Renny? You look so thin, my mother says.

—Just fine, Ma, never better. Big new job, another cover shoot. *Roundup* magazine.

Here it comes.

—Oh, Renny, that's wonderful. Your father would be so proud.

I know he would. Garbageman's boy makes good. Big-shot fashion photographer, one of the youngest ever to make it like this. My own apartment in Manhattan. Beautiful women in the city on my arm and my cock, money in the bank and more off the books from Reza, surviving and thriving in a city with 20 percent real unemployment. Yes, Ma, I think Dad *should* be proud.

As always, instead of venting what's boiling in my head, I say:

—Yes, Ma. Do you have everything you need? Any problems with the—in the neighborhood?

—No, no, everything's fine, dear. I have everything I need right here. In fact, it's more than I need.

Here it comes again.

—Here, take this.

—Ma, come on.

—Now, Renny, you listen to your mother. Take this and put it away. Your father wanted for you to have it, and you will. Don't argue with me. Take this and put it in the bank. Save it for—for tomorrow.

—Yes, Ma. Thanks, Ma.

Like always, I take it. Resistance is futile; this ritual seems to make her feel a little bit better. When my father found out he was sick, he set up an annuity for my mother, secured by his pension and what life insurance he could get through the department. Since he died so quickly, Ma wasn't saddled with impossible medical bills. School didn't cost her much, and the church helped out here and there. Dad made sure Ma would be able to stay in the apartment as long as she lived, and she never spent anything on herself, just kept at me to keep my grades up (in *my* school? I got straight A's in my sleep) so that maybe someday I'd be able to go to a good school and get a good job. The minute NYU said yes, I was gone.

It's not like I use it for myself. Anything from my mother—plus a lot more from me—goes to settle her bills and fill in any gaps, like now, when so many pension funds are on the ropes. She's pretty much taken care of as the widow of a city worker back when pensions were guaranteed and there was money at the ready. This sort of thing has been up in the air since the crash, especially with both the city and the state broke, and no more federal money coming in for city agencies. I'm not alone; there are probably thousands of people in this kind of jam these days. Though I doubt too many of them have come up with my ways to make ends meet.

As for my *legal* job, well, Mom has every issue featuring my work, and that's good enough for her. They're all kept neatly in my old room, which I usually stop into after taking Mom's money, and pretend to use the bathroom while I check on message traffic from Reza's network. Ma keeps everything exactly the way it was. My old trundle bed, a fraction of the bed I sleep on now. My old desk, with that ancient color photo printer. A bulletin board, a few posters from bands I shot that are long since gone. And my first cover, framed, with the early taxiscape technique that first turned heads.

And my one remaining photograph of X, the one I took of her in the pagoda at the Botanical Gardens in Brooklyn. There's nothing stylized or put on about the shot—she's just looking at me through the lens, very matter-of-factly, a warm look, but (I see it now) a hint of reservation. I took this picture four years ago, before the bottom fell out of the world.

Don't ask why, she said when she told me she was leaving.

I keep this photo here at my mother's, where it's safe. I destroyed all the others.

I've shown Ma my apartment (since it's so difficult getting her to leave her own, I had plenty of time to clean up and secure anything suspicious). I come out and check on her on a regular basis, say, once every other month, or when I feel some sudden irrational need to visit Queens, like now. I still can't believe Eyad's dead.

After extricating myself from the family homestead, I flag down the first hack I see. It's a big roomy Toyota Shorthorn—you'd call it a Sienna. One thing about Queens, there's no shortage of fucking cabdrivers.

•

Afternoons are for acceleration. The recovery from the previous night's excesses, the anticipation of more come evening—this is my prep time.

First, break up the shipment. I never carry the whole load, because if you get nailed, it's better to be below the minimum for a distribution charge. I keep several extra disc cases for transport at all times. I check in with Reza via a coded message and await his response. This will be the location of my pickup driver, in whose cab I'll stash the Specials. This driver hangs around the speak I'm working, to be summoned by me when I've made contact with a client and secured payment. I send a text message to the driver (easier to code and therefore harder to trace than an actual call), who arrives with a presorted amount of product ready to go to the customer, who goes for a short ride. The client gets his purchase, the driver makes a few bucks, and I'm nowhere near the switch. A clean deal for me, even cleaner for Reza. The only one at risk is the cabbie, and no one thinks about the cabbies. Since Reza started operating—I'm not sure exactly when that was, and he's not the most forthcoming type—we've never lost a shipment or a cabbie to the TLC or NYPD. It's a sound system for these unsound times.

I whack up the shipment three ways—one half, two quarters. Half goes into my stash box upstairs. One quarter goes into a DVD box to give to the driver once I call him. The remainder I stash in the suit I wore the previous night, hanging on my inside closet door. Then I mix myself a perfect Manhattan, fire up a fresh Davidoff, and start calling my clients. I don't want to think about what happened to Eyad.

It's only about half an hour before I have the first quarter accounted for (you don't offer product over the phone, you just ask if someone will be where you are later, nothing illegal about that).Then I start to lay out my route. The first stops of the evening are in Williamsburg, making the rounds of the legit bars near the busy corner of Manhattan and Driggs avenues, along with a couple of tonight's adjacent speaks. Since the speaks are rarely in the same place twice and are always a minimalist affair (less to leave behind in case of a raid), they're generally set up near legitimate bars, in order to draw off their clientele. (Where there are drinkers, it goes without saying that there's usually a market for less legal substances.) I send Reza (or whoever handles his online logistics) a Google Maps snapshot of the area so he can arrange for a driver and a password, which I will have in my phone before arriving on site. If I need to resupply, this driver will be on hand for a quick round trip (I'll have him drop me a block or two from my building—the less we know of each other, the better), just long enough for me to tank up on Specials and get back to the action. Reza can switch out the cabdrivers at any time, so it pays to keep an eye on the phone.

It may not seem like the best system to you, but it's been goddamn effective. My record is two whole Fast Forties in one marathon night that began at the close of one wild stock market session (one of my clients called it Triple Witch or something) on a Friday afternoon and continued until noon the next day. I was on nicotine, alcohol, and adrenaline for a full twenty-four, but I gave Reza every dollar before I crashed. A breakthrough moment in our relationship—he gave me my Jaquet Droz watch on top of my commission as a reward. I went home and slept for sixteen hours.

Since then I've enjoyed a much better rapport with Reza, if not the rest of his crew. I don't really know how many people Reza has working for him. I try not to ask too many questions or spend more time socializing with his other employees than necessary. Some, like Arun, are easy enough to get along with. But there's something about the guys Reza keeps around his office that makes me uneasy. I made the mistake of drinking with them once, and it took me two days to straighten out. They speak something Slavic-sounding, Polish or Russian, and they smoke like chimneys.

These guys and the cabbies—all these people are labor. Guys like the Prince and I, we're management. We cultivate the clientele and maintain the supply chain. We look the part, we dress and speak well enough to put the appropriate window dressing on Reza's operation. It's a living. It's also a hell of a lot more streamlined than fashion photography. You get an assignment, you have your quota, you meet your numbers. There's little room for complaint and no margin for error—either you bring Reza the money or you don't.

Which is why I can't stop thinking about Eyad. No one's ever stolen from Reza, I don't know why they'd even bother. There's plenty of money in his operation to go around, and you get out of it exactly what you put into it. That's why I'm at this level and haven't risen up to where Prince William is. The difference between us is that he wants to do this for a living. I don't see it as a long-term career. There are other things I'd like to be doing, and they don't involve cabbies being tortured and murdered. Of course, they don't involve Fast Forties, either, and they don't pay what Reza does. And I need the money, it's as simple as that. The fashion gigs pay well, but that's a high-bullshit-factor business, and the more time goes by, the more magazines, designers, and stores go under. It's too choppy to stake my whole life on. Reza's brand of product, however, always seems to be in demand.

I know I could do more for him. He could use an organizer, someone who's come up through the ranks and knows his system, someone he can trust. Someone whose services command more than the 10 percent he pays me now. I'm just not sure it should be me.

Another half hour sees the second quarter of the shipment accounted for, this time with the downward-spiral crowd on the LES. I'm not as big a fan of this scene as I should be, it being full of colleagues from the photo trade, but the scene is too druggy, too much coke and smack. Does that sound strange coming from me? It shouldn't. I don't use drugs, period. Why take the risk? Hardcore drug abusers are notoriously unstable, lack good judgment, and call attention to themselves in the stupidest of ways (usually while loaded or jonesing). This crowd is too jaded, too numbed, too burnt, and therefore always looking for more. What's more, the fortunes of this crowd are as unstable as their personalities. My clientele (carefully built up over time) consists of more level heads (which, if they desire expansion, do so in a discreet manner and controlled atmosphere—I'm not tossing out handfuls of pills to the concert crowd at the McCarren Pool) and the financially secure (no arguing with broke junkies for me, thank you). This is how I can shift Fast Forties as quickly and smoothly as I do. This is why Reza likes me. That and the fact that I've never stolen from him. (Eyad, you didn't, did you?)

The final half is arranged while I'm drying off from the shower, my second (or is it third?) Manhattan sweating in its crystal prison, the first butt of the second half of the pack smoldering in my Jensen ashtray. This is the Capitale crowd, which will be out in force tonight at Le Yef, as I suspected. This being the richest crowd (my favorite, at least for business), it always accounts for the bulk of my sales (these took me forever to cultivate, and as you have seen, I don't put up with them any more than I have to—but this is also why Reza likes me, because I have *contacts*).

Clean, dressed, and properly primed for the evening, I call Reza's driver. I never know who it will be until he shows up. I almost wish it were Arun. A bad day has turned out for the best after all.

●

—Brooklyn Heights has too many Russians now, Dagmara replies to someone's suggestion.

We're in Punch & Judy's on the LES (one of the few remaining legitimate bars whose owner lucked out with a good long lease, and who wisely invested his profits in security when the city began its tailspin), a welcome break from the grittier bars and speaks I've had to trammel through these past few hours. It was a great relief to connect with this bunch while I was making my rounds, even if I have to endure Dagmara's eternal whining about where to move. (Christ, those coked-up drag queens in Lucky Cheng's give me the creeps. Forget androgyny, they look mummified.)

Dagmara is Polish and carries her history like a sea anchor around her neck. She's from some region that changed hands innumerable times between Poland, Russia, Prussia, the fucking Austro-Hungarian Empire, the fucking Nazis . . . honestly, she can go on all night about it (and does). It's completely out of place in New York, and in America, for Christ's sake. People come here to leave behind the prejudices of their dismal home countries, not carry them around like some diseased badge of pride. America in general and New York in particular provide an *escape* from history, a *refuge* from all the bad blood of a thousand faceless generations that have nothing at all to do with who you are and what you're doing here now. I never understood why people at NYU wasted their time taking history (although I did like that one paleontology class), packing into the Erich Maria Remarque Institute on Fridays for wacky old Professor Judt's lectures. Why study history when you can live it?

—What's wrong with Russians? somebody says.

—You *obviously* don't know about the history between Poles and Russians, Dagmara says with that half-smile, half-sneer so common to Slavic women that makes her (despite her golden tresses, ice-blue eyes, and lithe figure) a cold fish to me.

—What about near Park Slope? You know, out by Greenwood Cemetery, by the highway? It's cheaper there, someone else says.

Dagmara shakes her head with exaggerated sadness.

—Too many Serbs, she says.

—So forget Brooklyn. Try the Bronx. Arthur Avenue, somebody else says.

Dagmara gives *that* contributor a withering, jaw-agape-beneath-the-eyebrows stare.

—And live with a bunch of *Albanians*? Don't be ridiculous, she scoffs, obviously above it all. (Playing haughty, while a favorite pastime of hers and other women like her, only underscores the extent of her hypocrisy. Her fallen-aristocrat posturing isn't ridiculous enough to be pathetic. Like *she's* never traded blow jobs for blow in the men's-room stalls at the Odeon. Kiss my crown jewels, *principessa*.)

I'd be paying more attention to the details of this group, but I've got a nice easy buzz going, and I've become quite fixated on Dagmara's new friend N. Now, *this* is a woman I can handle. She has the tawny pelt and leonine features of the best *Boricua* beauties, while her full, slightly pouting lips and silky smooth brown hide belie a hint of African blood. She wears a simple, almost Grecian-style tunic of a shade complementary to her skin, which drapes itself in succulently baroque formations around her perfectly proportioned promontories. *Hispanicus Afro-Carribeanensis divinae.* The rest of the crowd is lost on me. We are in our own room, sharing our own language, she and I, now. When she taps a fresh Dunhill on the box, I'm ready with my Peretti, and we slide outside. When Dagmara first introduced us, she said she'd picked N up on the Brooklyn supper-club circuit. She can't mean they're together, surely. N is a cool, masterfully composed facade banking fires I sense emanating from within. Dagmara is all coldness and complaint. Most likely they shared a cab from one of the supper clubs, which started springing up a couple years ago after the great wave of restaurant failures began in '08. Since no one other than a handful of chefs with the richest backers could afford to rent spaces, the chefs started illegal supper clubs, held wherever they could bribe a landlord for a night. If you know someone who can get you on a list, you get a number the morning of, call that night for the location, then show up and pay at the door, cash only.

The speaks operate on basically the same principle, only with a cash bar, and entrepreneurs like me plying the currents of the chemical trade upon taxi-yellow dhows . . . oh, Eyad, you poor dumb fuck. The chef calculates his fees based on his operating costs for the night (including bribes). A savvy landlord might host several different clubs (or speaks) per week and will keep at least one gas or water line working (in his own name or that of a tenant long since gone). Everybody wins. Since the brick-and-mortar economy priced itself clear out of reach, the floating economy has grown at breakneck speed. No need for corporations and contracts and codes and leases loaded with legalese. That's the *old* economy. Ours is a *young* one, and it has plenty of room to grow. That's what worries me.

But here, now, with N, thoughts of the macro get very much micro. N's dress follows every curve, plane, and peak of her body, her smooth, muscled legs encased in saddle-colored harness-style boots (my God, this girl). Getting her to come with me to Le Yef is a small matter. So sorry, Dagmara dear, it's plus-one only, I'll get you in next time, promise.

—That was artfully done, N says in a low-timbered, slightly husky voice that makes my cock thicken and roll around in my pants like some large animal waking up from a nap. Once we're outside, I spot a Toyota Jersey slowing for a trio of loud out-of-towners too drunk to score, and grab N's hand (that first touch, the first physical contact of the evening, there's nothing like it, no chemical can duplicate it, no photograph can convey the jolt and rush) and pull open the door on the opposite side of the drunken porkers, who realize too late what's happening as I give orders to the driver in my best level-and-decisive. We're lucky—the legless muffin-tops only hurl curses as we take off (one of them is throwing up on another one, anyway). A quick check of the driver and his hack license to make sure he's not one of Reza's (it's always awkward to run into one socially, you don't want too much recognition, it might shed light on the business, or so Reza says). All is well, and I can turn my full attention to the goddess sitting next to me with the wryest of smiles, leaning her head on one index finger, the overheads along Houston Street giving her an otherworldly halo (my God, this girl).

—Is this sort of thing typical for you? she says.

Is it her voice or her self-assurance that are sounding an echo of X?

—Only on Mondays, I reply, trying to edge closer. This is the tricky bit: trying to convey maximum interest while appearing aloof. Our game is all about appearances.

—Did you really meet Dagmara at a supper club?

—Are you really just a photographer?

—I really am. But then I'm so much more, too.

She laughs, a pearly peal of fine teeth draped in shades of coral velvet. I feel a flush of relief up the sides of my rib cage. Laughter is the fulcrum on which the lever of seduction turns. You'll know when you've missed it, later, alone, needing an on-screen hand to help your own jerk you off to sleep.

There's a deliciously full silence as her laughter dies down and we gaze into each other's eyes. Very slowly, gently, and deliberately, I place my left hand over her right one.

I'm counting the seconds in my mind, feeling each one pound through my ears and gums, when I feel her fingers (strong, supple fingers that promise many tactile talents) lace themselves to mine. She does The Drop, that utterly feminine gesture of dropping her head, releasing a stifled laugh as a puff of air caught in a smile, and looking away, running her free hand through her hair.

Traci, Dagmara.

•

Tonight's incarnation of Le Yef is at the top of the old Toy Building on Madison Square at the western edge of the axial mess where Fifth Avenue, Broadway, and Twenty-third Street skewer each other. At the southern end is the Flatiron Building, indomitable even in its coat of soot and grime, defiantly proclaiming its survival in this as in other bad times. Along its eastern edge running north is Madison Square, once home to open-air U.S. Open broadcasts, Pakistani parades, absurd lines for designer hot dogs, Tagalog death-metal concerts, and a dog run that was one of the most pedigreed puppy pens in town. Now that the corporations bordering its rim have collapsed, as have the attempts to turn their shells into luxury housing, all that's left are cracked hexagonal paving stones and weed-choked flowerbeds in which vagrants (driven mad by the communal bottles of paint thinner passed around the benches by the bus stops at the north end of the park) pretend to swim. The best time to be here is toward sunset on a very late afternoon (at rooftop level; you wouldn't want to be near the park after dark), when the western facade of the former New York Life Insurance Building (taken over by the same Arab company that bought the one that bought Barneys) turns the exact shade of chewable baby aspirin.

I love the view from up high, overlooking Madison Square—pure Steichen. N would be a natural for this setting. I could construct a whole series around her, and I know Marcus fucking Chalk would eat it up.

The entry to Le Yef is routine—make The Call, give the password to the security goons just inside the door (out of street view) by the freight entrance down an alley by an adjacent building a block away (no, don't bother asking for it, they change it every half hour anyway; that keeps those who don't have The Number out). The lobby is dark to save power (and discourage attention), but the elevators work, because the owner gets paid by promoters of Le Yef, or dispossessed *ronin* chefs like Matt Hamilton or

Akhtar Nawab, or perhaps by someone like Reza. I'm pleased to see the number of heads N is turning as we make our way to the elevators, and even more pleased that either excitement or air-conditioning has brought N's nipples (not too large, not too dark, not too heavily girdled, simply perfect) up through the thin fabric of her dress.

And we have the elevator all to ourselves.

This is how it happens.

Can softness have a taste? Her lips are cumulus clouds wrapped in rose petals, but her jaw is firm, her tongue well toned and animated. There is strength in her shoulders, the web of her back, the brace of her pectorals as they cantilever her breasts out toward my shaking fingers. This woman has power, poise, that was evident in her carriage as we strolled across the alley arm in arm past throngs of jealous onlookers. She has the strong self-assurance of a woman confident in her abilities, and the smooth levelheadedness of one secure in her financial position. (I could easily lose myself in a woman like this—in my world, it's rare to meet someone so three-dimensional.)

The door opens, and after we peel ourselves wetly apart, we step into paradise. What was once a showroom for meaningless wares has been converted into a vast arena for the serious business of hedonism. The bar (jerry-rigged, collapsible, but backlit and equipped with portable refrigerators and dishwashers tapped in to the building mains) dominates the field of vision. No fewer than three bartenders are on station, with barbacks running resupply up the freight elevator from the liquor stash in a panel truck in a lot next door. Tonight's lineup appears to be: Chris, a black Adonis with a magazine visage, NFL physique, and ruined knees (now artificial); Song-hee, an androgynous Korean girl with a bleached hairdo straight out of anime and two railroads' worth of healed track marks up both arms, which she always covers with long sleeves (I saw them when I photographed her naked for *Zyklon B* magazine—had to use one of my pseudonyms to avoid messiness between the mags, if you ever see a photo credit for Gianni Giovanni Frangipanni, that's me); and V, willowy and raven-haired, an eye-patched lesbian with whom I once passed a dark and stormy night (she's never told, and neither have I).

Then there are the Staff Girls.

The Staff Girls of Le Yef are legendary, handpicked for their beauty and charm by the even more legendary LA, one of Le Yef's promoters. I've never met her, but LA's hazy background and fastidiousness for effectively creating the twenty-first-century courtesan have raised her to near-mythic status. She appeared on the scene right after 9/11, making a name for herself first around the Meatpacking District (how she managed to operate right at the police cordon, I have no idea), moving slowly south and east, tapping in to the bulging credit lines of the recovering financial sector. I've heard a story that her first backer was somebody who made money in soy milk but went broke when food prices started to spike a few years ago. (He was killed live online by some of his employees after he announced he was cutting salaries. He wasn't the only one, but that clip set the record for intraday page views on Cloaca.com.) I'm not sure how she connected with Reza, but they worked a couple of early speaks together after the '09 crash. Whatever business they may have done then, they're completely separate entities now, and you don't bring up her name in front of Reza if you know what's good for you. Since he supplies markets she doesn't deal with, they can at least coexist, albeit uneasily. LA's a promoter, a party planner, par excellence. She's assembled a terrific system of cutouts between herself and her vendors (including the landlords she bribes for locations and the cops, firemen, and Con Ed guys she pays off), and she's never been linked to drugs (she's supposed to be some sort of fitness freak). Or, as is the common misconception, prostitution. Both markets readily served by Reza, courtesy of a payroll full of obliging cabbies and a small management team of savvy operators such as yours truly. LA's girls are decidedly *not* hookers. Nor are they entertainment in the conventional sense. They don't sing or dance (we've evolved beyond the need for talent). They're the quintessential fashion accessory. They're paid to make a party look good. LA turned the recognition of a simple fact (a party full of beautiful young women is a party you'd want to go to and stay at) into a sizzling business. She's made all the glossies (gushing sycophantic praise, lots of cheap hemline-level photos) and the papers and news websites (hand-wringing, moans about corruption, vice, spreading disease and drug use, moneymaking in an age of moral decline, yadda yadda). No one likes to see a woman getting ahead (especially unemployed men), let alone one who's thriving at a time like this.

And of course there's the crowd. They are legion. There are the old-timers (thirties and up, the money behind the club) and there's my target market. Here are Cameron and Kyle, Dylan and Ryan, Tucker and Tyndall, Forest and Savannah, with all of their consorts (all flavors), every one of them gawking and fawning over N. She's surrounded but keeps her composure admirably amid the idle flattery and inane chipmunk chatter. (The trick now is to drift far enough out of earshot so I can do business, but not out of arm's reach. There's no way I'm letting a prize like N be on her own in Le Yef: Too many predators are eyeing her, waiting for their chance. I should know, I'm one of them.) I let the girls and gayboys squawk and flap and whinny about her while I (maintaining a delicious one-handed tether) get their boyfriends lined up. It's more practical to send them in groups, and they usually go in threes (legally, a cabbie has to let a fourth in the front seat, but a fifth is against the law, and you don't want that) after surreptitiously giving me a cumulative stack of hundreds. These go into a dedicated jacket pocket (never, *ever* fuck with the money, not just my rule but Reza's). There must be a full moon tonight, they're lining up like lemmings. I ask Tyndall to bring us a couple of Chris's specials, a delicious concoction of fresh lime juice, ginger beer, and—if Chris knows you—a magnanimous pour of Old Plantation, shaken to a froth and served on shaved ice; being with N is putting me in an island mood. Chris comes back with the drinks at about the time N pulls me close and says:

—Are you really *just* a photographer?

—Yes, he is, Tyndall says right on cue (obviously hoping for some freebies). The youngest one ever to shoot the cover of *Malathion*.

—*Roundup*, too, I say, carefully holding my enormous cocktail aloft for a communal toast. Whistles, catcalls, and applause follow as I twine my drink around N's and we sip from each other's glass, gazing into each other's eyes, before breaking into laughter. (This is where I live. It's not always bad.)

N is playing with my fingers and brushing deliciously against me when she feels the lump of cash in my jacket pocket.

—That bulge is a little north of the one I'm supposed to be interested in, isn't it? she inquires with a small wry smile.

Oh, fuck me poorly.

—Tell me, when you were growing up, did you always do what you were told? I say. (I know this sounds contrived and pretentious, but believe me, I've thought this situation through dozens of permutations, and this is one way that puts the ball in her court but leaves both of us an out while saving face. Of course, she could call the cops as soon as she clears the door, but I don't peg her for that type.)

—Never, she responds immediately.

Crisis avoided. Commence Phase Two.

I pull her close and kiss her, drinking in the sweetness of her tongue, our teeth touching. I'm lost in the moment (though not so lost that I can't sense the flashbulbs popping around us) when a baritone voice I don't recognize says:

—Hello, suckers.

Turning toward the voice, I am confronted by my recent past. It's the blonde from the Broome Street Bar, Our Lady of the Abdominals. Tonight she's in a skintight silk crepe tank top that shows off the topography of her arms and shoulders, which display all the peaks and valleys of a dedicated gym rat. There's no doubt about it, I am face-to-face with the one and only LA. It's only because I didn't recognize her from countless photos that I dared to hit on her that night in the bar. She never goes anywhere without some primordial specimen of XY-chromosomal overload. Currently, she's flanked by a creature that is human only in name, impossibly wide, skin more leather than flesh, eyes spaced too far apart and too orange in hue, a jaw built for pulverizing bone.

—Well? LA drawls in an unmistakably L.A. accent. Aren't you going to introduce us?

I gather my wits enough to make the introductions. N asks how I know LA, confusion (and something else, something unknown) in her eyes.

—We met downtown, LA says. She turns her head a fraction and whispers something inaudible to her saurian consort, who silently melts away through the readily yielding crowd. I babble something appropriately vague about the night in question and quickly throw a few compliments over the verbal mess. But LA's not listening. In fact, she's not looking at me at all. She's got her eyes fixed coolly on N, who does not shirk her gaze.

I was doing so well with N, but LA is throwing me off my game. I try to get back on track with:

—Business is clearly booming.

—Indeed it is, LA says sideways to me without taking her eyes off N. You should tell your boss he needs to learn how to share. There's plenty for everyone.

It's like vertigo when you realize a situation has been completely out of your control. LA has just talked business out loud, in public, in front of a total stranger, and with *me* in the lens. She didn't mention Reza's name, but she did mention my *boss*. If N's a cop, or if anybody's running surveillance in the room, or if somebody's making movies nearby with their phone . . . It's true what they say—nothing kills an erection like paranoia.

—We should have lunch, LA says to N.

—Glad to, N replies in a voice that is so much goddamn steadier than mine, I want to spit. Instead I laugh too loudly and start suggesting options.

—Not you, LA says with an icy finality I feel in the base of my spine. I'll call you, you bring her there, you can pick her up afterward if you like. This isn't about you. She turns to look at me for the first time with a triumphant smile. I swear she can hear my cock shriveling.

And with a final look (it's not sexual, it's not, it's desire, but more like for something you'd want to buy, to own, LA is gone, melting into a crowd of gushing toadies, a massive black-suited brachiosaurid materializing off each of her sculpted shoulders.

—What was that about? I ask N, who's not quite shaken but is visibly stirred. You know who she is, right? Have you two met before? Was she coming on to you?

Yes. No. No. N has gone cold; the woman who was ready to mount me five minutes ago has completely disappeared. Bring her back. *Please* bring her back. This version of you has tough hide, a hard shell, and spines. This woman *doesn't want me*. She chews a thumbnail, then, with a wave of her hand and a jerk of her head, she seems to shrug off the coldness. The glow returns to her skin; she takes a long pull of her drink.

—What just happened? I ask.

—Not sure. What'd she mean about your boss?

—Not sure.

I want to pursue this further, but my phone's leaping around in my pocket like a *paco*-crazed squirrel. There's a photo on the screen of an empty nest. Fuck! I need to resupply. While N most likely has an inkling about my extracurricular activities, there's no need to broadcast it for her and anyone else she may meet in life. On the other hand, there's no way I'm leaving her here alone. Although I'm not really sure *what* LA's game is—N is gorgeous, but if LA bats for that team, she's got an army of Staff Girls to choose from. What else could she be after? Something on me? Something on Reza?

Crunch time. I send a text message to the number of the cabbie working product at this location for the night. This will appear on a phone given to the cabbie earlier by Reza or one of his minions and won't show up on the GPS meter installed in every taxicab by order of the TLC. I take N's hand and tell her we need to be going. It's not fair to her—it's by far the shortest night I've ever spent at Le Yef, but it's also the most eventful one, so N can't possibly claim to be bored, given the night's erratic course. I'm apologizing to the bartenders for cutting out so early, Chris and V can't take their eyes off N, though Song-hee appears to be on autopilot—I hope she's not using again—when Kyle returns, clearly feeling no pain. Dylan is with him, but judging from his anxious sobriety, he hasn't taken a cab ride yet.

—Surly fucking African, Kyle says with a smile, oblivious to the impact of his words on Chris. Can't you at least get drivers who speak English?

—Renny, are you out? Dylan says with concern, too anxious to stay in the closet. I've got this super-hot wrestler down from Bowdoin for the weekend, and—

—No worries, lads, I say breezily, stepping between them and N and trying to shift the group away from Chris, who, at maybe six-two and two hundred pounds, would tie both these nimrods in a knot, but that would cost him his job at Le Yef, and Renny's Rule Five is, Befriend Bartenders Everywhere, They Are Your Infantry. Thirty minutes tops. I'll call when it's ready. Ante up.

Below waist level, out of common eyesight, hundreds fill my hands.

If this doesn't scare N off, nothing will. But whatever went down between her and LA seems to be carrying her now, regardless of business.

—How 'bout a change of scene? I say to her softly, taking both of her hands in mine, kissing their smooth backs.

She doesn't speak, doesn't smile. But she looks me fully in the face and nods, once.

Exeunt.

Thankfully, we don't attract nearly as much attention leaving as we did arriving, though we do have to share the elevator with one of my clients, who at least has enough discretion to maul his girlfriend instead of talking to me. I wouldn't mind doing some of that myself, but N is clearly experiencing some residual effects from her first trip to Le Yef. Getting her back in the mood will take some work. But, as they say, this is what I do.

Out through the loading dock, down the alley to Twenty-fourth Street, under the skywalk, to where Cipriani used to be. But it's out of sight, and there's the Dodge Angus, right where it should be. A quick glance down the block registers Arun's Hereford (he's working Flesh tonight), and sure enough, there's Luigi climbing in. Didn't notice him upstairs, he must've been there for a while, getting his load on. Arun will drive him to whichever location Reza has arranged as his brothel tonight, and maybe make an extra few bucks on the side slinging him some smoke, which is suicidal in my book, but Arun doesn't think Reza really minds. Why would he? His operation is bringing in more money than any of us can know, since we're working different parts with no way to tally up total volume. You've got to hand it to Reza, he could teach the MBA program at Stern all by himself.

My cabbie does wear a surly, jaded expression; judging from the name on his hack license (Ngala), he is most likely African. N stiffens at the less than pristine interior, the driver's sullen glare in the rearview. I'm nonplussed by the separate seating, but the driver straightens when he sees me. We've never met, but Reza has probably told him about my hair. I give him my address and tell him *Vite!* When in doubt, Reza says, you can always go French with Africans. A most well-traveled executive, Reza.

We're rocketing up Tenth Avenue before I reestablish physical contact with N, and this time there's no mistaking our intentions. She's not shy about it. Flipping up the armrests between our seats, she straddles me, one hand gripping the passenger strap, the other locked on my cock in a Wimbledon-worthy forehand grip. I'm trying to push her dress up above her waist, flailing for balance in the swerving cab, gasping for air while she bastes my tonsils with her dexterous tongue. (My God, this girl.) I'm starting to worry that I should've put on a condom back at Le Yef, not that I had the chance, when the Angus lurches to a stop and Ngala-whatever-the-fuck raps on the partition with his knuckles. We're at my building already, he got us home so fast that I lost track of the journey. That's how it is with the best cabbies—though, granted, I had some worthy distraction. N is arranging herself and returning the driver's unfriendly expression with one of her own as I fork over the money (the GPS meters can trace every trip the taxicab makes while it's running; Reza made it clear from my first day on the payroll that I would pay for every cab ride I took, since freebies and drivers missing their day-rate payments would attract unwanted attention). Here's the next hurdle: making the re-up on the sly without tipping off N. I tell the driver to circle the block—no one remembers cabs that leave, only cabs that linger—and guide N inside. I want so badly to touch her, there's heat radiating from her lower body that's liquefying my insides while turning my cock to pulsing veined granite. I give her an absurdly chaste kiss and tell her I'll be back in five minutes; she asks where the bathroom is, I show her, and when I hear the door close, I bolt to my bedroom and pull the rest of the stash from its lair. I run awkwardly, painfully, to the front of the building (ever try running flat out with a raging hard-on?) just as Ngala is completing his lap around the block. I jump in and tell him to make a loop around Morningside Park. Five minutes and fifteen bucks later, the stash is replenished. I give Ngala a twenty and bid him *adieu*, which earns me a scowl. *I* can't help it if he doesn't like his job. No one's *forcing* him to do this.

When I've double-locked the door behind me and followed the soft glow of candlelight into my bedroom, I find N with her back to me, facing the wall, studying my Mall Seasons series, wearing nothing but a sterling belly chain just above the inverted tulip bulb of her impossibly perfect ass.

—Where were these taken? she asks in a near-whisper.

—Central Park, the Mall, next to Sheep Meadow, I whisper back. My throat's constricted and my hands are shaking slightly, but the rest of me is throbbing.

—They're beautiful, she says over her shoulder, not quite looking back at me.

—No. You are, I say, coming up behind her.

Let there be no underwhelming descriptions of the ineffable glory, the mystical transmutation, that occurs when two like-minded lovers of equal prowess and appetites (unhindered by age or familiarity) collide. Her body is an instrument that is mine to learn to play, to spend eternity seeking to master. We are outside time, N and I, as we seek out every minute unit of pleasure to be wrung from the other. Up against my display wall, spread-eagled across couch and coffee table, on rug and bedspread and bath mat and chair back. I cannot get enough of her. Each part of her becomes a lightning rod for further sensation, each crevice a new receptor quest. I can keep track only with condoms. On our third, when I am (very deeply, very slowly) thrusting into her from behind, she drops her head, her thick hair falls away from her neck and dark block lettering—AETAS ANIMA—across her cervical vertebrae reveals itself to me (I *live* for moments like this!).

Finally sated, languid, tangled up in linens and limbs, sharing a Davidoff, my semen drying in her hair, I'm telling her about the garden behind Donna Karan's flagship store, and which positions (ostensibly for photography, at least at first) would be ideal for the heavy stone chairs by the fountain, when she says:

—Renny, how many women have you fucked this month?

If sudden, the question is not entirely unexpected, and having faced it before, I'm ready with a counter.

—I don't view relationship development conventionally. People meet, they interact, they come together and drift apart, that's the nature of the universe we inhabit, and our social patterns naturally reflect that. It's when you start imposing *conventions* on that movement, or worse yet, *legislating* them, that the trouble starts. I think that people need to collide, to bounce off each other a few times, in order to determine if they're really a good fit for combining. If not, it's best they keep moving. Because otherwise you get stuck in a vicious cycle of expectation and disappointment, and everybody ends up getting hurt. Throw kids and property into the mix, and you've got our seventy-five percent national divorce rate. I think at our age, it's best to earn some practical experience about what kind of person would make for that ideal combination, if there really is such a thing. But learning that takes a lot of trying, a lot of mistakes, a lot of movement. And I think it's best to keep moving.

That came out better than I thought.

N exhales smoke through her smile.

—Well, now, that's the most I think you've said at one time all evening. Is it supposed to be my cue to get dressed and leave?

—No, no, a thousand times no. I have had a truly exceptional time with you, and I want it to continue.

It's true. I don't want this night to end. I've made my Fast Forty, set up my twenty-thousand-dollar *Roundup* gig, got some extra drink and cab money from Ma, and had this extraordinary encounter with this extraordinary woman. Only two things mar this day: Eyad's death and that strange occurrence between N and LA. Whatever it is, I feel neither bodes well for me.

—Since we're taking non sequitur shots, mind telling me what was going on between you and LA? There is something, isn't there?

She gets that serious look again and starts to withdraw. But I'm not letting her off the hook so easily this time. And where's she going to go? Her answer, after a long pause, surprises me.

—She was sizing me up. She was appraising me, N says with a touch of weariness, of resignation.

—I see, I say without meaning it.

—Do you ever get the feeling that your direction in life is preordained?

That you're not really free, you're just playing a role in a script that's already been written?

—Absolutely, I say softly. It's funny how she managed to express the vague uneasiness that I think resides in every young person so concisely—another echo of X.

—Is that why you do what you were doing tonight? For the one she called your boss?

I surprise myself and say:

—Yes. And tomorrow I'm going to have to get up and do it all over again.

I'm surprised by how much that prospect, ordinarily exciting, seems frightening and unwelcome.

—Well then, N says, stubbing out her cigarette and moving the ashtray off the bed, we'd better do more of what we came here to do, while we still can.

She softly aligns her fingernails in perfect formation along my scrotal seam and arcs the tip of her tongue unerringly into my urethra.

My God, this girl.

FISH FACE

SANTIAGO HAD A PLAN.

Or at least he did until he met More. Before then, the plan looked something like this:

Into the academy at twenty (after doing his obligatory two years at CUNY for the deflating department requirements and in order to get his parents off his back), out with full pension at forty (assuming a pension fund existed by then). In between, gather as many of the relevant certifications, degrees, and initials after his name to take it to the next level. Teacher, lawyer, fed, judge? Santiago hadn't made up his mind what that next level would be, but he'd long since decided on the tool that would help him get there: the combination baccalaureate/master's program in police studies at the John Jay College of Criminal Justice in Manhattan. He was pretty sure the combination of undergrad and graduate degrees would separate him from the cops who clawed their way to the hallowed gates of OCID.

Naturally, this didn't come easily for an Anticrime cop with a second job. Anticrime officers were considered the NYPD equivalent of trashmen: knuckle-dragging thugs who hauled the most noxious human garbage off the streets. Investigations were unheard of, initiative seemed unwarranted, and the whole credit scheme brought sneers and jeers from the rank-and-file veterans.

However, John Jay being what it was, Santiago was able to use some of his patrol time as field credits for the Criminology Research Internship (SOC 430-31), his Patrol Function class (PSC 204), his Investigative Function class (PSC 207), his Psychology of Criminal Behavior class (PSY 372), and his big

Computer Applications in Criminal Justice seminar (CRJ 255), which gave him access to COMSTAT reports before they entered general circulation, something achieved by few officers below command rank.

All of which was greatly facilitated by McKeutchen, who was impressed by Santiago's zeal and actively supported his quest for degrees. McKeutchen had long and loudly bemoaned what he saw as a lowering of standards for each successive class of recruits (the force had been straining to make its minimum intake for the past seven classes, and seasoned veterans were retiring in increasing numbers each year). Academic requirements were eased (though the department somehow managed to hold the line at abolishing the requirement of a clean criminal record) in favor of military service, something that was hardly lacking among the thousands of veterans of the Afghan and Iraqi campaigns. The resulting influx of young gung-ho servicemen with itchy trigger fingers occasionally made for rather incendiary news feeds and some headlines in the few remaining newspapers around town, but hey, you couldn't have everything.

Santiago had known the day he transferred to the CAB unit that he'd have a rabbi in McKeutchen. The captain was paternal and encouraging and, Santiago suspected, had an ulterior motive as big as his ass.

This was confirmed within a week of Santiago's transfer. McKeutchen had confided to Santiago one day in his office as he sat in his reinforced chair demolishing a tuna melt sandwich in a way that made Santiago feel sick.

"Economic extremes breed social ones," McKeutchen said around a mouthful of melt. "Social extremes, in turn, breed political ones. Witness the recent Republican victories at the state and congressional levels. It's just Dem fatigue, same as GOP fatigue after Afghanistan and Iraq. So, people voted for change. Now, four years later, inflation, layoffs, and plunging home prices have conspired to make the natives restless. They exercise their displeasure through the electoral franchise. Out with those greedy corrupt DNC fuckers, they cry. Up with the right, in with a new mandate, the red banner of change!" McKeutchen emphasized his point with a massive bite. The ends of the sandwich gaped at Santiago, and the pink goo within swelled menacingly toward him. "Of course, it didn't work. Now that the elections are over, there's nothing left to distract the public from the ugliness of reality. The 'new' mandate looks a lot like the old one: disruptive tax code changes, austerity budgets, and forced housing subsidies. All for the greater good, we're told. But there will be no balm for our pain. Now people who've lost their jobs and their homes slide down through the layer cake to the stained cardboard slab at The Bottom. Reclaiming their previous status becomes a myth. They have no incentive and no hope. They seek solace in self-medication. When this fails to offer relief, they become bitter. Inevitably, they blame their situation on others, as is human nature. Occasionally, they punctuate their feelings with sharp objects, firearms, or the ever popular IEDs. Which is where we come in." The sandwich vanquished, McKeutchen licked his fingers and smacked his lips loudly; the sound reminded Santiago of the surgical documentaries he sometimes watched on cable during late-night insomniac channel-surfing. "The recent rise in, shall we say, large-scale discontent among our citizenry begs the question: Where do these good people get the goods with which to cut up, light up, and blow up one another with the frequency that has sadly become the workaday norm?" McKeutchen wiped his fingers with one paper napkin, then blew his nose in another. Something solid hit the inside of the paper with an audible *pock*. "Explaining the current scenario of decay and depravity I leave to those with higher learning and pay grades. Myself, I am concerned with bad guys getting through the cracks while everyone's distracted by the carnage in the foreground." McKeutchen pensively inspected the contents of the napkin, an augur divining the future from entrails. "There's something new happening here, a change in the shape of the street. It's more, whaddya call it, *amorphous* than what I'm used to. The more brick-and-mortar businesses collapse, the bigger this shadow game gets. The speaks are taking over from the bars, and there's an ocean of shit moving through them, but since the whole game floats, there's no way to pin it down. There're profiteers working this chaos, naturally, but not your garden-variety mopes, no sir. All this takes money, planning, logistics, and a lot of muscle."

McKeutchen paused for effect, which was undermined somewhat by a stifled belch. "The difference between organized and disorganized crime today is measured in billions, in nautical miles, and in international borders. Where were you when they sold the Chrysler Building? The same thing's happening on the street. And I just can't believe it's the bottom-feeding knuckleheads pulling it off. They don't have the brains or the manpower. There's too much dope out there, too many guns, too much black-market business."

McKeutchen folded his arms, braced himself on his elbows, and leaned over the desk intently, causing it to creak under his bulk. "OCID should have its arms buried up to the shoulders in the ass of this beast"—Santiago winced at the unfortunate choice of imagery—"but it doesn't. Something's wrong. Something is rancid in OCID. The machine's not doing its job, at least not for *us*.

"I want to fix it."

Santiago gaped at his CO. "You want to ghost *OCID*?"

It was unprecedented, unthinkable. There had been enough departmental investigations in the NYPD's checkered history, but the most successful ones had been spearheaded by the feds and backed by the state. For a CAB unit—street sweepers, drag haulers, cabbie cops, call it what you will—to go undercover in a top-tier investigative unit like OCID was simply unheard of. And dangerous.

McKeutchen flashed an imp's smile that quickly reverted to his customary golem's glare. "Indeed I do. But I can't just stick you in there. You've got to earn it. And you can't do it alone. I want to send at least two teams to OCID, maybe more as time goes by. The officers recommended will have to be absolutely stellar, on paper as well as on the street. They've got to make and break real cases, not just rack up the credits in this bullshit program. We need to get a handle on the speaks. Who's running them, how they're being supplied, where they're going to pop up next. If we can crack just a few of them, interrupt the supply lines, get some people to flip, we can find the money. Once we do that, we follow it right to the top."

There was a slight ringing in Santiago's ears and a drumbeat in his wrists. In his mind's eye, he saw dawn breaking over snowcapped mountains and heard the sustained bleat of horns calling for war. At that moment, he would have followed McKeutchen into hell. Or East New York.

But that was before he met More.

•

Interior, undercover police taxicab, night.

Stale was the first word that came to Santiago's mind that night before getting into his cab. It was nothing new. Stale odor of junk food, stagnant coffee, sunbaked vinyl, and much maligned radio and scanner. Stale feel of old aluminum and tired plastic, fake leather fraying off the steering wheel. Stale breath and perspiration, stale aftermath of countless exertions in the backseat by drags desperate to avoid jail. Stale subway smell on the clothing of the innocuous, somewhat disheveled-looking white guy in the black field jacket and plaid newsboy cap taking up the front passenger seat.

Santiago's new partner, assigned by McKeutchen himself, didn't bother to look up from the stapled printout he was reading when Santiago (in full street gear, hoodie and vest, watch cap and drag-stompers) slammed his bulk behind the wheel. He didn't look up when Santiago introduced himself. He didn't even look up when Santiago laid down the rule, that no matter where they were, if they got a call that Santiago's parents were in immediate danger, they would drop whatever they were doing and go straight to them, lights and sirens and backup. Santiago would do the same for the other guy's family if he requested it. Which was, of course, completely illegal.

No response.

"Hey, *cabrón*, I'm talkin' to you," Santiago snapped, shifting in his seat so that his massive shoulders blocked the garage lights coming through the driver's-side window.

That got the stranger's attention; his head came up and around, and for the first time Santiago was confronted by what he would forever think of as the Fish Face.

Several branches, boughs, and twigs of Santiago's family tree lay in southern Florida, and since childhood he had been making visits to various cousins and uncles, almost all of whom were blue-water fishermen. Some of Santiago's happiest memories were of sitting in an angler's chair on the stern of some relative's rickety old boat, a cooler full of Presidente within arm's reach, plying the waves for kingfish and tarpon and marlin. Whenever Santiago found himself looking into the eyes of what he managed to snare from the depths, he was taken aback by the utterly distant and alien gaze of the fish. Looking into the eyes of the fish was looking across a chasm of evolution; he felt none of the empathy, the recognition, he otherwise did when confronting people, livestock, or pets. The wild fish represented something other, something older, something *else*.

Looking into the eyes of Everett More, Santiago felt that same distance, the same lack of mammalian warmth, the same disconnect between species. This fucker More did not read like a human. Santiago was dumbfounded. He did not know what sort of opponent he was facing, and this made him, for the first time in quite a long while, feel something that bore a vestigial resemblance to fear. He would admit this to no man.

They stared at each other for too many seconds. Finally, Santiago decided to break the ice. "What're you reading?"

More blinked once and folded the top sheet of the printout over, holding the packet up four inches from Santiago's face. The printout did not quiver or shake at all. Santiago read: ANTIGEN CARTOGRAPHY: FROM VECTOR TO VACCINE, by A. N. Chakramurtii; Chuasiriporn Duang-prapha; and Lo Dingxiang, each of whom had various initials and suffixes after their names, as well as the name of some university Santiago had never heard of. He had no idea what he had just read, although it occurred to him that this was not the sort of reading material that "uncles"—undercover police officers—typically pored over between drag hauls.

Maybe More had some extracurricular job activities, too.

Santiago realized one of the things creeping him out about More was that he didn't seem to blink much. That, and there didn't seem to be any heat coming off him. In Santiago's experience, a face-off would cause some noticeable responses: elevated pulse, flared nostrils, perhaps the first tinge of sweat—the hallmarks of a body preparing for combat. More gave off no such spoor. If he was uncomfortable, sitting half-twisted in the front seat of a Crown Vic facing a cranky cop nearly twice his size, he showed absolutely no sign. Santiago wondered if More could hold that position indefinitely, and decided he could. He blinked his tingling eyes, mentally brooming away images of coffins and ghostly white men hanging upside down by their feet.

He decided that the best way to proceed was to initiate some sort of dialogue. "Did the captain tell you who I am?"

That at least took the Fish Face away. More went back to reading his printout. If having nearly come to blows with a new partner barely two minutes into the first assignment had rattled him, More didn't demonstrate it. *It's like I'm not even here,* Santiago thought.

"You don't talk much, I'm guessing."

Nothing.

"If you *can* talk, say something," Santiago attempted in a somewhat less grumpy tone. For him, this was reaching out.

"This car sucks," More gargled. Santiago could barely make out the words behind the phlegm. More's voice—what there was of it—sounded like it came from beneath a storm drain caked with alluvial mud. More sounded like he hadn't spoken a word in years, or maybe he had an errant sliver of bone growing sideways through his larynx. But he *had* spoken; that was something, at least.

"You just noticed?" Santiago turned back to face front, grabbed the leaden steering wheel with his left hand, cranked the key with his right, and miraculously, the tired old V-8 coughed to life.

They passed that first patrol in silence. Seven hours and four drag hauls and not one word. The hauls were, in sequence: a UPS driver in the Flatiron District getting a blow job in his truck from a transvestite prostitute; a purse snatcher outside a church in Murray Hill, too stoned to run a straight line; a pair of college football players outside a Third Avenue tavern, too sodden with beer to make their punches connect; and a derelict hopped up on *paco* who was terrorizing patrons of a sidewalk café on Madison Avenue with a broken bottle, stalking the tables, screaming about how much he didn't give a fuck.

Santiago had let More take the lead on the last one, just to see how he'd handle it. It was quite a sight, though a short-lived one. Showing no ill effects from being cooped up in the front seat for hours, More became pure liquid as he slid soundlessly from the cab. The junkie never saw him coming, never heard More identify himself as a police officer, never heard himself being told to drop his weapon and put his hands on his head, because More did none of these things, although he was required to by law. More simply appeared in a blind spot off the derelict's right shoulder and, well, did *something* that was too fast for Santiago to see. The junkie made a loud, croaking noise, dropping the bottle harmlessly in the gutter and clawing for his throat, his legs collapsing beneath him. More cuffed him, dragged him by the scruff of the neck, and threw him in the back of the cab in under ten seconds, oblivious to the café patrons, who were too terrified even to film the event with their phones. Santiago double-checked to make sure More had secured the drag's manacles to one of the heavy-duty steel rings bolted to the armored partition between the taxicab's front and back seats. By the time he had, More was back in the front seat, reading his printout. Santiago noticed he'd swung the overhead visor to the side and diagonally across his window, effectively blocking out the amateur videographers who were now falling over one another trying to get footage with their phones. *Cops,* live, New York City!

It was an extremely slow patrol, given the state of things in the city. A good night for a rookie to break in. Except that More was no rookie, Santiago knew in his heart. When they went end of watch, Santiago turned to ask More what unit he'd transferred from, but More had already slammed the door behind him. He hadn't said a word during the entire patrol. He'd had nothing to eat or drink and hadn't asked for a bathroom break. Stranger still, he hadn't asked how many credits their hauls would bring in. *Anybody* who transferred to Anticrime asked that right up front.

It was just as well, Santiago reflected later, that if there were any off-duty lawyers in the crowd watching More's Anticrime debut, they'd chosen to sit that one out. More had ignored maybe half a dozen procedural regulations while breaking his Anticrime cherry. That in itself was nothing new; Anticrime was rough, dirty work, hence the credit sweetener given to entice recruits who would otherwise pull nice cushy shifts in uniform patrol or Traffic. But More stood out. He'd acted with ruthless efficiency and a blatant disregard for individual rights. Santiago turned this over in his mind during the silent patrol and decided that, until such time as More's MO proved dangerous to his own career path, he was okay with it. Whatever happened, Santiago felt reasonably confident that McKeutchen had his back covered. After all, McKeutchen had assigned him this wackjob partner, which would come to light should there be an IAB inquiry.

In fact, Santiago thought, More might be a blessing in disguise, albeit a mixed one. All business, yet somehow completely aloof. Wrapped up in his own little world, though not so much that he couldn't take care of business when necessary.

Quiet, quick, and out the door.

Like he didn't really care, almost.

Definitely a weird one.

●

"*Flaco?*"

"*Gordito?*"

"Is he married?"

"Is he gay?"

The interrogation had begun without warning about a month after Santiago started working with More, when he'd opened his mouth about his new partner to his John Jay coffee-klatch companions, Lina and Yersinia.

The girls were Mexican-American, born to immigrant families from that country's rural south, a bit younger than Santiago, and widely different from each other in temperament. Lina was soft-spoken and demure. She had neat penmanship and took excellent notes, which she sometimes shared with Santiago when he missed a class or arrived late after a long night of drag hauling. She dressed in old-fashioned argyle and corduroy, which almost completely masked her comely figure, and wore huge glasses that distorted her fine Indian features. Lina had ripped through Introduction to Criminal Justice (CJ 101), finishing at the top of her class, and decided on the spot that she was bound for the DA's office, via Fordham Law School. Sometimes Santiago thought he could picture her, twenty years on, heavy and matronly, dwarfed by towering piles of case folders in a hideous green office on Centre Street somewhere, still wearing those ludicrous glasses. Too bad.

Where Lina was a slow, methodical, sweep-and-clear type of student, Yersinia was all search-and-destroy. She embodied every cliché about hot-blooded Latinas in a way that at times seemed self-parodying. Yersinia smoked menthol 100s and swore like a truck driver (in English and Spanish, sometimes simultaneously) and seemed to be on a lifelong kick of bitchiness. Every male in the building under the age of eighty turned to watch her sashay by, all black and red and mesh and leather, her ebony hair shining under the fluorescents, her ripe curves ever on display, to Lina's embarrassment (and, Santiago suspected, envy). Yersinia went through men the way Lina went through legal pads, and seemed to enjoy gloating over each lovelorn nitwit she canceled.

Santiago privately speculated that while Lina (who, for all he knew, was still a virgin) would be a delicious neophyte to initiate to sexual maturity, Yersinia would be a no-holds-barred fight for survival. Lina was an inoffensive diversion; Yersinia was a pest, a twenty-four-hour bad-news channel to which his mind always returned.

Despite the inevitable underlying flirtatiousness among the three, nothing had ever progressed beyond their meetings in the cafeteria, where they gathered to caffeinate and vent and trade stories. They were young hungry people who wanted access to what the school's degrees offered them, and despite the playfulness their age produced, all three were quite serious in their academic pursuits.

They had met in Drugs, Crime, and Latin American Society (RJ 250). It made for some good bull sessions for the three, which naturally segued into Santiago's (primary) job. The girls would grill him about police requirements and procedures, and he in turn would pick their brains about the finer administrative points of law enforcement. Meetings after his court dates were grist for the mill, as were headline-grabbing crimes; the girls always wanted to know if he'd shot anyone. And they loved hearing about the CAB characters he found himself working with.

Like the Narc Sharks (aka Detectives Turse and Liesl). They were the stuff of which legends—or maybe nightmares—were made. They had transferred to Anticrime together from Narcotics, having worked their way north along Manhattan island through Precincts Thirty to Thirty-four. No one knew when or how they had found each other, but they were inseparable. Beginning with street-level buy-and-bust operations, they had developed a fearsome reputation as case crackers and head breakers. Endlessly inventive and openly contemptuous of what they referred to as "the hand that squeezes the nuts" (i.e., the law), they had a simple credo when it came to closing cases: By Any Means Necessary. When word of the credit package went through the ranks, they had smelled blood and signed on. If there was drug activity in any sector, they would find it first. They quickly established themselves as top credit scorers; even McKeutchen didn't want to know the specifics of how they operated. Santiago had no fear of the sneaky little fucks, but sometimes, when the three of them snarled and squabbled in the station, he found himself thinking of one lion facing two hyenas, struggling to keep both in view. The Narc Sharks, he speculated, should have gone to Iraq or Afghanistan but were born street cops, and if they had enlisted, they probably would have been indicted for war crimes. A drug dealer in East Harlem suppos-edly put out a contract on the Narc Sharks, then went to ground pending word of their demise. The dealer was found dead in a third-floor walk-up around the corner from Rao's, shot nearly thirty times. The hit was ulti-mately pinned on some local gangbangers who could barely read or write yet somehow managed to intercept cell phone calls from the dealer, which led them to his hideout. The Narc Sharks had donned collared shirts and ties and slicked back their scraggly manes and sworn under oath that they'd had no contact with the defendants, who howled and screamed from their seats and had to be forcibly removed from the courtroom. A pending IAB investigation withered and died on the vine as two members of the gang suddenly overdosed on hot shots. That they did so while in Central Holding in the Courthouse District turned a few heads, but the story was quickly replaced by a spate of fresher, more attention-getting crimes, of which there was never any shortage.

The girls always asked about the Narc Sharks, and Yersinia even wanted to meet them, but Santiago absolutely forbade it. Knowing what Liesl and Turse did on the job, he had no desire to know how they comported themselves off duty. Not with anyone he knew. And not the way things currently stood between the Narc Sharks, himself, and More.

It had happened several months earlier, on Gas Fight Night, the second time the fledgling CAB unit nearly went extinct.

It had started typically—the Narc Sharks bitching about vouchers for gas. When gas prices first topped seven dollars a gallon, NYPD brass ordered paper trails for each and every fill-up of police vehicles citywide, with a cap of no more than one tank per shift. Cops from Kingsbridge to Brownsville gristled at this new directive, since subsidized gas was taken for granted by most patrol cops and all senior officers, who suckled at the gas nipple for their personal vehicles as well. Now they were not only being called to account for their consumption, they were having to go into their own pockets just to keep their cars running (which, since some dipshit EPA report came out in the *Times* stating that the average NYPD cruiser spent half its useful life stationary with the motor running, now had shift supervisors driving *their* cars around looking for cops burning gas just to idle, as cops were wont to do). Stations with their own pumps became covetous posts. McKeutchen, ever prescient, guarded his pump with the ferocity of a mother bear (ordinarily deskbound, he was known to physically chase off non-CAB cops looking to suckle at his ninety-one-octane teat). He had one rule only: Keep the Paper Trail Clear. This did not go down well with unconventional cops like the Narc Sharks, who preferred to keep their doings as nebulous as possible.

Things had come to a head one fine spring evening when the city endured one of its cold, damp, foggy rains that lasted all day and into the night and drove New Yorkers to drink, order in, and watch adult pay-per-view, doubtless what most of the CAB cops finishing their shifts were planning on. The Narc Sharks, however, were all fired up about whatever it was they were doing after work and couldn't wait to get out the door. (It might have actually *been* work, Santiago didn't know for sure and didn't want to know.) When the duty sergeant, an elderly alcoholic marking time until his thirty-year pension, waved the gas vouchers at them, they treated him to the sort of high-intensity ass-chewing normally reserved for the most troublesome drags. That had brought McKeutchen into the fray (he despised his men fighting among themselves), and soon everybody was screaming, and suddenly Santiago was in the middle of it, with Turse in his face calling him a shit-sucking, drag-fucking spic, and Santiago closing the gap between them, and Turse going for his gun, and Santiago locking up Turse's right hand and arm with a *tenkan* variation of the *sankyo* immobilization technique he'd learned from the aikido instructors at John Jay, and there was Liesl coming in from his nine o'clock going for *his* gun, and then More slid fluidly between them, deftly pinning Liesl's arm to his belly in a maneuver Santiago didn't recognize, and smoothly pivoting his body, whipping his right foot upward in a vicious clockwise arc that caught Liesl high on the inside left thigh with a muffled *thwap*. Liesl's eyes rolled up in their sockets and he sank like a stone. In almost the same motion, More had this weird little pistol out, a pinprick of green light visible beneath the huge muzzle bore, which also registered unwaveringly on Turse's right cheekbone. More wasn't even breathing hard.

McKeutchen started bellowing strange things like "Not my men" and "Not cops, not cops" at More. Santiago had never backed down from a fight in his life, and he'd learned firsthand how time and events could seem distorted through the carnival mirror of combat. McKeutchen's ravings only added to the confusion.

It was only much, much later, after everyone's evening plans had been ruined, after they all were finally allowed to reclaim their weapons after mandatory disarmament, after McKeutchen had screamed himself hoarse about how they were supposed to be fighting fucking *crime*, not *each other*, after he'd given the entire CAB unit a dressing-down that reminded Santiago of the drill sergeant in *Full Metal Jacket* (except Liesl, who came to after the speech was over and McKeutchen had released everyone—except More, whom he'd sequestered in his office with the door locked and the blinds down), after he'd faced down a glowering Turse, who was helping his groggy partner to their cab, only after all that did McKeutchen's odd exclamations come back to him.

What the hell was he talking about? *Not cops?*

McKeutchen's door banged open and More slouched out. If he'd suffered any ill effects from his extra time in McKeutchen's personal toolshed, they did not register. Santiago found his head filling up with too many questions too quickly. He started after More, then stopped, then tried to phrase some of his jumbled thoughts, but what came out was: "Hey . . . thanks . . ."

But More was already gone.

•

Their first patrol together passed into memory quickly enough. There'd been other, nastier drag hauls: the elementary-schoolers who'd pushed a wheelchair-bound paraplegic in front of a bus; the teens who'd tied their middle-aged teacher to a chair and set her on fire; and the pack of marauding gay twentysomethings, fried on meth, whom they'd discovered gang-raping a male FIT student between Dumpsters on West Twenty-seventh Street, in the now-defunct Nightclub Alley. And some fruitless poking around into a fast-cooling case the Homicide dicks didn't want, some Arab cabbie named Eyad who'd apparently picked up the wrong fare, one with psychopathic tendencies and a toolbox. It was a halfhearted effort that yielded little more than the crime scene itself, which happened to be in close physical and temporal proximity to the fiasco on Broome Street. Beyond that, they had nothing.

Santiago grudgingly came to admit that while More wasn't exactly the best company, he was more than up to the job. More never hesitated to throw down with drags (who gave him ample opportunity), but he never seemed to get carried away, either. The Narc Sharks, Santiago knew, were up for at least one brutality complaint (one of their drags, who'd ended up in St. Vincent's ICU, turned out to be the son of a senior market analyst at Urbank) and were having a hard time keeping their interview date with IAB, for which McKeutchen discreetly provided cover.

The front-line CAB investigators (McKeutchen had declared to a snarling crowd of reporters during a press conference that more closely resembled a horde of refugees clamoring around a WFP truck) were now "actively engaged" in what he referred to as Operation Coploscopy, targeting the drug trade in the city's bars. Santiago knew McKeutchen was using this as a cover to get up on the speaks, but since he had an email from the mayor's office demanding immediate action to curtail the surge in drug-related violence around the city (having hitherto kept a straight face, McKeutchen turned positively gleeful as he flashed the hard copy for the pod of obese, hungover cameramen), he was putting on a show to keep

City Hall and the council from his door (and using the operation's name on-camera as a dig at the assholes who'd come up with the gas caps that had nearly caused his unit to self-destruct).

The insertions had been going on long before McKeutchen's press conference. On Santiago's team, More had silently agreed to take point, since he looked so unremarkable. Santiago had been working with More long enough to see the human features behind the Fish Face: A fine web of creases ringed his eye sockets, and fine straight lines made nearly indiscernible axes across and down the tight fleshless planes of More's hard-edged cheekbones and jaw, as though he'd spent a lot of time in someplace very hot, or else very cold and bright. Under the station-house fluorescents, these lines aged More nearly a decade, but in the gloom of a bar, they effectively disappeared, making More seem like just another raggedy-ass student, a look he sometimes enhanced with an unlit cigarette in the corner of his mouth, or by turning his newsboy cap around backward. He'd even borrowed one of Santiago's hoodies, which fit him like a circus tent and stuck out the top of his field jacket like a poncho. It was perfect—More looked like a bum.

Santiago knew that he himself would stand out where More could blend in. With his height, wide shoulders, narrow waist, and memorable hands and eyes, Santiago commanded a certain amount of attention whenever he walked on a set, and his deep voice and direct manner would be remembered. More, on the other hand, faded into the nighttime crowd of revelers like a plank in a parquet floor.

Santiago was amazed by how quickly More could adjust to his environment. More would pick up on words and phrases and immediately rearrange and repeat them in new sequences, at varying speeds, and (to Santiago's frustration) without a trace of the raspy gurgle that he used for talking to his CAB colleagues, including his partner (which he almost never did). To look at him, he was a nobody; to listen to him, even less so. Santiago became convinced that More had done undercover work for another unit, maybe Robbery or Narcotics, maybe Homicide, maybe even the DA's vaunted HIU, going toe to toe with gangbangers in all five boroughs. But that didn't explain More's physical prowess, nor did it account for his odd detachment on duty: More behaved as though he were on autopilot much of the time. Santiago had considered and then dismissed the idea that More was on drugs (too well controlled). If More were an IAB plant, he kept no written records and expressed no interest in the other members of the unit or its CO. Granted, he could've been wearing a wire during their patrols, Santiago would never notice. After six months, Santiago hadn't figured out where on his person More kept that strange little gun. When More had been publicly introduced by McKeutchen to the rest of the CAB team (who'd barely noticed), More slowly and visibly took a very ordinary-looking Glock in a very ordinary-looking waist-clip holster and put it in a drawer in his desk, which he locked. Not once had Santiago seen More retrieve his weapon from its resting place. Maybe he was trying to duck an old brutality charge, or maybe he had a bad shooting on his record and was on probation. There were too many questions, and Santiago figured McKeutchen had at least some of the answers.

But those could wait. Operation Coploscopy was Santiago's ticket to the big time, real investigative work. The press, the council, and even the mayor's office were up in arms about CAB cops doing the work of seasoned city detectives, but this was ignoring a very basic fact: The city homicide rate had breached its 1990 peak and was rising every quarter. Stressed by budget cuts and forced retirements, the Homicide Bureau, the ME's office, the courts, the holding facilities, even the Corrections transports were backlogged and overworked. Somebody had to pick up the slack. CAB wasn't alone. Other bureaus were picking up more man-hours on drug-related murders and collateral killings. Pundits theorized that blending the roles of otherwise distinct departments would have a detrimental effect on the police, the judiciary, and individual rights. From Santiago's point of view on the yellow-and-black tip of the CAB spear, it was at least holding back the tide, creating new and potentially helpful surprises as novice officers improvised techniques and procedures for infiltrating the network of the city's three-thousand-plus bars.

That response was what had brought Santiago and his *extraño* partner to the Broome Street Bar the night two morons tried to fillet each other on the sidewalk. The night More had (for the second time) whipped out his little big-bore and saved Santiago's ass. And the night when, in their sector (in which they *of course* were the only available unit), the mutilated body of a cabdriver named Eyad Fouad had been discovered near the Holland Tunnel entrance on Dominick Street, inside yet another restaurant padlocked for nonpayment of taxes.

Eyad Fouad was Egyptian, born in Alexandria and a legal U.S. resident. According to his TLC license, he'd been driving a cab for two years. He was not on any known watch list. He had no violations and had never been summoned to the taxi court on Rector Street. He had no known medical problems, nor records for treatment of depression or violence.

But the gasoline used on him had not quite obscured the fractures and dislocations Eyad suffered before immolation (the postmortem would confirm these were inflicted while he was alive). Eyad had been put through the wringer, slowly and carefully, by someone with time and expertise.

Santiago jumped on this one immediately because Homicide nonchalantly dumped it in his lap without so much as a thank-you.

He jumped on it because it meant more credit for him in his Investigative Function class (PSC 207).

He jumped on it because slow torture was out of keeping with the frenzied drug killings that were the usual type of homicide around town.

But mostly, he jumped on it because More did.

For once, More showed interest.

In a dead cabbie.

Huh.

(ANDANTE)

REZA COVERED HIS EARS as another 747 drifted down toward tarmac that began just a few yards from the water's edge. He was leaning against the front fender of an Audi RS9 that glimmered in the light pollution softly emanating from the airport. A second car, a tricked-out Honda Akuma sedan, idled nearby. Two men sat in its front seats smoking nervously; a third was out in the weeds with a suppressed STG-2000-C assault rifle with FLIR optics. The man called Reza never would have dreamed of coming to this meet without backup, but he had little faith in his troops. Especially given the ones they'd be up against.

He absently crushed the long paper filter of a Kazakh cigarette in two dimensions, Russian-style, before lipping it up and cupping his hands around a gold Dunhill lighter that spat a three-quarter-inch blue tongue of flame. He held the gas jet to the plug of black tobacco at the cigarette's end long enough to be sure he had a good draw going; they went out all too easily. A taste acquired long ago in a prison he didn't care to remember.

The man who'd called the meet liked this sad little spit of land near JFK International because police surveillance aircraft could not overfly the airport directly, and the roar of the jets undermined the efficacy of most listening devices; infrared was usually distorted by the amount of heat generated by the airport lights and the exhaust streams of the planes. The marshy terrain made exceedingly difficult the advance insertion of any personnel other than trained frogmen. The man who'd called the meet knew about such things, having learned them in campaigns in Ingushetia, Dagestan, and Chechnya, where he'd added to his already fearsome reputation by matching the savagery of rebel fighters with his own. He'd been drafted into the army during the second Chechen war, plucked from his home in Magadan on the Sea of Okhotsk, where he was sent following a homicide conviction (just how many deaths he was charged with was unknown) in his hometown of Kiev. Magadan was a relic from the days of the purges, when Stalin sent his enemies east packed in boxcars for a weeks-long trip in temperatures reaching forty below zero. Reza once knew a Turkish criminal sentenced to Magadan. The inmate had bribed a guard for his cell phone charger and hanged himself with it the night before his transfer.

The man who had called the meet—whose first name was Miroslav but who was usually called The Slav in hushed tones because of his background—was Reza's boss. Reza did not know who The Slav worked for and knew better than to ask. The Slav was known to be a high-ranking officer in one of the five major syndicates (Reza didn't know which and was happy to remain ignorant) that sprang up in the wake of the USSR's collapse to divide up the country's riches, and then, armed with the capital from their wholesale plunder, had set out to carve up the rest of the world. Multilingual, ravenous, and utterly ruthless, these men kept up the most enduring traditions of organized crime: Bigotry is for losers, work with whoever you can profit from; always be willing to work with existing local networks when entering a new territory; and last but not least, use reliable subcontractors (and cutouts) wherever possible to maintain distance between the organization's strategists at the center and those far out on the tactical edge of things.

•

Which was where Reza came in. Now a naturalized citizen, Reza had arrived in New York in the early 1990s with only a smattering of English and a criminal record he'd paid dearly to have expunged. As a new arrival from a former Warsaw Pact nation, he'd been screened (though not too carefully) by Immigration, whose employees seemed more concerned with whether he was carrying any diseases and if he'd start paying taxes like a good resident than with scrutinizing his bona fides. Reza did what many a good immigrant had done before and would continue to do afterward: He got a hack license and went to work as a New York City taxi driver.

How easy it had been, in those days before 9/11, even before the '93 bombing, for a cabbie who didn't have to send money home to support a family of God knows how many in the middle of God knows where, one who had some decent connections, to make good money and put it to good use. Of course, he'd had his sponsors. Those who had cleaned up his record, who'd paid to get him into the country and set up in a shitty apartment on McGinnis Boulevard in Queens, expected a healthy return on their investment. Reza understood his role perfectly—he was a plant, an independent contractor that the organization was looking to grow for long-term gain. He'd never be one of the inner circle, but he was fine with that. He'd always worked best alone.

It hadn't taken many nights behind the wheel—ferrying home horny drunken youngsters from the East Village, the Lower East Side, and SoHo to the Upper East Side, Chelsea, Williamsburg, Carroll Gardens, and Park Slope—for Reza to figure out where the action was. He'd put out his feelers carefully, seeing which bars were best for women, which ones for drugs, which ones for the commerce in both. New York City nightlife in the '90s was a far easier market to work than contemporary southeastern Europe. Typical nights along Orchard Street, Driggs Avenue, Avenue A, or Houston Street were driven by the same hormonal and chemical propulsion as the region he'd left, but with no government or police supervision and none of the seething tribal malice that always simmered just beneath the surface of all the then-EU hopefuls. No, it was the same as working the summer crowd at Laganas, except these people had no sense of danger, no limit to their appetites, and more important, no limit to their credit cards. He felt he was witnessing an entire generation underwriting its life on someone else's expense account, and he knew he'd fit right in. God, these Americans are incredible, he remembered thinking repeatedly in those heady early days. The men who'd become his first clients had the same lack of scruples as their contemporaries in the Ionian Sea and points east, with none of the business sense. They'd film their girlfriends having sex with them, or with other men, or with each other, and then post it on the Internet. *Unbelievable,* Reza thought, *these morons give it away for free!* No wonder the U.S. had gone the way of its mother nation, the UK; its young people were dumber than dog shit, they seemed well aware of that, and they continued on their aimless course unperturbed. A miraculous place for an operator like Reza.

Full of energy and flush with cash from his cab shifts and initial ventures in flesh and narcotics (and far less encumbered by the expenses faced by his fellow cabbies, thanks to his handlers), he'd spent night after night drawing up new schemes for ever larger returns. The American appetite for marijuana and cocaine was bottomless, and Reza repeatedly mentioned that to his handlers, had even given volume and percentages out of what he was able to glean from his contacts in the bars. "Not your department," they'd told him. "There's a network of wholesalers we deal with; that works much more smoothly and attracts far less attention. Your input is noted. For now, we're sticking with pills."

Very early on—ironically, about the time a new Italian mayor was beefing up the police presence around the city—Reza had investigated more niche markets for party-oriented substances in vogue in the city's bars and clubs. He'd met some British kid, like the ones he remembered from the Greek islands but sharper, who was seeking a connection for lab-grade pharmaceuticals straight from the manufacturers. The kid had asked Reza if he could come by any Ketamine, Rohypnol, or especially MDMA. "We'll get back to you on that," Reza's handlers had told him when he'd relayed the request. Reza had given the Brit a conversational shrug and promised to keep in touch.

He'd had better luck with his first legal business, a pack-and-ship place along a busy stretch of Queens Boulevard, not far from the TLC Building. He was dumbfounded that Americans made it so easy to move vast amounts of freight, any size, by any means of transport, sometimes as quickly as next-day delivery. In Bulgaria, moving a container of English cigarettes or Italian beer sometimes took a week of cajoling, intimidation, and bribes. But with a Photoshop-equipped computer and high-resolution color printer, a postage meter, a bank of postal boxes the police never bothered to check, and an account with a marvelous agency called Federal Express, he'd be able to bring the best of Istanbul right to Astoria!

"Very good, Reza," his handlers had said. "This one will earn you some points with the brass." They'd commandeered a slew of the postal boxes (various sizes) for themselves, and he'd had to stay up late a few nights designing and printing letterhead for bogus corporations that the organization opened and closed on a revolving basis, with multiple "offices" in Liechtenstein, Grand Cayman, Panama City, and Zurich. FedEx charges to these corporate accounts would be billed to fraudulent company credit cards (another sideline business Reza explored beneficially).

Meanwhile, he'd grown his fleshpots. It had always surprised him how easily American girls would open their arms and legs to anyone with ready cash and an exotic accent, and even more so how many such young women, particularly in the East Village, would be willing to enter into an informal arrangement for services rendered in exchange for what they claimed were difficult necessities in life—a guarantor for an apartment, a letter of recommendation for a job or school, or loan collateral (oh, how Reza loved exploring this avenue for income!). He quickly recognized the dynamic commercial potential in party girls. Within eighteen months he had a string of tough barmaids, sycophantic waitresses, bored salesclerks, self-deluding artists, strung-out filmmakers, and aspiring actresses milking cash from barroom Casanovas from Gansevoort Street in Manhattan to Metropolitan Avenue in Williamsburg. Reza was careful to treat his talent in that casual, just-one-of-the-guys manner they all seemed to respond to, never making threats or hitting them, and always ready with a few bucks or something more as needed. Not only did the girls stick with him through their most productive years, they procured new assets for him, since more arrived every fall, a bottomless wellspring of young, willing, needy talent.

Excellent, Reza! his handlers had exclaimed. It's always good to make use of local merchandise. Girls are a much bigger pain in the ass to move than guns. Transshipment points are the worst, they never want to go, we have to insist, and merchandise gets damaged or lost that way. Those fuckers at Interpol and Europol are always busting our balls about that.

Flush with cash from eager orifices, Reza expanded his mercantile horizon. He still drove a cab, and during the long hours of each shift, he daydreamed of cabs and contraband, a checkered yellow distribution network that would support his burgeoning empire of sex, chemistry, and software. (Reza was keenly interested in the American addiction to wireless handheld devices; he marveled at how many people simply could not do without every fucking new application that seemed to appear week after week.) Reza knew better than to try and cheat the taxi meters—the garage owners' greed was legendary, and any anomalies between the driver's trip sheet and what he brought to the cashier's window at shift change would result in instant termination, possibly prosecution.

But that was a sucker's game, nickel-and-dime stuff. Reza was much more interested in the brokerages that provided drivers with the loans to secure the all-important medallion, the permit allowing any moron the chance to operate a taxicab in New York City. Since Reza had arrived in the city, the price of a TLC medallion had more than doubled in two decades (it currently stood at nine hundred thousand for an individual medallion and $2 million for a mini-fleet owner). To set up a front company that could access lines of credit for those amounts gave Reza a painful hard-on while he sat behind the wheel. He envisioned a vast vertically oriented network that funded, secured, maintained, and operated a golden armada of mobile profit centers; that doubled as nondescript ferries of a wide range of products and services (with access to all airports, ports, and railway stations) widely desired by the general public and foolishly deemed illegal by the authorities, thus stoking demand while—

Forget it, Reza, his handlers told him flatly. The organization's not interested in a bunch of dirty fucking taxicabs. The brokerage idea's a good one, though. We'll look into it.

Reza was not discouraged by their dismissal. He knew his idea was a good one, and he continued to hone and refine it.

While he did so, 9/11 came and went.

Interestingly, despite the initial investigation of the yellow cab fleet by the TLC, NYPD, FBI, and some worthless nonsensical agency known as the Department of Homeland Security, Reza (who had spent many a sweaty night following the attacks tending to his bolt stash of fake passports, overseas SIM cards, Krugerrands, and cash in half a dozen foreign currencies) was completely overlooked. After all, by then he was a naturalized citizen with a fixed address and clean criminal and tax records (a necessary sacrifice, for Reza hated paying taxes more than anything else). Moreover, he was an experienced non-Muslim cabbie, and the TLC was desperate to maintain the pool of experienced cabdrivers, which was depleted by arrests, deportations, early retirements, and general flight from the industry, going so far as to streamline the reentry process for the drivers who had left the business but returned once the dust had settled or once they'd secured new funds from God knows where.

The attack didn't bother Reza. He hardly noticed. It certainly didn't surprise him; the greedy camel-fuckers thrived on screwing things up for others, it was just how they were. Like that thieving little fuck Eyad, who deserved everything he got. The only way in which 9/11 impinged on his life was that he had to give free rides for a couple of weeks afterward. That nearly killed him, throwing away money like that. But his garage owner, a dissipated old Irishman who reeked of liquor even when Reza showed up for his shifts at seven-thirty A.M., had insisted. Reza had hated the faded, white-haired octogenarian who sat in the dispatch booth listening to annoying music full of lutes and whistles and accordions, who lived on whiskey and cut-rate cigarettes, and errantly pissed against the side of the garage several times a day.

But Reza did concede the ghostly old Irishman one point: Taxicabs were rivers of gold, no doubt about it.

As the city recovered, Reza tended to his businesses as a horticulturalist would his garden, and fruition followed. This period had been Reza's first real experience in New York during hard times; 9/11 had merely exacerbated a recession that had begun the year before in a flaming conflagration of dot-com destruction. As New Yorkers (with memories scorched by the attack) quickly forgot the tech-boom implosion that crashed to earth the year before the towers did, they eagerly embraced the new religion of better living on credit. Reza silently watched a whole new crop of suckers flock to this latest delusion—that they could transcend even the go-go '90s with a whole new soaring mountain of excess built on debt. Real estate replaced the thirst for tech stocks; a new bubble rose like a sinister phoenix from the ashes of the old. For prescient opportunists like Reza, it was the ringing of a great dinner bell, inaudible to the prey.

Ever the hardworking immigrant, Reza had sold his shipping store to UPS and migrated to the East Village to keep a closer eye on his core businesses. In the immediate aftermath of the attack, many downtown property owners panicked and sold, in some cases offering renters the option to buy their apartments cheap. Reza had bought two adjacent apartments in a well-maintained prewar building on the corner of East Tenth and Avenue A with a view of Tompkins Square Park, and combined and renovated them for next to nothing (thanks to his handlers, who saw this as rewarding his years of service with the easy gift of city permits and Pakistani work crews overseen by Ukrainian foremen, a small matter). Now a new property owner like many of his neighbors (though, unlike them, free of debt), Reza watched the value of his new home swell like his penis did each day now, sometimes several times a day, thanks to his happy menagerie of bimbos from Washington Heights to Bushwick, whose tight pockets were full of drugs and cash for their bar tabs, all courtesy of *Tio* Reza.

He had plenty of girls and plenty of product and was moving more each year, thanks to his cultivation of a small network of cabdrivers and distributors, in particular one ambitious little fuck with a dumb hairdo and an even dumber name, said he was a fashion photographer or something, had been introduced to Reza by the British bastard. Still, the new kid had the contacts and proved himself regularly with clockwork earnings, as well as procuring a somewhat higher grade of talent for Reza's service sector. Reza still stayed up late nights with legal pads, crunching numbers (with the help of a top-of-the-line Sony laptop), by the light of a single lamp (now a Danish designer model), trying to visualize a diversified empire of real estate, software, moneylending, narcotics, and flesh, all connected by a taxicab-yellow transportation network, and all under the organization's protection.

His epiphany came at the end of a long, aggravating Tuesday, which he'd ended with a high-test bottle and a ditzy blonde whose name didn't matter. He'd been staring at the whorls and patterns made by the rising smoke from his cigarette (now a premium English brand, no longer export-ed to the U.S. but available to seasoned anglers in the shadow economy's waters, such as Reza), while the blonde (eager to please after he'd tossed her half a gram of premium flake) tried vainly to succor vitality from his exhausted glans.

He'd been worrying about money all day. A larger income meant more to hide, and the organization had been painfully precise about his taking steps to ensure clean transfer of funds without calling undue attention to himself from banks or regulators. Those from less polished quarters, the chis-elers and competitors, the organization handled with Swiss efficiency—one phone call from Reza and the problem disappeared.

It was not lost on Reza that he resided at a point of intersection be-tween the white and black economies of the world, and problems in the latter were much more readily solved than problems in the former. What was needed was a machine, an engine to conglomerate and streamline his businesses in a manner that funded itself while providing solid legal cover for all illegal operations and revenues.

His epiphany came in a climactic expectoration of enlightenment that nearly asphyxiated his cokehead consort. Reza knew just what he had to do.

The following day he secured a home equity line of credit from Urbank, a sweetheart arrangement that allowed him to draw the maxi-mum with a pay schedule that was essentially his to call, without penalties for early payoff of principle. The loan officer was a client of Reza's who promised clean paperwork. Reza, in turn, promised a discount on the loan officer's trade, catering to his peculiar tastes, which would certainly earn him a prison sentence were they publicized. The credit line ran to seven figures, available immediately.

Next, Reza worked up a prospectus on his laptop, burnishing and polishing the armatures of his dream machine. When he felt confident the presentation was solid enough, he took a big belt of Polish vodka and called his handlers to request a meet.

It went better than expected, although all things were relative. When he was finished with his pitch, the handlers stood silent, frowning at him. One of them went to the other side of Reza's large apartment to make a call. When he returned, he said: You will come with us.

They took him and his laptop downstairs to an idling Audi QX TDI with blacked-out windows. Reza made himself comfortable in the plush backseat. He thought things were going well. His demeanor changed somewhat when he was bookended by two large, unsmiling men who took away his laptop, then handcuffed and hooded him. The Audi moved off, Reza marveling at how quiet its diesel engine was. He figured things might still be going well, considering how the organization did things. The fact that he was not allowed to see the route suggested he would remain alive for some time after reaching the destination. He did not bother trying to guess, knowing they would drive in circles to defeat the purpose. He grimly settled for trying to not soil himself. After all, he had a pretty good idea what was happening.

He was finally going to meet The Slav.

●

The Slav: a slab-sided monolith of horrific certainty. His presence drained the air from a room. Outdoors, the environment seemed to rearrange itself to accommodate him, as though the earth knew who was standing on it. He swathed himself in black calfskin that kept his gigantic body in shadow; the airport lights formed a penumbra around his shaved skull that gave the impression of a hideous mockery of a halo. Only the Slav's face and hands were visible, framing the mind that measured Reza's fate and the hands that could all too easily enforce it.

The Slav had no visible joints. His head simply rose out of his massive upper body in the manner of reptiles. He had no wrists; his enormous hands (the digits thick as rifle grenades) sprouted from arms like concrete pylons. Girth implied midsection; the Slav had none. His frame was impossibly wide and geometrically solid. What light there was around him was imprisoned in his eyes, shining with an opacity that obscured iris and retina. The Slav rarely blinked. He looked like an early amphibian that clawed its way out of the primordial sea, stood on dry land for the first time, and decided that it all belonged to him.

Reza once saw The Slav naked in a bathhouse near Brighton Beach. His tattoos stretched from just beneath his clavicles to the wings of his pelvic girdle, circling his rib cage front to back, an atlas of stopping points on a long road of criminal and military history. The bathhouse meet was to discourage electronic surveillance; Reza had been subjected to both strip and body-cavity searches (including a nasopharyngeal probe). The Slav had watched expressionless, men on either side of him in leather, wools, and furs, dripping sweat on a fearsome array of weapons, motionless in the steam.

That was years ago. Since then the pendulum had swung from right to left and back twice, with no visible improvement. Now was a new time of crisis, new fertile ground to exploit.

The Slav stood in front of Reza, impassive as he was on their first meeting, impervious even in the wake of a 747 roaring overhead on approach. When the squeal of the landing gear hitting the tarmac reached them from across the water, The Slav spoke, his voice clubbing the air between them into submission.

Reza did not speak The Slav's native Ukrainian; The Slav did not speak Reza's native Bulgarian. Russian was forbidden while discussing business in urban environments, as The Slav was too rich a prize for myriad police and intelligence services (replete with Russian speakers) the world over. For business, Reza and The Slav spoke Romanian. Since he was Bulgarian, Reza's Romanian was pure southern Bucharest. Since he was Ukrainian, The Slav's was northern, rougher, inflected with the murderous tinge of Chişinău.

"*Haideţi să-l,*" The Slav rumbled. Let's have it.

Reza shifted his cigarette from left hand to right, opening his left fist, which had hitherto been clenched around a tiny ten-megabyte flash drive containing his monthly operations report. He held it aloft on his open palm; it was snatched by a shadow from behind him. Reza knew his men would be disarmed by now; he hoped The Slav would not kill them. This was one of those rare moments in life when being careful *could* hurt.

For the next three and a half minutes, Reza recited a carefully scripted spiel of revenues, expenditures, receivables, and requirements, the litany of operations. Reza was hitting the high points; the details were laid out to the smallest denomination of various currencies and meticulously mapped out in tables and pie charts on the flash drive. Reza's voice was steady, as were his hands. The tremors came before and after he was in The Slav's presence; now Reza was calmed by an overwhelming sense of finality. If The Slav wanted to kill him, he would do so, and (Reza's sniper notwithstanding) there would be absolutely nothing Reza could do about it. Such certainty removed the anxiety of the unknown.

Reza didn't mention the problem he'd had with Eyad; The Slav wouldn't care about his personnel problems. He would've handled things the same way, Reza thought.

The Slav inclined his head marginally when Reza finished his presentation. "*Bine făcute,*" he grunted appreciatively. "You've done well. What I don't like is the size of our market share. New York is for sale, and I don't like waiting in line."

Reza's sphincter tightened. He'd known it would come to this. He did his best not to squirm.

"You know what we want," The Slav said.

The pressure in Reza's colon was intense. "*Ştiu,*" he replied, hoping The Slav would not hear the turmoil in his voice. "But these things take time. Abruptness gets noticed. We can afford to move slowly. There's plenty of business for everyone."

The Slav snapped his fingers; Reza nearly jumped. A rustling noise came from behind him. Reza groaned inwardly as two shadows, black-swathed, with night-vision goggles over their balaclavas, dragged his sniper, groggy and unsteady on his feet, in front of him. One of the shadows unslung the sniper's rifle from his shoulder and held it by the barrel, muzzle up, to The Slav, who took it one-handed by the grip.

"I don't blame you for taking precautions," said The Slav slowly, effortlessly holding the eight-pound rifle dead steady, the suppressor muzzle resting lightly against the hollow of Reza's throat. "But the next time you put a sniper on me, I'll make you eat his kidneys. *Înţelege?*"

Reza was rigid with fear. He was trying desperately not to fart.

In one disturbingly smooth motion, The Slav withdrew the rifle, flipped on the safety, popped out the magazine, and cleared the chamber, all without looking. One of the shadows caught the ejected round on the fly. "STG," The Slav said with a smile that made Reza's stomach torque. "I carried one myself in Ossetia. I commend you on your choice of weapon." He made a dismissive motion with one hand, and Reza's sniper hit the ground with a groan. "*Pe curând,*" The Slav said. "I look forward to your next report."

No long goodbyes for military men, Reza thought as the Slav's squad mounted up and drove off in a matter of seconds. Just as well. As the last vehicle's taillights disappeared through the reeds, Reza loosed a long, relieved volley of flatulence.

His men took that as their cue to remove their hands from their heads and get up off their knees. They were Poles who did not speak Romanian. The two gunsels helped the groggy sniper to his feet.

"*Moja głowa jest zabicie mnie,*" the sniper moaned. "Why'd he take my rifle?"

"Yeah, what the fuck was that all about?" asked one of the support thugs. Reza was looking at the place where The Slav had stood. He could still feel the suppressor muzzle against his throat. He was not aware that he had moved his hand to where the rifle had touched him until the tip of his cigarette grazed his chin. There was no pain; as usual, the Kazakh had extinguished itself.

"The rest of your lives," Reza growled.

PART II

CARNIVAL OF THE DAMNED

THE SACKLER WING

I'M SITTING IN THE COPY SHOP that serves as a front for Reza's office. It's payday, meaning I make my Fast Forty drop and take my 10 percent commission. Ordinarily, this is a fairly brisk matter—I don't like hanging around the office. Reza is tense enough these days, but there seem to be more overseas heavies here than usual. One of them, some steroid mongoloid as big as a fucking house, is in the office all the time. I don't know if Reza is feeling heat from Eyad's death—supposedly the cops are looking into it, but they'd never learn enough to follow the trail here—or if he's pissed about what's been happening in the speaks. Too many fights, too many ODs. I'm only on Specials, euphorics—when was the last time you saw someone fighting-mad on Ecstasy? But who knows who's slinging what else on the circuit. Prince William deals a little powder, I know that for sure. I don't—I've never touched powder, neither personally nor professionally. Then there's smoke, ice, who knows what other kinds of pills besides Specials. This is what happens when the party goes on too long: What started out pretty turns painful, at an unpredictable rate.

While waiting to be summoned, I'm catching up on the latest slasher yarn by C, a British novelist I was once fortunate enough to photograph (though, sadly, not to swive). I'm probably one of the few people my age reading hard copy. There's a good reason for it—phones stay off when you're in the office, and you don't turn them on until you're out on the street. Besides, I like books, another lamentable casualty of our age. This author has special meaning for me, too. Long have I dreamed of the day

I could entice her back to town, to the Metropolitan Museum and the inner sanctum of Dendur, where I would ravish her upon the temple's altar, carved kings and goddesses looking on, until her screams of joy echoed off the two-thousand-year-old stones . . .

Yes, I'm definitely in a Metropolitan mood. I'm due to meet N there in an hour, all the more reason to get in and out of the office fast. Sitting here waiting on Reza's whim is just tedious. I'm actually excited—I haven't been on a real date in years. X was the last woman you could say I dated, someone I had a connection with higher than pelvic. Someone I liked, someone with whom time shared made for a little bit of light in the city's lingering gray. Someone not connected with business, with the speaks, or with Reza. Especially not with Reza.

N is . . . different. Yes, she and I spent our first night together at Le Yef. And yes, LA did invite her to lunch, something I'd like to hear more about, and something I want Reza to never, ever hear about. But she's much more independent, much more self-assured. She has the air of someone who knows what she wants and how to get it, someone older than she is. The more time I spend with her—and it's been whenever I can, L has been chiding me all week for ignoring her electronic come-hithers—the more I'm convinced N is headed in one direction: up. She's got the focus, the drive, the hunger. She energizes me, something I haven't felt since—

—He's ready for you, Re-ni.

Reality has a way of shattering the fondest reveries, and at this moment it manifests itself as Edek, one of Reza's Polish rent-a-thugs, who looms over me and jerks his head for me to follow. Normally, his garrulousness extends to grunts and curses. This is why I try to avoid spending time with the rest of Reza's crew. They aren't the sort of people I want to remember or be remembered by.

At the back door, Jan, Reza's Tin Man, jerks his head for us to head into the inner sanctum. Jan is a gun nut. You rarely see him out in public, because Reza doesn't want to take the chance that he'll get busted on a weapons charge. I don't know how he gets all his iron, and I don't care. That's not my end of the business. Jan must have had some time off, though. His head is all bandaged up.

—Rough night? I ask him, trying for levity. Jan glares at me with blackened, bloodshot eyes and I decide to disengage. We head inside.

How to describe the lair of a modern black-market tycoon? You'd expect custom, premium, high-end/low-profile, no? No. Reza's office looks like a small showroom for used office furniture, which is exactly how he wants it. Chipped desk, battered file cabinets, black swivel chairs with broken hydraulics. Deep Zone Project playing softly in the background.

This is called hiding in plain sight.

The man himself is seated at his usual place, next year's Sony Mercury notebook on the desk in front of him. At his nine o'clock, the new gorilla is in a chair watching HGTV on a wall-mounted flat screen with—I surreptiously risk a second glance to make sure—a lollipop in his mouth. As Jan ushers me to sit down, I catch the end of the latest IAD spot featuring the great Arnaldo Mazur's rich baritone over the backing track of Beethoven's Moonlight Sonata: *Immodium. Stop the Squirts.*

—Love what you've done with the place, I say. It's a lame line, but I don't care. Usually, I'm not this glib in Reza's presence, but today the whole routine seems flat and distant, like a bad foreign-language gangster movie. And I have better things to do, with someone far above all this.

Reza closes his laptop and adjusts himself in the chair to give me his full attention. He might be forty-five, he might be sixty, I don't know for sure. His wiry brown hair has receded a bit across the wide Slavic steppe of his forehead, and the hard slopes of his face bear the ravines and gulleys of a life not easily lived. But his jadeite eyes have the avaricious glint of a much younger man's. I don't know how long he's been at this or how much longer he can last. He's in it for the long haul, unlike me. I've got no designs on his job. I just want enough to get out and start over clean and well capitalized. Let Prince William be Reza's golden boy, I don't care. Jan and Edek, they're hired muscle. The lollipop goon is an anomaly, though. Maybe that's another reason Reza's been so cranky lately.

—Same as always, Reza replies in his inscrutable accent. I know he's from Hungary or Belarus or one of those places where everyone savors tiny cups of eye-watering coffee and speaks ten languages, but I like to think of him as Russian. Jan materializes off my left shoulder and I hold up my messenger bag. With a well-practiced sequence of movements, Jan pulls out the Tumi computer case within, handing it to Reza, who, with equal economy of motion, activates the machine sitting downstage right on his desk. It's a Cummins JetScan two-pocket that can sort large bills from small or sift new bills from old. I know because I have the same one at home. The day I made my first commission from Reza, I asked what model he had and went out and bought myself one. There will be no difference between my count and his—see Renny's Rule One. Reza extracts the cash from a waterproof parcel I special-ordered online and runs it though the Cummins. No beep—a Fast Forty in full. While Reza counts his money is one of the few times I get to see him smile.

—Right on the money, as usual, Reza exhales. He punches some numbers on the machine, pops the adhesive band on several of the stacks I meticulously sorted last night, drops them in the JetScan, and lets it trill. Abracadabra—my 10 percent commission, which he silently passes to me. I'm stowing the cash in my bag's inner pockets when Reza says distractedly:

—Oh, I have something for you.

I figure it's my ration of Davidoffs, and I'm half-right. Reza slides open one of the panels in an ancient sliding cabinet behind his desk, pulls out two cartons of Davidoffs, and slides them across the desk. Then he reaches back inside the cabinet and pulls out something that hasn't been seen in this town since Bergdorf's went bankrupt: a pair of Vass boots, three grand at least. Reza plonks them down on the desk in front of me, picks up his cigarette, and takes a long, smoky Slavonic drag.

—These should be a good fit, he says through smoke.

—Well, *thanks*, I say, trying not to ham it up. I guess Reza's funk has ended; he's throwing me an extra bone. No point insulting his generosity. Reza inclines his head slightly and gives me a wave, my signal to go. The boots are in the bag and I'm on my way to a better place, swaggering a bit. Jan gives me half a sneer as I saunter out the door. The gorilla hasn't moved a muscle the whole time.

I'm happy, and it's been so long that it feels foreign. I've got cash in hand, a snazzy new gift from the boss, and a lady-in-waiting. I feel so good that it's not important to wonder how Reza knew my shoe size.

•

As the cab crests a hill on the Eighty-first Street traverse in the park, I see smoke rising from the cook fires in the New Amsterdam settlement. Originally, it sprang up in the playground just across from the Met, but when it got too big, the city ordered it moved to the Great Lawn deeper inside the park, so the tourists wouldn't have to look out on a shantytown. I've shot quite a few images of it from the balcony of Belvedere Castle—my nod to Jacob Riis. Couldn't make a dollar, though; the big content agencies have shooters living on the grounds, no shortage of Squalor Feed. Supposedly, a couple of movies are being filmed in there.

I hop out down the avenue to avoid the logjam at the taxi rank and stroll along the neoclassical facade in my fancy new kicks—taking care to avoid the concrete blast barriers, police kiosks, and rolls of concertina wire—to the huge pile of stairs at the front entrance. I love this place, I always have. I haven't been back since X left—we used to come here all the time—and when you have this in your hometown, it becomes easy to take for granted. But no one should. A terror attack on the Met would be terminal, an attack on history itself. Humanity would have few supporters left on earth if it came to that.

Naturally, those in charge of the place have considered this, too, and taken precautions. They'd already started work on the system the last time I was here with X, and I see it in all its terrible splendor. Walking through the doors into the Great Hall, I see that the entire lobby-level gift shop is gone, having been turned into a massive security center fronted with blast-proof walls of hardened steel. The nearest adjacent wall alcove, which used to hold an arrangement of flowers in a huge Grecian urn, sports a massive white ball turret with three long barrels trained on the front entrance. I know these are cameras and X-rays and other prophylactic counterterror gadgets, but it feels like there's a huge multibarreled cannon aimed at you when you walk in. The security center is supposed to have interconnected detection systems running throughout the museum, so they can see whomever, wherever, whenever, doing whatever.

We'll see about that.

When I pass through the scanner, the alarm goes off, like I knew it would, and I hand over my titanium Thoth to a guard. I'm traveling light; I cabbed it back to my place to drop off my bag and stash my cash, then took the same cab over to the museum. I've brought only my pen, my phone, and my special gift to a lady who's fast becoming someone special.

N is standing by the information booth in some kind of pale gray diaphanous tunic that makes my throat catch. She could be one of the statues in the Greek and Roman galleries come to life. When we kiss—publicly, unabashedly, as if we need to—a warmth spreads from my mouth back through my face into my chest.

—I missed you, she says, holding both my hands. I can't remember the last time anyone has shown me this kind of tenderness. I'd almost forgotten it was possible.

N asks where we should start, and I figure she probably wants to check out the new Anonymous show, which produces a smile from her that could light up the entire Great Hall. I pay for the two of us, and down we go through the ages, streaks of orange and black as Attic amphorae drift by in the background. I'm so comfortable with her, our conversation is easy and unforced, none of the inane small talk I usually have to put up with. I almost don't want to ask about her lunch meet with LA, though I know I'll have to.

Anonymous is upstairs in the modern-art wing (thank you, Lila Acheson Wallace). You don't see much new art these days, no market for it. But Anonymous doesn't seem to be in it for the money. There's so much urgency in each canvas, so much fear and chaos. No wonder he (or she) is being hailed as the consummate painter of our time. N and I are stopped in our tracks by one huge canvas titled *The Slow Evisceration of Saint Anton* that is so unspeakably violent, it could only be the product of a disturbed mind recklessly provoked into psychotic rage.

—What was this guy *thinking*? N asks, wincing at the grotesquerie in front of us.

—Definitely a bad brain day, I say, clucking sympathetically. We move on.

I want to show her Tomonori Tanaka's new stuff, so I guide her past the Impressionists, through the aisle of Rodins, down the ramp, and hard left into modern photography (thank you, Henry R. Kravis). This was always where X and I wound up; after she left, I still came to the Met, though I found this room too painful to enter. But now we glide through it easily; it's as though N has exorcised X's ghost. My God, this girl.

I gently steer her across the hall, down a short flight of stairs, and back five centuries. We stand on a cloistered terrace, leaning our forearms on the veined marble railing overlooking a Renaissance courtyard. I've always thought this was a nice mellow spot for conversation, and it's as good a place as any to ask N how things went with LA.

When I do, N's lightness fades; her countenance becomes that of a person who's been asked to recount something unpleasant. I can't imagine LA would have roughed her up in public. A wave of protectiveness washes over me, something I don't feel for anyone these days except my mother. Naturally,

I'm dumbstruck when N tells me that LA wants to hire her.

—What do you mean, hire? I ask incredulously. I'm not sure how to take this. If N joins the Staff Girls, there should be nothing to worry about, since LA doesn't deal in women—only spectacle—and her security goons would make short work of any moron who got the wrong idea. But an ugly green plume of jealousy is rising in my gorge as I imagine the likes of Timo and Luigi drunkenly monopolizing her. I don't know what to say about it—N and I have just met, and while this past week has been a bona fide whirlwind, I don't know how Serious we are. I don't even know whether I'm ready for Serious, if it's been too long.

—It's not about that, N says in a more soothing tone, as if sensing the knots in my stomach.

—No? What is it, then?

—She's branching out. She wants to trademark the Staff Girls, get them into the mainstream. She says she's already got some big contracts in media, cosmetics, jewelry . . .

N continues, but I'm having trouble concentrating. LA is branching out. She's expanding her territory out of speak country into legitimate business. She wants to have one foot in the light and one in the dark—she wants to do what *I* do, but on a much larger scale. She's amassed her illicit capital to invest above street level.

LA wants to get ahead of Reza.

And I think she might.

I snap back into focus when N says:

—She mentioned your boss, too.

—What. What did she say. What about my boss. Did she call him by name or—

—Take it easy, baby, she just mentioned you and *the guy he works for,* nothing specific. She made it sound like . . . competition.

You could call it that, I say to myself.

—She had a certain look in her eyes when she was talking about you two. I can't really describe it, but I got the impression she doesn't like your boss much, you know?

Oh, honey, you have no idea.

N shifts along the railing to face me more fully.

—Renny, maybe you should . . . find some other gig. You've had a lot of success with your photography for someone so young. Who knows, maybe it'll be *your* pictures on the wall in that gallery we were just in. Someday soon. Maybe if you . . . stepped down from whatever job this boss of yours has you doing, you'll have more time to focus on your photography. You keep telling me that's what you want, right?

She puts her hand on my neck, just below my ear.

—Now's the time, Renny. Carpe diem.

My mind is in overdrive. N can't possibly know how this development has realigned things. If she joins LA's team, I'd have eyes inside LA's camp. It could be dangerous—I don't relish the thought of becoming Reza's spy, but I'd have a much better chance of knowing which horse will win this race. And which one to back.

I can't deny this windfall for N, either. She'll make good money, real money, legal money, which I can boost with my commissions from Reza. I could get gigs shooting N and the other Staff Girls for the high-end fashion conglomerates, the ones that were big enough to survive the crash—with Marcus Chalk as a reference, this should be a snap. N and I could move in together, build a fast nest egg, and do what X did when she dumped me for that Wall Street guy—*escape*. Get away from Reza, LA, the speaks, this putrefying place. We'll have cash in the bank, kick-ass portfolios of high-profile work, in the prime of our lives. At last, I can see a way out.

Not just yet. It'll take us maybe two, three years to get there. But we will.

I really can have it all.

I pull N close and kiss her on the balcony of the Vélez Blanco castle, and there's plenty of heat in it as well as something else, a deeper kind of warmth beneath the fire. This is—New.

—Come with me, I gasp when we break apart. N's eyes are shimmering wet, but she can't be sad, those must be the tears of joy I've always heard about but never seen. We half-walk, half-run through ancient Near Eastern art (bearded warriors with elongated faces and hollow eyes follow us out), across the Great Hall balcony passage, past yards of Korean ceramic, through ancient Chinese art (thank you, Charlotte C. Weber) and stumble breathless into the Sackler Wing, the finest collection of Japanese art this side of Tokyo.

The air is always hushed here as you pass the great carved Buddha, and more humid, thanks to the near-silent Noguchi fountain. I have to consciously restrain myself from pulling N down onto the tatami mats in the *shoin* room with its vast ancient plum tree scroll—security would be all over us. The special gift I have for N requires privacy and sepulchral quiet.

I lead her by the hand into the Asian art library. This was a study center up until the crash, when staffing cuts caused it to revert to a documentary film theater. Gone are the rows of books and computer terminals and long tables, but they put in some cheap old pews, and we settle on the farthest corner of the last one, me with my back to the wall, N seated to my left. Koto music drifts around us from hidden speakers. There are two elderly Asian tourists up in the front row and us in the back. No one else.

With as much sleight of hand as I can muster, I pull out N's gift. You're probably wondering how I was able to smuggle a small metallic object past all that security downstairs. Sorry, trade secret. Suffice to say that I go in and out of some of the most heavily defended places in town night after night, often holding large amounts of cash. One of the few fringe benefits of my job is getting to learn all about security.

N's eyes widen and her hand goes to her mouth to stifle a gasp. The gift is a Little Something by Jimmy Jane, just over five inches long, with a platinum finish. It's silent, insertable, and completely waterproof—fun for the bathtub and dishwasher-safe for all you clean livers out there. I twist its base to its slowest setting and slide it beneath N's tunic, up between her smooth tan thighs to a place I've become very familiar with in a very short period of time.

N arches her back and closes her eyes. She slowly brings her arm up across my chest, bringing her hand to my face, her fingers lightly stroking my right ear. On the wall-mounted screen in front of us, Phoenix Castle rises through a mist of cherry blossoms.

—*Mi pobrecito*, she murmurs wistfully as I increase the vibrator's speed, what are we going to do about you.

EAU DE DEAD CABBIE

MORE BOTHERED SANTIAGO.

It wasn't anything he said—More could go whole shifts without speaking, and often did. Nor was it anything he did or didn't do, at least as far as the job was concerned. More easily held his own in a fight, taking down even the most violent drags with little apparent effort, and (best of all) giving Santiago the collar—and thereby the credits. OCID didn't look so far away after all.

It wasn't even that More was clearly uninterested in any kind of bonding bullshit. No pictures of family on his phone (come to think of it, Santiago had never seen More's phone; he didn't know whether More even had one). No drinks after work for More, though they were starting to become more commonplace among the other CAB cops, as the camaraderie born of a small group in near-desperate straits coalesced. Santiago had picked up on More's barroom trick of touching only the water back of his usual shot-and-a-beer when working the bars. More never showed up to work with a hangover, never had the reek of metabolized alcohol oozing through his pores. Whatever he was, Santiago concluded, More was not a drunk. More's job routine was simple: Appear out of nowhere at the beginning of a shift, haul drags until end of watch, then disappear again. Santiago's second job and classwork prohibited him from double shifts (not that the department had any OT money), but McKeutchen had told him that, if the situation arose, More would work doubles with him.

"He likes you," McKeutchen told Santiago in his office late one night after his shift. "You don't bother him."

"Nothing bothers him," Santiago countered. "And that bothers *me*. Six months on shit detail, he doesn't even blink. Shit, I don't think he *can* blink. Nothing that happens to us out on the street gets to him. He doesn't talk, he doesn't want any credits—Cap, what gives?"

McKeutchen shrugged his meaty shoulders, his smile thin beneath curtains of fat. "He's ESU."

That was the heart of the matter, nagging at Santiago while he was pumping iron or scrubbing clams or poring over his textbooks. The Emergency Services Unit liked physically aggressive officers and was infamous for grueling training and qualification standards. Santiago had heard all the stories about ESU trainees fast-roping from choppers onto rooftops in driving rain, or doing rope climbs from river barges up the Triboro Bridge in full riot gear. ESU replaced the earlier SWAT units of the NYPD, which wanted an updated paramilitary force to deal with any contingency, never mind the Atlas patrol wannabes pulling guard duty around Rock Center and Grand Central, posing for the news cameras with their black tac helmets and slung M4s . The cops who survived the ESU induction were given the "special" rig-out of weapons and medical training, as well as learning advanced communications and imaging systems. They cross-trained with the department's air and marine units and received visiting instructors from the FBI, various military branches, even foreign security and intelligence agencies whenever somebody got a feeling that al-Qaeda wanted to hit the Javits Center (not that there had been a convention in town for the past three years). The ESU was an elite province of the NYPD, and those cops usually had their pick of plum assignments when they transferred. If they survived.

Not that ESU had given Santiago a scrap of information about More. When he finally got through to a lieutenant at the ESU command in Brooklyn, the conversation went like this:

SANTIAGO: More, I'm trying to find out about Detective More.
LIEUTENANT SHIT-FOR-BRAINS: Who?
S: More, Detective More!
LSFB: Detective-Specialist More? The new sniper guy?
S: You have more than one?
LSFB: We have snipers, and we have sniper instructors. It depends on the course being given—

S: Just tell me which one you're teaching him!

LSFB: Teaching him? He teaches *us*!

S: Say what?

LSFB: Who is this again?

S: Detective Santiago, CAB Group One.

LSFB: If they don't tell you who you're working with, why should I? (Click.)

Why would a cop leave the ESU to haul drags in a dirty fucking taxicab? And why would said cop forgo the arrest credits that could take him above the vaunted ESU, maybe all the way to OCID? It wasn't that More was riding on Santiago's coattails; the guy hauled more drags in one night than Santiago did in two (or most of the other teams did in five). More did more than his share of heavy lifting, but for what?

And where did More go after he finished his shift? McKeutchen shrugged and said he probably went back to the ESU in Brooklyn. Or picked up extra CAB shifts on the weekends. Santiago knew that was a lie, because the weekends belonged to the Narc Sharks, who frowned on any other cops (even brother CAB cops) poaching on their turf. In the same way civilians used to look forward to the weekends as a time to party, the Narc Sharks viewed weekends as a bonanza of credits. The holding tank bulged with their drag hauls from Thursday night to Monday morning. The only other team in the unit whose credit count was remotely close was that of Santiago and More, perhaps owing to More's loose interpretation of individual rights.

The night Santiago decided to investigate his partner did not begin in any unusual way. For weeks, the drag hauls had been getting worse. The sort of random "stranger violence" that typically occurred at night in neighborhoods emptied by the real estate bust was now taking place in otherwise low-crime areas at all hours, a trend confirmed by a monthlong series of consecutively grim COMSTAT reports. To make matters worse, a new hobby with the street moniker "mad-dogging" was threatening to become a city pastime. The activity had begun as a form of separation anxiety for the thousands of newly unemployed who could no longer shop at the stores nor eat at the restaurants they once took for granted. Crowds would form at the windows, looking in at those lucky enough to enjoy what they could not. The first incidents were merely disruptive and profane. The spiral did not take long.

Groups of youngsters began trying to outdo each other with feats of daring, such as running through restaurants tearing tablecloths off, sending knives and broken glass flying in the faces of terrified diners. Soon widespread reports of drunken and drug-fueled criminal entries were clogging the airwaves. A new charge, EAR (entering, assault, and rape) was being entered on indictments around the city (the cops referred to it as "taking it in the EAR"). The ensuing drop in restaurant traffic drove dozens of establishments out of business; merchant security responses, such as full-body friskings required upon entry, closed dozens more. Streets formerly resplendent with glittering, prosperous stores stood lined with shuttered, padlocked gates. The surviving stores bristled with the sort of countermeasures usually reserved for the UN: security cameras, armed guards, concrete blast barriers. Ever looking to the classical past, Ralph Lauren had festooned the doors and windows of his stores with barbed wire, and deployed jackbooted private K-9 security guards with massive drooling Rottweilers and Alsatians in his twin mansion flagships on Madison Avenue.

The store closings were a body blow to the city's tax revenue. The dying restaurant scene, together with the City Council's ill-conceived price caps on landowners (meant to keep businesses and tenants in their locations) begat a parallel economy of illegal restaurants and bars. This shadow world of mobile clubs—their locations often available only hours before opening time via a coterie of electronically linked insiders—allowed for a resurgence of a sophisticated drug trade that remained frustratingly out of reach of the overburdened police department, stretched thin as it was by a surge in violence fueled by cheap, highly addictive street drugs like *paco*. Since the well-organized, exclusive mobile supper clubs and speakeasies did not have anywhere near the levels of violence borne by the brick-and-mortar businesses of New York, The Powers That Be at City Hall and One Police Plaza did not deem them as immediate a threat as the wave of EAR crimes (known among the rank and file as "EARgasms"). Hence fewer police investigations, hence a burgeoning underground nightlife the likes of which hadn't existed since the repeal of Prohibition in 1933.

Except for a few crusty pain-in-the-ass dinosaurs in the chain of command who refused to toe the party line on the grounds that it was strangling the city. Men like McKeutchen, who had nurtured and cultivated loyal pups like Santiago, grooming them to follow in the paw prints of salty NYPD dogs like Joseph Petrosino.

"Who?" asked Santiago.

"Get the fuck out of here," growled McKeutchen. "More, wait here a minute. Shut the door."

When he looked back on it much later, Santiago would decide that had been the last straw, McKeutchen shutting him out on that fateful night. The captain had done that periodically over the six months Santiago and More had ridden together. Santiago had come to think of himself as McKeutchen's golden boy, and the sight of an interloper like More getting the same preferential treatment made him feel left out and jealous, something he would admit to no man.

So he decided to test his budding investigative skills on More. After all, he reasoned, if you can't trust your partner, who can you trust?

●

It probably wouldn't have come to pass, Santiago thought later, if he'd just let the drag die.

They'd rolled on an assault call straight from dinner, takeout from Santiago's favorite Peruvian restaurant in Spanish Harlem. Santiago had thrust his order of *parihuela* at More (who never seemed to eat anything, the weird fuck), fired up the siren and wig-wag lights hidden in the Crown Vic's grille, and screeched the cab over to the Conservatory Garden along Central Park's northeastern edge at 103rd and Fifth.

Jumping the front wheels onto the curb, Santiago put the lights on an unconscious nurse, and a drag geeked to the gills on *paco* and doing his best to separate a moaning, drooling geriatric from her oxygen tank–equipped wheelchair, which would probably retail on the street for enough dope to kill the drag and six others like him. Santiago figured the nurse had wheeled the old bag of bones across the street from the Cardinal Cooke Health Care Center to take the evening air. Up jumped the junkie, and here they all were.

As usual, More was out the door before Santiago brought the car to a full stop. As usual, the drag never saw him coming. This time, however, More used a short, vicious technique Santiago didn't recognize, although there was no mistaking the loud crack that followed. The drag took one look at the fractured radius poking through the skin of his forearm and promptly passed out. The broken bone had severed vital vessels on its way to the great outdoors, and a pool of blood formed rapidly under the drag's inert form, spreading in a zigzag pattern through the mortar of the garden's old brick sidewalk.

Santiago, with blood thumping in his ears and wrists, cilantro rice sticking to his forehead over his bulging eyes, pointed out that the suspect needed emergency medical attention.

"Why?" rasped More.

"What do they teach in ESU school, how to burn the fucking police manual?" Santiago gasped as he tried to pull the drag's wounded arm above heart level without doing further damage. "Help me tie this off."

"Why?" More repeated, as still as the unconscious junkie.

"More, just shut up and HELP ME!" Santiago bellowed. He didn't know which was more frustrating: that he was telling a nearly mute man to shut up; or that he had been partnered with said mute, who, among other things, seemed okay with letting an injured suspect publicly bleed to death. Santiago saw all his prospects dribbling away with the junkie's blood, and knew what he needed to do was to get the suspect across the street to the hospital, then get himself straight with McKeutchen. If the junkie died later, fine, his own ass would be covered. More could go take a flying fuck, there were plenty of other eager-beaver applicants for CAB who wouldn't jeopardize Santiago's career on a routine drag haul.

As things turned out, Santiago might have hoped for better.

The trio of burly orderlies who rushed across the street when they saw the taxicab on the curb with an overturned wheelchair in front of it weren't prepared to like the cops, who they figured had just run over their ward. When they found out the drag had coldcocked the nurse, who was well liked and respected around the hospital, as well as terrorizing an invalid octogenarian who never raised her voice to any of the staff, well, they weren't prepared to guarantee the young thug's safety once he was brought onto the premises. Things did not improve when Santiago asked to speak to the chief of staff and instead got a quivering resident whose pupils were clearly dilated by something stronger than coffee. The resident said, like, they had no beds, and, um, maybe they'd be better off taking this, uh, patient down the street to Mount Sinai?

"What about the Hippocratic oath?" Santiago demanded, growing more disgusted by the minute as the drag kept leaking on the bricks. From behind him More made some kind of coarse glottal sound, while in front of him the ursine orderlies openly snorted and sneered.

"Can you at least tie him off so he won't bleed out while he take him down there?" Santiago asked through grinding teeth. But he could see it was a lost cause; the orderlies were bundling up the old and young victims and carrying them across the street, and the resident was, like, I mean, y'know, see ya.

Santiago felt very much like he was back in the waiting room of St. Vincent's being told that Bea Goldberg was basically toast and nothing in that great fortress of medical knowledge, technical wizardry, and pools of public and private funding could save her. Briefly, he wondered if he could manage a head shot on the wired young resident at this range.

More's latex gloves snapped him out of it. All CAB cops rolled with gloves and masks in their kits, as standard as badge and cuffs. (Guns were another matter, and Santiago reminded himself for the umpteenth time to ask More what piece he carried and where.) Santiago watched, fascinated, as More tied off and splinted the drag's arm in under a minute using the drag's own belt and a ballpoint pen. "Damn, they teach you good knots in ESU, huh?" Santiago offered lamely, his earlier adrenaline rush ebbing.

More ignored him and pointed to the back door of the cab. Santiago opened it and started to reach for the drag's foot to heave him inside, but More snapped the latex twice against his wrist, and Santiago nodded, reaching for his own gloves. With the infection rates what they were (current HHS estimates claimed one in three New Yorkers had herpes, while one in six was HIV positive), no chances were taken with bleeders, biters, or open wounds.

They managed to get the drag levered into the backseat with a minimum of cursing (More his usual silent self), then clambered into the front. Santiago called it in and left word with the ops dispatcher to tell the CAB duty sergeant to raise McKeutchen ASAP, knowing there was little chance of that. The duty sergeant was an alcoholic wreck named Felch who was marking his last thirty days before retirement and could hardly be bothered to sign his name. Santiago could hear the phlegmatic wheeze in Felch's voice over the radio and wondered how sauced he already was.

Checking the time, he smiled for the first time that night. There was one person he could count on who would help salvage this mess.

And she had just started her shift at Mount Sinai.

•

They managed to roll the drag up on a gurney next to the nurses' station in time to catch Esperanza Santiago chewing the ass off some nitwit nurse. "You'll like this," Santiago told More, who ignored him, as usual.

They awkwardly carried the unconscious drag between them, each with a hand on the back of his belt and one on his frayed collar, since putting his arms over their shoulders would probably soak them in blood of dubious origin (never mind killing the drag). There were no gurneys or staff anywhere, so they propped the drag upright in a chair in the waiting area, More looking around for someone to deal with the imminent pool of blood while Santiago filled the pass-through section of the NTU with his bulk. On the other side stood his sister, Esperanza, in her starched whites, a stethoscope around her neck, a blood-pressure cuff in one hand and a clipboard in the other, with the phone cradled against her neck and an expression of annoyed determination on her face. Santiago knew the look, and the conversation in which she was involved, quite well.

"*. . . no debe ser más de doce horas. Asegúrese de que el paciente tiene un montón de líquidos. Si pulso y la temperatura son constantes, después de doce horas que usted pueda cumplir. Asegúrese de que todos los funcionarios que entran en contacto con el paciente use guantes y mascarilla en todo momento, y se han ordenado en un modo en espera, con las restricciones en caso de* DO NOT INTERRUPT ME WHILE I'M SPEAKING *en caso de que el paciente recaídas. Usted me llamó para solicitar ayuda debido a que no saben cómo manejar este paciente, no me interrumpan mientras estoy dándole instrucciones sobre cómo hacerlo. Estoy tratando de explicar cómo se puede salvar el culo y las de sus compañeros de trabajo, no necesitan más retrasos. Si usted tiene un problema con eso, pruebe con otro NTU. Tres del CC, doce horas, del médico y comprobar que la puerta.*" She slammed down the phone. "What?"

Santiago pointed to the drag in the chair, his jerry-rigged arm sling listing badly, a small stain on the floor slowly spreading. Esperanza took in the sight at a glance, then rolled her head in a three-quarter circle, coming to rest with her eyes fixed in exasperation upon Santiago, a trait common in the women of his family that had been demonstrated countless times over countless meals. He heard her slap on the gloves, heard her page the attending, heard her shout commands, but all he saw was the scar on her right temple, above and to the left of her mole.

The scar was barely visible to anyone other than Santiago, Esperanza having learned to artfully conceal it with makeup and hairstyle. Cosmetic surgery, even for someone in her profession, was an inordinately expensive luxury that she could not justify, preferring to wear it as a reminder. Though they had long since stopped talking about it, Santiago was secretly proud of her for retaining it.

The scar's giver was a piece of shit named Nestor, who'd been in the tenth grade heading for trouble when Esperanza came into the eighth. She was just beginning to form then, with budding curves and glowing skin punctuated by a mole near her right eye which gave her a look that seemed to set boys' teeth on edge. Nestor was in a loose confederacy of loud, reckless boys who everyone, including Santiago, could see were destined for prison or early death. They roughed up younger students, disrupted classes, and threatened teachers with violence (making good on at least one of them, although no arrests were made). By the time Esperanza was unlucky enough to catch Nestor's attention, he and several others in his group were openly using drugs, and a few were suspected of selling them. Not that anything was done about it, not in a school where students outnumbered teachers nine to one and the only security came at the beginning and end of the day, when NYPD school squads were deployed (and which, in down years, were the first units to be cut when budgets were slashed). Really, it was better to stay out of the way of boys like Nestor until graduation or something else took you away from the zoo that was George Washington in the waning years of the crack wars.

Nestor was the worst of the worst, the dynamic of coalitional aggression embodied in a punk. He wasn't even the gang's leader—that title definitely belonged to Alejandro Zayas, a vicious brute in his own right who was silently regarded by the student body as a rapist, probably responsible for at least two girls quitting high school with burgeoning bellies. Nobody came for Alejandro, which emboldened him into progressively more brazen behavior. And if Alejandro could do it, then runner-up Nestor, with chips on both shoulders, had to outdo him, to prove himself even more of a badass and thereby keep himself from being eclipsed by Alejandro's shadow.

The fledgling Santiago had warned his sister about the looks and leers she was getting from Nestor when she was unfortunate enough to pass by him in the halls or cafeteria, where the close proximity of so many enervated young bodies made the air a viscous soup of pheromones and tension. The slightest provocation, real or imagined, could set off an explosion.

Santiago had memorized his sister's class schedule that semester and tried to follow her between classes. But he couldn't always be where she was, and she had to tell him for years afterward that there was no way he could blame himself for not being there the day Nestor dragged her into a bathroom and tried to rape her. Tried, because Esperanza kicked his kneecap hard enough to get out from under him and flee, though not before he'd connected a solid right to her cheekbone, one of his rings tearing the flesh near her mole. Esperanza staggered but did not stop. She ran and ran, all the way to her father's machine shop, where Victor hugged her to his chest and smoothed her hair and told her everything would be fine, all the while glaring over her shoulder at his youngest son, who had seen her from a school window running as if the devil himself were chasing her, and who unbeknownst to her had sprinted behind her all the way from school and stood panting in the shop's office doorway, reading a new meaning in his father's silent scowl.

It took about three weeks. Santiago shadowed Nestor around school and beyond, learning his habits, watching for patterns. Santiago knew Nestor wouldn't think twice about him, might not know him at all. Still, Santiago was careful not to be seen while Nestor was in the company of Alejandro and his cronies.

Three weeks.

At the end of the third, Santiago knew what time Nestor would be by himself, under the stairs on Fort George Avenue just behind the school, smoking a blunt and sucking on a bottle of Cobra, tripping on the raindrops falling from the crosshatched beams of the overhead trestles. Santiago knew how long it would take Nestor to finish his smoke and a good part of his bottle, how long it would take for him to sink into a righteous daze. He knew exactly where the light reached up under the stairs at that time of day, even when the sun was out, so he knew where to crouch a little beyond that, in the dark, watching Nestor get his lift on. Watched and waited for thirty-two minutes, with a seven-and-a-half-inch length of three-quarter-inch cold-rolled steel pipe he'd brought from his father's shop.

Nestor had scarred his sister's face on the plane of her right temple, just beyond the zygomatic arch. Which was where Santiago began, proceeding down across the jaw hinge and the outer edge of the mandible, across the right clavicle and scapular acromion, down the humerus to the lateral epicondyle at the outer elbow, the ulna and carpals, the ribs, sternum and xiphoid process, then crossing to the right iliac crest of the pelvis, hammering the femur until he felt it crack, then pounding on the patella until Nestor's right knee was concave. Though Santiago did not bother to conceal his face, he doubted Nestor would have recognized him. The pipe was easily disposed of in a nearby storm drain; Santiago had not been away from his scheduled detention long enough to be missed. Not that he would have been. After all, what was one absent sixth-grader?

Santiago saw Nestor once, years later. He was on his way from CUNY to his parents' house for dinner, checking his messages to see if he'd have a date later that night, when he caught sight of a misshapen form beneath the subway stairs on Nagle Avenue by West 213th. Gingerly peering through the slats, he made out Nestor's misaligned face, his body slanted at an impossible angle over a cardboard pallet, a plastic bottle of Fleischmann's in his one good hand. One eye was closed; the other was white and dead and permanently half-open, seeing nothing.

Santiago went to dinner.

•

Esperanza got the drag stabilized and into the rotating OR queue. Since the formation of the Triage Nursing Unit during the riots, all incoming patients were sorted by severity of condition and assigned a numbered bracelet that could be monitored anywhere in the hospital. Mount Sinai's image had been tarnished somewhat over the years as the number of suicides, assaults, and overdoses mounted following the Panic of '09 and the riots. Since the hospital's foundation had been largely wiped out by the massive Jagoff fraud at the end of '08, and with city and state funding nonexistent by mid-'09, the staff (caught between the demands of the City Council for free treatment and the screams of the unions for full compensation for those sidelined by budget cuts) members were left to cope as well as they could. Things had peaked when a woman admitted for the removal of two precancerous moles on her back wound up having both legs amputated. The ensuing public outcry and investigation made for a fierce crackdown throughout the hospital hierarchy. Which meant greater than usual reliance on the midlevel managers who ran the daily routines of the hospital, making sure the little things checked out (like screening the dwindling blood supply for HIV, double-checking the time clocks on the donor organs, and making sure the residents weren't raiding the pharmacy for recreation or commercial gain). On senior TNU nurses, for instance. Like Esperanza Santiago.

"*Coño*, you think this is your own private clinic?" she growled at her younger brother, her words punctuated by the snapping of latex as she peeled off her gloves and slammed them into a wall-mounted container marked BIOHAZARD.

Santiago recounted their Waterloo outside of Cardinal Cooke. Esperanza shut her eyes, shook her head, and exhaled loudly through her mouth. "That kid should be strung up."

"Or become a patient there. I can arrange it." Santiago smiled in spite of himself. His sister had always been his best friend, and being around her made even the most ridiculous drag haul a little more bearable.

Esperanza did not share his levity. She grabbed him by the elbow and steered him inside behind the TNU desk, away from More, who slouched in a chair in the waiting area, looking blank. He fit in well among the patients on the queue, many of whom looked like they'd been brought in from sleeping on the streets or dragged bleeding and vomiting from barroom floors. Those conscious enough to take notice of his presence seemed to slink away from him. The seats behind and on either side of More stood empty, even though the room was two-thirds full. "Is that the new guy?" she asked quietly.

"Yeah. Don't tell me you think he's cute."

"*Carajo*, give me some credit. He looks like a bum, or one of those students they bring in on an OD." Over the past year, the number of overdoses had tripled. The *paco* cases were usually goners, since the drug pushed cardiac rates far beyond human endurance (not to mention the psychosis it usually triggered). But the tox screens on a good portion of the others revealed high amounts of extremely potent lab-grade pharmaceuticals such as ketamine, GHB, and MDMA—party drugs, nightclub drugs. This had not been lost on Esperanza, who'd relayed the information to her brother, who'd brought it up with McKeutchen, who'd assigned them to dig up the speaks any way they could. (Which, naturally, made the dicks at the Detective Bureau laugh their asses off. Anticrime? Cabbie cops? Running *investigations*?! It was too funny to be true.)

"So why'd you ask about him?"

Esperanza's voice dropped even lower. "That kid you brought in has a compound fracture of the radius. That's the *inside* bone of the forearm. Usually, with a fracture like this, it's the ulna, the *outermost* bone, that comes through the skin. You follow me?"

Santiago sensed something coming that would make this bad night worse. "So?"

"*¡Escúchame!* You know how much force it takes to cause a break like that? And precisely how you'd have to apply it? And then there's the blood loss."

Something bad was nudging at Santiago. He'd felt it earlier, when More broke the drag's arm, but he'd been too distracted to think it through. "Yeah, that bugged me. I've never seen a break cause that kind of bleeding. But so what? It's just the way the bone came through, right?"

"No, that's what I'm trying to tell you. A fractured bone doesn't just randomly sever the radial artery, not when it's fractured by somebody else. That kind of damage is deliberate. That break was *meant* to kill. Don't tell me anyone in the NYPD, even the ESU, gets taught that kind of lethal hand-to-hand. And if you're telling me the *flaco* out there can do this to someone whenever he wants, you need to tell McKeutchen, like, *now.*"

Santiago heard the timbre of Esperanza's voice, saw the fear in her eyes, and knew that she was right. He had never looked forward to getting into the battered Crown Vic with More, but now he liked the idea even less. He did not mention this to his sister, who could be cold as ice with patients but would probably freak out if she knew her baby brother was riding with a sniper instructor who could break bones and use them as internal saws.

"*Joder,*" he breathed. Who the fuck was this guy?

•

"We need to check out the cabs," More said without looking up from a man lying motionless on a gurney.

Santiago was always taken aback whenever More spoke. "What cabs?"

"We've been trying to figure out how the speaks resupply. In six months we haven't seen any hand-to-hands, no dead drops, nothing. We haven't found any evidence the big deals are going down in legal bars. Liesl and Turse haven't, either, and you know they'd run down trace evidence even if it was microscopic." More was using his unclouded voice, free of phlegm. His ability to switch this on and off rattled Santiago to no end.

"How the fuck you turn your gargle mode on and off like that? Why the fuck can't you talk like a normal person? When the fuck you decide to start talking all of a sudden?" Santiago's pulse and voice had risen, his hands were opening and closing involuntarily, and his palms were damp. He was acutely aware of the distance between him and More, of his position directly between More and the TNU stand, where Esperanza stood calling up what little hospital security was available, of the weight of his Glock 25 in its hip-mounted paddle holster.

More seemed oblivious to the 220 pounds of armed, agitated Dominican in front of him. In his unsullied voice, More continued: "That dead cabbie we're looking into. Eyad Fouad. He's got a friend." More stood abruptly with something in his right hand, and Santiago had his Glock pointed half an inch below the brim of More's plaid newsboy cap in two and a half seconds.

"Not bad," said More with the left side of his mouth creased in what might turn into a smile in a year or so. "Could use more work." He held out his right hand with the object extended.

For a few long seconds, Santiago's eyes went back and forth from the object in More's outstretched hand to his passive, almost sleepy eyes. He reached out and took the object but did not lower his weapon until he had read the writing on the object twice, intermittently, his eyes darting between it and More.

A TLC hack license for one Jangahir Khan. The guy on the gurney was another cabbie, and for the first time Santiago registered the smell, the cloying, carbonized perfume of charred meat. Before Khan got the bullet through his left eye that had finished him off, someone had taken something very hot, a soldering iron or acetylene torch, to him.

"You can tell your sister she can free up this gurney," More said, reverting to his wet-gravel voice. "This guy won't need it anymore."

Now Santiago knew what was bothering him about More.

He was getting interested.

Joder in all its forms.

RIVERS OF GOLD

AH, THE EYRIE. SUCH MEMORIES.

The studio is an empty white loft at the top of a dingy-looking slab on Dyer Avenue right above the Holland Tunnel. Packed full of similar photography shops and their attendant software retouching companies, the Eyrie sits atop them all, ringed with windows on all sides, affording the best natural light a shooter could ask for. Careers have been made here, mine being one of them. I did it the old-fashioned way—I stole a client from the photographer I was assisting. A whole year I slaved away for that moron, putting up with his tantrums, his complicated lighting setups, and his now-fueled round-the-clock shoots. He was a hack, but he had good connections. I had school loans, an invalid mother, a lease coming due, and no word from the art schools I'd applied to. You'd have done the same thing.

The cab hurtles down Ninth Avenue past boarded-up storefronts and restaurants long abandoned by their owners, salt shakers on tables but the chairs all gone. Here in the backseat, I'm feeling good about things. I feel like there are possibilities instead of pairs of bleak choices. And N is in all of them.

Twelve stories up, the cavernous loft is filled with the kind of New York sunshine you get only at high altitudes, and which Marty has thoughtfully sought to temper by draping the walls in luminescent damask. He's setting up the kliegs by the eastern wall, and I notice that (a) he's playing MC Cancer on the PA, which sets my teeth on edge, and (b) he's in a tank top to show off his tats. Normally, I wouldn't mind; the work really is first-rate, huge twisting fish rendered *kingyo*-style, the colors in the scales changing shade with each motion of his arms. The problem is that I don't want him dominating the attention of the delicious Miyuki. (And where the fuck *is* she?) I can see the wunderkind Retch, two-time Oscar winner for his artful portrayals of conflicted, tormented young men, piss-drunk at eleven A.M., being fawned over by Donny and Marie (hair and makeup), while the *favoloso* Tony Q flits and floats amid his lineups (good God, is that an Augusta Shai Hulud original? That jacket has to be ten grand, and Retch looks like he's going to ooze all over it), clearly oiled up on some mixture of his own, feeling no pain.

—*Caballero*! Tony trills.

Let the games begin.

Leaving the drudgery of lighting, loading, and everything else to Marty (who stoically drops his eyes behind his round eighties-style glasses and silently bends to his tasks), I confer with Tony and boy wonder Retch, who reeks of vodka and is sweating 80-proof. I unload eleven Specials on them as discreetly as I can, the odd one going to the extra, R, at Retch's slurred request. R has been a stand-in on several of my shoots and is a textbook runway runaway, a tangled mane of thick brown hair, scrawny with brown teddy-bear eyes and incongruously large breasts, says she's nineteen but probably left home as soon as she grew profitable curves. R has no difficulty rationalizing the exchange of fellatio for spots on the most high-profile shoots, no matter how menial, which ensures that she gets them.

Tony promises the balance due for the Specials consignment at Le Yef later. Tonight it's in the empty Bryant Park Grill, long since closed. The restaurant is in the park behind the library on Forty-first, which stays open thanks to the posthumous benevolence of some of its donors (you can almost hear the wails of their deprived, dependent offspring). The BPG went under, well, I don't remember now, there've been so many. The park was beautiful before the association supporting it went broke. Now it's just another public latrine, its coffee kiosks looted, its gardens razed.

With Retch drunkenly ogling R's décolletage, Tony informs me that Miyuki's flight is late and that her publicist will call the minute they're on the ground. That's fine; the more time I have to rent the space, the more I charge *Roundup*. Johnette will be none too happy, but thankfully, she's nowhere in sight. In fact, there's no one here from the magazine. That's odd—usually, the clients have a rep on the shoot to make sure they're getting their money's worth.

I decide to use the lull to calm my fears about Señor Soccer Ball Light, which is sitting on the floor not ten feet from where Retch weaves on his stool. I make a show of picking it up and taking it to the changing room, where I carefully place it on the floor beneath the makeup counter. There will be no disco light show today.

With the important business (the Specials) out of the way, and since I can't proceed with the shoot until Miyuki arrives, I devote myself to the task of checking my messages while Marty finishes setting up the lights and preparing the cameras. A photographer's job, after all, is but to point and shoot. I've already paid my dues.

The first message is from N, saying she can't make it tonight. That's three nights in a row. I can feel my frown. I knew she'd get busy working for LA, but something's not right. I need to get on this. Fuck.

Two more calls from L, who's sounding impatient about why I haven't gotten back to her. She's such a control freak, always wants to be the one calling the shots. She can be the one to wait for a change. I haven't figured out how to break it off with her, but given the nature of our relationship, it shouldn't take much.

The last one is Joss. She's inviting me over, wants to talk about *size matters*, says she'll make it worth my while.

Shit. A week ago I'd have been thrilled by the prospect, but now I wish she hadn't called. Her veiled reference to size, aside from the obvious pun, is code for a bulk order for Specials. I could probably unload a whole case, maybe more. I find I just don't want to. But this is Reza business, I can't say no. It also sounds sketchy. Is Joss planning a franchise of her own? And doing the deal at her place—no fucking way. Renny's Rule Number Three: No House Calls. Keep It in the Cab.

I'm so caught up over what to do that it must be five minutes before I notice the change in the studio. The music has gone off, Tony has disappeared, and so have Kid Retch and R. Only Marty is in the room with me, quietly taping down cables.

—Where is everybody?

—Beats me, says Marty, his default answer for everything. Probably smokes as much dope as Arun, though I'd be lost without him. This shoot is slipping out of my hands. If someone from *Roundup* walked in right now, I'd likely lose the gig. No, sir.

I commence prowling the Eyrie, starting with the wraparound terrace. It'd be just my luck if Retch took a drunken dive off the building. But the only one outside is Tony, smoking and gabbing away on his phone. I make a complete circuit of the outside and start working through the ancillary rooms. Office, kitchen, bathrooms—all empty. The only place I haven't checked is the changing room, and there are noises I can't place emanating from behind the closed door.

How best to describe walking in on a catastrophe? Since I'm a photographer, my mind records the sequence in frames. In the first I see myself reflected in the long vanity mirror. In the second frame is Retch, swaying slightly on rubber legs, a drunken gargoyle's leer on his slack face, his (uncircumcised) cock in both hands, piss flowing freely. Frame three is R, on her knees in front of Retch, not eagerly but dutifully drinking his urine, swaying to keep her mouth in line with his wavering stream.

In the last frame I see myself again, features contorting in horror, as they both turn to face me and Retch pours rivers of gold all over the twenty-thousand-dollar oscillating icosahedral soccer ball light I stashed in here for safekeeping, and for which I am wholly responsible.

●

The job is gone, destroyed, poof, and with it twenty grand and my cover shot. Instead, I'm on the hook for *another* twenty grand, plus the cost of the rentals, which I've sent Marty to return along with whatever story he can cook up.

The commission I made this morning won't begin to cover the cost of this disaster. I need to collect on the Specials I sold Tony Q on consignment before the shoot went to shit—or, more accurately, to piss. Retch lurched unsteadily out of the Eyrie with R in tow, not a care in the world. If I see him at Le Yef tonight, I'll kill him. Actually, I'll ask Jan or one of Reza's other goons to do it, maybe even that big fucking lollipop guy.

Think. Get the money for the Specials from Tony tonight, and move the rest of the first half of the package during the remainder of Le Yef. Wait. Joss. Bulk order. Must keep second half of package on reserve for her tomorrow. Wait. See her *tonight*. Sell through first half at Le Yef fast, sell second half to Joss, then pay off Reza and the soccer ball light tomorrow. I'll be behind on everything else, but I can pick up another package from Reza and start moving it tomorrow. Within twenty-four hours, I should be back on track. *Yes.*

This plays out in my head while we're waiting at the light on Fifty-seventh and Tenth. On the southeast corner, I notice a woman squatting with her back to the wall of an office building, arms around her knees, crying. This is an all too frequent sight around the city these days, men and women whose worlds have imploded, overwhelmed by the cold, stark enormity of their plight, unable to think their way out. People crying all over town. We were all so happy once, not so long ago. I move my Marathon Cyber SEX into position. Two frames: Lost Soul.

Not me, goddammit, I've worked too hard and come too far. Not *me.*

•

Prince William grabs me as soon as I clear the velvet at Le Yef.

—We must talk, my son, he says quietly.

After I grab a double thyme Verkhoyansk on the fly, he steers me to one of the standing-room-only tables by the boarded-up front windows and says:

—There's trouble afoot.

Oh, fuck. This day can't get any worse, it just can't.

—What's going on?

—Reza's moving on Le Yef. Wants LA's turf and her operations. It's on, my son. Full-blown war, and we're in the middle of it.

I take a big pull of my drink and make a point of slowly smacking my lips. I'm nowhere near calm inside, but in my world, appearances are everything.

—Now, why would Reza do a thing like that? I ask, focusing on keeping my voice level.

Prince William is giving me a look I haven't seen. I sense he's sizing me up, but I don't know for what. I continue as carefully and steadily as I can:

—And why now? After all this time? They have an arrangement—LA makes money off the clientele we bring to Le Yef, Reza makes money supplying them. Through our *cabbies,* I feel compelled to point out. LA has the hottest can't-miss event in town, but we supply the party favors. LA doesn't have Reza's taxi network.

Prince William looks away, tightening his lips. I want to grab him by the scruff of the neck and shake him. Then a penny drops.

—Is this about Eyad?

Now the Prince's head comes around. He looks grim.

—There's been another one. Something Khan, the Prince says, downing a yellow-colored shot.

I'm having a hard time putting it all together. Prince William's words are jarring something loose in my head, something I'm not sure I want to examine.

—*Another* one? You mean Reza killed Eyad? For Christ's sake, what *for*?

The Prince gestures with a swizzle stick.

—Eyad was skimming. The other one, who knows? And it's not about Reza. It's the organization *behind* Reza. They've been putting pressure on him to raise more cash in a hurry. The organization wants more money, and they want it bloody fast. I trust you've noticed the Lollipop Man round Reza's gaff? He's meant to speed up operations. Those two dead cabbies are *'is* 'andiwork. Muscle. Not just for Reza but *for* Reza, savvy?

The amorphous thing in my brain is taking shape. It's ugly. I try to make some headway.

—What's the rush? Why would they make Reza kill his own cabbies? And why do they want Le Yef? Reza has an understanding with LA, a business relationship, they've had it as long as I've been working for him. And Le Yef's a gold mine. Why stir up trouble and risk the cops getting involved? Our arrangement runs smoothly. Hell, Le Yef's the only event on the whole damn speak circuit that hasn't turned into a free-for-all.

Prince William sighs as if he's dealing with a slower sibling. I'm not feeling as impressed by him as I have in times past. Right now I want to strangle the prick.

—You're right, it's a gold mine. And the organization wants it. They're not content with having a finger in the pie, they want the whole pie. New York City, he says.

I'm feeling clumsy and slow, like I'm tripping through a dream.

—This doesn't make any sense. The city's always been an open market. It's too big for one player to corner it. Nobody's ever done that here, never.

Prince William looks me in the eye.

—Not until now. Whatever happens, make sure you know which side you're on.

I try to ask him how the hell he knows all of this, but suddenly I'm hemmed in by a pair of megatheriums. One of them puts a huge paw on my back. It's hard and heavy and carries the potential for catastrophic damage.

—Please come with us, one of them intones.

•

I'm on my knees on the floor of the former BPG's men's room, downstairs from the party. At least they won't be able to drown me in one of the toilets; the water was shut off ages ago. The megatheriums are behind me, a huge heavy hand on each of my shoulders, pressing bone against bone, though not quite hard enough to make me scream. LA, who stands before me resplendent in skintight gym attire, her chiseled abdominals inches from my mouth, must want me for something.

—You know, Renny, I like to think of myself as fair-minded and even-tempered. Your boss, Reza, is not. That's upsetting the balance of things, which upsets *me*. LA slaps me lightly with her right hand, then softly brushes her fingers against my cheek. Reza, she says, is not willing to share.

She punches me in the same spot she was rubbing. I see it coming, and there's nothing I can do about it. LA's workouts are paying dividends; I taste blood in my mouth and the bathroom fades out for a moment. The hands on my shoulders never waver.

(That *CUNT*.)

She goes back to stroking my face and continues.

—Your friend out there showed some shrewd business sense, coming to me to parley. He figures with a war on, he can play both sides against the middle and still get paid. What do you think, Renny? Would you like to get paid?

My brain is struggling to absorb what she's telling me while trying to shake off the effects of her punch. I manage to say:

—I'd like to get paid.

LA backhands me hard, the other side of my face this time, but the taste of blood in my mouth is stronger. The goons don't budge. (I will not cry. I will *not* cry.)

—Then I suggest you find another party to peddle your wares once you resupply. I'm keeping tonight's shipment for my trouble.

(Oh shit oh fuck oh FUCK ME. She's taking the Specials, I'll have to make up the cost to Reza on top of what I already owe for the light . . . this day *cannot* stop getting worse.)

LA draws back her arm for another blow and I can't help it, I flinch and feel the burn of tears at the corners of my eyes. LA lowers her arm. Her smile makes my stomach drop like a high-speed elevator.

—Give Reza my regards, she says.

She jerks her head at the twin golems and turns away toward the sinks.

I'm hauled to my feet so hard, my arms feel like they'll come out of their sockets. The goons half-pull, half-drag me out of the bathroom, past the clumps and hordes and gaggles of stunned onlookers. I've never been thrown out of anywhere, I've always known how to play it smooth. I can't handle this. It's worse than the beating. There's no fame like infamy. I will *not* cry. (Not here.)

There's a momentary pause while one goon gets the door. Just long enough for me to look back toward the men's room. Just long enough to see another guard ushering a woman inside. Just long enough for me to see that it's N.

●

Ngala whatever-the-fuck is his usual surly self, though surprisingly blasé about having just been held up and ripped off by LA's thugs. When I ask him if they took the stash, he shrugs and points to the partition. He doesn't care about losing fifty thousand dollars' worth of coated, easy-to-swallow, lab-grade Ecstasy tablets. His cab isn't damaged, that's all he's worried about. I put him on my list of people I'd like to kill. The list has grown very long since this morning.

Retch. Tony, who never showed up tonight and still owes me for ten Specials. LA and her whole earpiece-wearing muscle menagerie. Prince William, who's making a deal with LA behind Reza's back to hedge his bets about who wins the war. (That PRICK.) Marcus fucking Chalk, who will never hire me again. Johnette, who made sure of it. (That CUNT.) And Reza, who's expecting his money and is accustomed to my prompt deliveries.

So who's on *my* side?

Prince William. Phone's off. L. Phone's off. N. No, I'm not calling N. I don't know where I stand with N. I don't even know where she stands anymore. I am definitely not calling Reza or any of his retinue. Marty. Phone's off. There are two dozen numbers in my phone, but there's nobody I can talk to, nobody I can trust.

I have many contacts but no friends.

Wait—Joss. I stab the call through the phone, angrily gesturing at Ngala to wait. He wants to go back to work. He will, but for me. Thunder sounds off in the distance. We're supposed to get hit with a storm tonight. Perfect.

Joss lives in the penthouse of a brownstone on Sixty-ninth and Second with a fabulous glassed-in living room cantilevered out over the street, doubtless guaranteed by Daddy. After having Ngala drive me home to pick up half the remaining batch of Specials (I leave the other half in my stash as backup), I have him drop me on First under the cool neon sign at Goldberg's, the last indie pharmacy left in town. It's a five-minute walk to Joss's place. She buzzes me in just as it starts to pour.

The girl who opens the apartment door upstairs is jailbait. Small breasts nestled in a man's blue oxford shirt knotted in front, exposing a midriff not quite free of baby fat, with a silver hoop in her navel and jean shorts cut off right below the crotch. She's actually wearing pigtails. I put her at seventeen, maybe.

—Rough night? she asks with a wry smile.

—Joss called me, I grunt impatiently.

—Do come in, she says, gesturing with the drink in her hand.

Joss is splayed out on the couch with a pile of fashion magazines, each open to a piece illustrated with my photos. She's turned the lights down so she can watch the lightning. The wraparound glass is thick; the drumming of the downpour seems faint and far away.

—Renny! Joss squeals, jumping off the couch to embrace me as if we're old friends. There's been some drinking going on, though not enough to seriously hamper things. Joss is making a lot of body contact, pressing herself against me, her arms locked behind my back. Not long ago I hoped for this, and after the day I've had, I might even revisit the sentiment, but I wasn't expecting her to be babysitting. If she's put off by the condition of my face, she's not letting on.

—Meghan's my cousin. She just got back from school. I've been telling her all about you, Joss says playfully, with a gleam in her eye.

—Yes, you seem to be quite the man of many talents, Meghan says from the bar that separates the open kitchen, where she's building a G&T

that would drop a horse. Naturally, she brings it to me.

—To business, Joss says, clinking her glass against mine and then her cousin's.

—What exactly did you have in mind? I ask. I want to close the deal, take my money, and get out of here so I can start on damage control, not to mention figuring out what the hell is going on. There are too many wild cards now. Reza. LA. Prince William. N. What kind of hand will I be dealt?

—How much have you got on you? Meghan asks. Joss just sits there wearing a bright smile. I notice for the first time that she's not wearing much else, gray gym shorts that LA would probably admire and a tank top that does not indicate the presence of a bra. What's going on here?

I take a long pull of my drink and survey the two of them, then slowly pull out the disc case. This is crazy, but it's been a crazy day. And I need this deal. Their eyes light up.

—How much is in there? Meghan says, all business. Quite the budding young entrepreneur. America's Future.

—Two fifty.

—What're you asking?

—Fifty large.

—No problem! beams Joss.

—How do we know if it's good? Meghan asks.

I take another belt of my drink, then set it down and pop open the case, extracting two tabs and handing them to Joss, who hands one to Meghan. They neck theirs and chase the pills with gin.

—I'll be right back, Joss says, hopping off the couch. Renny, make yourself comfortable. Meghan, make Renny feel at home. Out she goes, presumably to get the money.

This is all for show. Meghan is obviously setting up a franchise at her college, or more likely her boarding school, and she's talked Joss into putting up the money. Assuming a 20 percent markup once she starts distributing, she and Joss can split the profits, even keeping a small stash for themselves. With the money they make, the stash would end up paying for itself—free Specials, which they can keep or sell as they choose. Very smooth.

—Very smooth, I say to Meghan, who's standing behind the couch.

—Funny, Meghan says, coming around the couch to me, that's what Joss says about you.

There's a strange glint in her eye, but the drug shouldn't kick in for a few minutes yet. I figure I'll watch them lift off, then take my money and go.

But Meghan is standing between me and the door, smiling in a bad-girl way, almost absently untying the knot of her shirt. She shrugs it off, and a wave of nostalgic lust washes over me. Meghan's newly budding breasts are exactly like those of B, the girl with whom I spent the excruciating summer of my fifteenth year, being carefully tutored in the playing of that most magnificent instrument that is the female body.

Still smiling, Meghan steps close to me. She slowly pulls down my zipper and unsheathes me, her fingers lightly circling the head and top of the shaft with a butterfly's touch. My cock swells up so hard and fast, I can feel the blood draining out of my brain. Behind her Joss appears, naked, and cups Meghan's left breast with her left hand, fingers lightly tweaking the nipple, while her right hand comes around Meghan's hip and grips my cock with a seasoned authority I would not dare challenge.

Which is how we all end up on the living room floor beneath the glass roof, Jim Hall's *Concierto de Aranjuez* playing out of my phone through Joss's superb sound system; me kneeling behind Meghan, thrusting very deeply, very slowly, one thumb gently but firmly in her ass, guiding; Meghan's head between Joss's thighs, her mouth expertly working on her cousin's precious portion. Meghan has the most terrific vaginal grip I have ever experienced. Rule One goes flying out the window and dies silently on the rain-spattered street four stories below, followed by all the others.

Well, wouldn't you've thrown them out, too?

●

It's only much, much later, emerging from a cab in front of my house, the eastern sky slowly giving way to gray, drifting in the fugue state of a man who has just had one of the most horrific days and searing nights of his life, while reaching for my keys, that I realize I never got the money.

HADITH

"NOW, THERE'S SOMETHING you don't see every day," Santiago remarked. More, in unusually gabby agreement, nodded.

They were watching roughly three hundred cabdrivers at afternoon prayer, kneeling on rugs in the taxi holding lot at La Guardia Airport, facing Mecca and the Grand Central Parkway. This was overflown at an obtuse angle by big transatlantic inbounds from Benin, Bahrain, Medina, and Ankara. Desperate to keep foreign money coming into the city, the state assembly (with much public and vocal support from Representative Dick Lamprey, D–New York) had in late 2008 pushed through an emergency tax-free revenue bond issue (as was the fashion in fund-raising for flat-broke cities) to retrofit the airport for the big 747-300s and A-380s that had international range but needed more room to stop. The issue was rated triple-C with a 10 percent yield, and Albany wrote in a clause forcing New York to buy at least 25 percent of the bonds. When Mayor Baumgarten (I–New York) pointed out that the city couldn't afford the bonds at face value, let alone the interest payments, he was shouted down by the coterie of assemblymen around Governor Janice Anopheles (D–New York) and the coven of City Council members around Speaker Isabella Trichinella (D–New York), as well as a particularly venal snub by Senator Theodore Usanius Rickover Davidson III (D–New York), on Baumgarten's own financial-news cable channel. The bond bubble lasted just long enough for the new runway extensions to be paved. When it burst and the state defaulted on the issue, the city treasury was gutted. Mayor Baumgarten had boxcars of shit thrown at him daily by the unions while he performed wholesale amputations of the Sanitation, Health, Education, Fire, and (of course) Police departments. (It was his emergency decree for the latter that earned him the enmity of the rank and file—police officers requiring new service weapons would henceforth have to purchase them out of their own pockets, an executive order derogatorily referred to in the press as "The Big Gun Rule"; the cops called it Phallus Magnus.) He kept the airport construction crews on schedule, though, and the renovation was completed on time and, to the surprise of all but Hizzoner the Mayor, under budget. Now new waves of affluent travelers shopped in the airport's sterile boutiques hawking must-have NYC curios like T-shirts and coffee mugs and model NYPD prowl cars and bright yellow toy taxicabs. They bought tons of fattening snacks and splurged on gallons of sugary cocktails at the airport's new food courts and bars. All in all, the rehabbed airport added a thousand new jobs and hundreds of thousands of dollars to the city's moth-eaten economy, which otherwise would have been siphoned off completely by those bastards in Newark. This made the Port Authority (which owned the airports) very happy and was considered one of the few silver linings in an otherwise pitch-black tapestry of the city's history.

This new wave of jaunty travelers also lavished tens of thousands of dollars on taxicabs to the city from the airports; why bother figuring out the buses and trains when your home currency kicks the shit out of the U.S. dollar? Cab rides everywhere, from the airports, from the hotels, to the theaters (those few that were still open), to the high-level executive meetings (mostly at various Interbank offices around town, since the forced compaction of the banking industry had allowed the company to swallow up whole buildings at fire-sale prices), and to all the parties on the illegal club circuit for which the city had become internationally infamous.

All of this was being spelled out to a placid More and a smoldering Santiago by the head of the de facto drivers' union as they stood in the taxi holding lot.

In an effort to combat the mounting sense of frustration caused by an investigation that no one seemed to want him to pursue, over the murders of cabdrivers nobody cared about (not to mention doing so with a partner who seemed less and less coplike with each passing day), Santiago had decided to go on his own. When they'd first pulled up, their beat-up hack blending perfectly into a veritable sea of cabs, Santiago thought they'd question a few drivers. The very sight of a badge, however, made most cabdrivers' mouths snap shut. Santiago tried repeatedly to get something, anything, from the cabbies about the killings, but it was always the same thing.

"*Les bus sont emparés de manière lente,*" said a Senegalese.

"*Etot prokliati autobus uzasno medleno iediet,*" said a Russian.

"*Yeh busen saali Itni Dheere chalti hain,*" said an Indian.

They were getting nowhere fast, and Santiago was getting annoyed even faster. Then he had an idea.

After confirming the identities of the victims and securing the names of the garages where they worked, Santiago had gone to the one place he thought might be able to guide him through the city's Byzantine taxicab industry. It wasn't the city's Taxi and Limousine Commission (those fuckers never returned his calls). While a student at CUNY, Santiago had spent a fair amount of time at the Dominican Studies Institute on Convent Avenue in Harlem. He still kept an eye on various DSI goings-on, and he remembered seeing something about the formation of a long-term research project on Dominican taxi drivers within the last few years. Reaching out to Pedro Heredia, one of the project's researchers and a fleet owner himself, Santiago had been advised to meet with the lead organizer of the drivers' "union" (which was more in name than fact, since under state law, cabdrivers were classified as independent contractors and therefore prohibited from official union organization).

Who now stood before him.

"*Trate de no mirar,*" Heredia had warned him. "Don't gawk at her. She's touchy."

Baijanti Divya was nearly seven feet tall and wore the longest, loudest sari Santiago had ever seen. It was iridescent, in the exact shade of a Creamsicle. She had large hands and a long neck, both of which shimmered with gold. (If it was real, Santiago thought, she had a night job that paid much better than labor organizing.) A filigreed gold braid was suspended between her left earlobe and nostril. A crimson *bindi* flared between her shaped eyebrows. There was no way in hell Baijanti Divya could keep a low profile, Santiago thought. It wasn't her nature.

"You have two cabdrivers murdered in as many weeks," she said in a deep voice that resonated oddly in Santiago's tympanum. "Yet you suspect the drivers to have been complicit in criminal activity?"

Fucking More. It was his fault they were coming on like the cabdrivers were to blame for getting themselves killed. Barely speaks for six months, then boom, two cabbies get whacked and he's looking for Keyser Söze. All this shit about looking at *the cabs, the cabs*. Why was More so interested in a couple of garden-variety robbery-homicides in the middle of a fucking crime wave? The NYPD clearly didn't give a shit about a couple of cabdrivers. Not that Santiago accepted this, but why was More so hung up on it?

"We have to look at all the possibilities," Santiago replied in his best Polite but Official, since More was back in his mute mode. "You said yourself the industry is rigged against the drivers. Maybe one of them was skimming."

"You clearly have little grasp of the way the industry is structured, Detective," she said in that voice that was making for unusual signal traffic in Santiago's amygdala. "Taxi drivers cannot 'skim,' which I presume from your usage means cheating the meter. You cannot cheat the meter. All meters in yellow taxicabs in this city are attached to non-navigational GPS units, the presence of which is mandatory in all TLC-licensed New York City taxicabs. The drivers themselves are required in most instances to pay the maintenance costs for these meters and, in some cases, for their installation. The meter records the place and time of each and every fare. It is also connected to the engine of the taxicab. If it is tampered with in any way, it shuts off. All meters are connected to a central mainframe, which the TLC claims is used to send text messages to drivers alerting them to areas of high fare demand or traffic problems, but which in actuality is a surveillance system by which the TLC can keep track of all on-duty cabdrivers at all times. No city cabdriver is allowed to operate a taxicab with a broken meter; broken credit-card swipes are permissible, since the drivers can still conduct cash transactions. But a broken meter is prohibited by regulations. Any cabdriver operating with one would be immediately pulled off the road by TLC enforcement, or your own NYPD colleagues, and could easily lose his license and his job. A cabdriver would have to be suicidal to try to cheat the meter, Detective, and you have already described this as a homicide investigation."

Damn. She was tough, this one. Smart, too. And then there was that voice! "Would a cabdriver be able to hold back some money when he goes off duty?" Santiago asked.

"There are two kinds of cabdrivers, Detective. There is the lease driver, which applies to the majority of the drivers you see in this parking lot. Lease drivers pay a fixed rate per shift for the use of the taxicab. This 'day rate' or 'lease rate' is due in cash at the end of each shift. In addition, the gas tank must be filled before shift change. To use an example, the second victim, Jangahir Khan, worked a day shift for the Sunshine Taxi Corporation in Queens. He would be paying, I believe, one hundred and eighty dollars per shift. If he did not make that on duty, he would have to make up the balance out of his own pocket. The cabdriver who does not pay his shift rate would most likely not be permitted to work another shift for that garage. I should also point out that if he incurred any tickets during his shift, he would be responsible for paying those as well, or risk losing his license and possibly his job.

"The second kind of driver, the owner-operator, owns his medallion and taxicab, in principle. In actuality, the case is most often that he has taken on massive loans. The current market price of a TLC medallion is just over six hundred thousand dollars. If Mr. Khan or the first victim, Eyad Fouad, were owner-operators, they would have had to come up with over sixty thousand in cash to secure the medallion, then work off the remaining ninety percent as best they could. This can take a lifetime, Detective, and sometimes cannot be done. I remind you that this is only for the medallion. They would then have to secure funds to buy the car and have it prepared for taxi use, a process known in the trade as a 'hack-up.' They would have to pay all costs associated with the hack-up at the TLC. Failure to pay any of these costs would render their taxicab legally inoperable. No money means no cab, and no cab means no money. This is all just to get the cab up and running. Once they do that, owner-operators must pay for gas, insurance, maintenance, emissions checks, garaging, and the city road tax. Whatever is left feeds their families. It is not," Baijanti Divya concluded, "an enviable position to be in."

Her voice was causing a traffic jam in Santiago's mind. He tried to focus. "How would they get that kind of money, especially with the new loan regulations?" By 2010, after the subprime meltdown, commercial real estate collapse, and coast-to-coast credit card defaults, getting any kind of loan practically required one to sell his vital organs.

"Mortgage lenders for the taxi industry offer ninety percent financing, often on terms that could politely be called usurious," she replied smoothly, making Santiago's jaw clench. "These lenders have made themselves indispensable to the industry, even more so since the banking crisis."

"Where do they get their financing?"

"Typically, they would make arrangements with the banks," she said. "Given Urbank's rapid growth, it is able to exert a greater amount of influence over the remaining brokers. Call it a leverage on leverage."

"How else would an owner finance a fleet outside of brokers and banks?" More asked out of nowhere, startling Santiago so much that his teeth clacked. There was no trace of phlegm in More's voice. His ability to switch from a quasi-gargle to clear speech was getting on Santiago's nerves; he badly wanted to pound More's head down to somewhere near his sternum.

Baijanti Divya's luminous green eyes moved over to More. "There are many places one may find money, Detective," she said, and the new, faint note of coyness in her voice made for bad driving conditions in Santiago's head.

"Like where?" he blurted out.

Without taking her eyes off More, Baijanti Divya said, "I believe you are asking me to confirm something you already know."

Now Santiago was lost. The conversation had taken an abrupt turn, and he had been thrown out of it. Airhorns and smokestacks blared in his head. "What do you mean?"

"I believe your colleague is referring to the Javaid Tariq Corporation. It is, shall we say, an experimental paradigm, a pilot program for an aging industry," she said. "I'm surprised you haven't heard of it; most drivers would give quite a bit to be able to work there. At the risk of sounding trite, it's a taxi corporation designed to provide better returns for the drivers as well as the owners, who, of course, are drivers themselves, as required by TLC regulations. It's also only half a mile from where you now stand."

"*Namasté*," More said, tilting his head slightly in her direction.

"*Shubh kamanaye*," replied Baijanti Divya, smiling.

"What the fuck?" groused Santiago.

•

"You want to tell me what happened back there?" Santiago grumbled.

"She's sharp for a *hijra*," More gurgled.

"Okay, before you tell me what that means, tell me what fucking language you were speaking and how you know it." The last thing Santiago wanted was more linguistic surprises from his ordinarily taciturn partner.

"Hindi. Rosetta Stone." More was watching the jumbo jets lumber into the sky.

"You speak Hindi? Is that part of your ESU training, too?" Santiago was unconsciously pressing down on the gas as they hurtled creakily onto the expressway. More made a noncommittal sound in the back of his throat. "You were sent to Mumbai and Delhi to do CT stuff, is that it?" Santiago growled. In the wake of 9/11, sending NYPD "specialists" abroad for counterterrorism cross-training had become all the rage. Until it got too expensive.

"Jammu and Kashmir, actually," More replied, and this confused Santiago, mostly because he thought he detected a trace of wistfulness in More's voice, buried beneath the phlegm.

"So what's a *hijra*?"

"Intersexual. In India they're called 'The Third Sex.' "

The traffic mess in Santiago's head congealed into a horrific pileup involving semis, school buses, and a runaway freight train. He tried to speak, with mixed results. "Wait. You. She. Not. A *man*?"

"Could be a transvestite, a pre- or post-op transsexual, or even a hermaphrodite. There's a long history of them in South Asia," More said distractedly, apparently working through a bolus in his throat.

For a moment Santiago considered shooting More, a thought that had come to him more frequently of late. He just as easily dismissed the thought: If they were going to work their way through the entire yellow-cab labor pool, he might need a translator.

Intersexual?

Fucking More.

•

Javaid Talwinder was a well-contented man. His eldest son, Tariq, had submitted fitness reports on the two new hires, both good Punjabi boys only two months in-country. The new Moneymap GPS meters Tariq had insisted upon were paying off. Even after Javaid's weeklong instruction course, it would be unreasonable to expect any immigrant to assimilate and memorize the entire road network of the five boroughs in under a month. The in-dash Moneymaps used real-time navigational software, updated hourly, so no driver had called in lost. News reports on construction, accidents, and road closings arrived on each driver's screen in real time, along with TLC alerts on conventions, hotel checkouts, and airport volume, so drivers could follow the money and avoid being tied up in traffic. Thanks to the regenerative brake option (expensive but worth the cost once put into practice, he reflected), the Moneymaps never went dead, which meant the meters never cut out, which meant the cabs stayed on the street and the drivers stayed out of the TLC's kangaroo courts. *A moving cab is a river of gold, an idle cab is a money drain,* Javaid thought, echoing the mantra of the old Irish supervisor who'd broken him in years before.

Manesh, the foreman in charge of keeping the cabs running, appeared off Javaid's left shoulder as though by magic. "Need your signature, *bhai.*" Manesh's voice rumbled out from, Javaid guessed, beneath his collarbones. He held out a clipboard in one huge, oil-stained paw. To his delight, Javaid read a list of familiar words and numbers comprising the final shipment for the bolt-on turbo/intercooler upgrades for the cabs, which would enable the Hondas to keep up with any five-, six-, or eight-cylinder cabs on the road, but which were also completely reversible (a necessity, come inspection time). The inventory was complete—Manesh had a full set of replacement parts in-house for each and every cab in the fleet, just as they'd planned. Barring true catastrophe, no cab would spend more than one shift off-road on a lift with Manesh tearing at its guts. Javaid happily scrawled his name on the freight bill and beamed at Manesh, whose dull amphibian gaze never changed, and sent him on his way. *Allahu akbar,* he thought, turning to face the front lot through the three open garage doors. *God truly is great.*

Then he spotted the beat-up Crown Vic stretch taxicab drifting creakily to a stop not twenty yards away as the delivery van quickly backed out, and he thought: *Bhenchod.*

For a moment he figured this was just another driver leaving the garage for greener pastures. He mentally called up the speech he'd rehearsed for turning away new job seekers; Javaid's team was handpicked, and his garage was already fully staffed. Interlopers were not welcome. He'd chased quite a few off already.

Something about the taxi appeared wrong to Javaid. The paint scheme was right; the medallion was right where it should be, at eleven o'clock on the hood; there was grime on the front valance and inside the wheel arches that no car wash would ever touch. As his eyes drifted over the cab's hood, he caught it on the edge of his vision—the license plate was not the standard TLC sequence. This plate had six consecutive numbers bookended by matched capitals. This cab was not a cab. It was a—

The driver was big and brown, and even at a distance, Javaid could make out the same sort of hands Manesh possessed—mechanic's mitts. As the driver closed the gap (long strides, a slight swagger), Javaid's hopes for connecting along familiar South Asian ground faded in the face of Hispanic hostility. Puerto Rican, Javaid guessed. Maybe Cuban or Mexican. Javaid had a cousin who owned a greengrocer on the Upper West Side full of such men; they broke down cardboard boxes and stacked cans of condensed milk and cupped Newports in their tattooed hands when Javaid's cousin wasn't around.

The man who got out of the passenger side was *mamuli*, nondescript. Caucasian, smaller than his companion, his form lost in a black army jacket and hooded sweatshirt, he moved on silent trainers and seemed to fade into the tarmac of the parking lot.

The big Latino was already in his face, all frog eyes and bull neck. "Police department, Detectives Santiago and More, Citywide Anticrime," he said in a voice that oddly echoed Manesh's in timbre.

Javaid was well versed in dealing with hostile authority figures and put on his best expression of courteous compliance. "Yes?"

"We're pursuing an investigation into the deaths of two cabdrivers during the past two weeks," said the big dark one. "We're treating these as homicides. Our intelligence suggests that the victims may have tried to gain employment with your corporation at some point within the last year. We'd like to review your employee application records."

Khun? Murder?

"Of course," he managed, finding a small outcropping of stability in his professorial mannerisms of long ago in Lahore.

The garage was nothing like those along Vernon Boulevard. It was too new, too clean, too spacious. The outer lot, Santiago guessed, ran to maybe two or three acres, with new blacktop, split into more or less three areas. The first was the front lot they'd pulled into (fenced, with concertina wire running along the top and floodlights mounted on each corner post, along with what appeared to Santiago to be CCTV cameras behind all-weather plastic housings, much like those deployed above traffic signals citywide to catch tags on light-jumpers, speeders, and hit-and-runs). The floods and cameras were arranged so that the entire front lot would be covered day or night.

The front lot consisted of a compact, inverted U-frame car wash (complete with soap guns and vacuum hoses, like those he remembered from his childhood back in the DR) and—More had caught this when they first rolled up to the garage doors—two brand-new diesel pumps (B-100 blend). Every garage Santiago had ever seen boasted lifts and grease monkeys trying to wring a few more miles out of each battered cab, but not every one had its own pump, let alone two, let alone *diesel*. The garages he drove by along Tenth Avenue in Manhattan were usually located along side streets next to gas stations, and the cabbies would drive right off the lifts to tank up. Santiago wrote a reminder in his phone to check with Traffic, DEP, and the TLC about new pump applications and permits. This place had been planned out by someone familiar with the industry, someone who would know all the bureaucratic requirements set down by the TLC for garage and fleet operations. Santiago bet himself there would be a large filing cabinet somewhere in this man's office that contained every receipt for every payment for every permit the outfit required.

"You're an ex-driver," Santiago said, no question in his tone.

Javaid smiled for the first time since the foreign cab rolled onto his lot. His teeth were yellow and bore all the marks of hard wear. "No, Detective, I am a *current* driver. TLC regulations specify that owners of mini-fleets, which are defined as corporations containing two or more medallion taxicabs, must themselves drive a minimum of twenty hours per week. I do, as does my son."

The son had been standing just behind his father's right shoulder, a look of open hostility etched into his features. There was no question of family resemblance, the kid had his father's high cheekbones, coriander coloring, and a good deal more hair, cut the same way as his father's. He wore jeans and a teal-colored T-shirt with a VW logo and the words EAST LONDON ALL STAR DUBS CLUB on the front. Behind him, three lifts (brand-new, their rails painted a brilliant red to contrast with the undercarriages of the cabs they would support) ran the length of the main service area. The far wall contained a series of heavy-duty metal racks and shelves, reaching almost all the way up to the ceiling, each containing a row of what Santiago realized were all the components of the driveline, arranged by weight and size. The rack closest to the floor held new tires, with laser-printed signs designating front and rear neatly taped to the wall above each group. Above were gleaming new alloy wheels, arranged the same way. Above those, stainless steel brake rotors, their machined surfaces catching a dull shine from the overheads, were neatly arranged alongside large black calipers with the word ALCON in silver dropped-out type. The next rack up contained odd-looking pinions and springs that Santiago guessed were suspension components. The place seemed purpose-built to service taxicabs and put them back on the road in the shortest amount of time possible.

"My compliments to the chef," Santiago said wryly, with a sidelong glance at Javaid, who was positively beaming.

"Thank you, Detective. Manesh and I spent many nights planning the layout for the service area. Our objective was simple—no taxi should spend more than one shift in the shop. A taxi on a lift earns no money. Manesh was the fastest taxi mechanic on McGinnis Boulevard. I knew when I had a fleet of my own, I wanted him to be the one who would maintain it." Javaid nodded toward the gorilla in overalls, who was looking at the floor—not averting his eyes, Santiago realized, but keeping watch on something on the floor. What the hell was he doing? And where the hell was More?

As if in answer, More emerged ducklike from behind the cab he first approached, walking on his haunches, his eyes roughly level with the cab's headlights. He showed no concern for having a man Santiago's size, within arm's reach of a wide array of heavy metal tools, plodding a few feet behind him. Tariq also took notice of More's reappearance and seemed annoyed at having to divide his spiteful glare in two directions. Santiago knew he had to maintain control of the situation—More did not seem to give a shit—and keep the jittery cabbies cool. That brought him back to the cabs themselves.

Which were hardly TLC standard issue. The cab on the nearest lift was a brand-new Honda Fit, painted an outrageous mix of the usual yellow and black, laced with a red-white-and-blue-striped pattern that Santiago knew he'd seen somewhere but could not readily identify. The wheels were brand-new alloys, but their style was also vaguely familiar and seemed foreign in an old-fashioned way. The dome light was a smooth wide fairing, like an eyebrow ridge over the windscreen, with a second fairing running perpendicular from the middle rear of the eyebrow partway down the center of the roof—a long dorsal fin that Santiago guessed housed an integral satellite antenna.

"And an LCD display for advertising," Javaid said with a clairvoyance that rattled Santiago and made him wish More would say something so that he could yell at him.

But More just kept peering over his nose at the car from about four inches away, so Santiago was grateful when Javaid stepped into the breach. "This is our model taxi of the future, Detective. The Honda Fit TDI. My son calls it the 'Fat.' " (This elicited a sound halfway between a snort and a chuckle from More, and even Santiago couldn't resist half a grin.) "It has a two-point-two-liter i-DTEC turbo diesel engine with a combined fuel economy of forty-five miles per gallon, with a fifteen-gallon fuel tank and a new catalytic converter system that breaks down NOX pollutants *without* urea injection, as well as diesel particulate filters fitted on the exhaust and good for the lifetime of the car." Javaid paused to let the detective catch up. "Honda does not ordinarily supply taxi fleets, although some individual owner-operators have successfully introduced them into service. Manesh came up with an aftermarket titanium suspension upgrade that met TLC fleet standards."

Santiago nodded, his mouth tightly closed. He had not understood a thing but hoped he looked like he did.

More's voice, brittle from lack of use, sounded distant and alien as it rattled off the concrete floor. "There hasn't been a diesel medallion issued since 1984," he muttered. "How'd you get one?"

How the fuck did More know *that*? Santiago raged to himself, bruxing his molars. He should be getting credits just for being partnered with this prick.

Javaid smiled even more broadly and benignly, a proud patriarch with teeth like the Burgess Shale. "By giving the TLC what it asked for, Detective. While it's true that the TLC, as well as the mayor's office, would like to see a fully hybrid fleet by the end of the century's first decade, it acknowledges that there is no way to meet all the demands placed by various political lobbies around the city. For instance, there is no way to make all taxicabs wheelchair-accessible, not for any technological reason but simply because the percentage of riders requiring such vehicles is minute relative to the mass customer base. Nevertheless, the lobby for this portion of the customer base has made itself known to the municipal powers that be with a successful legal and public-relations campaign, and thus the city agencies find themselves bound to answer their citizens' call. This is easier said than done, given the city's current fiscal constraints.

"Based on these conditions, and armed with our experiences working within the industry for several years, we—my son, my foreman, and I—devised a new, more efficient mini-fleet, one we could make work for ourselves. You see the results before you." Javaid spread his arms and opened his hands. "This corporation is entirely self-sufficient. It has its own medallions, its own taxicabs, its own service area and fuel supply. Behind the office, there"—he pointed toward a door behind the hulking foreman—"are the drivers' lockers, toilets, and showers. Any time a driver needs a bathroom, he can find one here." Javaid's smile cratered for a moment into a hard grin. "I can assure you, Detectives, being seated at the wheel for twelve hours a shift without a bathroom break is not what the human animal was made for. I can give you the names of at least three drivers who now require dialysis three times a week because of it." The grandfatherly smile returned. "Ten cabs, three men to a cab. Three eight-hour shifts instead of two twelve-hour shifts. The drivers choose shifts based on seniority, that is, number of years on the road. Top man gets first pick. Free parking on-site for staff vehicles." Javaid paused as though preparing himself for something unpleasant, Santiago wasn't sure what. "Health insurance for all staff."

Fucking More did it again. "Taxi drivers are independent contractors. Under state law, they can't unionize. So how'd you get them health insurance?"

Javaid's smile went from grandfather to grand inquisitor. "You seem to know a bit about the business, Detective. May I ask how?"

"No," More grunted nasally. "Suffice it to say I bothered to check. How'd you get the insurance?"

Santiago felt like he was watching a tennis match. Something was being lobbed between More and Javaid, and he wasn't getting it. He settled for keeping watch on Tariq and the big blank-faced mechanic, who still stood uncomfortably close to More. But Santiago sensed a change in the pressure between the cabbies and the cops. It took him exactly three and a half seconds to grasp what it was. More had gotten their attention. He had shown interest in what they had to say, and now they were reciprocating. The tension coming off the cabbies was changing to curiosity. *It's working,* Santiago yearned to tell More. *You've got 'em. Now reel 'em in. But for Christ's sake, clear your throat.*

Javaid was standing up very straight, looking down intently at More, who seemed to have no circulatory issues with squatting indefinitely on the cold concrete floor. "This is a private corporation, Detective," Javaid said, speaking slowly and evenly, though in a softer tone than one begging confrontation. "We have contracted with a national health insurance provider through a local hospital network, which offered us a group rate for our employees and also offers limited coverage for dependents. A fixed percentage is withheld from each employee's wages, calculated by the amount of quarterly premiums charged to the corporation." His smile warmed up a couple of degrees. "We also have an IRA program set up for—" He halted abruptly in midsentence.

"Where's the real money coming from?" More asked in a clear voice.

Javaid sighed. "I don't suppose you know what a *hawaladar* is, Detective? No? He is, shall we say, the bedrock upon which the Islamic financial system has rested until very recently, and he still is, for millions of disenfranchised Muslims around the world with totalitarian governments over their heads, religious or secular, and no vast lakes of oil beneath their feet. Simply put, his job is to transfer monies from one party in one location to a second party in another. This transaction may, and often does, transcend international borders. There are no records kept. One could think of it as the world's oldest off-balance-sheet transaction. It is based entirely upon trust, and the *hawaladar*'s relationship with his clientele may stretch across generations."

The cops said nothing. The big one, Javaid surmised, had no idea what he was talking about and masked his ignorance with stolid silence, trying to look like Manesh. The one on the floor didn't move; his breathing was lost beneath his baggy clothing, and he didn't seem to blink as much as biology required. Javaid pressed on.

"Such was my family's relationship with our *hawaladar*, who received my family's patronage since long before I was born," he continued. "Our *hawaladar*'s eldest son is now an executive at the Abu Dhabi Investment Authority, what you here call a sovereign wealth fund. The Gulf League states are enjoying unprecedented wealth and constantly seek new opportunities for investment. Having already spent large amounts on faltering international financial institutions, such investment groups are looking for, shall we say, less risky ventures, with a more reliable return on equity. For a minute fraction of the sums the ADIA spends on capital infusions for banks and brokerage firms, the amount required to purchase land, plant, equipment, and medallions, a taxi corporation run by veterans of the industry can obtain hard assets, real estate, and experienced management with a built-in line of succession."

The big cop was losing some of his composure, Javaid thought. His lips were parted, and he appeared to be sweating slightly.

"More, what the fuck is this shit?" Santiago snapped.

Immobile, More replied, "New York's broke. These guys come along with money from Abu Dhabi ready to pour millions, maybe billions, into an industry central to city infrastructure. The U.S. can't audit a foreign country, and even if it got a list of accounts, there'd probably be a broker's name, or a lawyer's, nothing more."

While speaking, More had somehow gotten to his feet with neither a rustle of clothing nor a crackling of joints. "We're not here to hurt you. We will need copies of your financial statements, receipts of purchase for equipment, copies of inspection certificates by the TLC, DEP, DOB, every city agency you went through to obtain permission to set up your operation. You seem to have gone to great lengths to put this corporation together legally; all we're asking for is a copy of the paper trail. Can you oblige us?"

This one didn't bluster like the big one did, Javaid thought. Concise and to the point. He should have gone into business instead of frittering away his life on this *ujar*. But that was no concern of his. The business was legal, and there were reams of paper to prove it. Once Urbank and the ADIA were brought in, it was out of his hands.

More turned to Tariq. "Why the Minilites? Couldn't you get Sunraysias?"

Whatever More's words meant, they had a truly shocking effect. The kid's features twitched, his shoulders relaxed, and he *smiled*—actually smiled, baring eggshell-white teeth in a regimental alignment that Santiago knew the NYPD's dental plan would never cover.

"Not for Honda, and they'd never fit over the brakes we got," Tariq replied. He spoke the Queen's English, clarion London, not a trace of his father's accent. "Dad thought the Minilites would give a more classic look, and the vendor had a fitment package for Honda ready to go. It's all in the paperwork."

Santiago had no idea what was happening.

"Tell your painter he did a great job," More said with an incongruous grin, pivoting neatly on the ball of one foot and sliding just out of range of the bolt cutter. "I hope the filmmakers don't sue you." He slid to a stop between Santiago and Javaid and held out a card to the latter. "Let us know when the copies are ready. If you've got a scanner, you can email the files directly to Detective Santiago."

The motherfucker had even swiped his cards! Santiago couldn't believe it. This guy broke every rule in the book.

Then again, Santiago cautioned himself, this guy was no cop. That was becoming clearer by the minute.

"Tell me," More continued nonchalantly, "do you get many drivers from other garages applying to work here?"

"Of course," Tariq said with the same pride in his voice as his father's. "Every driver in town wants to work with us. We only pick those we think are the best qualified. We can afford to be choosy."

More, riding the drift upward: "And do you keep records of all those applicants?"

Father and son exchanged glances. Santiago could actually see, hanging in the air, the weight of their mutual wrangling over the decision to open up to the cops or not.

More, you motherfucker, Santiago raged silently. *See what clearing your throat once in a while can do?*

•

Santiago knew something was wrong as they walked back toward the battered hack, which stood out in stark contrast to shiny new Hondas, resplendent in their unusual livery. Santiago still couldn't place the paint scheme. Now, however, he got curious. More had pulled out his phone.

It was bigger than a standard iPhone and covered in thick heavy-duty plastic. It reminded Santiago of a pygmy version of the device his asshole brother carried on the job (Rafa was a UPS driver); he bet himself it was waterproof and impact-resistant. He hadn't seen where More pulled it from, but noticed that he kept it next to and slightly behind his left thigh, with his hand concealing it from forward view. Santiago's antennae went up.

"Wassup? Your date cancel on you or something?" Santiago didn't know why he said it. More didn't seem like a guy who went on dates; he seemed like a guy who snatched women off the street in a van.

"Two o'clock, fifty meters, behind the Dumpster, gray four-door,"

More said in a low, clear voice with no trace of interference. He sounded like he was already on a radio.

Without turning his head from More, and without changing his stride, Santiago let his eyes move left to the edge of his peripheral vision. It was there, all right. Might as well have been lit up in neon: UNMARKED CAR.

"So?"

More was working the phone with his thumb without looking at the screen. "The plate's coming up as a delivery van for a flower shop. That means two things. One, it's stolen."

This guy is going to drive me batshit, Santiago thought. How the hell could he run a plate so fast? "Two?"

"Whoever sent the car doesn't want us to find out who they are."

Now Santiago felt uneasy. "More, we're cops investigating two murders. Nobody would fuck with that."

"Detective, we start out looking for drugs in bars, which leads to dead cabdrivers, next we've turned up a money pipeline to the UAE. Now we've picked up a tail. Maybe this guy Javaid is on the level, we'll find out when we check the paper trail. But one thing about SWFs is you don't know where every dollar comes from or where it ends up. Maybe this *hawaladar* backed a legit cab company. Who knows what his other projects are? I think whoever's in that car might be able to tell us."

Now Santiago got nervous because, for the very first time, he thought he might have seen the beginnings of a smile. "So let's ask 'em," he said, reaching for his badge.

"I've got a better idea," More said, reverting to his razor-wire voice. They had reached their cab, and More was in the driver's seat and had the engine ticking over before Santiago had his hand on the door. He yanked it open, stuck his head inside, and said, "May I remind you I have the keys?"

"I copied them. Get in."

"You fucking did—"

"Get in." More had his Fish Face on. Whatever it was, it was going down *now*.

Fuck me, Santiago thought bitterly as he jumped inside, pulling his right leg in fast before it was severed by the closing door; More already had the cab moving.

More drove fairly slowly off the lot and past the intersection where the unmarked squatted, then punched the gas as soon as they were out of sight.

He had his phone to his ear, barking orders in a tone Santiago had never heard him use but recognized instantly. More was giving commands like he expected them to be obeyed; he was acting like he was *in charge*. Santiago heard him telling something to somebody, somewhere, and caught the call sign for the NYPD Aviation Unit, at which point he reached for his seat belt and buckled himself in securely. *Fuck me*, he thought again.

"McKeutchen says you came up through Traffic," More said, his voice clear and strong. Santiago noticed that More had his left foot lightly resting on the brake pedal while his right more firmly pushed the gas. The speed hovered at thirty-five. The tail car filled the rearview, gaining on them.

What are you getting at now? Santiago moaned inwardly. Why couldn't he have a normal partner like everyone else? "Yeah."

"Show me."

ALLEGRO CON BRIO

INTERLUDE II

"VA ROG, TE IMPLOR," Reza pleaded, "you've got to listen to me."

"*Nu, tu ascultă-mă,*" rasped The Slav in his ear. "There is nothing to discuss."

"But you're going to destroy everything we've worked for!"

"Reza, you need to understand. We're on a tight schedule. We've got to have our positions secured as soon as possible."

"But why? It's taken years to get to where we are, and planning our moves has worked beautifully. The authorities had no idea, and we almost never had to do anything that would get their attention, like we're doing now. It's a mistake to—"

"No, Reza, disagreeing with me is a mistake. Let me put it in terms you can understand. This problem with the other club owner, the one who won't back down? This is not a problem. This is why I sent you Baby-*fata*, to keep you on schedule."

Reza involuntarily glanced over at Baby-*fata*, who was enormous even sitting down. As always, he had a lollipop stuck in his mouth. Raspberry, this one smelled like. From the line of his massive shoulders upward, he looked to be about nine years old. His soft brown eyes had long lashes, and his hair was very fine in the manner of mongoloid children and brushed forward from the back of his head. Reza blinked away the memory of what Jan had told him about how Baby-*fata* worked, up close, which tools he favored.

"Her organization is simply an obstacle to be cleared away, with whatever usable elements absorbed into our operations. *De ce ai de a face un mare lucru din asta?*"

Reza knew his next words were vital but must be chosen with care. Delicately, he said: "Four dead cabdrivers in as many weeks brings unwanted attention from the police."

"*De poliţie?*" roared The Slav in his ear. It took a few breathless moments for Reza to realize he was laughing. "They can't even afford to buy themselves guns! They're almost as bad off as the ones we have at home. They're nothing to worry about."

"But—"

"Reza, shut up and listen. You think Prokhorov took over Renaissance by dragging his feet? No. He wasted no time seizing his opportunity. That is what you are there for: to secure our opportunities. The only difference is, I'm not screwing around with banks or financial firms, at least not beyond the necessary footholds. I am an old-fashioned guy. I relate to older, more well-established values. Like land. Land is power, it always has been, see? Long before paper money, credit, and *blestemat* securitized debt, there was land. And it will retain its value long after the worthless idiots who went broke speculating on it are dead. Land, and the intelligent and enduring uses made of it. Look at the Park Row Building, Reza, a timeless masterpiece. Wouldn't you feel more secure owning that than some worthless investment portfolio you can't even touch? And that could become worthless overnight? Like that moron Deripaska. Is that what you take me for? *Nu?*"

Reza swallowed hard. He tried not to look at Baby-*fata*, who seemed interested in nothing beyond his lollipop. "*Desigur, nu.*"

"Good. Then you understand my point, that things must be accelerated. We are not the only ones interested in owning New York, Reza. The very institution through which we conduct our overseas financing is looking to consolidate its position in New York. In fact, the Arabs are investing in a number of upgraded legitimate business projects around the city. They're even backing some new kind of taxi garage, would you believe it? They're letting some fucking Pakistani cabbies run it. Who knows, maybe you worked with them once." The Slav unleashed another salvo of awful laughter in Reza's ear. "So you see, time is running out. New York is for sale, and despite the economic turbulence, there is no shortage of potential buyers. I do not intend to be late to the auction; nor will I be outbid for the choicest items that go under the hammer. I *am* the hammer, Reza, and you would be wise not to forget it."

The connection was severed and the line was empty, save for a few whorls of dissonance as the scrambler and satellite link faded out. *Baby-fata*—Babyface—reached out one massive paw, and Reza gingerly placed the secure cell phone into it.

Acest scop și nu ar.

•

```
DATE:_____
TO: NID,_____/JSOC,_____/DoD
FROM:_____ /_____
SECURITY CLEARANCE: DARK SECRET
RE: Domestic deployment of HUMINT/SCAR asset MORE,
EVERETT NMI (hereafter "Subject")
```

BACKGROUND: Subject born on or around mid-April 1980 in Shoshone, Lincoln County, ID. Official birth certificate missing. Subject's mother identified as Loretta Grace More; father unknown. Mother's medical records indicate multiple treatments for complications related to alcoholism; no record of Subject's treatment for fetal alcohol syndrome.

Little data available RE Subject's early years. Mother worked as waitress/barmaid at Cal's Bar & Grill on District Hwy. 24. Mother had multiple citations for DUI; one for solicitation; one arrest for D&D, no charges filed. County records show Subject attended _____ school in _____. Subject first applied for library card in 1987; state library records show Subject renewed card until enlistment in USMC in 1997. (NOTE: Lack of personal data suggests possibility that Subject falsified age to meet enlistment requirements.)

Subject underwent basic training at Marine Corps Recruit Depot, San Diego, CA. Early evaluations indicated aptitude for endurance; Subject underwent SERE training at NAS North Island facility as well as Camp Pendleton scout/sniper training programs; Subject qualified for Coronado BRC training program in 1998. Upon completion, Subject underwent ASC at USMC Quantico, VA. From Quantico, Subject attended eight-week USMC Combatant Diver Course, followed by three-week (Ground/Tower/Jump) airborne qualification at USAAS Fort Benning, GA. Upon completion, Subject TRUEX-qualified.

Subject's first combat post was with _____,
Kosovo, 1999. Subject returned to USMC Pendleton in 2000.
(NOTE: Subject did not go home while on furlough, instead
volunteering for intensive language studies and advanced
communications/TGO training.)

Upon initiation of Operation Enduring Freedom (fall
2001), Subject selected for advance insertion with 3/75th
Rangers and 23rd STS as part of an ITG FORECON contingent
for securing FOB "Rhino" following Operation Crescent
Wind, October 2001. (NOTE: Subject should be considered
at this stage a "Green Side" operator.) Subject witnessed
firsthand the friendly-fire mishap between USMC gunships
and USN SEAL recon team during local area operations.
(NOTE: While no casualties were suffered, the incident un-
doubtedly had a pronounced effect on Subject's inclination
toward FAC [Forward Air Controller] training.)

Following the establishment of Rhino as a FOB for 15 MEU(SOC)
and 1 SASR, Subject was involved with push on Konduz.
Due to CJSOTF requirements, such as _____,
Subject accompanied SASR on at least one and perhaps more
long-range reconnaissance patrols, which often took him
near or in some cases across the border into Pakistan.
(NOTE: This period saw Subject building extensive contacts in the SOF community, particularly among US ODA SOF
TACPs, as well as SASR and NZSAS units.)

Upon hearing of the friendly-fire accident involving ODA
574 on 5 December (NOTE: An inadequately trained TACP
caused a JDAM to be dropped on his own unit's position,
resulting in at least 25 killed or wounded, including
a near-miss for soon-to-be-installed President Karzai),
Subject immediately requested transfer to JSOTF-N (TF
Dagger). Request denied.
Subject returned to LRRPs, staying out for longer and
longer periods with mixed SOF units; longest patrol
recorded was 41 days. Upon returning to base, Subject
volunteered whenever possible for training in local area
languages (e.g., Pashto, Dari, Punjabi, Urdu, etc.) before resuming patrols.

Subject's activities eventually attracted the attention of OGA _____ /_____. When approached, Subject formally requested TACP (or FAC in USMC parlance) training. Upon completing his first Afghan tour of duty (late 2002), Subject did not go home; instead, Subject was promoted and transferred to the Udairi Ridge TACP facility in Kuwait. (NOTE: Udairi is not a formal facility, nor exclusive to any one branch of service. Other attendees were present from USMC, as well as USAF/STS and OGA _____ units.)

Subject returned to Afghan theater in late 2003, assigned to _____. Subject returned to long-range patrols, often involving mixed personnel and equipment. (NOTE: During this period Subject's unit patrols grew longer, with a rate of engagement well above most JSOC units. Cross-border incursions became deeper and more frequent.)

Subject's unit was ambushed on_____ in _____. Although seriously wounded, Subject nevertheless called in a JADAM-equipped B1B (NOTE: How Subject was able to raise this specific aircraft, with these specific munitions, all the way from the airbase at _____, is unknown) and guided in a "danger close" airstrike. Enemy force completely destroyed; Subject's unit exfiltrated to _____ and successfully extracted by joint SOAR/MWSS airlift. Subject medevaced to Rhine-Main, Germany.

During his convalescence, Subject was visited several times by _____ and _____ _____, as well as _____/_____ throughout early 2004. (NOTE: Subject declined to have family members notified; no inquiries from Subject's family were recorded as to his condition or his prolonged absence.)

Following an unexpectedly early release, Subject did not go home. Subject (promoted again) reported to USMC Camp Lejeune, NC, where he remained throughout 2004 and into 2005, with several brief details to Washington for _____

_____.

During this period Subject trained and was solo-certi-

fied for fixed-wing flight in _____, _____ and _____
. Subject also temporarily detailed to _____ for
cross-training with members of _____ and _____ in
both reconnaissance and tactical deployment of UAVs.

With the official formation of MARSOC in 2006, Subject
returned to Afghanistan. (NOTE: Subject should hereafter
be considered a MARSOF operator.) Subject (now command-
ing a mixed SOF/AMF unit with unconventional equipment,
such as SASR Parenties and RSOVs, as well as "Gator"
and "Prowler" ATVs, even using retired "Chenowth" DPVs
and M1030M1 motorcycles, all modified for communal JP8
fuel) resumed cross-border patrols throughout northern
Pakistan, traversing the entire country at least once,
crossing the LOC and infiltrating the Jammu-Kashmir region between Pakistan and India. Subject's unit achieved
unprecedented engagement and enemy kill rates, while
setting new standards in CAS efficacy.

However, allegations of repeated engagement with Pakistani
forces eventually forced the recall of Subject's unit
to base in late 2010; following surge of conventional
forces in-country the following year, Subject's unit was
disbanded. Subject concluded his fourth Afghan tour in
Kabul, studying languages and new airlift applications
for combat vehicles. (NOTE: Studies of comparative combat weights of an array of vehicles, such as IAVs, LAVs,
Bradleys, and UK Warrior APCs, including classified rub-
ber-track combat fitments, were found in copies of his
personal computer files when he returned stateside in
2010.)

Subject did not go home. He is presently assigned to
_____ based at _____. Subject currently holds
the rank of _____; he has been awarded the Navy & Marine
Corps Commendation Medal, three Combat Action ribbons,
two Purple Hearts, the Bronze Star, and the Silver Star.

COMMENTS: Two themes recur throughout the Subject's career, namely, his continual striving for self-improve-
ment and his focus on optimizing CAS. Subject was clearly set on Force Recon from the beginning. His burgeoning
interest in CAS, from the ground and eventually above
it, should come as no surprise, given his long-term im-

mersion into the SOF community, particularly among TACPs
and LRRP groups. Likewise, his early sniper training
proved to be complementary to the FAC role, a blending of
skill sets seen elsewhere among SOF TACPs/FACs deployed
in both Afghanistan and Iraq.

Such a remarkable degree of achievement within the given
time span warrants mention of the fact that the Subject
lacks all semblance of a normal home life, which can conflict with the demanding long-term mission requirements
of SOF life. Subject's FITREPs, while impeccable, indicate a solitary personality, though one not incapable of
functioning within and supporting a larger unit. (NOTE:
In basic training, Subject showed disdain for typical
hazing measures taken against new recruits, e.g., tattoos, branding, etc. Several incidents of injuries of
cadets within Subject's training platoon are on record
as arising from such alleged activities; no charges filed
against Subject, nor did Subject report any complaints,
or medical treatment for injuries sustained.) This is
not to imply that Subject is incapable of unit solidari-
ty or reckless with the men under his command; according
to debriefings of those in his unit ambushed at _____,
firsthand accounts confirm that Subject refused extraction
until every man in his unit was accounted for and the
remains of those KIA were recovered for burial. Such behavior is consistent with the highest aspirations of the
USMC for its recruits.

Subject's psychological evaluation suggests a highly
systemic thought process, combined with a shallowness of
affect and a degree of self-discipline almost frightening
in its intensity (a conclusion supported by Subject's
ability to assimilate new languages well into adult-
hood). Subject's ability to blend into new environments
and fluid situations recommend him highly for this mission.

EQUIPMENT/WEAPONS QUALIFICATIONS: Subject is well versed
in the following communications systems: AN/PRC-150; DCT;
AN/PRC-148; MPLI and MBITR; AN/PRC-117F; AN/PRC-138.
Subject is trained in the use of the following surveil-
lance/TGO systems: SIDS; AN-PVS-14;AN/PVQ-4; ANP/PEQ-1A
SOFLAM;MS-2000(M).

Aside from advanced unarmed combat training, Subject has displayed an unusually high degree of proficiency with the following small arms: 5.56mm M4A1 (all SOPMOD configurations); 7.62mm M40A1 and M40A3; 7.62mm M14 Mod 0 and Mk 11 Mod 0; 12-gauge JSCS; 9mm M9; and .45 MEU(SOC). Subject also qualified with M82 and M107 long-range .50-caliber sniper rifles, as well as the 25mm M109 AMPR. (NOTE: Subject also became familiar with a number of undocumented weapons systems while serving in mixed SOF units in Afghanistan.)

Subject is combat dive- and jump-qualified, FAC-certified, E&E-driving-certified, and fixed-wing/solo-pilot-certified for both _____ and _____ aircraft.(NOTE: Subject's flight certification is civilian.)

MISC.: Any references to the unit known as "More's Machine," or to the Subject's alleged nickname "Ever," are wholly unsubstantiated.

PART III

कंअघञइखअञदकृं

CONFLAGRATION

"PUT SOME TALK IN YOUR TAINT"

SANTIAGO FELT LIKE he'd been dropped into a mobile switchboard manned by speed freaks. More was working his phone, calling in air surveillance on the chase car behind them, while telling Santiago to call the Traffic Ops dispatcher to get some uniforms to block downtown Second Avenue traffic at East Sixtieth Street, on the Manhattan side of the Queensboro Bridge, and then to position some ALPR cars along the Sixtieth Street corridor between Second and Fifth avenues in case the stationary cameras mounted on the traffic signals at key chokepoint intersections missed the tags on the chase car.

"Identifying your target is as important as taking it out," More explained in his command voice. "The ALPRs are for backup in case whoever's behind us gets away. Maybe the computer guys can dig up something from the fake plates. But I've got a faster way to find out who's in that car." He outlined his plan in broad strokes as they rolled toward the city.

Santiago listened, thinking it through. When he could visualize More's plan, it brought a smile to his face.

"Hell yeah," he said half to himself, the radio mike in one hand, his phone in the other, grinning like a kid being let in on a devious prank. "Oh, hell yeah."

They used the highway time coordinating between Aviation, Traffic, and other NYPD units. Santiago started wondering exactly what the fuck More was up to when he said to raise Central on the radio and have them scramble a surge patrol from the Police Academy on East Twentieth straight up Third Avenue. Surge patrols were blocks-long motorcades of police cruisers cobbled together from various precincts in a mass emergency CT response. It was mostly for show and a pain in the ass for all other drivers; even the cops hated them. After a shouting match with the dispatcher, Santiago got McKeutchen on the phone. Wherever More was taking this, Santiago wanted his ass covered.

He noticed More using his left-foot braking while simultaneously goosing the gas, expertly weaving the old taxicab in and out of traffic. He held his speed to about fifty and used his signals. Santiago noticed two more things as they took the Northern Boulevard exit off the Queens Midtown Expressway: More was driving like he hadn't made the tail yet; and one of Aviation's birds, an Agusta A-119 Koala in NYPD blue and white, popped up over Long Island City, hovering over the Costco on Vernon Boulevard. The first part of More's trap was in place.

Wherever More had learned to drive, he was no slouch. He hit every light on the green or yellow, never stopping as they sailed down Northern Boulevard to Thirty-sixth Avenue, then cut left down Crescent Street. It took them a little out of the way but also kept them out of Queens Plaza gridlock; Santiago saw the speedometer creeping toward sixty as they headed for the entrance to the lower roadway ramp for the Queensboro Bridge.

The *lower* roadway?

"Yo, why you takin' the lower roadway, it's commercial, it empties onto— OH, SHIT!" Santiago put a death grip on his overhead safety strap.

If More noticed the red light at the ramp entrance on Queensborough Plaza, he paid it no mind as he put the cab into a perfect 45-degree drift from the outer left lane on the street all the way onto the inner right lane of the ramp access, tires shrieking. Santiago cursed More in two languages as he struggled to lock in his seat belt, his knees bouncing into his chest as they climbed the ramp onto the bridge, accelerating between a cable company van and a UPS truck.

"Feet wet," More quacked as they soared out over the East River.

Juggling the radio, his phone, and constant checks of both mirrors, half-blinded by the dappling sunlight hammering in on them through the bridge's massive steel latticework, Santiago realized that More had cast off any semblance of stealth, hitting the siren and lights masked in the cab's grille. Their taxi was the bait, and the tail was the prey. It was a car chase in reverse. Santiago cursed again. Being trapped in a dirty fucking taxicab piloted by an ESU psycho, barreling across one of the busiest bridges in the city toward one of the worst intersections in midtown Manhattan during midmorning traffic? It was almost like—

"You ever watch *Lethal Weapon*?" Santiago asked, his right hand white on the safety strap.

"Wazzat lahk oan de teevee?" replied More in a spuddy, soyish corn-pone drawl.

"Just—just—" Santiago stammered in exasperation, vainly flailing his huge left paw, the one gripping the radio handset.

More was really pushing the old Crown Vic, the speedometer touching seventy as they slalomed between vans and trucks. The tail had to work hard but was keeping up. Their pursuers, Santiago noticed, drove more like cops than More did. He thought he caught a whiff of something burning, maybe leaking exhaust fumes or smoldering transmission fluid, and silently prayed that More wouldn't blow up or crash the old cab before Santiago had a fighting chance to get clear of it.

Santiago's stomach was doing strange maneuvers as More slammed the cab between vehicles, all the while gaining speed on the downhill toward the off-ramp. The Roosevelt Island tram, which ran parallel to the bridge's north side, would be passing overhead any minute. Santiago imagined the looks on the faces of tourists and commuters as they watched a runaway taxicab plow head-on into the side of a slow-moving bus. He looked down the off-ramp in horror and saw that the two uniformed traffic cops, visible from afar in their fluorescent yellow vests, had apparently not been notified of the situation and were nonchalantly waving on southbound traffic along Second Avenue, with no clue that More was guiding a two-ton missile down on them at seventy-five miles per hour.

"More," Santiago began.

More showed no response. The speedometer cleared seventy-five and kept moving. Santiago could see a woman with a stroller crossing Sixtieth, yakking away on her phone, the kid, too old and fat to be wheeled around, contentedly lazing with one arm draped over his head, both of them oblivious to the danger.

"More, slow down," Santiago attempted.

One of the uniformed cops finally noticed the Crown Vic hurtling toward him and frantically threw up his arms, trying to stop oncoming traffic and clear the ramp and yelling at the woman with the stroller, who paid him no mind, lost on her phone.

"MORE, YOU CRAZY FUCK!" Santiago conceded.

The Crown Vic hit the intersection at eighty miles an hour, More drifting the cab slightly to the right of the tramway terminus to shoot across Sixtieth Street. Santiago briefly heard the woman's scream as they smashed her stroller all the way down the street to the stairs of the old Serendipity, long buried in a sea of trash; Santiago glimpsed the stroller kid setting a new land speed record, sprinting up Second Avenue. More kept accelerating, and the burning smell intensified. The elastic central articulation of an uptown-bound M101 loomed directly in front of them. Santiago screamed and time truncated for him again; they missed the rear of the bus by inches, and Santiago, looking south past the Fish Face, saw sixteen NYPD cruisers heading broadside at them before being blocked by the ruin of the old Bloomingdale's, now little more than a public latrine. The surge patrol crossed the T of their rear bumper, and Santiago heard the screech of their pursuers' brakes, trapped on the east side of the avenue with cops all over them.

More finally reduced speed. He turned and offered the soft, childlike smile often associated with the hopelessly insane and asked, "Was it good for you, too?"

"Watch the fucking road!" Santiago yelled as they bounced over cavernous potholes left unrepaired for years, bleeding off speed. More put the car in a controlled skid at the corner of Madison and fishtailed them northbound as Santiago's phone rang. McKeutchen.

"Congratulations, assholes," he growled into Santiago's ear. "You two just turned the whole fucking city upside down. Meet me at the CPP. *Now.*"

Santiago cut the connection and relayed the orders to More. "If I lose my shield over this, I'm going to kill you."

"Take a number," More replied wetly.

•

The Central Park Precinct was a relic from the days when horsepower was measured in feed and dung. A row of stables converted to mixed garage/ office/storage/junk space lay nestled on the south side of the Eighty-sixth Street traverse, across from the reservoir. Here cops on cushy patrol beats parked their three-wheeled ATVs along footpaths designed nearly two centuries earlier, the great green gift of Olmstead and Vaux, now peopled with joggers, dog-walkers, bird-watchers, tourists lost in their maps, homeless lost in their minds, and the occasional contraband entrepreneurs doing business under cover of the Ramble. The CPP was an ugly little atoll in a sea of urban bliss.

Which was none too peaceable at the moment. With the cab safely out of sight behind a row of NYPD vans, Santiago stood in a huddle with McKeutchen, two deputy commissioners (Operations and CT), the chief of detectives, and just for laughs, the chief of organized crime control, in whose bailiwick lay the OCID command that Santiago coveted. His prospects for a detail to OCID looked tenuous at best.

"What the fuck are you talking about?" barked the OCC chief, an ursine brute named Randazzo, who looked as though he wanted to pull one of Santiago's arms off and gnaw it like a buffalo wing. "A drug ring that uses *cabs*? The TLC has every hack in the fleet wired. There are cameras inside half of them now, there are the GPS meters, there are cameras on every major intersection traffic signal and TLC enforcement in unmarked cars. The cabbies can't take a piss without somebody knowing."

"And you say they're connected to these, what, *speakeasies*? We haven't had those in almost a hundred years," pointed out the DC Ops, a sullen, barrel-chested pug named Devancy. "Back then, the cabs were for getting johns to hookers. A cabbie serving drug customers today would be rolling in cash. So where's the money?"

"Why'd you call in air and a surge patrol?" asked the Counter-terrorism chief, a quiet umber slab of a man named Derricks who never took his eyes off More.

"And why the fuck were you guys playing cat and mouse with a fuckin' *Treasury* car?" moaned the chief of detectives, a tiny saffron-colored dweeb named Saffran, who squirmed and fidgeted as he spoke. The day had turned sultry and humid, the kind on which New Yorkers blasted the AC and threatened the power grid and prayed for rain, and the chief was clearly uncomfortable with his clothes and with the situation.

The Automatic License Plate Recognition cars Santiago had called in had transmitted the tail car's plates to the Real Time Crime Information Center, a hive of supercomputers on the eighth floor of One Police Plaza. It had taken longer than usual to get a hit because of all the cutouts, but the wonks had finally turned up feds. The big surprise was that the tail car was from Treasury, not the FBI, as everyone had suspected at first. Nobody knew why the Treasury Department would want to spy on a CAB team. Between that and More's joyride, the hornet's nest at One PP had been sufficiently stirred up. Hence the unusual and unofficial powwow of pissed-off police chiefs in the park. McKeutchen was doing his best to run interference for his men, but he was outranked and outflanked. That pissed *him* off.

And Santiago was the focal point for the whole group's enmity.

McKeutchen stood just behind Santiago's right shoulder, stolid in the armor of his fat. More, for his part, was ignoring everybody, poring over the taxi for damage.

Santiago had the bizarre feeling of being summoned to the principal's office to explain a troublesome sibling's urinating in a school water fountain. He saw his gold shield and OCID assignment shimmering like a desert mirage, his Plan swaying on feet of clay, yet in the midst of it all, he noticed something different: He did not blame More. His partner, gurgling psychopath though he was, had called it and played it through, and Santiago no longer felt like shooting him. This revelation notwithstanding, Santiago knew he would have to find out once and for all just whom he was rolling with.

He was working up an eloquent line of bullshit when a second taxicab squealed into the CPP's lot, blaring speed metal through its gaping windows (from the radio, a low screeching voice full of ball bearings screamed, *"Sto-o-o-p the SQUIRTS!"*). *Subtle*, Santiago thought disgustedly. If their pursuers hadn't been able to find them before, they'd have no trouble now. His mood darkened further when the cab's doors opened and Liesl and Turse, the Narc Sharks, clambered out, grinning all over themselves.

"Mierda," Santiago said under his breath. Tilting his head toward McKeutchen, he asked, "What're *they* doing here?"

"I told them to come," McKeutchen replied in his best Shadowy and Inscrutable. "If you guys are gonna crack this thing, you're gonna have to learn to work together. No," he said quickly, cutting off Santiago's broiling response, "More's in this, too. You guys pull this off and you're a team. We all pull this off, we're a *unit*. Sabby?"

Santiago nodded distractedly. He was watching DC Derricks, who had ambled over to More, who had popped the taxicab's hood. The two huddled over the engine bay, out of sight and earshot. Santiago got the Narc Sharks in his face. Liesl wore a faded, torn Sex Pistols T-shirt; Turse wore a yellow one with I ❤ TO FART emblazoned in brown across the front.

"Burnout's name is Arun Ladhani. Cabbie for the Sunshine Taxi Corp. Two priors for possession back in '98 and '99, misdemeanors, both suspended. Clean TLC test records for years. He's dirty," reported Liesl through a mouthful of cashews.

"GPS printouts of his trip sheets going back the last three months show him coming back repeatedly to a handful of locations, several times each in the same night. The last one was at the old Toy Building, where the second victim, what's-his-name, Jangeroff, was working just before he disappeared. He's fuckin' filthy," Turse informed them, spraying chewed-up pieces of cashew onto Santiago, who was hovering dangerously close to a personal event horizon.

Sensing this, McKeutchen added: "Those reports your sister was feeding us about all the ODs? I had these two run them down. I had a hunch they were connected to the speaks somehow, and they were. But we had no eyes on buys anywhere. And since we didn't know where the next speak was gonna be—"

"—we started looking for the ones that already happened," Liesl finished.

"We figured we'd start with the night the first victim was discovered, when you two were playing mumblety-peg with those drags on Broome Street," Turse put in. "With the cabbies' GPS trip sheets, we could see who was driving where on any given shift. We did digital overlays of driver routes shift by shift and found the patterns."

"It's the cabs," McKeutchen explained. "You get a couple cabbies on your payroll, disable the onboard cameras, have them drive around the block, do the handoff inside, maybe through the partition or in some hidden compartment, whatever. The switch is in the cabs."

"How'd you know to look at the cabs?" Santiago asked, perplexed.

"We didn't. He did," Liesl said, nodding toward More, who was still huddled with DC Derricks.

"Your partner's a fuckin' genius," said Turse. "We find this Arun guy, we find the dope." This stung Santiago, who had back-channeled the information they'd gotten from the Talwinders and Baijanti Divya to McKeutchen.

"We find Arun, we can roll up a whole fuckin' *network*," Liesl said excitedly. "Who knows how many cabs they've got working?"

"Who knows how long they've been running this scam?" Turse said, all jazzed up. Santiago was starting to catch the narcs' buzz. Busting a single crooked cabbie was one thing, but this was their first real crack in the speak wall, and it meant a mountain of credits for the cops who broke it wide open.

Santiago realized that McKeutchen had staged this scene for their benefit. The chief of detectives was bitching sotto voce and scratching himself all over. "I fuckin' hate this," he griped. Santiago couldn't tell if he was referring to the course of the case or the weather.

"Put some talc in your taint," offered McKeutchen, deadpan. The chief stopped scratching and looked at him with an expression that could kindly be described as incredulous.

Eager to avert further contributions of this sort by his CO, Santiago jumped into the conversation with both feet. "Okay, I'll bite. The drugs in the speaks come from cabs that circle the party zone. They pick up and drop off customers and make the switch on board. We got a line on one of the cabbies, maybe we flip him. Then what? What if he doesn't know where the next one is until it happens? If we bug his cab, we don't get anything that we don't have already. If we pose as cabbies, it's just buy-and-bust, no big deal. Where's the dope?"

"Where's the money?" glagged More, silently materializing between the Narc Sharks, who jumped at the rattle of his voice. "We find that, we get the key to their communications, locations, everything."

"Who the fuck're you?" DC Saffran asked, glaring at More.

"He's ESU," McKeutchen answered, and Santiago picked up a subtle tone of urgency in his voice. "CAB volunteer, partnered with Detective Santiago here."

The Narc Sharks were frothing by now. "Let's roust the good Mr. Ladhani and hook his nuts up to a car battery," Liesl suggested. The chiefs looked like they'd bitten into lemons.

"You know where this Sunshine place is?" Santiago asked, playing along for McKeutchen's sake.

More coughed. "I've got a better idea."

"Oh, shit," Santiago sighed.

"Hear him out," McKeutchen ordered.

"Who the fuck *is* this guy?" Chief Saffran whined, tugging his trousers out of the valley of his ass.

•

While More rode with the Narc Sharks to see Baijanti Divya about his absurd plan, Santiago took some time for himself. He had a friend at the Real Time Crime Center, and on a hunch, he gave her More's name and asked her to see what she could dig up. Then he drove down to the public library's main branch, dumping the cab in its loading bay behind the abandoned Bryant Park Grill.

Between CUNY and John Jay, Santiago had spent plenty of time at the main branch and become friends with David Smith, a librarian who went out of his way to help writers and researchers. Smith looked a bit like a balding, bespectacled beaver, but he knew every inch of the library and procured materials in almost no time flat.

Santiago was sick and tired of playing catch-up with More. It was time to get ahead, and part of that meant learning the taxi business. With a notepad and pen, he attacked the pile of books and printouts Smith had turned up on the industry, taking up the end of a common table in the main reference room. He sponged through the hansom-cab days of horse-drawn buggies. He soldiered through the strikes and plowed through the taxi wars of the 1930s, when cabs were torched and brains spilled out of cracked skulls during some of the worst union violence in city history. He absorbed the rise of Checker and the fall of the unions; he even dug up the scandal surrounding the diesel medallion issue More had mentioned earlier. He clambered over the peak in cabdriver murders in the early 1990s, the driver protests and the Plexiglas partitions that followed. He glided through the free rides cabbies gave in the weeks following 9/11, the FBI raids on cabbies' homes in Queens and Brooklyn, the deportations. He saw Baijanti Divya photographed at the head of the 1998 and 2004 strikes, and the protests for fuel surcharges after Katrina, Iraq, and OPEC sent gas prices through the roof.

He called Smith over and thanked him for his help, complimenting him on how quickly he had pulled the material together.

"No big deal," Smith said. "I just gave you the same stuff I pulled for the other guy."

Santiago went rock-still. "What other guy?"

"The cop. The one who said he worked in an undercover cab."

Santiago sat back down in the chair he had just stood up from.

"Describe him," he said quietly.

"Well, he kinda looks like a bum," Smith said, "or an NYU student. That's what I figured he was until he showed me his badge."

Santiago felt the room pulling away from him. "What else did he ask for?"

Smith shrugged. "Said he wanted to check out the roof structure."

"Check out the roof structure," Santiago repeated almost inaudibly.

"Yeah. We don't usually allow that, but y'know, he's a cop and all . . ."

"Yeah," Santiago whispered, "he's just a cop. Show me where he went," he added, then, very slowly, he leaned over and began softly hitting his head against the varnished tabletop.

●

Santiago's friend from the Crime Center texted him as he robotically headed down the marble stairs to the library's Fifth Avenue entrance. He thought he would sit on the stairs and watch the pigeons until he could trust himself to go back to the station.

He read the message twice. His friend had accessed possibly every law-enforcement database in the country and gotten only one hit on a More, E., nearly one year earlier, a moving violation in Jacksonville, North Carolina.

Santiago pulled up the GPS in his phone. What the hell was in Jacksonville, North Carolina? The Hofmann State Forest. The Paradise Point Golf Course.

And the U.S. Marine Corps base at Camp Lejeune.

"I gotchu, *carajo*," Santiago snarled loudly, scrambling a squadron of pigeons into the air.

He hit every green light on the way to the station. Once inside, he printed out a hard copy of More's violation, a speeding ticket on State Route 17, and stormed into McKeutchen's office, slamming the door behind him. McKeutchen was so startled he dropped his magnifying glass, with which he had been inspecting a large gob of orange wax he had just excavated from his left ear.

"Problem?" McKeutchen asked around the wad of gum in his maw. It was apple-flavored, his favorite. Santiago slammed the printout on McKeutchen's desk hard enough to make the lamp bounce. McKeutchen stared at the paper for a good thirty seconds, saying nothing. He even stopped chewing.

"What is he?" Santiago asked, trying very hard to keep his voice level. He was angry and hurt and confused, and for the first time in many years, he felt almost like crying.

McKeutchen looked sullen and pouty. Santiago put his hands on the desk, leaned into McKeutchen's face, and barely managed to growl, "WHAT IS HE?" before recoiling from the awful reek of apple gum. He sank into one of the visitors' chairs on the far side of the desk.

McKeutchen sighed. "Force Recon."

Santiago felt the room slowly beginning to rotate. "Explain."

McKeutchen laced his fat fingers together. "Uncle Sam is worried about our situation. He views it as something of a dark time in our august city's history, what with riots and EARgasms and the wholesale breakdown of society. Little things like that. Since he went broke bailing out every industry in the country, Sammy's looking for someone to bail *him* out. Now, to do that requires a shitload of money, and since ours isn't worth much anymore, we have to get it from outside the country. When you mix government and money, two things happen: (a) The government fucks everything up royally, and (b) wondrous opportunities arise for bad guys all over the planet who have buckets of dirty money that they need to wash clean.

"As far as I've been told, and I damn sure haven't been told everything, somebody thinks there's dirty money mixed in with the clean money flowing in from overseas, mainly from sovereign wealth funds. This somebody knows very well that there's no legal way to do anything about this, since said funds aren't subject to the laws of our great nation, and since they are under no obligation to disclose their investors. How do you audit a foreign country? Never mind that the first account you ask about is a lawyer who tells you to get fucked in every orifice in triplicate." McKeutchen paused to let this soak in.

Santiago felt dizzy and nauseated. Speaks, drugs, dead cabbies, and sovereign wealth funds. Spooks in DC and batshit marines in cabs. Maybe he should have stayed in Traffic. No. Fuck that. Santiago wasn't in a graduate program at John Jay for nothing. "The Posse Comitatus Act keeps the military and law enforcement separate."

McKeutchen pointed both index fingers at Santiago, his hands still laced together. "Wrong. The PCA was a product of Reconstruction. After the Civil War, the army had garrisons all over the South, where they had bushwhackers and the Klan and other upstanding citizens exercising their constitutional right to be assholes. It was bad enough that the army was stretched so thin, but to make matters worse, the civil policing it was forced to carry out meant it was getting sucked into dicey political situations that Congress figured federal troops had no business being in. The states had to police themselves.

"The PCA itself is a statute from 1878. Title Eighteen, look it up. It is *not* a constitutional provision. It's supposed to keep the military from prosecuting civil law enforcement, and to a large extent it does that. But the military can and does get involved, and it started long before 9/11 and the Patriot Act. It's not like there's no precedent. Federal troops have been deployed on U.S. soil two hundred times in two hundred years. Today we've got marines on the border with Mexico and army BCTs garrisoned around the country as emergency first responders. We've got whole corridors of U.S. airspace designated for use by military aircraft only. The Coast Guard does drug patrol offshore and the National Guard gets to clean up after every hurricane, mudslide, and brushfire, not to mention every major riot except our own, since so many Guard troops were still in Iraq. See? There are no boundaries anymore.

"There've been enough court rulings over the years *upholding* military involvement in civil law enforcement, providing it's a 'passive support role.' Since the pendulum has swung back to the right, somebody in D.C. probably thought they could squeeze an operator like More through. Shit, by the time the Defense Authorization Act was passed in '06, the PCA was pretty much gutted. Who's to say where an enemy is anymore? We got homegrown wack jobs sending anthrax through the mail and flying planes into IRS buildings. Whether it's drugs, terrorism, WMD traffic—it doesn't matter. The battle's not just *over there, over there*. If shit goes down here, or if somebody at the top of the food chain *thinks* something's going down here, the military can get involved. And it does. But not like this. At least not until now."

McKeutchen moved his laced hands behind his head and leaned back in his chair, which cried for mercy beneath his weight. "We've arrived in a realm," he continued, "that makes me ever so slightly anxious. The system always made for a clear distinction of duty—troops for overseas, cops here at home. That distinction no longer applies. It's not just that military units are training for domestic deployment, now they're being *deployed* domestically. It's not just in a *support* capacity anymore, it's *operational*. Using somebody like More, buried in the biggest police department of the biggest city with the biggest financial center in the country, is a logical step up from what came before, but it's a big one. I don't know what the legal grounds are for this operation, if there really are any, and I can't say I like it. More says he won't make any arrests, question any suspects, or show up in court. From what I've seen and what you've told me, he's kept his word."

Santiago's head was swimming. "Why More?"

"He's Recon. Actually, he's MARSOC, Marine Special Operations Command; they finally came up with that back in '06 for Afghanistan. They needed someone who could get into places quietly, gather information, and pounce when the time was right. More's background is deep-penetration covert reconnaissance with an attack component built in. He's career military, and my guess is, he got loaned out to the spooks once or twice, too."

Santiago's hands were shaking; he clenched his fists. The light in the office seemed too bright. "And ESU?"

"It was easy for them to embed More into our ESU. They cross-train with military instructors, and with all the troops coming home from Iraq and Afghanistan and no jobs around, a lot of ex-soldiers become cops. The elite troops, the hard cases, tend to gravitate toward ESU; it's their kind of work. For More, it's perfect camouflage, if anyone's watching."

"Are they?"

McKeutchen frowned. "Dunno. This thing today with Treasury, I don't know why they were on you. Maybe you're poking around in something they've got going on. Maybe it's something they don't want anyone else knowing about. I don't know. I keep asking, but they don't tell me shit. Command chewed my ass out today, but aside from that, they're being very cagey. Most of them don't know about More, and I for one would like to keep it that way as long as possible." McKeutchen nonchalantly raised his right leg and unleashed a growling low-register fart. The smell of his apple gum neutralized the odor but was even worse.

Santiago gripped the edge of McKeutchen's desk. "Why you?"

McKeutchen's eyes drifted over to the single portrait he kept in the office, of a young marine in full dress blues. The marine was McKeutchen's only son, Michael, from his first marriage, which had ended before Santiago was born; Michael had been killed along with dozens of his comrades in a suicide bombing in Beirut in 1983.

"I'm a friend of the Corps," McKeutchen said, his voice soft. "They helped me over the years, and once in a while, I help them."

Santiago used the desk to help lever himself to his feet. He took a deep breath. "Cap," he said in a shaky voice, "I want you to tell me exactly what the fuck is going on. But first ditch that fucking *gum*."

THE DEMOLITIONED MAN

THE PRINCE AND I ARE DRINKING our appetizers in Bar Blanc
Bistro, trying to figure out what to do next.

I don't know how this place stays in business; they must have a lease
that runs for centuries. They're serious about their security: The screening
area juts out of the front vestibule onto the sidewalk, where the windbreak
entrance used to be. Or maybe Reza has taken it over. Sooner or later, we
all end up working for Reza.

The 3B is a well-stocked hunting ground tonight. Besides the Prince
and me, the only other male customer is some middle-aged geek at the end
of the bar with his nose in a book; otherwise, it's all women. As usual, the
Prince is seated with his back to the wall in the last banquette on the left,
facing the front door, so he can see the new trade walking in. I'm trying to
keep him focused on my problem, but I'm competing with every size six
who sashays through the door.

A few weeks ago, this would be pretty close to my vision of paradise.
But right now I'm such a wreck, I'm not even paying attention. Jossie and
that little bitch Meghan are gone. I can't get hold of N or even L, and I'm
not sure what I'd say to them if I could. I don't want to eat and I can't sleep.
I can't even fucking masturbate. Nothing, not my private pictures of N, L,
or any woman I've photographed in flagrante delicto can stir me; not even
the madonna of Redtube 721 can hoist my colors. What's *happening* to me?

It doesn't help that Prince William is so calm about all this. Granted,
he didn't just lose a big chunk of a shipment of Reza's on top of blowing a
Roundup cover and getting stuck with a twenty-thousand-dollar equipment

fee and getting screwed—literally—out of the other portion, which would have helped to cover the loss. I still don't know how the Prince knew about the dead cabbies or Reza's war with LA. The Prince doesn't know about the remaining Specials I've got stashed at home, and I see no reason to enlighten him. I don't trust him anymore.

He signals for another round of appetizers (an appetizer being a truffle oil–infused shot of Absolut 100). I put up with his nonchalance because I need his advice, and because I can't afford the drinks, and because I need money, fast.

—She's still not answering her phone? he queries, his face a handsome mask of innocence.

—For all I know, she's ditched it by now. I went by her house first thing, and no one answered the bell. They'd pretty much lifted off by the time I left, who knows where they wound up?

Most likely, they've already left town. Maybe to Joss's parents' place in Wainscott, maybe back to Meghan's *school*. What difference does it make? Joss is loaded, she's got plenty of plastic, and they've got a box full of Specials—MY FUCKING MERCHANDISE—at zero cost basis. Face it, boyo, you got played by a couple of white-bread, private-school, trust-fund bunnies. Renny, you stupid fucking *amateur*!

The Prince purses his lips and pretends to be deep in thought. He's enjoying this, the sadistic bastard. There's nothing he likes more than watching someone impaled on his own hook.

—Have you told him yet?

Oh yeah, sure, I told Reza I lost his goods, I can't make payment, I'm in debt up to my eyeballs—of *course* I told him all that. I knock back my appetizer and glare at him silently.

The Prince takes on the air of an older, wiser man counseling a wayward youngling. (I can't stand being in this position.) He sips his drink leisurely, savoring the moment. (I want to strangle the prick.) He smacks his lips and says:

—I've seen this kind of situation before, and there're two directions you can take. Either you tell Reza the truth and throw yourself on his mercy, or you find another way to replace what you lost.

For a second I'm too dumbfounded to speak. It doesn't last.

—What *I* lost? *You* were at Le Yef with me when LA jacked the cab. *You* can get hurt by this, too.

I'm undone the moment the words leave my lips. Reza doesn't care who loses what, all that matters is getting his money. The Prince could easily make up the difference on his own. This is his aloof way of asking if I'm ready to get off my high horse and handle powder, and I'm not (I *never* touch powder). It occurs to me that as experienced a swindler as Prince William could come up with any number of ways to compensate for some product gone astray. It also occurs to me that if he's been slinging powder and rocks for so long, he's probably been supercharging his profit margin with *paco*, garbage made from garbage to be consumed by garbage. No wonder the Prince is never short of money—he's got his own private revenue stream, pushing the by-product of Reza's product. Since he's just repackaging the junk that Reza's chemists would most likely throw away, it's the perfect skim. No flies on Prince William; as long as Reza gets his money, why should he care about the Prince's sideline enterprise?

Then again, he might like to know. And maybe, just maybe, I can use that to my advantage. Knowledge is power. At this point, what do I owe the Prince? A cheat and a liar and a dope dealer is he, par excellence.

My friend.

But I say:

—I'd have better luck throwing myself on the mercy of Marcus Chalk.

Prince William's eyebrows rise; he hadn't considered this. *Roundup* is the legitimate side of the street, way off his patch.

—Not a bad idea, that.

—Oh, come on. He'd humiliate me.

—Reza would do far worse, he replies evenly.

Oh, shit. Would it really come to that? Reza would have me work off the debt; he wouldn't actually *kill* me over this, would he? After all I've done for him? A two-tone text alert sounds from the Prince's lapel pocket. He pulls out his phone while I turn and signal for another round to keep my hands steady. When I turn back, he's frowning at his phone.

—That was Arun. There's been another one.

—Hers or ours?

—Ours.

—Who?

—Raj.

One of the cabbies in Arun's group. LA has taken the offensive in the taxi war.

We sit there, not looking at each other, not liking the news. I'm not liking how calm the Prince is while I'm coming apart. I'm not liking the fact that Arun told *him* first that another cabbie's been killed.

Most of all, I'm not liking how fast my pool of options is shrinking.

In the dictionary, *prevail* comes before *pride*.

•

I'm in Mangia across the street from the 9 West Building, wringing the last drops from my debit card, when someone says:

—Hey, Renny!

Jesus! It's almost enough to give me a heart attack. I turn to face my old roommate and partner in crime from college, Brian. It's already been three years since we last saw each other and swore we'd always keep in touch. And we have. Email and Cloaca are the primary ways of my generation to say we're catching up with each other, without the actual catching-up part. Ah, the memories. Setting up Bar Bobcat on the top floor of the library. Three A.M. condom runs to Sixth Avenue. Bluffing our underage way into Any Orifice night at Crash Site. Tag-team sessions with C, M, Y, and K . . . but that all changed when Brian met Jeannie. I will never understand the depth of their attraction. Jeannie is a frumpy, dumpy thing with bad skin and a spine-rattling laugh. But once bitten, Brian was a goner. Upon graduating, he went straight to Stern. And I, having seen my prospects shot down one after another, went to work for Reza. Now they've done the dance, house in Mamaroneck, he takes the train to some office somewhere, she works close to home and makes the daily round trips to school for the monkeys. This is the sort of thing we once laughed at. I'm hoping he didn't see me put a cup of coffee on plastic. Then again, he might be someone I can tap for a loan.

I've been tuning out most of the backstory when Brian says the thing I least want to hear:

—And I can't rock the boat now, since Jeannie's pregnant again and we need to finish out the basement for the—

For the kids. I already know where this is going before he finishes. There's no point in asking him for anything. Trying to mask my creeping depression, I absently wonder aloud where he'll find the time to be young.

—Young? Young? Renny, this *is* being young. I needed to lock down the house while I still have a full-time job so I could get a mortgage. At least we've got the place and can fix it up while we have paychecks coming in. Who knows what'll happen tomorrow? You have to be old in order to be young.

I don't know what to say. I wonder when they'll find the time to enjoy their children, or if they will, but I keep my mouth shut. For all our differences, it's good to see him.

—It's good to see you, I manage.

—You, too, man. Hey, I gotta go. Keep in touch.

—Right.

Watching him run out the door, I can almost see the dark cloud of my situation roll back in like a malevolent fog. This cup of coffee is probably the last thing I'll be able to charge. My cards are maxed out. Everything I owe, I've put on credit. Where did it all go? (*On you. On everyone around you. On those who used and abused you.*) I never thought about saving, never thought about putting money into the things Brian did. Well, I did want to buy my apartment, but I was depending on Reza for that, and unless I can make up for the shipment LA took, fast, I doubt he'll be in an eleemosynary mood. As I look at all the panini on display behind glass, my stomach growls. I'm starving, but I don't have enough to buy a meal. It won't be the first time I've called a box of Carr's dinner.

This is how it happens. Right when you're at your lowest, the friend you once thought was the brother you never had pops up and shows you everything *you* did wrong by showing you everything *he* did right. Then he vanishes like a ghost, and you know in your bones that's all he is now, and all you are to him: evanescing memory.

This is how it happened.

•

The receptionist in the waiting room at *Roundup* is getting nervous. It's been almost an hour since I asked to see Marcus Chalk, and of course she said he was out. I said I'd wait and I'm still here, waiting. She's started cupping her hand over the phone receiver to muffle her voice; by now she's probably informed the whole office by email about the guy who won't leave, and would someone please call security?

It doesn't matter. I'm pinned to this settee by entropy. I've got my earbuds in and thumbed up the Only Ones' "Another Girl, Another Planet," repeating it over and over. On my phone's screen, the front page of the magazine's website features a bevy of beauties arrayed behind a naked and glorious N. Wrapped around N, her gym-toned arms deployed over key strategic points, is LA, striking a pose at once provocative and proprietary. The gaudy headline in the foreground reads EXCLUSIVE! THE STAFF GIRLS OF LE YEF.

I don't want the receptionist to call the cops. With leaden limbs, I pull myself to my feet. On my way out of the office, I catch a glimpse of Johnette as she emerges from behind one door and disappears behind another. Our eyes meet for an instant: There is no gloating, no sadistic leer, no malice in her face at all. She sees me, or perhaps through me, and then she's gone.

•

There's no rational explanation for why I park myself on a bench across the street from the lobby of the *Roundup* building. It's another one of those unfinished parks, abandoned when the money ran out, a fitting place for my vigil. I have to see Marcus Chalk. I've got to try to explain what happened and see if I can straighten things out. Maybe, just maybe, he'll give me another chance. If I've got money coming in from *Roundup*, maybe I can work out a schedule with Reza for paying back the cost of the lost Specials.

And here he comes, nodding to the doormen, one of whom raises a radio to his mouth. There's a stunning woman with him. Even at this distance, her confident, indescribably seductive bearing beckons to me.

I should have known. L magnificently fills out a carnelian iridescent chiffon asymmetric suspension cocoon dress, every inch the *belle du jour*. It's so decadent. So last-decade. So very, very L.

I tear my eyes away as they share a laugh and the inevitable kiss. A throaty burbling sound gives me something else to focus on. A valet for the building roars up in a glossy black Audi RS9. I blink furiously through my tears to make sure I read the license plate right. I have. This is Reza's machine. The valet jumps out and holds the driver's door open. Marcus Chalk holds out a folded bill while L slides behind the wheel. I can almost hear the rustle of silk across leather, bunching between the flesh of inner thighs softer than rose petals, and even then I can't get hard. Everything's falling apart.

Marcus Chalk walks slowly, grinningly around the front of the car, in my line of sight for a good three or four seconds, but he doesn't see me, intent as he is on the prize behind the wheel. In he gets and off they go. The roar of the engine does not quite mask the growl in my guts.

Sooner or later, we all end up working for Reza.

•

I know the mood is bad from the stillness that greets me as I make my way cautiously into the dragon's lair. Jan doesn't bother with a jacket now, and the pistol in his shoulder rig looks like it could bring down a helicopter. He opens the door for me but stays outside and pulls it shut behind me.

This is my one shot to make things right with Reza. I've come in on my own instead of running away. I've still got half a load of Specials stashed at home that I can probably start moving tonight. Plus, I've got an ace in the hole—Prince William's sideshow *paco* operation. I'm auditioning for the role of my life, literally. But I can do this.

The lights are off except for Reza's desk lamp, which illuminates a near-empty bottle of raki and an ashtray heaped with the crumpled paper filters of those awful foreign cigarettes he smokes when he's angry. The air is thick with the stench of burning hair they give off, laced with something else, something fruitish but synthetic. Like candy.

As usual, Reza is in his chair behind his desk—no sign of the goon with the lollipop, which is a big relief. Reza's laptop is open on the desk in front of him, but he's looking at the wall-mounted screen, which appears to be showing a real-time surveillance feed, the timer counting in the lower-right corner. The camera is positioned obliquely over a bed on which a couple is clearly engaged in rough, almost violent sex. The man behind the woman is large and muscular, with an elaborate tattoo snaking from his right nipple over his shoulder. I've seen him before—yes, he's one of the security goons who dragged me downstairs for my bathroom meet with LA at the BPG. But the woman on the bed . . . wait, it isn't a woman, it's a man. It's Prince William. His lips are drawn back from his teeth in a rictus of strain; tears of joy shine on his cheeks.

—You knew about this? Reza asks through a cloud of evil-smelling smoke.

Holy shit. I figured the Prince was hedging his bets by playing both sides, but I never imagined he'd do something like this. Or that Reza would find out so fast.

I've got no choice. I have to play my trump card now. In the steadiest voice I can muster, I say:

—Reza, he's working a scam on you. He's been freelancing, selling *paco* that he makes off your merchandise. He knew you were moving on LA's territory. He tried to recruit me for her. I wouldn't play ball, and she beat—she had her men beat me up. Look at my face, Reza, you know I'm not lying.

Reza is looking at me wordlessly, his hard eyes glinting through the smoke and gloom. He's listening; maybe I'm getting through to him. He's got to know about the missing Specials, there's no point trying to cover that up. If I come clean, I should be able to bring him around, make him see that all this wasn't my fault.

—So, says Reza, picking up his cigarette, you wouldn't play ball.

Slowly, very slowly, he turns his laptop around to face me. There's a split-screen display on it. One window is still, showing the front page of the *Roundup* site with LA wrapped around N.

The other window shows another surveillance feed. It's from the Great Hall at the Met, one of the cameras in the big cue-ball turret by the security center—how the fuck did Reza get that? The camera zooms in on a couple happily embracing, oblivious to the crowd around them.

It's me and N.

Oh no.

—So, Reza grunts, pushing his laptop to one side of his desk, how long you been seeing this *curva*?

There are so many questions piling up in my head that I don't know which one to start with. In fact, I can't speak at all. I'm just standing there with my mouth open when Reza makes a beckoning gesture and someone, no, some*thing* locks me in a terrible grip, all over, worse than the one LA's goons put on me. Now I really can feel my bones grinding together, and I try to scream but can manage only a broken croak. Something sharp pokes me in the back of the neck, and for a split second I think I'm being injected, but no, it's a stick.

A stick from a lollipop.

That is much, much worse.

I'm bent over from the waist, my upper body slammed onto the desktop, my right cheekbone taking the hit. Reza's back is to me, his profile partially obscured by the darkness and the high back of his office chair.

The samovar is nowhere in sight, just a near-empty bottle of raki and a glass, along with a battered old Zippo and a wide, flat cigarette box marked KAZAKH. I'm watching N and me kissing on the laptop, a lifetime away.

The force pinning me to the desk is immovable, a glacier sealing me in wood. A fierce orange point from the end of Reza's cigarette flares against the blue glow of the TV screen on the wall.

—You think I didn't know? he growls.

I can't tell which screen he's looking at, so I don't know whether he's talking about me or Prince William, but it doesn't matter, I need to make my case. In this position, with the pressure on my back, chest, and face, every word is excruciating.

—Reza, wait, I can explain. It was—

—You almost got away with it, Reza says to the screen. His voice isn't slurred, but there's a rasp in it I've never heard before.

—No, I stammer, this has nothing to do with—

Reza makes an indistinct motion with his cigarette and the world streaks away from me, leaving a vacuum immediately filled with something far beyond pain, beyond agony, a realm of sensation I can only imagine is the province of the dying. This is the kingdom of the Lollipop Man.

Even in the dark, with my head being ground into Reza's desk, I can see it all clearly. Prince William (having obviously infiltrated LA's camp through the back door) has been trading sex for information, playing both sides against the middle. That's how he knew about the dead cabbies, the war, everything. That's how he knew to set me up so *I* would take the fall. If LA wins the war, he becomes head of distribution. If Reza wins, I'm still dead, which eliminates further competition for him downstream. Prince William would have seen a conflict like this coming from miles away, and would have known he'd need a fall guy, but not one of the cabbies, because who gives a fuck about cabbies? No, it'd have to be someone higher up the line, higher than Arun, someone in middle management. Me. This can't be happening, but it is.

—Reza, listen to me. I'm not working for LA. *He* is. *He* set me up so that you would blame me. The girl was just somebody I met at Le Yef. I'm not even with her anymore.

Reza raises his right arm and the couple on the screen disappears. He takes another drag of his cigarette, making the air more fetid. I'm going to be sick in a minute, from the smell if not from the pain.

—Even if you were telling the truth, he says slowly, there's no way I could trust what you say.

—No. Yes. You can. Reza. I'll make it up to you. Just give me a chance to make it back. I'll pay you back every penny, I swear. We can work this out—

—*Tăcut!* he barks.

I'm losing sensation in my arms and legs. The thing on my back apparently can hold me in this position forever. And Reza's just getting worked up.

—You want to *negotiate?* Reza spins in his chair and leans into the light. His eyes are bloodshot, his face flushed and sweaty, his teeth bared. My master is a gargoyle, and he has set a demon upon my back. I can hear a strange keening sound coming out of me. Nothing seems real but the pain.

—*Hristos,* you Americans, you're such fucking babies, Reza growls, and sucks the cigarette up to pinkish-white radiance. I try to move, but the mass on my back is immense and unyielding.

—No, wait, Reza, I didn't mean, please DON'T–

—Renny, you *take* orders, you don't *give* them, don't you understand? Reza hisses.

He slowly brings the tip of the cigarette down to the left side of my neck, just below my ear, where L and N once let their tongues play, and the last thing I'm aware of is the smell of my own flesh burning.

FISH FACE ULTOR

"WHO SENT YOU?" SANTIAGO ASKED.

"Classified," More burbled.

Santiago thought he might have better luck keeping things abstract. "What are you?"

"I'm a scar," More coughed.

"You gonna be a fuckin' scab, you don't start giving me some straight answers," Santiago bristled.

"I'm part of a recon SCAR/HUMINT element, Twenty-sixth MEU(SOC)," More said in his clear disc jockey voice, free of phlegm.

Even after years of NYPD acronym-speak, it sounded like More had thrown a bowl of alphabet soup at him. "In English?"

They were leaning against a wall of glass six inches thick, which formed one side of a holding tank roughly a square acre in size. The tank was filled with cold, murky seawater and was situated in a far corner of the New York Aquarium campus on Coney Island. More had finally agreed to talk after asking Santiago to sign out an M4 from the armory for him, and after Santiago had spent a full minute cursing him in English, Spanish, and what little Creole he knew. Then he'd signed out the carbine. Impulsively, he'd signed out the Benelli, too. Both weapons were stashed in a locked compartment behind the spare-tire brace in the Crown Vic's trunk.

"SCAR stands for strike coordination and reconnaissance. That's what I do. Some people call it deep recon. I get into hard-to-reach places and gather intelligence. If I get the order, I coordinate an attack."

"You just go in guns blazing?"

"I call in the airstrike, then my unit goes in to mop up."

Santiago thought about that. Somebody in Washington had seen fit to embed a crazy-ass jarhead who did *airstrikes* into a CAB unit of the fucking NYPD in order to . . . what?

"Why are you here?"

"Classified."

"Oh, no. No, no, no, *cabrón*, that song don't play no more. I ain't into this Commando Cracker bullshit. I'm a cop. I chase shitheads like the ones going around killing cabbies, and I will catch their sorry asses so I can get my second grade and my credits and go to OCID with the real cops and kiss all you wack-job motherfuckers goodbye forever. *Comprende?* I don't need some motherfuckin' marine whose head is still stuck in Iraq—"

"I was stationed in Afghanistan."

"—wherever the fuck, who thinks he can start raining down fuckin' rockets and bombs in the middle of New York fuckin' City like it was his own private fuckin' artillery range—"

"I'm a FAC, not an artie spotter."

"—who doesn't talk for weeks at a time, and when he finally does, he sounds like a busted radio, who waits six months before telling me what the fuck is going on, and then only after half of One PP comes down on *my* fuckin' head, who had McKeutchen play me like a fuckin' fish on a hook . . . Why the fuck are we at an aquarium?" Santiago had to catch his breath after the tirade.

More gestured with his chin. "Meet Carl."

Santiago turned and almost went for his gun. Whatever breath he had managed to catch stalled in his throat, making him wheeze and cough. "*Coño . . .*" he whispered.

The shark was a juvenile, no more than six or seven feet long, but already broad across the gills, its signature dentition visible even with its jaws closed. The stark white of its belly clashed deeply with the bronze-brown skin of its sides and back; Santiago could barely make out the dorsal and caudal fins, though the sweep of its tail was visible enough in the murk. The shark lazily drifted in a clockwise azimuth across the window where the men stood, one depthless black eye cocked vaguely in their direction. Santiago tried to keep it in sight as it swam off, but roughly twenty yards out, it simply vanished, fading into the dark waters of the tank.

Santiago turned back to More, who hadn't moved a muscle but whose face seemed somehow younger and slightly more animate. He liked being here, Santiago realized; maybe this was where he went after he finished his CAB shifts. Oh, Jesus, there was no getting back into a cab with More after this, no sir.

"I never saw the ocean until I was seventeen," More said. Non sequiturs were not More's style. "Spent a lot of time in it during training."

"How nice for you," Santiago whispered, making sure he had a clear draw. Don't hit the glass, he told himself, don't hit the fucking glass, *el tiburón* will be mighty pissed if someone shoots a hole in his tub.

"Don't bother asking who or how," More croaked. "I wouldn't tell you anyway. But we need to work together on this. We have to trust each other. If it makes you feel better, I'll tell you what I can."

Santiago pulled himself together. "What's wrong with your voice?"

"I was out on a long patrol with my unit and we were ambushed. I took a piece of an RPG in the throat. The surgeons couldn't go in through the back of my neck because of my spinal cord. Sometimes the scar tissue presses on my larynx and I have to work to speak clearly."

Santiago blinked. "You mean it actually hurts you to talk?"

"No. Just takes more effort. Need to make each word count."

"Where did this happen?"

More hesitated a moment. "Bajaur."

"Where the fuck is that?"

"Northwest Pakistan."

"We never went into Pakistan."

"Right," confirmed More.

"When was this?"

"Classified."

Santiago tried again. "Why were you in Pak—"

"Classified."

Santiago changed course. "You said you're a SCAR. Does that mean you're a soldier or a spy?"

More considered this, his eyes searching the waters of the tank. "Technically, I'm tactical, but because of my operational background, I'm an intelligence asset, too. So I guess you could say I'm both."

"So you're, you're what, scouting a landing zone? The marines are gonna invade New York?" Santiago could not believe the shit coming out of his own mouth.

"No, just me. This is an OGA operation."

More soup. "OGA?"

"Other government agency."

"Which one?"

More blinked slowly at him.

"Oh," Santiago said, feeling like he was back in kindergarten. "Them."

They were quiet a moment, scanning the tank for the shark.

"Look," More gargled unexpectedly, "don't ask why they're putting operators like me into the police department. I don't make policy, I'm just one of the people who execute it. The bosses are worried that some of the money pouring into the country might be dirty, and to judge from what we've turned up, they're right. Somebody built a network here, probably over a long period of time, and it's moving drugs and other stuff through speaks connected by cabs, and they're washing the money through some other part of it we haven't turned up yet. Treasury must've been working this from another angle, and we stumbled across each other."

"Why would the Treasury Department care about an NYPD murder investigation, let alone a CAB case?"

"I'm not saying they do, just that we came up on their radar while checking things out on the supply end, and they probably got curious. I think it's all part of the same thing. They're following the money, which we've been after all along, but we found dope in cabs instead. There's probably FBI mixed up in this, too, maybe state police. That OCID division you like so much might even be involved."

Santiago was feeling more lost by the minute. "Why would so many different outfits be conducting separate investigations? Why not do a joint operation? It worked for—"

"Because," More cut in, working his throat again, "the government's a lot like Urbank. It has lots of people in lots of places doing lots of different things, and the big picture's usually not very clear, especially when it comes to intelligence work. One of the bosses who knows I'm here is supposed to try to coordinate all that, but not every agency head tells him everything that's going on. Sometimes it's competition, sometimes it's ignorance. When there's big money involved, it's like boiling a solution: All the different molecules speed up. Sometimes they collide, like with the Treasury team."

"So how much of One PP knows what you're doing here?"

More shrugged. "The commissioner. Maybe the DA or the AG. I'm not really sure. But they were told to keep it close."

A penny dropped for Santiago. "And DC Derricks?"

"Yeah. As head of CT operations, he had to be kept in the loop."

"What were you two talking about at the CPP?"

"He was curious. Said he'd heard about me through the SOF grapevine. He asked me if I was the only one."

"The only what, exactly?"

"The only SOF operator embedded in the NYPD right now."

"Are you?"

More's Fish Face came back, coinciding with the shark's reappearance. Looking at the two of them, separated by a few feet of water and glass, Santiago thought he'd been mistaken. More did not look like any creature Santiago had ever pulled from the depths. He was no game fish. He was an apex predator, like the shark gliding through the cold dark water beside him.

"I don't know," More said flatly, and Santiago's blood ran cold. The thought of an unknown number of highly trained, battle-hardened head cases like More being turned loose in New York with badges and enough firepower to take out entire city blocks and no sense of restraint (legal or otherwise) scared him. Even worse than More's driving did.

"You know, there are laws against this kind of thing." Santiago figured it was worth a shot.

More snorted, an ugly sound. "Officially, I'm here to help with drug interdiction. On the books, that's legal. The Corps got stuck with drug detail a long time ago, I don't know why. The ESU embed is perfect cover; I really do sniper training, your guys need it bad. Volunteering for CAB duty was my idea, and as far as I know, it was never an issue. Until today." More leaned in closer. "Law is reactionary in nature, Detective Santiago. It's always playing catch-up, and it always will be. But with New York City going down the tubes, the bosses figured it's time to get proactive. I'm not supposed to make arrests, interrogate suspects, or testify in court. I'm not supposed to interfere with the *process*." Santiago thought he heard the faintest hint of a sneer from More. "And don't worry, you'll get all the credits. Anything else?"

"What were you doing on the roof of the library the other night?"

"I'd been doing some research on the taxicab business, just to get some background. The last time I was there, I noticed some delivery vans parked down the block on the Fortieth Street side. Guys were carrying in boxes of booze, stereo speakers, stuff like that. I wondered why someone would be setting up a party in a restaurant that's supposed to have been closed for years.

"When you're a scout/sniper, you get used to sitting in places for long stretches. You watch and wait, and if you're patient, eventually, you get some good intel. I'm very patient. When that librarian took me up to the roof, I ditched him and stayed up there. The crowd started showing up around nine-thirty. I watched the taxi traffic with this"—More held up what looked like a mini-Maglite—"it's a night-vision monocular, and I took down some of the numbers off their dome lights. Arun's cab came back twice, and so did another one Baijanti Divya is running down for us. I stayed up there just long enough to see the security guys work. Looked like they knew what they were doing. I saw them toss some kid out like trash. Then I left. They never saw me. Anything else?"

Santiago's situation had been so drastically altered in one day that he didn't know what to ask. "What's that weird-looking piece you carry?"

"A Heckler and Koch P2000SK chambered for forty-five GAP rounds."

"What's wrong with a nine?"

"Forty-five's for force recon."

"So why do you keep yours locked in your desk?"

"I got that from ESU. Glock sells to police forces all over the world. My weapon was custom-made for me at the RTE shop in Quantico, same as for all recon operators."

"I thought you jarheads were all married to your rifles."

"We are."

"So why'd you ask me to sign out an M4 for you? Don't you have your own? And couldn't you just get one from ESU?"

More made a sound that might have been a sigh. "Detective, try to keep up. I'm not supposed to be here. I'm supposed to be inconspicuous."

"You call what you did to that drag *inconspicuous*? Lemme tell you something, if *I* can make you, anyone on the force with half a brain probably could if they cared enough. The only reason I made you is 'cause I gotta *work* with you."

More frowned. "How *did* you make me?"

Santiago explained about the speeding ticket he'd dug up through RTCC. More listened, looking into the tank, and nodded once. Santiago could almost see him mentally giving himself a demerit for carelessness. "Hey, it was a year old. Anyone else would've missed it," Santiago reassured him.

"You didn't."

"Like I said, I have to work with you. And you know, whatever you did in Afghanistan, that shit won't play here. You want to look like a cop, you gotta think and act like one, not like you're goin' out every shift to smoke some Taliban motherfucker shootin' RPGs and shit. They may be drags, but they're still people, they got rights."

From More, a noncommittal grunt. They were quiet for a time, watching the shark follow its ancient circle. "They'll be releasing Carl in a few days," More said with a uvular rattle. "Captive white sharks die if they're not released soon after capture. They weren't made to be cooped up."

Santiago wondered if More was trying to tell him something.

"When we start rolling up the network, you won't always see me," More continued, as though they were discussing shoelace colors. "We'll have to keep our comms clear. I need a handle for you, something nobody else knows, in case the guys we're after can monitor NYPD signal traffic."

Santiago thought about this. Where it came from, he didn't know, but somehow it fit. "When I was a kid, I played a lot of basketball. I used to get in pickup games at the park with the older kids." He pictured them, nineteen or twenty, impossibly tall and bulked up, fresh out of jail. No fouls. "They called me Six."

More nodded. "Six. I like it."

Santiago dreaded asking it. "So what did they call you?"

More did his impression of a smile forming in geologic time. "They called me Ever. Ever More. Get it?"

●

Nuts. Completely fucking nuts. That was Santiago's impression. But here he was, behind the wheel of the Crown Vic, holding a laptop far more expensive than anything he'd ever worked on. Baijanti Divya sat in the passenger seat. They were parked in a bus lane on Twenty-sixth between Fifth and Madison, on the northern border of Madison Square Park. More was on the roof of the Flatiron Building, with a camera that had an obscenely large telephoto lens. Once he had the eyeball on Arun Ladhani, high-resolution images would be sent to Santiago's laptop, from which he could beam them to the phones of the half-dozen CAB volunteers who the Narc Sharks had asked, cajoled, or threatened into being part of this lunacy. More called the photo-transfer system SIDS. McKeutchen had said hell, why not, the department didn't have the equipment for this kind of stunt, but they'd need an independent confirmation of the eyeball before they took down the burnout. Hence Santiago's present companion.

They were on a ridiculous schedule. Baijanti Divya had organized a massive driver protest after the identity of the third cabdriver victim, Raghuram Rajan, was released. Santiago had pointed out to the CAB force that while victim number three had been shot twice in the head, the postmortem showed no indications of torture, as with the first two cabbies. This looked more like a straight hit-and-run. They'd kicked it around a CAB Group One huddle before rolling out.

"Maybe they didn't have time to break out the toolbox," Turse proposed.

"Maybe somebody saw them jack the cab," Liesl suggested.

"Maybe it was someone else," More expectorated.

"Enough fucking maybes. Pick up the burnout and the other one, see if we can get one to roll on the other. But do it fast. Three dead cabbies and a big fucking protest drive is *not* helping our cause any, gentlemen." In spite of the long odds and short shot clock, McKeutchen was visibly pleased at the progress they were making, and at the fact that they were finally working together, albeit grudgingly. He no longer held More in his office for private meetings, yet he seemed able to keep the rest of the department from sharing More's secret. Santiago did not press his CO on the state of things with One PP vis-à-vis More.

Baijanti Divya agreed to confirm More's recon of the burnout cabbie but had stressed that the other one was to be treated with care. When Santiago asked why, she made a point of looking at More.

"This man, Detectives, is a refugee from one of the worst conflicts raging on the planet. He is from a town near Goma, on the border of Rwanda and the Democratic Republic of Congo. He has lost his entire family to the ongoing proxy wars there, and was repeatedly victimized as he struggled to make his way here, where becoming a cabdriver was one of the only occupations open to him. All cabdrivers have difficult lives, but his is an extreme case. He has no relatives here, and there are few people with whom he can communicate in his native language. If he can make enough money and learn enough English, he may be able to assimilate, assuming he can survive. For now, driving a cab is all that he has. Becoming involved in your investigation will likely jeopardize his standing with the TLC, which will inform both the FBI and ICE, which will ultimately decide his fate. This man's life has been a violent, dangerous river. Now that he has found a reasonably calm eddy, I would like to see him stay there as long as he likes."

Baijanti Divya crossed her arms. No gold or traditional dress for her today, Santiago noted. Today was an olive-green one-piece garment covered with pockets and zippers. She looked like Che Guevara in drag on the flight deck of an aircraft carrier.

"We'll try to make things as easy as we can for him," Santiago assured her, though he wondered how they'd pull it off.

That was before the cabs started massing at the north end of Central Park, near where his sister was working. She had taken some shots with her phone and sent them to him; the lush green of the northeast corner of the park clashed sharply with the bright yellow blob that seemed to stretch from 110th and Fifth all the way to the East River bridges. Santiago had never seen anything like it. This was much, much bigger than the taxi lot at the airport. It was a seething yellow mass made up of angry, frightened cab-drivers. The NYPD had mobilized auxiliaries in riot gear and staged a dozen motor cops at the corner of each major crosstown artery from Ninety-sixth to Twenty-third. There were three mobile command posts parked along the route and two choppers from Aviation hovering motionless over the park, along with half a dozen helicopters from various news agencies. Santiago idly wondered if there weren't one or two high-altitude drones up there, their cameras sending high-resolution feeds back to Washington, and maybe More could make a call . . . More gave him the Fish Face, and Santiago skulked off to the cab in disgust. His mood lifted only when Baijanti Divya joined him.

It occurred to him that while he would admit to no *man* what he thought or felt about More, Baijanti Divya did not technically qualify. Despite having had his earlier impressions sufficiently shattered, he had to admit there was something about her that went beyond the sort of intuitive female radar he had been subject to in the course of his life, from his mother and sister on. Baijanti Divya had something the women of his experience did not. He did not believe in psychics, ESP, spiritual mediums, or any of the other pop-psych garbage littering cable television. While he accompanied his family to church for the usual occasions, he felt no connection to the divine, nor did he hold much faith in his fellow man. His upbringing and vocation had thoroughly cured him of that. Still, there was something ethereal about Baijanti Divya that he couldn't put his finger on. And while he couldn't read her interest in More, he was absolutely convinced that she knew *what* More was, and had known since their first meeting at the airport. This was all gut, no rational explanation.

Cabdrivers all over were making for the staging area uptown, OFF DUTY on the dome lights. Several of them appeared to be listening to the same Punjabi radio station, with the same Bhangra tune pumping out of their lowered windows. Even Santiago thought it was a pretty good beat.

"It's 'Sonne Da Challa' by Vikrant Singh," Baijanti Divya informed him.

How the fuck does she know what I'm thinking? Santiago thought. More had said she was some kind of tranny, intersexual, whatever. Said there was a tradition of them over there. How did *he* know about that? Were there people like Baijanti Divya in Pakistan as well as India? Why would a crazy motherfucker like More know about them? Maybe the whole cross-dressing thing helped with deep recon. And why had she decided to help them?

He was just about to sound her out on this when she said, "You and your partner haven't worked together long, have you?"

"What? Uh, about six months or so, give or take," he sputtered.

She smiled, a lovely sight, especially compared with the looks he usually got these days. "I'm confirming an observation. I don't suppose you know his background?"

She knew. But she couldn't know. McKeutchen had kept More under wraps and trusted Santiago to do the same. Was it the Narc Sharks? DC Derricks, or maybe that dweeb Saffran?

"What, you want his phone number?"

"What I want is of little consequence in this context. If the government sees fit to spy on cabdrivers, all it needs to do is look to the regulatory agencies overseeing the industry. But I fear this matter is deeper and more serious, with cabdrivers being caught in the middle of a dangerous game between extremely dangerous opponents. I want to protect those in the industry from what promises to be an ugly confrontation between your department and men in cabs who are not cabdrivers, although both sides are using them for their own purposes. What I want, Detective, is a safe and decent taxi industry, which has historically been anything but. The taxi business is an integral part of the city's infrastructure, and it has provided a starting point for generations of immigrants who come to this country to help build and support family structures the world over. The man you seek is an exception, one whose corrupt ways are well known to those in the trade. The time of his reckoning is long overdue, like your investigation. I want the livelihood of the rest, the decent, hardworking majority of the industry's labor pool, protected for as much time as it has left."

"Left?"

Baijanti Divya sighed, looking through the windshield. "They say that some *hijra* can predict the future. I don't know if I can, but I sense the time is coming when the occupation of cabdriver will be rendered extinct, replaced by automation. The amount of overregulation, health hazards, cost overruns, insurance, and whipsawing fuel charges has reached a zenith. It won't be long before someone creates a cost-effective robot cabdriver that doesn't sleep, doesn't eat, doesn't get kidney trouble sitting behind the wheel for days at a time, doesn't speed, doesn't get lost, and maybe doesn't get into accidents. It will constantly broadcast its location to the TLC, never talk back to customers, and never stage a protest like this one today. That's him," she said, pointing to the screen. Santiago looked down. The image of a young Indian man standing beside a cab stared back at him. The man had disheveled hair, mirrored sunglasses, and an easy smile, and was gesturing to a small group of cabdrivers parked in the plaza. More's photos indicated the man was laughing while pointing to the side of an abandoned building on Twenty-fourth.

The passenger door slammed. Baijanti Divya was heading for the corner of Twenty-sixth and Madison, where a cab idled in front of a boarded-up restaurant behind the Federal Courthouse, a dark-skinned man with a bushy white beard and dark turban behind the wheel. She slid into the passenger side, and they were gone.

It was too bad, Santiago thought as he keyed the transmission sequence out to the CAB team's phones, that he wouldn't be there to watch her go by standing in the bed of a pickup at the head of ten thousand cabs bisecting Manhattan lengthwise along a golden filament two miles long. It really was too bad. He hoped More would take a long-view shot, just for the record. Maybe it would end up in some book somewhere, someday.

•

The CAB station hadn't seen this much activity since the riots. Three interrogation rooms were booked, one for the cabdriver known as Arun Ladhani, an Indian national; and one for a cabdriver named Wiliad Ngala, in from the DR Congo on a shaky work permit. Working from the Narc Sharks' analysis of the taxi trip sheets surrounding past speak locations (with More's rooftop observations thrown in), the drivers of those cabs on duty during the corresponding shifts were quickly identified. Bhaijanti Divya had made positive visual ID just to be sure, and here they all were. Somewhere along the way, CAB group one had accidentally become an effective police unit. McKeutchen was so happy he forgot to replenish his supply of apple gum, to Santiago's relief.

The third interrogation room was on loan to two teams of feds. The FBI team was comprised of two squat special agents, Saltarello and Bassadanza, and their supervisor, a towering, cadaverous deputy SAC named Totentantz. They were arguing jurisdiction with the supervisor of the Treasury team, a dapper mocha-colored man named Reale. His two burly underlings, Gilliard and Rondo, glared at Santiago and More, clearly itching for a fight. They had been in the tail car during More's mad sprint across the Queensborough Bridge.

The feds were sitting on one Mark Shewkesbury, head of the True Apothecary Fund, one of the new feeder funds started by Urbank under the strict new federal regulations imposed in the wake of the Jagoff trial several years before. They had surprised him at his office earlier in the day, while he was kibitzing with a state assemblyman whose name was well known to the cops: a fat swarthy Greek named Ommatokoita who sat on the financial oversight committee. The congressman had hauled (considerable) ass when the feds came in (his name not being on the warrant), and Shewkesbury had started howling for a lawyer. That stopped when they cuffed him to the table in the interrogation room, at which point he began rambling incoherently. The feds grudgingly told the cops about Shewkesbury's financial records, which showed a series of payments to "Bacchanal Industries," which turned out to be a premium brothel in a brownstone on West Eighty-third, just off the park. When the Narc Sharks (accompanied by an armored ESU team More swiftly whistled up) took the door, they found a bonanza. "Six different kinds of pills and counting," panted a breathless Liesl into his phone. Even better was the company computer, the hard drive of which a slender young woman in lingerie tried vainly to fry before Turse drew a bead on the center of her forehead and gently advised: "Don't fucking move, dear." Both Narc Sharks had GTL light/laser attachments on their Glocks, along with tactical Fobus holsters that permitted a concealed carry for the modified rig, which were hardly standard issue. "I wonder who gave them the idea for those," Santiago muttered, glaring at More, who shrugged.

So the feds were arguing and stealing angry glances at the cops, the Narc Sharks were writing their own ticket to OCID, and Santiago was stuck with More, two surly cabbies, and Shewkesbury, who had stopped ranting and now stared, glassy-eyed and drooling, at the old Micronta clock on the wall, watched through the one-way glass by Santiago and McKeutchen.

"Guy used his own credit card at a brothel," Santiago said, shaking his head. "How can people who are so successful be so stupid?"

"Y'know, maybe Oswald Spengler was right," McKeutchen observed.

"Who?"

"Get the fuck out of here," McKeutchen growled gleefully. "Get the mope his translator."

Santiago started to walk off, but More tapped him on the shoulder, shook his head, then tapped his own chest and vanished into the stairwell. The lawyers from Legal Aid and the TWA insisted on a translator who spoke either Swahili or Bantu for the Congolese cabbie, who glowered through the glass as if he'd done it before. Santiago figured he'd try his luck with the Indian burnout first.

Closing the door of the interrogation room behind him, Santiago surveyed his prey. Short, spindly, expensive-looking haircut poorly maintained, with a short-sleeve plaid button-down over a T-shirt that read I LOVE GRAVITY. This was Santiago's first full-length CAB interrogation, and since he knew he'd be in the spotlight, he wanted to make sure he did everything by the book.

"So," he began, "you want a—"

"Fuck you, man," snarled the little brown cabbie.

"Okay, so you *don't* want anything to eat or drink." Santiago smiled. This would be easier than he thought. He pulled out the second chair and sat backward on it facing Arun. "Guess why we picked you up?"

"Fuck you, man."

"It wasn't 'cause you had any outstanding summons."

"Fuck you, man."

"Wasn't 'cause you failed a drug test."

"Fuck you, man."

"Wasn't 'cause your license expired."

"Fuck you, man."

"Who's Nightclub Guy?"

That tripped him up. This time Arun hesitated just a moment before repeating his favorite line.

"We know the switch is in the cabs. Where do you re-up?"

See previous line.

"Who does the money?"

Ditto.

"Look," Santiago said in his best Reluctantly Helpful, "we've got you on conspiracy and possession with intent to distribute. Your trip sheet shows you making runs to Newark, so we can make it interstate trafficking, too. You're looking at fifteen years minimum, twenty if I tack on an obstruction charge."

He was getting somewhere. The cabbie was morosely silent; he had no idea the charges being leveled at him were baseless, there being no dope in Arun's cab, and no cash other than what the cabbie had on him at the time of his arrest. Still, he was acting like he was already facing the judge. That was fine with Santiago, who wasn't sure where any part of this fucked-up case stood on a purely legal basis.

"You give us a name, we give you a deal. Otherwise, call your union head."

The cabbie snorted. "Who—the *chaakha*? What's she gonna do for me?"

This was such an unexpected break that Santiago nearly dropped the ball. "Probably nothing. Your hack license is history, most likely your personal one, too. The Legal Aid lawyer you'll get will just ask the judge for leniency. That means half the maximum, if you're lucky. Say ten years minimum. Unless you play ball with us." Santiago hoped he wasn't overdoing it.

The cabbie looked down at his lap. Santiago got the feeling that he'd been through this before and was getting sick of it.

"Get it from the African," the cabbie snapped, startling Santiago. "I don't give a shit about him."

Throughout his life Santiago had repeatedly, sometimes violently, experienced the seething racism between black and brown firsthand. What was true in New York and Hispaniola apparently held on both sides of the Arabian Sea. He would never understand it. He shook his head, got up, and left the room.

McKeutchen gave him a firm pat on the back after the door closed behind him. "That was a ground-rule double, kid. Not bad for your first time at the table, not bad at all. Now, if More gets that translator, we might get out of here by dinnertime."

But the evening rush hour was nearly over when More came up the stairs behind a gigantic bald man with glossy black skin who wore the smallest sunglasses Santiago had ever seen, shaped to cover the almond arc of the eyelids rather than the bony ocular orbit. Extra chairs were brought into the second interrogation room for McKeutchen, More, Santiago, and SAC Totentantz. Wiliad Ngala exchanged a few gruff-sounding words with the translator, then nodded once.

"*Tafadhali,*" the translator said, gesturing for Ngala to begin. The room's hidden recording devices were already running.

"I look at you policemen," began Ngala, "and I wonder if you really know what you are up against. Far be it from me to debate the efficacy of law enforcement, as I have seen firsthand what becomes of society in its absence.

"I was born in Ndeko, just north of Goma, which, as you may or may not know, is on the border between what is bemusingly called the Democratic Republic of Congo and Rwanda, with Uganda to the north and Burundi to the south. I grew up in the refugee camp nearby at Kibati. For as long as I can remember, there has been trouble between all these nations, which are superimposed over a map of tribal battle lines going back centuries. When the Hutu began slaughtering the Tutsi in earnest in Rwanda about twenty years ago, each of these surrounding nations picked a side. When the militias blurred the national boundaries by melting into bush and town, massing periodically for hit-and-run massacres on each other's villages, I was just a boy. I played in garbage and drank polluted water and thought nothing of it. This was simply the way the world was, why fight about it? I never knew my father. My mother passed away when I was five. She wouldn't stop vomiting blood and died before I could bring a doctor back to our house. By 'house' I mean whatever slabs of plastic my brother and I could drag together from inside the zone where the UN troops patrolled. Going into the woods alone was much too dangerous.

"After the Ugandan troops pulled out, the militias came through the streets. They were boys not much older than my brother and I, drunk and stoned and barely strong enough to carry their weapons. Everyone knew what became of those who were captured and forced to join the militias. We stayed just long enough to see the first killings. Boys forced people out of their homes and stores, made them kneel in the street, and executed them. Those victims from rival tribes were disemboweled and their entrails eaten raw.

"My brother and I ran into the woods. After two days, when the shooting died down, we decided to cross the river. A group of others we had met up with while traveling offered to help us across; they said they knew of a fisherman with a boat. We believed them. But after they had gathered us and several others into a clearing, they demanded that we hand over all our money and possessions. My brother and I ran back to the woods. The *gumagumas* opened fire and my brother fell down. I went into the woods and stayed for another two days, gathering whatever rainwater and insects I could to survive. On the third day, I crawled out to see if they were still there, but they had gone. I dug a makeshift grave for my brother by the clearing where he was killed.

"I lived in the woods, starving, moving from place to place along the river, staying off the roads. I heard bits of news here and there—so many names, Matata, Ngudjolo, Nkunda, warlords came and went. I grew up on the river, always trying to head west, doubling back to avoid soldiers and militias. There was no point in going north, since the LRA controlled the woods. I was lucky not to have been shot by Ugandan or Rwandan security forces; your government trained them well.

"Everyone told me if I could get to Kinshasa and somehow get across into the Republic, it would be as though I had died and gone to heaven. Clean water, all the food you could eat, drugs for malaria and cholera, even air-conditioning. After a year, I finally made it across with the help of some men who worked for drug dealers bringing in cocaine from South America. I worked for these men for a year, showing them the best crossings, until I had enough money to get to Brazzaville. There I worked for another year cleaning toilets until I qualified for passage to the U.S.

"I arrived here in the spring of 2009, just in time to watch the city fall apart. Some other Africans told me I could find work as a cabdriver, which is what I did. I was on the job maybe six months, living in a homeless shelter, trying to save what money I could, when I was approached by someone I recognized as another drug dealer, who said he could triple my pay. I believe you have this man sitting in the next room.

"When you are starving, Officers, when you have not known a real home since childhood, when you have watched everyone you have known and loved die, when you have seen children turned into monsters who eat the flesh of their elders, you are hard-pressed to turn down such an offer. It was a small matter for me to ignore the rude and distasteful ways the people of this city demonstrate to cabdrivers, for I have seen people do much, much worse. But such aloofness puts neither food in my belly nor a roof over my head. The man in the next room explained how the system worked; in its way, it's effective and elegant. I was always paid cash at the end of each night's work. Dealing with my annoying contact was also a small matter. For the first time, I had enough money to influence my own fate. I had enough to eat. If you do not send me to prison or deport me back to Africa, perhaps I will one day be able to save enough money to go back there on my own. They say that the shooting has finally stopped, that the warlords are all in jail or dead. Maybe someday I will be able to go back and find my brother's bones and give him a proper grave."

The enormous translator took off his minuscule sunglasses and began to cry. The cops were silent. McKeutchen's fat face was pressed into a doughy visage of grimness. Totentantz and More were expressionless. Santiago experienced a gnawing hollowness in the pit of his stomach; he desperately wanted to leave the room. Ngala reached out and gently patted the translator's enormous shoulder but continued to glare coldly at the cops in front of him.

Everyone in the room except Ngala jumped when More snapped, "*Et qui pourrait être votre contact?*"

The huge translator was so shocked, he stopped sobbing. Ngala grimaced angrily at More, then lowered his eyes and muttered something in Swahili.

"He has very unusual hair," the giant translated.

The room went dead silent except for the faint drone of the overhead fluorescents.

"Holy shit," Santiago breathed. "We've got him."

●

More suggested the Benelli, but Santiago was already through the outer door lock. The inner ones took some doing; the kid must have spent money on new cylinders.

Their initial search did not yield much. The walk-in closet held finery the likes of which Santiago had never seen or touched; he didn't recognize any of the labels. There were more pairs of shoes, boots, and silly-looking sneakers than he had owned since his feet had stopped growing. The bathroom had two sets of thick, velvety towels the colors of dried herbs. The bed was a standard queen but covered with all manner of opulent pillows and linens. Santiago was reminded of the time his sister dragged him into ABC to outfit his apartment (he had taken one look at the prices and left).

There was a wide mahogany desk and an even wider bookcase, ornate in an old-fashioned way, stocked with large-format art books with titles Santiago didn't recognize: Mark, Steichen, Singh, Snowdon. There was a shelf of smaller books, some of which bore yellow stickers that read USED.

And that was it.

For a few moments they stood silently in front of the four huge photos of the Mall in Central Park, each shot clearly taken in a different season. They were nothing short of stunning.

The desk looked promising. Santiago made for the computer, which took up most of it, along with a money counter and a top-of-the-line digital camera. When he tapped the space bar on the keyboard, the monitor filled with multiple images of a curvaceous Boricua chick wearing only a belly chain.

"How do you know she's Puerto Rican?" More asked over his shoulder.

"See that a mile away," Santiago said dismissively.

More was staring at the books. The bookcase looked like an antique, too, with an intricately carved mantel. More, however, seemed interested only in the books, inspecting the spine of each.

"File says he was an art history major at NYU," Santiago pointed out. There hadn't been much else to go on; the kid had no record at all, not even a parking ticket. Santiago picked up a book from the mahogany desk, a well-thumbed copy of John Lawton's *Life Before Mankind*, third edition. Santiago flipped it open at random to a page showing a scale drawing of a man dwarfed by what appeared to be a gigantic scorpion, with flippers. He squinted at the caption: *Species of the class* Eurypteridae *arose during the Ordovician and Silurian periods and attained sufficient size to become one of the Permian's top marine predators* . . . Santiago shut the book and tossed it back on the desk.

More was still inspecting the bookcase. "You thinkin' 'bout selling those on eBay?" Santiago ribbed.

"I would've killed for books like these when I was a kid," More said tonelessly. Without taking his eyes off the bookcase, he absently reached up into the left sleeve of his field jacket and withdrew a huge, slightly curved blade with the gleam of Damascus steel. A Stek. Santiago had read about such knives. He seemed to remember they were used by fishermen to cut through whale blubber.

Maybe it was the way More casually mentioned killing, or the familiar way he handled that knife, or the fact that he'd probably had it on him all this time they'd been working together and Santiago never had a clue. Whatever it was, Santiago didn't like any of it. He hoped they could grab the kid fast and get him down to the station quietly.

"More?"

More had dragged the kid's swivel desk chair over to the bookcase (as if anyone could balance on a swivel chair, fucking More). After examining the mantel from about two inches away, he worked the tip of the blade into the ornamental grommet.

"More, what the fuck're you *doin'*?"

The center of the grommet came free, revealing a hollowed-out compartment. More reached inside and pulled out what appeared to be an unmarked disc case. He cracked it open for a moment, then shut it and tossed it to Santiago.

Who spake thus: "Holy shit."

The mother lode, trails of tabs. There was enough in this one case alone to put the kid down for decades. Santiago wondered how big the Narc Sharks' haul was. Whoever the kid's boss was, his operation must be huge.

More came down off the swivel chair in one fluid silent motion and stood beside Santiago at the desk. Beside the keyboard was a printout of an e-mail conversation between the kid and a woman, probably the Boricua chick, judging from her name. The top line read: THERE'S REALLY NOTHING MORE TO SAY. Beside this, along the paper's edge, which was wrinkled from having had something colorless spilled on it and later dried, was scrawled a single handwritten word: VIVISECTION.

•

More was standing on the bed, probing at the ceiling plaster, when the kid came through the door, behind which Santiago silently stood. He recoiled in horror from the ragged-looking man on his bed holding a huge knife, and turned for the door only to find 220 pounds of Dominican blocking it. The badge on a chain around the big man's neck did not seem to register. The kid spun back to face the white guy, maybe to try to reason with him, as Santiago had known he would.

"You're the one who got thrown out of that party behind the library," said the mangy-looking maniac with the evil-looking knife. His voice sounded wet and rusty.

The kid spun back toward Santiago. Someone had definitely worked the kid over, Santiago thought. Greenish bruises, several days old, covered almost one whole side of his face, while the other was misshapen by fresh swelling. Farther down, on the side of his neck, was a livid flesh wound only partially concealed by gauze, the tape coming loose. Over the years, Santiago had seen plenty of burns, both self-inflicted and the other kind.

"You're the one from Barneys," he stated. He couldn't believe it; he'd seen the kid under a month ago, flirting with a cute Latina saleswoman named Janet Nuñez, who'd loudly and bilingually declined Santiago's own advances the week before. "Guess what we just found?" Santiago waggled the disc case at the kid.

Who looked like his head was going to explode. He opened his mouth to say something, but only a sickly sort of gurgle came out. More stepped silently off the bed and came up behind him. Although he hadn't seen him do it, Santiago was greatly relieved to see that More had sheathed the knife.

"Who's Nightclub Guy?" asked the bum through a throaty rattle.

"Y-y-you're the one from the bar, Broome Street," the kid sputtered.

"Who is he?" More repeated.

The kid turned and raised a finger toward Santiago. "And y-y-you were in the cab, F-F-Ford H-Heifer—"

More drove the stiffened fingers of his right hand into the kid's right kidney, folding him up like a lawn chair. More caught him on the way down, wrapping his left hand around the kid's jaw and cheekbones. He bent him backward over his knee. The kid made a noise that Santiago had heard before. "More."

Fingers tightened around the kid's face, driving the insides of his cheeks between his teeth. "Who's Nightclub Guy?"

The sound coming through the kid's nose went up two octaves.

"More, you're hurting him." Santiago took a step forward.

"No, that's not hurting him. *This* is hurting him." More slipped a thumb around the kid's jaw, under his tongue, then drove it straight upward toward the soft palate. The kid screamed through his nostrils as tears coursed down his face.

"More, stop it!" Santiago was halfway to them. He saw More pull something out of his pocket with his free hand. Santiago's gun was already out, though he wasn't sure whom to aim for.

"Get some whiskey," More rasped, "we'll have ourselves a down-home barbecue."

He flicked open a battered old Zippo (Santiago could make out an eagle, a globe, and an anchor on one side) and thumbed up a huge blue-tinged flame two inches from the kid's bulging eyes.

There was a low-pitched wet rumble, accompanied by a noise like cardboard boxes being torn open, and the kid's pants and the carpet around his feet turned wet and dark. The smell stopped Santiago in his tracks. For the first time ever, he saw a true expression on More's face: rank disgust. More let go and stood up and back, and the kid sank into his own product, crying and babbling incoherently.

Santiago looked at More in disbelief. He had never seen someone literally scare the shit out of someone else, and the gnawing sensation he'd felt in the interrogation room came back. He wasn't sure how long they stood there, watching the kid in his fetid puddle. But at some point, Santiago waved More off and holstered his weapon. Gingerly, he helped the kid to his feet. "Come on," he said numbly, "come on."

The kid eventually stopped crying, although he continued making vague noises. He made odd little clicks as he got to his feet and strange wet sounds as he made his way to the bathroom.

And he screamed like a dying rabbit when he tried to close the bathroom door behind him and More kicked it down, hinges, hasp, and all.

•

Now it was Santiago's turn to be mute. Everything he had seen, heard, and found himself robotically participating in since they'd broken into the kid's apartment conspired to rob him of speech. A cold, logical part of himself had looked at the various angles and permutations and deduced that More's plan made sense, especially given the manpower constraints. The self-preserving, rationalizing part of him held that this was a sure way to get his second grade. A purely avaricious part of him said, *Hey, fuck it, think of the credits you'll rack up when this is all over, OCID, here we come!*

But a larger, amorphous part of him, one that he thought of as the gray area connecting mind and heart, was shocked and cringing. This was not police work as he had been taught. More's actions were well beyond ordinary regulations, even beyond drag rules. They cast aside basic empathy. More had gone Afghan on the kid. Never mind that it was totally illegal. More had broken all the rules he said he was operating by, the ones he'd supposedly promised McKeutchen to observe. It was . . . cold. Santiago shuddered to think what might have happened in that apartment if he hadn't been there to intervene. And it was only going to get worse.

Once the kid had cleaned up and pulled himself together long enough for transport (Santiago insisted that More drive, while he sat in back with the kid, who wouldn't sit behind the driver and huddled in a corner trying to keep out of More's line of sight in the rearview), and McKeutchen had a chance to talk the kid down, it all came spilling out, or enough for McKeutchen to start mobilizing his troops.

"Nightclub Guy is Reza Varna, our primary target. Bulgarian national, here legally since 1991. He's behind the brothel Liesl and Turse just took down, maybe some others. Our intel is that he's also behind the Century Club." The Century Club was an incongruity, a plush start-up in the midst of wrack and ruin. Varna (the kid wouldn't call him anything other than Reza) had somehow scooped up the space formerly occupied by the big Barnes & Noble on Twenty-first and Sixth. Two floors, over fifteen thousand square feet. And he'd turned it into one of the city's hottest new restaurant-lounges, with one simple rule: A C-note got you in. Booze, live entertainment (they couldn't wait to see what that was), whatever was on the menu, one Ben Franklin covered it all. The place had been going gangbusters, there were write-ups everywhere, it had been hailed as a new business model for the times. "But intel reports Varna's command center is around the corner, behind a copy shop on West Twentieth," McKeutchen finished.

"Intel" was sitting in one of the interrogation rooms guarded by Santiago, who told More he'd open fire if he tried to come inside. The kid was a complete wreck, rocking in place on a chair, eyes pinwheeling, whispering to himself. Every so often he'd blurt out the names of cows and some of the cabbie suspects they'd been questioning, and Santiago put it together that the kid identified taxicabs by breeds of cattle. He wondered how long the kid had been frying his brains off Varna's pills; there couldn't be any other explanation for how he'd ended up so far gone. The kid's forthcoming re-up under the Manhattan Bridge, that was a joke; Varna obviously set the kid up to be killed, and probably would've killed the two cabbies they'd picked up if they weren't safely in custody. Which was why he was sitting on the kid for God only knew what madness More was cooking up next, while the Narc Sharks and a mixed CAB/uniform team took the Century Club and a nearby copy shop, supposedly Varna's HQ.

"Go!" McKeutchen shooed the troops out. He stashed More in his office, then came into the interrogation room alone.

"This is beyond fucked up, Cap," Santiago observed redundantly.

"This is true," McKeutchen muttered. He was watching the kid with sadness in his eyes. Leaning one meaty paw on the table, he whispered, "Don't worry, son. It's almost over."

"*What* is?" Santiago snarled, making the kid twitch. "Don't tell me that crazy motherfucker sold you on this."

"Indeed he did."

"Are you fuckin' *kidding* me? He can't *do* this! Everything about it is—"

"Kid," McKeutchen growled, laboriously turning his bulk to face Santiago, "I don't like this shit any more than you do, but we're stuck with it for now. This isn't about Varna, it's about who's *behind* Varna. Whoever More's handlers are, they've been after this guy for years. Right now, while we roll up Varna's network here, there are guys from DC working signal intercepts, Reale's guys from Treasury are going through bank transfers, SAC Totentantz scrambled a priority watch on bridges, tunnels, airports, train and bus stations, and the ports. They're coordinating with Interpol and Europol, who've been working on the routes for the dope and whatever else Varna brought over here. This is big, kid, bigger than me, bigger than you. This one here"—McKeutchen nodded at the kid, who had mucus running from his nose to his chin—"is somebody Varna might just want badly enough to pop up for. I know you wanted to roll with Liesl and Turse on this, but More figures that's an empty nest. Varna's probably in the wind by now, but if he's not, if he sticks his head out for anything, it'll be to get this kid in order to cover his tracks. You don't wanna do it, fine. But something like this doesn't just come along once a week, or once a year, or even once a lifetime. You want OCID, this is your ticket." McKeutchen put a hand on Santiago's shoulder. "I know you can protect him," he said quietly, "and I know More will protect you."

Santiago glanced at the kid—beaten, broken, maybe even insane—and thought, *This is how I make my big Plan work. Use this fucked-up kid as bait to flush a bunch of Russian gangsters, or whatever Varna's crew is, so that More can fucking snipe or bomb their asses. And I get to dangle the bait.*

Swell.

●

More said he lived out on the edge of Flushing near Kissena Boulevard, not far from where Victor used to take Santiago and his siblings to baseball games at Shea, before it was sold and torn down to make room for a development project long since gone bankrupt. More's apartment was in a crumbling three-story building that stood alone on one corner of a block that once was bulldozed and graded for development. The nearest inhabited building was nearly a hundred yards away. The bottom floor looked like a crash pad for any derelict who—

"No," More blatted, "I sealed all points of entry and egress. Don't touch anything. The window frames are wired, the stairs are booby-trapped. Bring the weapons."

"Wha-wha-what the fuck? You mean IEDs and shit?"

"Don't touch anything," More repeated in his crystal-clear voice, and Santiago wished the guns were loaded. He struggled awkwardly up two flights of groaning stairs, peeling paint, and gouged-up carpeting. The place smelled of dust, old linoleum, and time gone by. Not unlike the inside of their Crown Vic.

"Careful there."

Trip wires on the third flight. *Coño*, Santiago thought, *I should be getting paid in gold for this shit.* "What, ain't you got a homing beacon for smart bombs someplace?"

"Here," More said, opening four dead bolts on the third-floor door in a slow, deliberate sequence.

"That was a joke," Santiago reminded him.

"No, it's not," replied More.

The apartment was nearly empty. The western wall had most of the furnishings, if you could call them that. A workbench took up the majority of the lateral space, with two vise grips set into the edge. Peg-board had been tacked up, and a variety of tools hung from it, most of which even Santiago the machinist's son did not immediately recognize. On the far end was a laptop computer, encased in the same heavy-duty plastic as More's cell phone, surrounded by what appeared to be language software modules. Next to it on the floor was a green box with a thick antenna and brightly colored buttons; then an afterthought of an open kitchen with a hot plate and an ancient refrigerator. On the opposite wall was a closet secured with four shiny new dead bolts. There was a bedroll laid out in the center of the floor. The only other things in the apartment were the maps.

Street maps. Tunnel maps. Sewer maps. County maps. Maps of all the waterways in the tristate area (complete with data on depth and currents). Maps of all international, domestic, and commuter airports, heliports, airplane hangars, and flight schools. Maps of ports, docks, and dockside warehouses, marked with notes on off-loading capacity, types of cranes, and locations of the railway terminus closest to each. Maps of bridges (large red X's drawn on the caissons and stanchions, indicating, Santiago figured, explosive charges , fucking More). Maps of power stations and electrical grids. Maps of subway and bus routes and traffic signals with handwritten notes on duration and times of peak volume. Maps of all NYPD precinct houses and surveillance camera locations. Maps of MTA and DSNY motor pools. Maps of IRT railyards, Amtrak, LIRR, and Metro-North routes. Maps of all courthouses, City Hall, federal buildings, and post offices. Maps of hospitals (Santiago noticed a red circle around Mount Sinai and, to his horror, Esperanza's name and TNU extension jotted neatly in black). Maps of TV and radio stations, cell phone towers, fiber-optic cable hubs, and wireless dead zones. Maps of every retail branch and corporate office of Urbank. Maps with locations of taxi garages.

"Motherfucker," Santiago whispered, "you really *are* going to invade New York."

"Maybe next year," said More in a voice that could sell swimsuits in

Alaska. "Put the weapons over there." He pointed to the bench. While Santiago laid them out, he heard More unlocking the closet behind him. More appeared next to him with a hard plastic case, the letters JSCS stenciled on one side in white.

Santiago, disturbed by the speed and ease with which More stripped the Benelli to a handful of parts, quipped, "I love what you've done with the place. You should hang out with McKeutchen, watch HGTV together, pick up some decorating tips." A thought struck him. "No speakers. How you play your tunes?"

"No music," More croaked.

A high-pitched keening, very faint, sounded in Santiago's ears. "You don't listen to music?"

"No."

Santiago moved a bit farther down the bench. Farther from More. Coming around the side of the computer, he noticed the only evidence of any human occupant.

It was a photo, color, of what Santiago guessed to be More's unit in Afghanistan. Santiago counted twenty faces. The men were posed on and around a foreign six-wheeled jeep with—he double-checked—a motorcycle mounted on the back. The jeep bristled with machine guns, rocket launchers, and jerricans. There were some other vehicles in the background, jeeps that looked like Land Rovers, more motorbikes, four- and six-wheeled ATVs, and some weird-ass dune-buggy things with machine guns mounted on the front. Not a Humvee in sight. The men wore a motley collection of desert fatigues, scarves, do-rags, turbans, leather jackets, sunglasses, boots, and sneakers. Santiago counted one Yankees hat and one Raiders T-shirt. The men in the photo did not look like highly trained elite military personnel. They looked like extras from *The Road Warrior*. They looked like dirtbags. And they looked happy.

In the photo, More was kneeling, front-row center. He was not smiling, but he wasn't wearing his Fish Face. He looked . . . content. "Nice picture," Santiago said breezily. "When was it taken?"

"Right before we were ambushed," More mumbled. "Ninety minutes after that photo was taken, four men in it were dead. Three others were wounded, including me."

So much for levity. Absently, Santiago scuffed his left foot, which made contact with the green box on the floor.

"DON'T TOUCH THAT," hissed the Fish Face.

Santiago jumped back from the box as though it were radioactive. "Sorry, sorry, Jesus, man, what the fuck is it?"

"PLGR."

"In English?"

"Precision lightweight GPS receiver."

"And it does . . . what?"

More was reassembling the Benelli. "Gives coordinates. We use it for calling in airstrikes."

"So," Santiago said jauntily, "you're ready to call in an airstrike, how nice. What coordinates do you plan to blow away?"

"Here." More checked the action on the Benelli, then reached into the ballistic case and pulled out a box stenciled with the number 12.

In this environment devoid of music, the theme from *Deliverance* had been playing through Santiago's head. Now it changed to the theme from *The Exorcist*. "You have an airstrike ready to go on your own house?"

"Yeah." More took a handful of shells from the box and started filling the Benelli's sidesaddle. Santiago had never seen shells like these.

"May I ask why you did that?"

"If my position is overrun, I can't leave anything behind," More grunted. He loaded five shells into the magazine, checked the safety, and reached into the case for a tactical light, which he affixed to the barrel beneath the muzzle.

Santiago's inner soundtrack switched to the theme from *The Twilight Zone*. "And how do you intend to do this? You have a code word that I hope I don't accidentally say?"

"No," gurgled More, slipping a tactical nylon shoulder harness on the Benelli, "I just change the batteries every so often. The receiver resets to default coordinates. Itself."

Santiago watched More put down the modified Benelli and set to work breaking down the M4. He counted the seconds it took for More to break down the carbine. More went to the gun closet and came back carrying another plastic case. Santiago's eyes registered SOCOM and SOPMOD before he squeezed them shut in terror and frustration.

More stripped down the M4, tossed the receiver aside, and began reassembling the weapon with completely different components. A long ported barrel. A carbon-fiber hand guard. A thick sound suppressor. A vertical forward grip and bipod. A skeletonized stock. Along the flat top of the new receiver More attached a series of chunky objects Santiago could only assume were sighting devices for the shooter to draw a bead on a target in the dark, or maybe through walls. "What is that?" he managed.

More reached into the case and pulled out a pair of box magazines. Flashing his lunatic grin, he tossed one to Santiago, who caught it one-handed and nearly sprained his wrist in the process. Santiago had handled .223 magazines. This one felt like a fucking cinder block. He tossed—heaved, actually—the box back to More.

With the modified rifle assembled and loaded, More replaced the plastic cases (together with the parts removed from the police M4) in the closet. He pulled out something that looked (and smelled) like an old fishing net. This he slipped over his head, struggling a moment to get his arms aligned. With the thing on, More looked like a walking brush pile. From the closet of terrors he produced an elaborate piece of bondage headgear, to which was attached a monocular device that projected from More's face like some horrific insectine proboscis. Next came a three-tiered backpack from which two thick, ribbed hoses extended. The pack went on the back, the proboscis stuck out from the Fish Face, and the hoses went round and round the brush pile.

More hefted his modified rifle, which to Santiago looked less like a firearm and more like George Lucas's take on a cattle prod. More no longer looked like a bum or an NYU student. In fact, he looked no longer human. More had successfully transformed himself into a monster from a science fiction horror film.

"Season's open," said the monster.

Santa Maria, madre de Dios, Santiago silently prayed. *Please deliver me from this crazy fuck More.*

•

Santiago could not understand how cabdrivers did it.

Twelve hours a day, maybe more. Six or seven days a week. Being trapped in the vile yellow boxes was bad enough. But to be confined with a passenger (maybe more than one), with all their sounds, their smells, their elation or exasperation over the most trivial matters—that would be enough to drive anyone insane.

Worst of all was to be trapped in a cab full of fear.

It was raw, primordial, I-want-to-get-the-fuck-out-of-here fear, and it had oozed from the kid's pores since they'd bundled him into the Crown Vic's front seat. The kid had refused to get into the back with More, couldn't even look at him in the rearview mirror. He'd merely slunk down in the seat where Santiago had dropped him, feather-light and brittle as crystal, his eyes huge and glassy and sightless. Santiago took in the faces of the CAB backup team as they silently wrote Renny off for dead, and he wanted to swing massively at all of them, even McKeutchen. It was a suicide run, Santiago knew it, and he hated himself for being a part of it. McKuetchen had pulled rank to make him go. Oddly, it was the kid who'd decided it, back in the interrogation room, saying he'd be better off with them than those for whom More was laying another diabolical trap. The kid's voice was gnarled and caked, like roots pulled from wet earth, and it scratched Santiago in a place he could not define.

There hadn't been much room in the backseat, he reflected, not with McKeutchen's girth and More's huge black duffel full of mayhem. The captain had insisted on riding with them. Santiago knew he was there to keep the kid together until More could pull off whatever carnage he had in mind for whomever Nightclub Guy sent, but in the end it didn't matter. The kid reeked of fright and terror and shock, and Santiago was glad McKeutchen had the foresight to keep some EMTs from the closest hospital, New York Downtown on nearby Gold Street, standing by five blocks from the site, tuned to the same radio frequency as the CAB team.

The ride down to Chinatown had been awful, the usual rush-hour miasma paling in comparison to the fog of anticipation, tension, and terror swirling inside the Crown Vic. Santiago was sweating, the kid was bruxing and swallowing uncontrollably, and McKeutchen was loosing round after round of stress-induced flatulence. The only still being in the taxicab was More, who had gone someplace far inside himself to prepare for whatever maelstrom he was orchestrating. Santiago hated More on that long drive downtown, hated him fully and without reservation, and he swore to himself that when it was all over and they had Nightclub Guy's people in bracelets on their way to Central Holding, he would tell McKeutchen he was done with More for good.

He would have told More himself, except when they were about eight blocks from the site, riding down Henry toward Division with the bridge looming overhead, More left. Just left the fucking cab, stepping out of a moving vehicle on a darkened street strewn with broken glass, humping that huge black bag like it was filled with straw. If not for the sound of the passenger back door softly being closed and the kid jerking like he'd been hit by a Taser, Santiago might not have known. He scanned the street—discarded pallets, rusty fencing topped with barbed wire, cracked concrete and faceless, oblivious people—but More was gone. Looking back over his shoulder, he saw McKeutchen's broad head, half in shadow, shake slowly left and right. Santiago turned back, put both hands on the steering wheel, and squeezed until the tendons in his wrists locked.

Fucking More.

Santiago parked the cab about forty feet from the playground fronting the alley More had selected, he and McKeutchen taking turns getting the shotguns from the trunk so that Renny was never alone in the cab. Santiago didn't like it, the kid sitting in the front seat for anyone to see. For a moment he thought the kid would crack and run, but Renny seemed to have eased up somewhat. At least as much as a battered, borderline shock trauma case about to be murdered could ease up. Santiago figured that was only because More was gone.

Then they waited.

•

At dusk, Santiago walked the kid from the playground to the alley while McKeutchen repositioned the cab by the playground's entrance. The backup team was two blocks away. Santiago walked about three feet off Renny's right shoulder, his Glock in his pocketed hand, the Benelli on the Crown Vic's front seat with McKeutchen. At the end of the alley, between a struggling semi-permanent Chinese greengrocer and a thriving heap of garbage, they turned around to face the way they'd come. Back down the alley to the playground. Where Renny was supposed to meet Nightclub Guy's contact. For the umpteenth time, Santiago cursed the lunacy of it all. The kid would be alone, not wearing body armor, the nearest help a good hundred yards off. But that had been part of More's plan, and McKeutchen backed it all the way. How could he have gone with such a fucking—

"Six, Ever, radio check," crackled his earpiece. The kid didn't flinch more than a foot.

"Ever, Six, copy."

"Six, Ever—get out of there." More was using his command voice again. Santiago thought longingly of the shotgun, then felt a fluttering beneath his rib cage.

It was happening.

He glanced at Renny, mentally preparing to take him down should the kid try one last time to make a break for it. But Renny appeared to have gone into some sort of fugue state. His lips were parted and moving slightly, though no sound issued. Santiago doubted he'd be able to make the whole walk.

"Don't worry," he said, "the backup team's ready, and Captain McKeutchen and me will be watching you all the way. We've got uniforms at your mom's house, she'll be okay. Your dad isn't—" Santiago broke off, cursing, remembering too late what had been in the kid's file. No father.

Finally, Renny made a sound between a snort and a sigh, as though his wiring had frayed so badly, he couldn't decide which one he wanted. But something else came with it: "My dad," he whispered.

Santiago's radio crackled again. "Six, Ever, clear the area *now*." He didn't know what to say to More besides fuck off. It was happening.

"I gotta go," he said with a steadiness he did not feel. "We'll be with you the whole way." He forced himself to look at the kid directly, but Renny was staring in the vague direction of the playground, lost to him.

Santiago ran.

As arranged, he circled the block instead of heading back down the alley. He took the route with one hand on the radio, the other on his pistol, Renny in his head stumbling down the alley like a zombie. His heart was hammering by the time he reached the cab, the captain, and the Benelli, which was the first thing he touched. McKeutchen was in the passenger seat, his shotgun out of sight beneath the dashboard. Santiago brought the Benelli to port arms and cocked it, thumbing the safety off, the barrel pointing out the window behind the driver's-side mirror, just like he'd done during the riots. The street was full of people and devoid of cars. His pulse thudded in his ears. A minute passed. Five. Was it happening?

"Maybe Nightclub Guy called it off," he whispered to McKeutchen. "Maybe—"

But McKeutchen cut him off with a wave and a gesture of his chins. Squinting out through the windshield, Santiago only saw the vampish

Chinatown night.

"Uptown lane, just passed the traffic light," McKeutchen grunted, reaching for the door handle.

Santiago realized he'd been anticipating twin headlights—a car. But now he saw it, arcing slowly toward them past a row of ducks hanging by the neck in a greasy, neon-lit restaurant window. A single disc of light, like a phantom Cyclops, hovering impossibly high above the street. Santiago's sweaty fingers slipped twice on the door handle. The Benelli and the steering wheel seemed to fight each other, slowing him down, blocking his way. In the distance, he could hear the motorcycle's engine growl.

•

My favorite memory of my father is of him singing me this lullaby:

Sing a song of thunder
A long and echoing tone
A song to keep nightmares at bay
A song that's all your own.
Send it down the path you take,
Past every unknown zone,
Through wood and fog and snowbank break
Through pitch and glare and roan.
It always comes right back to you
As though it's always known
Just where you are and where you'll be,
You'll never walk alone.
So if you find yourself distressed
With faculties o'erthrown,
Just sing a song of thunder
And you'll find your way back home.

The sunlight never gets down here during the day, so the stone stores no heat and the dampness never dries. I've seen them clean up at night, but somehow it's never really clean, there's always garbage and the smell of decay. Reza would know how much I hate this place, its squalor and stench and darkness, the fetid, sclerotic eastern auricle of Chinatown with its teeming oblivious hordes. He would know because L would have told him. Sooner or later, we all end up working for Reza. I should have known that L was a liar and a manipulator. I should have known that N was an atavistic opportunist. I should have known because I am all of these things. I became them with every decision I made. I rationalized my life away. All the way down here, this awful alley beneath the Manhattan Bridge, where I'm going to die.

I used people, thinking I'd avoid *being* used, but now it's come full circle. *Wait*, I want to say to them, *wait, I'm not what you think I am.* Yes, I made bad choices, but what choice did I have? I had to survive, to rise, to *keep moving.* Is it wrong to want more? Is it a crime to want to live better than your parents did? It must be, for here I am, walking through the anteroom of hell. I can see the taxicab waiting at the curb next to the playground that will take me away. I hear the rising grinding roar of a Manhattan-bound Q train passing overhead, and now there is a closer roar, yes, a fiery chimera unfurling one great clawed wing toward me, and now I can see my father but I don't know the way home—

QUIETUS

SANTIAGO HAD NEVER seen a federal pissing contest settled so fast.

Treasury Agent Reale was figuratively bitch-slapped and sent scowling from the station in seconds.

FBI Deputy SAC Totentantz went stomping and braying down the stairs in minutes, vowing to bring down a full-bore Justice Department colonoscopy on the NYPD.

"Wouldn't be the first," McKeutchen muttered, hands in his pockets, chewing more of his disgusting apple gum.

They'd kept More bottled up in an interrogation room for nearly two hours. They'd stayed behind the glass, of course. More reeked to high heaven, a wall of putrefied offal and mulched vegetable matter, congealed oil and grease, urine, and ashes. There were still papers strewn about the floor where a city ADA had dropped them two seconds after entering, after More had given him the Fish Face and he'd dropped all his folders and half-stumbled, half-run out of the room. The only fed who'd been able to stand it was Totentantz, who seemed oblivious. More was oblivious to everything and everyone. He sat in a chair, hands in his lap, eyes hooded, utterly silent. Maybe, Santiago thought, More was immune to people: an enviable trait.

The man who'd shooed the feds off in such record time was a compact, dapper man in his early fifties, with a rough crevassed face that put Santiago in mind of star anise. His hands were square and his dark blue suit fit him like neoprene. He gave his name as Devius Rune. He offered no badge, business card, nor ID of any kind. He had two men with him who made Santiago feel like a kid on the playground basketball court again. Looking up.

"I had hoped," said Devius Rune in a measured, methodical voice, "to draw a bit less attention."

There were news crews and stringers and photographers and bloggers and students from the Tisch School of the Arts and the New York Film Academy and the Columbia School of Journalism swarming like gnats over the Sophie Irene Loeb Playground in front of the alley between East Broadway and Henry beneath the Manhattan Bridge, trying to get a few frames' worth of blood and gore. Not to mention about a million local gawkers, their camera phones held high.

"It was a clean shoot," McKeutchen repeated for what seemed like the umpteenth time that night. "My men identified themselves as police officers. The shooter drew anyway and made to fire. I was there. I'm not telling you anything I won't say in court."

McKeutchen was standing up for them all the way, and Santiago was supremely grateful, even if he was telling only half the truth. It had been McKeutchen's idea to go along that night, a Remington 870 shotgun in hand, for this very reason. More important than IAB, more important than the commissioner, more important than the DA, was Devius Rune. If McKeutchen could sell their story to him, the rest of the ducks would line up in a row.

"Oh, really," said Santiago in a dull monotone. There were still spots dancing on his retinas from the muzzle flashes. And what had followed.

"Yes, really. C'mon, snap out of it." McKeutchen was all business. Maybe, Santiago thought distantly, he'd been through something like this before.

Santiago certainly had not.

He could still feel the burn, from his hands to his shoulders, from the shock delivered to his muscles when he'd squeezed the Benelli's trigger. This was after screaming "FREEZE, MOTHERFUCKER" at the huge, leather-clad specter on a gigantic white BMW R14 GSX trail bike. After the specter had turned its helmeted head from the kid, shivering and crying just a few yards beyond in the archway where the underpass opened into the playground, toward Santiago and the muzzle of the Benelli, and still drawn out the suppressed HK MP7 they'd recovered later.

And around the same time that More, ensconced in the sniper blind he'd been in for hours, had fired a single .458 round from his modified rifle at a distance of forty-six yards.

Sitting in McKeutchen's reinforced chair, his fingers steepled together, Devius Rune did not appear angry. His shoulders were relaxed and his craggy features calm, almost slack. Santiago didn't know how he could be so at ease.

And he didn't care. He couldn't rid his mind of the sight of the figure on the motorbike coming apart in a cloud of fluid, the big BMW lurching sideways and pinning his left leg beneath, dislocating the hip joint with an audible pop.

More had loaded the Benelli with FRAG-12 rounds, each a 19-millimeter HE projectile that armed itself three meters from the shotgun's muzzle, designed to penetrate armor half an inch thick. Santiago's shot had severed the shooter's arm just below the right elbow, penetrating a Kevlar vest and detonating just beneath the right floating rib. More's shot had gone through the shooter's helmet and pierced the skull half an inch from the foramen magnum. A large amount of energy had been transferred in the process, resulting in a significant portion of the front of the biker's helmet—along with his head—being sprayed outward in a trajectory that ended in a neatly stacked pile of wooden pallets, which had supported several hundred pounds of star fruit only hours before.

Squarely in the middle was the kid, who wound up wearing a substantial amount of his would-be assassin all over his head, face, and upper body. In a bizarre twist, the paramedics treating the kid for shock found a lollipop stuck in his hair.

A crash DNA test ordered by Totentantz, cross-referenced with Interpol database records, would later identify one Ahmed Kadyrov, aka "Babyface," a Chechen enforcer for a multinational Eastern European crime syndicate rumored to be headed by a Ukrainian national, one Miroslav Tkachenko, aka "The Slav," among numerous other aliases. The Slav was a high-value target for law-enforcement and intelligence agencies throughout the Russian Federation, several Gulf League states, the EU, the UK, and the U.S. A State Department report claimed The Slav's fearsome reputation extended from a prison on Siberia's Pacific coast all the way to Paris; there were kill-on-sight bounties on him in a dozen countries.

"Which is where I come in," explained Devius Rune. "The Slav is one of my projects. He's a good example of how commerce becomes weaponized, how the economy is part of the modern battle space. National security isn't just about bombs and terrorists anymore, Detective, it's about money, how the bad gets mixed in with the good at the point where legal and illegal economies meet.

"Increasingly," he continued, "this city has become that point. Things are getting out of hand in New York. Some of us in Washington thought something had to be done."

He stood up abruptly, the way More had done in Esperanza's TNU. "You've been extremely helpful, Detective Santiago. More speaks well of you. Consider that high praise indeed. Usually, he doesn't say much at all. Captain McKeutchen says you have misgivings about legalities." He gave Santiago an index card, on which was typed DOD DIRECTIVE 5525.5. "Look it up. Makes for interesting reading."

Santiago was too tired for this. The rush was over. The kid was safe and the would-be killer was a puddle in a playground. The backup team (intercepted by CAB officers two blocks away) had promptly thrown themselves on the ground, shouting, "*Nie strzelać!*" The officers were still waiting on IDs.

Watching Devius Rune chatting idly, almost amicably with McKeutchen, Santiago noticed that he had lines around his eyes and mouth similar to More's, as though he'd spent long periods in cold dry weather squinting into the sun. Santiago wondered if Devius Rune had ever set foot in Afghanistan. Or heard the concussion from bombs he'd helped guide in. Or felt the bite of RPG shrapnel. He decided that he did not give a shit.

Rising slowly, almost painfully, he wandered over to the glass behind which More sat in an impenetrable cloud. He'd made his sniper blind in a mound of discarded pallets and garbage, the detritus of dozens of Chinatown markets and restaurants. Hence the rebreather apparatus he'd donned in front of Santiago. Nobody would have looked for him nestled beneath all the cabbage stems and dried fish and pork fat baking in the June heat; no one would think a human being could stand it.

And no human being could.

Except one.

Ever More.

The fuck.

He'd brought along his ballistic cases and returned the M4 and Benelli to their original states before the techs rolled up. Santiago didn't know what he'd done with them, but how easy it would be, he thought, to make a small insertion in his report. Just a deviation from the script. To go back to the way things were.

Not a chance.

"You keep quiet about this, Detective," Devius Rune said to him from behind McKeutchen's desk, "you'll get your second grade and that transfer to OCID."

"Where do you usually sit?" Santiago asked him. McKeutchen, standing in the corner, made a face that suggested acute constipation.

Devius Rune smiled, a terrible sight. "Most of the time, Detective, anywhere I damn please."

•

The next two days dragged by. Santiago had to type up his report and surreptitiously hand it to McKeutchen to fudge. This was easier than he would have thought, given that the unit was busy with evidence from the restaurant, the brothel, and the office. Two CAB teams were taken up processing the Polish gunnies they'd busted the night of the shooting under the bridge. The Narc Sharks had been interviewed twice (anonymously for print) and were packing their gear for the move to OCID. Santiago felt no envy. In fact, he felt nothing at all. The shooting had left him numb and listless. The weapons—restored to their original state by More—had been turned over without incident. Nightclub Guy was in the wind. The fund manager was due to be arraigned in two weeks' time and had been denied bail. The cabbies had delivered testimony *in obscura* and been released, even Arun. When Santiago had objected, McKeutchen said, "It's all for the best, kid. We've got more than we know what to do with. This is going to take months, maybe years, to unravel. And don't be jealous of Liesl and Turse. They're gonna have company. I'm gonna have to find myself someone as pigheaded as you to break in all over again." McKeutchen beamed, the effect mitigated by a mouthful of half-chewed peanut M&M's. Santiago looked away.

McKeutchen had made arrangements at St. Vincent's Hospital. The kid had his own room, better than most; nurses checked him at least once every twenty-four hours. McKeutchen was looking into rat-holing some department money—God only knew from where—for a therapist. He was there every other day. The first day Santiago went with him. When he walked into the room, the kid started screaming and yanking out his tubes. Shooed out by McKeutchen, Santiago vowed never to let More near the kid again.

While standing outside Renny's hospital room, hating himself, he was approached by a stout balding doctor with a quiet, self-assured demeanor and a nametag that read LOPEZ. Santiago disliked him on sight. Through his salt-and-pepper beard, the doctor asked Santiago if he was a friend of the family. Santiago had silently showed his badge.

"Ah," uttered the good Dr. Lopez, and looked at his clipboard. "Reynolds Taylor, age twenty-five, hair white-blond, eyes pale green. One hundred eighteen pounds at time of admission." Santiago looked through the window in the door. McKeutchen stood over the kid, who stared sightlessly, and an ancient woman, who seemed equally vacant. "Shock, borderline malnutrition, liver function off the chart. You may want to tell him to knock off the partying if he feels like seeing twenty-six." Dr. Lopez spun on his heel and walked off at a brisk pace.

Shock. It had been More's idea to use the kid as bait. He didn't care about the consequences, he just wanted whichever assholes from Varna's crew showed up for the kid's scalp. Not a thought for the kid, or the case, or the department. Just because More wanted it.

Because Nightclub Guy was More's mission.

Or, more likely, Nightclub Guy's boss. The Slav.

Fucking More.

Not that it would be a problem. Once Devius Rune had returned to Washington, More simply vanished. The Flushing site was abandoned. When Santiago called ESU to ask about More, he was told there was no such name in the department. More's name disappeared from the CAB duty roster, and his name was no longer spoken at roll call.

Within five days of the shooting under the bridge, Santiago felt fossilized.

His eyes kept coming back to the desk drawer once assigned to More, which still had the lock More put on it. Everyone except Santiago had apparently forgotten about it. On the fifth day, while McKeutchen was at the hospital, Santiago went through the lock and pulled the .45 and the IWB holster out of the drawer.

The holster was all wrong. Santiago had the torso for a shoulder rig and felt better with one. The .45 was another matter. The Glock 39 was a short-frame model, which felt spindly and small in Santiago's hands. The kick was something else entirely, bucking noticeably up and to the right, but manageable if you had hands like Santiago's. The barrel length was wrong, though, once he sent the target more than twenty yards downrange.

The range master came out as he was clipping up his third target and asked if he was married to the Glock. "What else you got?" Santiago asked.

He spent the rest of the afternoon firing .45s of all shapes and sizes. The venerable M1911 was great for range but proved bulky in a shoulder rig and slow on the draw. Glocks were too light. Compact colts and S&Ws appealed to him, even with the .45 ACP round's added kick, but only one of the pistols felt right in his hand.

Going on five P.M. that day, he burned some of his savings on an online order for a Springfield XD .45 compact with an accessory rail for a light/laser attachment and a Galco shoulder rig with provision for extra clips.

Back in his apartment, showered and shaved, Santiago strapped on More's Glock and sent a single text message.

Then he went home.

Back to Inwood. Back to the wooden-slat rumble of the 1 train above the seedy bars on Nagle Avenue. Back to the cell phone and barbershops along West 207th Street. Past his father's shop and home. Luis had made a haul. There was fresh striper and porgy and cod, and shrimp and calamari and mussels, and fresh cilantro and onions and tomatoes. His siblings were there, and their significant others, and Santiago was the only single one at the table. But it wasn't so bad. He was used to it.

The only awkward moment came when his asshole brother Rafa started running his mouth about the big shootout under the Manhattan Bridge in Chinatown and how it was probably a drug thing. Probably junkies. Probably on that new *paco* shit.

Santiago wasn't aware of staring until Esperanza gently touched his arm. Victor scowled. Santiago's mother said he looked like one of the fish Luis had delivered. Santiago lowered his eyes and said nothing.

After dinner, while others overindulged on flan and rum, Santiago, strong coffee in hand, braved the noxious cigar smoke generated by the males in his family to check his messages. The text he'd sent earlier read: TONIGHT. MY PLACE. MIDNIGHT. SAY YES. The reply was one word: YES.

As he said his goodbyes, his sister surreptitiously asked if he'd talked to McKeutchen about More. Victor was less encumbered: "You still working with the crazy fuck?"

"I don't know," Santiago replied, and for the first time in days, he felt like he was being completely honest. It helped.

He got back to Long Island City just in time to light the candles, set out a portion of his mother's homemade crab cakes, and make sure the bathroom was in order before the buzzer rang.

When he opened the door, Yersinia was leaning on the jamb wearing a belted trench coat like Columbo. She held out a foil-wrapped bottle. "For wrapping up the big case." She declined his offer to take her coat.

He went to work on the bottle. Porfirio Plata, the good stuff. "How do you take it?" he asked over his shoulder.

No response. Yersinia was a pest.

He turned. Yersinia was standing in the living room with her arms crossed, looking at the four huge photos of the Mall in Central Park that Santiago had liberated from the kid's apartment. She had shed her coat and wore only a silver belly chain.

"Well?" she asked over her shoulder. "Aren't you going to bring me my drink?"

It's fun to be right, Santiago thought as he cracked the seal.

•

THE WALL STREET JOURNAL ONLINE

(FOR SUBSCRIBERS ONLY!)

MONDAY, JUNE 27, 2013

Century Club Raid Uncovers Crime Ring

*   *   *

True Apothecary Fund head linked to chain of criminal enterprises, including swank Century Club, brothel, and the new notorious "speaks"

By Ronney Radiant

NEW YORK—A joint federal-NYPD task force conducted a sweeping series of raids last week on the Century Club, long touted as a lone success in today's downtrodden restaurant market, as well as a series of other private ventures around

New York City, including a brothel, a copy shop, and a taxi garage, as well as one of the highest-profile investment funds under the expanding aegis of **Urbank**.

The raids have ensnared a bizarre mix of suspects, including the head of Urbank's **True Apothecary Fund**, Mark Shewkesbury, several Polish nationals believed to be enforcers for a multinational crime ring, at least one unnamed employee of the posh Century Club in Chelsea, a string of suspects believed to be part of an Upper West Side brothel, and an unknown number of cabdrivers, at least two of whom are connected with the Sunshine Garage in Queens, according to unnamed sources. The cabdrivers are suspected of serving a network of illegal club-type parties, modeled after the illegal supper clubs that have sprung up around the city following an unprecedented wave of restaurant failures. Unlike the supper clubs, the nightclubs—or "speaks," as they are colloquially known—have nurtured a flourishing trade in illegal bar operations, drugs, and prostitution.

The violence simmering beneath the surface of this underground trade has exploded with lethal force. Three cabdrivers have been murdered within the past month, for reasons yet unknown. Following the huge cabdriver protest last Tuesday, which immobilized city traffic for hours, came the bloody shootout beneath the Manhattan Bridge in Chinatown on June 21. Eyewitnesses put a taxicab at the scene, later identified as belonging to the NYPD's new Citywide Anticrime Bureau (CAB), which uses taxicabs as undercover police cars.

In a near-simultaneous (though possibly unrelated) incident, other officers from CAB raided the offices of *Roundup* magazine after its editor in chief, Marcus Chalk, had been reported missing for several days, and after a surprise government audit turned up large deficits listed as "off–balance-sheet expenses."

A spokesman for Roundup's parent company **Malignant Media** Inc. could not be reached for comment. Calls to the office of Malignant Media's board chairman, pesticide tycoon Hugo Mugo, were not returned.

While the raids on the Century Club and the brothel (known commercially as "Bacchanal Industries") and Shewkesbury's arrest stem from a long-standing Treasury/

FBI investigation, it is unknown what triggered the raids on Roundup, the Chelsea copy shop (the name of which is being withheld pending further investigation), or the Sunshine Taxi Corporation in Queens. Both the FBI and the Treasury Department declined to comment.

The Polish nationals arrested in Chinatown following the shoot-out beneath the bridge, whose identities have yet to be released, also turn up in the books of the copy shop. It is unclear whether these men have any connection to the brothel, the True Apothecary Fund, or *Roundup* magazine. There was no information available on the status of the Polish gunmen. Calls to the Polish embassy were not returned.

Sixteen people and an unknown amount of narcotics and other contraband were seized in the raid on Bacchanal Enterprises, which operated out of a brownstone on West 83rd Street near Central Park. No further information is available.

Nor is there any further information on the shooting under the bridge, which one onlooker described as "a m——g war zone." The onlooker, who asked not to be identified, described the scene as "f——g disgusting" and "a s——d of blood."

The NYPD said a statement on the status of the cases was pending. City Hall spokeswoman Tsetse Fly said the mayor was "deeply troubled" by the raids and was withholding comment until "all the facts are in."

Baijanti Divya, executive director for the Taxi Workers Alliance, the de facto cabdrivers' union, stated: "I hope these sad events focus public attention on the plight of New York City cabdrivers, three of whom have been brutally murdered within the past month. Surely the TLC and City Hall don't want more protests like the one we staged last week. I call upon Mayor Baumgarten and the TLC to adopt stricter driver-security measures and better NYPD protection for New York City cabdrivers."

Calls to the TLC were not returned.

•

Detective (Second Grade) Sixto Fortunato Santiago put down his phone and shifted gingerly in his chair so as not to aggravate his bruised ribs. He did so favoring his right leg, keeping pressure off his sprained left ankle.

There was a dark knot on his forehead between his eyes, as though he'd been struck with a hammer. He carefully put his mug to his mouth, keeping the hot coffee well clear of the stitches inside his lower lip. Yersinia had ravaged him. He felt lucky to be alive. "Santiago, line two," Liesl called out morosely. He and Turse were inconsolable. Their big roll-up had hit the wall when NYPD divers fished out a corpse from the riverbed off Roosevelt Island. The corpse had a wallet and ID belonging to one William Rochester, a Brit. His wrists and ankles had been bound with piano wire, cruciform-style, to a sewage dredge, which had been floated out to the middle of the river and sunk in sixty feet of water at the center of the city's wave-turbine field.

A holdover from the earlier days of better-funded green energy projects, the wave-turbine program was resuscitated by the mayor after its initial failure in '06. It was now generating enough electricity from the East River currents to light twenty thousand homes in Queens, one small victory for the beleaguered administration.

But someone had used it to send a different kind of signal. Rochester's body had been carefully arranged so that the vanes of a turbine would collide with Rochester's head on each revolution. Ponk, ponk, ponk, Rochester's skull was batted by the slow-moving blades, the flesh of the neck slowly splitting from the shoulders, for however many days he'd been down there; only the ME would know for sure. The head separated from the corpse when the divers brought it to the surface.

Now the Narc Sharks had a hole in their chart for the middle management of the organization they'd titled CABS, CLUBS, & COOZE. The cabbies' lawyers had done a surprisingly good job of protecting their clients, who didn't know anything about the upper echelons—well, that was their story, anyway, and they stuck to it. There was only one other suspect the Narc Sharks could question.

"Can we see him *today?*" Turse whined.

Santiago shook his head. He had warned McKeutchen that if the Narc Sharks or any other investigator braced the kid before his hospital release, he would kill them. Renny was making slow but steady progress. He was off the bedpan though struggling to regain full bowel control. McKeutchen had visited him several times. After the last trip, he reported to Santiago that they'd had a detailed discussion on fighting the effects of diarrheal chapping. McKeutchen had suggested cortisone and Tucks, the kid had countered with wet wipes and Aquaphor. It was a textbook case of old school meeting new.

McKeutchen was working his magic to help with the kid's medical bills, since the mother obviously didn't have much, although she dragged herself to the hospital every day to hold Renny's hand and stroke his hair when the nightmares brought him screaming out of what little sleep Dr. Lopez could provide. They were doing all they could, McKeutchen assured him. Santiago stared out the window and said nothing.

He did that more often these days, thinking back over the case and how it had played out. Without More around, there wasn't much for him to do, as he was confined to desk duty until the shooting under the bridge was resolved. IAB seemed more than willing to clear things, but it was taking longer with the feds involved. Plus, someone in the ME's office had been making a stink about the condition of the suspect's body indicating a level of ordnance far more powerful than the standard arsenal of the NYPD, even that of ESU. The ME was asking for detailed ballistics reports on the weapons used on the night of the shooting. McKeutchen said he was on it, not to worry.

There was an e-mail message on his phone from Lina. It read: Y'S BEEN WALKING AROUND SMILING AND BEING NICE TO EVERYONE AND BUMPING INTO THINGS ALL DAY. THE NEXT TIME YOU GET PROMOTED, CALL *ME!* Her sig file photo was a baby seal, sound asleep.

There'd been no word from or about More, and nothing from Devius Rune. Santiago had looked up the document Bune had mentioned and found it interesting reading indeed, not least because it was much older than he'd thought, going back to 1986. The directive was almost as old as he was. Maybe it was a Cold War thing, setting guys like More loose at home to smoke out some KGB mole.

Or maybe it wasn't about enemies from overseas anymore. Maybe McKeutchen was right: Sometimes you had to break the law in order to maintain it. Santiago didn't know, and he didn't like not knowing. He'd dropped almost fifteen pounds since that night under the bridge. At dinner, his sister had said he looked svelte. His mother had said he looked sick.

He remembered the phone. An Inspector Sigurdardottir from Interpol was on the line. Dimly, Santiago listened to him describe, in better English than his own, human remains recovered by the Dutch police from a trap in a hydroelectric plant outside Rotterdam. DNA testing had identified the remains as belonging to a Reza Varna, a high-priority suspect in a large interagency investigation centered in New York. The Dutch cops figured Varna had gone into the sluice about a quarter mile above the trap, which was made of strands of ultra-thin high-tensile steel wires. The effect was similar to being slowly driven (by several hundred thousand tons of water pressure) face-first through a giant potato masher. Preliminary forensics indicated the victim had been alive, perhaps even conscious, when he'd gone into the sluice.

Sigurdartottir very courteously offered to email Detective Santiago the file as it stood, plus new reports as they were generated. Santiago robotically thanked him and hung up.

So much for Nightclub Guy.

He'd thought he could outrun The Slav.

Wrong.

Santiago felt lighter. He'd start getting his paperwork together for his OCID transfer request soon. His Plan was intact, his body would heal.

He wasn't so sure about New York.

AD: art director
ADA: assistant district attorney
ALPR: automatic license plate recognition
AN-PEQ-4: handheld laser illuminator
AN/PEQ-1A SOFLAM: special operations laser acquisition marker
AN/PRC-117F: man-portable multiband/SATCOM radio
AN/PRC-138: man-pack radio
AN/PRC-148: maritime multi-band inter/intra team radio (see MBITR)
AN/PRC-150: man-portable tactical radio system
AN/PVS-14: night-vision device
APC: armored personnel carrier
ARMs: adjustable-rate mortgages
ARS: Amphibious Reconnaissance School (USMC)
BCT: brigade combat team
BMW: Bayerische Motoren Werke (Bavarian Motor Works)
Boricua: Puerto Rican
BPG: Bryant Park Grille
BRC: Basic Reconnaissance Course (USMC)
CAB: Citywide Anticrime Bureau
CAS: Close Air Support
CC: Cubic Centimeter
CJSOTF: Combined Joint Special Operations Task Force
CIA: Central Intelligence Agency (U.S.)
CPP: Central Park Precinct
COMSTAT: COMparative STATistics (NYPD)
CUNY: City University of New York
DCT: data communication terminal

D&D: drunk & disorderly

DA: district attorney

DC: deputy commissioner

DEA: Drug Enforcement Agency (U.S.)

DEP: Department of Environmental Protection (NYC)

DMV: Department of Motor Vehicles (NYC)

DNA: deoxyribonucleic acid

DOB: Department of Buildings (NYC)

DoD: Department of Defense (U.S.)

DPV: desert patrol vehicle (UK/U.S.)

DR: Democratic Republic (Congo)/Dominican Republic (Hispaniola)

DSI: Dominican Studies Institute (NY)

DSNY: Department of Sanitation (NY)

EAR: Entry, Assault, and Rape

ESU: Emergency Services Unit (NYPD)

ECU: Engine Control Unit

EU: European Union

FAC: forward air controller

FBI: Federal Bureau of Investigation (U.S. Justice Department)

FDNY: Fire Department of New York

FOB: forward operating base

FORECON: Force Reconnaissance (USMC)

FUBAR: fucked up beyond all repair

GHB: gamma-hydroxybuturate

GCPP: Gnaeus Calpurnius Piso Partners

GOP: "Grand Old Party" (historical nickname for U.S. Republican Party)

H&K: Heckler & Koch

HGTV: Home and Garden Television Network

HHS: Health & Human Services (NYC)

HIV: human immunodeficiency virus

HUMINT: HUman INTelligence

IAB: Internal Affairs Bureau (NYPD)

IAV: interim armored vehicle

IED: improvised explosive device

ITG: initial terminal guidance

JDAM: joint direct attack munition

JSOC: Joint Special Operations Command (U.S.)
JSOTF-N: Joint Special Operations Task Force-North
KIA: killed in action
LAV: light armored vehicle
LES: Lower East Side (NYC)
LIRR: Long Island Railroad
LOC: line of control
LRRP: long-range reconnaissance patrol
LZ: landing zone
MARSOC: Marine Special Operations Command (U.S.)
MBITR: maritime multi-band inter/intra team radio (see AN/PRC-148)
MC: master of ceremonies
MDF: medium-density fiberboard
MEDEVAC: MEDical EVACuation
MEU/SOC: Marine Expeditionary Unit (Special Operations Capable)
MDMA: methylenedioxymethamphetamine (Ecstasy)
ME: Office of the Chief Medical Examiner (NYC)
MPLI: medium-power laser illuminator
MS2000-M: SOF strobe light
MTA: Metropolitan Transportation Administration
MWSS: Marine Wing Support Squadron (U.S.)
NID: National Intelligence Daily
NMI: no middle initial
NRO: National Reconaissance Office (U.S.)
NTU: Nurse Triage Unit
NYPD: New York Police Department
NYU: New York University
NZSAS: New Zealand Special Air Service
OCID: Organized Crime Intelligence Division
OD: overdose
ODA: Operational Detachment Alpha
OPEC: Organization of Petroleum Exporting Countries
PBA: Police Beneficiary Administration

PCA: Posse Comitatus Act (U.S.)

PLGR: precision lightweight GPS receiver

RPG: rocket-propelled grenade

RSOV: Ranger Special Operations Vehicle (U.S.)

SAC: special agent in charge

SASR: Special Air Service Regiment (Australia)

SCAR: Strike Coordination and Reconnaissance

SEAL: SEa, Air, & Land (U.S. Naval Special Forces, AKA DEVWARGRU)

SEC: Securities and Exchange Commission

SERE: Survival, Evasion, Resistance, Escape

SIDS: Secondary Imagery Dissemination System

SIM: Subscriber Identity Module

SIV: Structured Investment Vehicle

SOAR: Special Operations Aviation Regiment

SOCAFRICA: U.S. Special Operations Command, Africa

SOF: Special Operations Forces

SOPMOD: Special Operations MODifications

STG: Sturmgewehr ("storm rifle"—assault rifle)

STS: Special Tactics Squadron

TACP: Tactical Air Control Party

TDI: turbo direct injection

TF: task force

TGO: terminal-guided ordnance

TLC: Taxi and Limousine Control

TRUEX: "The True," USMC urban assault exercise (in conjunction with federal and local law enforcement)

UAV: unmanned aerial vehicle

USAAS: U.S. Army Airborne School

USMC: U.S. Marine Corps

USN: U.S. Navy

ACKNOWLEDGMENTS

Rivers of Gold is a work of fiction. May the world it describes never exist.

No book is written in a vacuum. The list of sources consulted is abbreviated due to space constraints; no slights are intended to those omitted.

First and foremost, my deepest thanks go to the cabdrivers of the Stan 55 Operating Corporation in Long Island City, Queens. None of them wanted their names used, so I will respect their wishes. But I will list the names of those not behind the wheel who allowed me to name names: Lincoln Stevens, Jerry Nazari, Richard Wyssak, and the incomparable Stanley Wyssak, who has been guru to other taxi-obsessed authors before me.

Delving deeper into New York's Taxi World: At the Taxi Workers Alliance, deep thanks to the canny Javaid Tariq; to Biju Mathew, author of *Taxi!: Cabs and Capitalism in New York City* (New Press, 2005); and, as always, to the sagacious Bhairavi Desai. At the League of Mutual Taxi Owners, thanks to Richard Curtis and Vincent Sapone. At the Taxi & Limousine Commission, special thanks to Chairman Matt Daus and the chimerical Allan Fromberg.

Bruce Schaller's frightfully detailed study *The New York City Taxicab Fact Book* (published online by Schaller Consulting in conjunction with the TLC in March 2006) is the most recent, most intensive, and last industry-wide study for New York City's taxi business that I could find. The industry desperately needs more statistics-obsessed taxi geeks, and I mean that as the highest compliment possible.

Lieutenant Richard Khalaf of the NYPD's Organized Crime Control Bureau was enormously helpful to me during the writing process, as was John Kelly at the office of the DCPI. Special thanks to Detective Investigator Chris Saffran (Ret.), a true chameleon in a ruthless urban jungle.

I am most grateful to Mark Zeller of UBS Investments for vetting the financial aspects of this manuscript for accuracy.

Thanks to the following on the *New York Times* Metro desk: Ian Trontz, Sewell Chan, William Neumann, and the prolix James Barron. (Can I have an expense account?)

No New York story can be told in one language, as New York is not a monolingual town. A special reserve of gratitude is hereby served up to my team of translators, who kept my manuscript from sinking into onomatopoeic ooze: Michael Adjiashvili, Aniruddha Bahal, Pria Bala, Jaspal Singh, and Thomas Thornton.

I am deeply indebted to Dr. Graham Hodges of Colgate University, author of *Taxi!: A Social History of the New York City Cabdriver* (Johns Hopkins University Press, 2007) for reviewing the manuscript. Likewise, special thanks to Dr. Burton Peretti of Western Connecticut State University, author of *Nightclub City: Politics and Amusement in Manhattan* (University of Pennsylvania Press, 2007). I delved deeply into *Dry Manhattan: Prohibition in New York City* (Harvard University Press, 2007) by Dr. Michael Lerner of Bard.

I owe a debt of gratitude to Dr. Steve Call of Broome Community College, author of *Danger Close: Tactical Air Controllers in Afghanistan and Iraq* (Texas A&M University Press, 2007) for giving selflessly of his time to help me with the manuscript, including schooling me in the finer points of airstrikes.

Bertil Lintner's *Blood Brothers: The Criminal Underworld of Asia* (Palgrave Macmillan, 2003) was essential in creating the backgrounds of Reza and The Slav, as was Misha Glenny's *McMafia: A Journey Through the Global Criminal Underworld* (Knopf, 2008). Special thanks to Jeffrey Robinson, whose book *The Merger: The Conglomeration of International Organized Crime* (Overlook Press, 2000) forever soldered my attention to the intersection of the world's light and dark economies. Likewise, reading *Lords of the Rim: The Invisible Empire of the Overseas Chinese* (G. P. Putnam's Sons, 1995) by the indomitable Sterling Seagrave pinned back my eyelids to allow for a nonobnubilated gaze to the east. Loretta Napoleoni's intricate study *Modern Jihad: Tracing the Dollars Behind the Terror Networks* (Pluto Press, 2003) helped carve the mechanics of Islamic finance into a mind not built for numbers.

Apart from my own meanderings around New York City, I relied upon several books for background detail: *The Works: Anatomy of a City* by Kate Ascher (Penguin Press, 2005); *Invisible New York: The Hidden Infrastructure of the City* by Stanley Greenberg (Johns Hopkins University Press, 1998); *Envisioning Information* by Edward R. Tufte (Graphics Press, 1990); and

Gotham: A History of New York City to 1898 by Edwin G. Burrows and Mike Wallace (Oxford University Press, 1999). For story's sake, I have taken liberties with some details of the locales; there is no long stairway down the hill behind George Washington High in Inwood, for instance, and the Eyrie is actually called Studio 450. More's route from La Guardia Airport across the Queensborough Bridge is as I drove it, though I would not recommend taking the Manhattan-bound lower roadway at high speed on a weekday morning to anyone who values his or her life.

Jeffrey Dunn and Topher Cox gave me the first hints that there were unsavory elements in the photography business, but it took James Sullivan of 1Prophoto.com to explain how supremely seedy the fashion-photo racket in particular can be (to him I attribute Renny's Moral Slide Rule). Thank you thrice.

For my allusions to the never-ending nightmare that is the Democratic Republic of Congo, the starting point was my 2008 interview with Bryan Mealer, author of *All Things Must Fight to Live: Stories of War and Deliverance in Congo* (Bloomsbury, 2008). For additional research, I relied upon the International Crisis Group's Africa Report #26, "Scramble for the Congo: Anatomy of An Ugly War" (12/20/2000), as well as reports from the U.S. State Department, the United Nations, and global news dispatches too numerous to be listed here. Any mistakes involving dates, place-names, or translations regarding this material are solely my own.

Those interested in reading more about interagency operations in Afghanistan should consult *Jawbreaker: The Aattack on Bin Laden and al-Qaeda: A Personal Account by the CIA's Key Field Commander* by Gary Berntsen and Ralph Pezzullo (Crown, 2005) or *First In: An Insider's Account of How the CIA Spearheaded the War on Terror in Afghanistan* by Gary C. Schroen (Ballantine, 2005). Also helpful were Leigh Neville's *Special Operations Forces in Afghanistan* (Osprey, 2008) and *Marine Force Recon* by Fred J. Pushies (Zenith Press, 2003). Thanks also to Lawrence Korb at the Center for American Progress.

More's arsenal is a mix of the real and the imagined. To the best of my knowledge, there is no Heckler & Koch P2000SK chambered for .45 rounds; however, I have no doubt the gunsmiths at the RTE shop in Quantico could produce one. Stek knives are very real and very expensive, hardly standard issue. The parts for More's modified rifle are all available on today's aftermarket for assault weapons. PLGR and SIDS systems are real enough; by now there are probably civilian versions on the market.

The inspiration for all my political characters may be found in Carl Zimmer's magnificently repugnant book *Parasite Rex: Inside the Bizarre World of Nature's Most Dangerous Creatures* (Free Press, 2000).

The Posse Comitatus Act and Department of Defense Directive 5525.5 continue to coexist, albeit uneasily.

A special round of thanks to those novelists who read my manuscript and lent me their craft: the wonderfully irascible John Lawton (author of *Second Violin*, Grove Press, 2008), who lent his name to Renny's favorite textbook; the latitudinarian and recondite Aniruddha Bahal (author of *Bunker 13*, Farrar, Straus & Giroux, 2003), the source of Arun's I LOVE GRAVITY T-shirt; and the lissome, lofty Dinah Lee Küng (author of *Under Their Skin*, Halban, 2006).

David Smith, formerly of the New York Public Library, was essential in helping me obtain research materials and finding me a quiet place where I could nail my hands to the keyboard and finish the manuscript before incontinence and dementia set in. Craig Finn and Tad Kubler are (as far as I know) alive and well at the time of this writing; their band, the Hold Steady, continues to publish music under the Vagrant label. I sincerely hope that Bea Goldberg is still with us. The shark is named after Carl Hiaasen. Arnaldo Mazur appears courtesy of Arnie Mazer.

These last few are part of a group of real people (or at least their names) inhabiting *Rivers of Gold*, alongside Ralph López, Matthew Hamilton, Akhtar Nawab, Devius Rune, Biju Mathew, Graham Hodges, Pedro Heredia, Raghuram Rajan, Tony Judt, Walker Evans, John Conn, Tomonori Tanaka, and The Slav. If you should happen to meet them on the streets of the city, be polite, especially to the latter.

Deep and humble thanks to the Dunn Books team: Chuck Dorris; Archie Ferguson; Steve Gaynes; Susan Heller; Jae Hong; Madeline Hopkins; Ed Katz: Arnie Mazer: Alan Neigher: James Sullivan; and Beth Thomas.

Finally, The Squirts. They are not of my making but are enjoyed by all. I first came across The Squirts in a novel I was reviewing for *Publishers Weekly*, but that was a decade and several computers ago, and I have been unable to find the correct source. However, proper credit must be given when due. Therefore, I say to the anonymous author of the untitled satirical golf novel published by an unknown press sometime around the turn of the century: Thank You for The Squirts.